*Sylvia gave him a sideways
look, her chin lowered.
"Why are you doing this?"*

Tony sighed. His hand was covered in blisters; he'd cheated death by working on the edge of a slick roof forty feet above the earth; he'd pretended to be a smuggler, knowing the government would see it as no pretense if he was caught; and just tonight had fought a man twice his size in defense of a woman he'd known only a week. A woman who'd become his acquaintance only because members of her gang had abducted him and knocked him unconscious.

Why, indeed?

Sylvia leaned closer, intent on his answer, her green gaze focused on his face, her lips slightly parted. He sat forward, cupped her cheek with his left hand, and kissed her. She stayed perfectly still, allowing him to brush his lips against hers, to caress her cheek with his thumb. He pulled back a bit, giving her a chance to escape should she want it.

She followed him, not allowing a break in contact. Fire coursed through his veins as their breath mingled, and she kept her lips pressed against his. Someone moaned.

They separated a fraction. "Good answer," Sylvia whispered.

Other **AVON ROMANCES**

Coming Soon

And Don't Miss These
ROMANTIC TREASURES
from Avon Books

SHIRLEY KARR

Kiss From A Rogue

AVON BOOKS
An Imprint of HarperCollinsPublishers

AVON BOOKS
An Imprint of HarperCollins*Publishers*
10 East 53rd Street
New York, New York 10022-5299

Copyright © 2006 by Shirley Karr
ISBN-13: 978-0-06-083411-1
ISBN-10: 0-06-083411-0
www.avonromance.com

First Avon Books paperback printing: February 2006

Avon Trademark Reg. U.S. Pat. Off. and in Other Countries, Marca Registrada, Hecho en U.S.A.
HarperCollins® is a registered trademark of HarperCollins Publishers Inc.

Printed in the U.S.A.

10 9 8 7 6 5 4 3 2 1

*To my mom, who proved that when the going
gets tough and the tough lose their hair,
laughter and love will hold us together.*

*To Mike, my own hero.
Thanks for putting up with the insanity.*

*My thanks to Betty, Jessica, Joey, and Maggie for
coming through in the clutch, as always. You make
me a better writer (whether I want to or not).*

*And my thanks to JD, for such an
inspiring body of work.*

Chapter 1

Lulworth Cove, Dorset
May 1816

Sylvia, Lady Montgomery, was a gently bred, gently reared female, yet found herself standing on a cliff, staring out at the midnight-black sea, waiting to buy smuggled brandy from one of humanity's most disgusting specimens.

She pulled her worn cloak closer about her shoulders, warding off the stiff breeze blowing in from the Channel. Moments later, a signal light flickered out in the cove, and Sylvia used her lantern to reply.

"You don't have to do this, my lady," Trent said, giving a steadying hand at her elbow as they picked their way down the steep cliff-side path. With no moon to guide them, they relied more on memory than sight.

She patted her pocket with the heavy purse, heard the reassuring clink of coins. "Yes, I do. You remember what happened last time Jimmy tried to take care of business? The captain nearly had him for supper."

"Aye, my lady."

Her brother-in-law was doing his best to fill her dead husband's shoes, but the captain had no patience for green lads. He preferred young widows, because everyone knew that widows were fair game for rakes, rogues, and scalawags.

As soon as she reached the base of the cliff, Trent headed back up, to keep a lookout for the Revenue agents.

The cluster of men on the beach parted, murmuring greetings and clearing a path to the water's edge for her, where the captain had just stepped out of the first longboat.

"Lady Montgomery, may I say you are looking especially fine this night?" He took off his hat and gave a low, sweeping bow.

She tried not to flinch at the overwhelming waft of odor his movements sent surging over her. Someone should tell him that all the cologne in the world would not mask the fact he hadn't bathed in the last decade, and that salty spray washing over the deck didn't count as a bath. "Good evening, Captain Ruford." She kept her breathing shallow. Would he take offense if she breathed through her handkerchief?

The captain put his hat back on, hiding his thinning,

overly pomaded hair. "Shall we adjourn to higher ground?" He took her elbow and led her back up the cliff path, out of the way, just as the next longboat slid onto the beach, followed by others. Men swarmed, forming chains to remove the casks from the boats and hide them in the caves. More than two dozen men moved about, only a single lit lantern in the entire cove, yet it was nearly silent save for the waves rolling ashore.

Attempting to finish their transaction as quickly as possible, Sylvia pulled out the purse.

"Ah, my dear, I had the most terrible time with the patrols on this voyage." Captain Ruford accepted the purse with a shake of his head. "I had to bribe more officers than usual, and I fear I cannot absorb the added cost."

Blast. She, Jimmy, and the villagers had barely been able to scrape up the usual funds to pay for this cargo as it was. Her head began to pound in time with the waves. "I am afraid we cannot absorb the cost, either, Captain Ruford. It is your expertise that we rely on, to avoid the patrols in the first place. You have assured me several times that no one knows this coast better than you."

"Aye, and no one does. However, the government lads are getting craftier, aren't they? I had to pay off several of them, and I won't take it out of my fee. You'll have to cover it."

"No." She fought to keep the anger and fear out of her voice.

Ruford lifted one hand to trail a fingertip along her

jaw. With the cliff at her back, Sylvia had nowhere to go to avoid his touch. "Unacceptable answer, Lady Montgomery."

She shook her head. "You have all our coins. There is nothing more to give you."

"That's not entirely true." Ruford let his fingertips slide down her chin, along her neck, to the fastenings of her gray cloak. She forced herself not to cringe.

She heard a growl from down the path, and saw Jimmy walking toward them, his hand on the pistol tucked in his belt. She waved him off. They still needed Ruford, and he hadn't yet crossed beyond what she could handle.

Ruford leaned in close, his putrid breath fouling the air even further, and lowered his voice. "I'm sure we can come to an amicable agreement." He rested his hand on her shoulder, his fingers toying with the curls by her ear. "Montgomery is rotting in his grave, my dear. It's long past time that you took another man to bed. Come aboard my ship for the night, and we'll call the debt paid."

She balled her fists at her side as indignation warred with nausea. However much she might wish, she could not end their business relationship. Not yet. The livelihoods of too many people were dependent on her actions. "Jimmy!" she called.

Her brother-in-law bounded toward them, his brow creased with concern, his hand at his belt, ready to draw the pistol. "Everything all right?"

"Leave the last cask in the boat. Captain Ruford will be taking it back aboard his ship."

"But—"

"I'll explain later."

He shot a worried look over his shoulder as he walked away, but passed the message to the men.

"I think that more than covers the added expense you incurred, Captain." Sylvia turned to walk up the path.

Ruford's eyes narrowed. "This time. I warn you now, it will not be sufficient payment in the future." He patted her derriere. "Pleasure doing business with you, my lady. I'm looking forward to our next meeting." He headed back down to the beach, calling orders to his men.

By the time Sylvia had taken a half dozen more steps up the path, the beach was clear. Jimmy and her men had taken the trail back to the village and the Happy Jack Inn, and Ruford and his crew were rowing out to his ship.

She sagged against the cliffside and shuddered. Ruford had been getting bolder, more offensive each time they met. The fact she still wore half-mourning in honor of Lord Montgomery was no longer a sufficient barrier.

Personal affront aside, losing that cask of brandy would set them back, a loss they could hardly afford. But, much as she wanted to help the villagers, there was no chance in hell she would ever spend the night with Ruford.

She'd have to think of something else next time, some other way to deter his advances. A way that wouldn't interfere with business, because the villagers still needed Ruford. Though summer had just started, under the best of circumstances the season was barely long enough to prepare for the cold winter weather and harsh storms. After the shipwreck last spring that claimed her husband and so many other men from the village, circumstances had been far from ideal. They needed the profit from the brandy to rebuild, to replace all that had been lost.

Ruford had made it clear on several occasions that he would only do business with the lord or lady of the manor on whose beach they landed their cargo. Jimmy may have inherited, but Ruford paid the boy little heed. So, Sylvia, the least supportive of the village's return to smuggling, had ended up the leader of the enterprise.

She reached the top of the cliff and strode for home, through the tall grasses, to the road that twisted and turned, lined with trees and overgrown rhododendrons, to the manor house. The path through the cave and tunnels was shorter, but she always avoided it. She'd never admit to being scared of the bats that made it their home.

"Set yourself down, missy, and I'll have tea ready afore the cat can lick his ear," Galen said as Sylvia entered the warm sanctuary of the kitchen.

"Bless you." Sylvia held her hands out to the fire blazing in the hearth. Within moments, a stool was shoved unceremoniously against the back of her knees, and the housekeeper set a tray of scones and tea on the hearth, before pulling up a second stool beside Sylvia.

"Did all go as planned?" Galen said around a mouthful of scone.

Sylvia nodded. Close enough to plan, anyway. She had time to grab only one scone for herself before Galen snatched the rest away and covered them with a towel. They'd be brought out again for breakfast in a few hours.

The estate's small herd of dairy cattle assured them of butter and cheese, and the village fishing boats brought in mackerel, but Sylvia could only tolerate so much fish and cheese before she longed for more variety. Like more pastry. Fruit. Even vegetables.

Slathered with creamy butter, the scone melted in her mouth. She followed it down with weak tea. As long as there was still even a hint of flavor left, Galen would hold off breaking out new leaves. But it was enough to wash away the lingering scent of Ruford.

"The captain required additional payment for bribes again." With the worst of her hunger satisfied, fatigue loosened her tongue. Galen was the closest she had to a confidante, even though the servant was old enough to be Sylvia's grandmother. "He is increasing his profits at our expense, and I don't know how to stop him. With so many repairs still to make, there's barely enough to go around when we get our full share."

Galen shook her head, iron-gray curls not moving a whit. "If only my Gerald were a few years younger. He'd show that peacock a thing or two!"

A few *decades* younger, perhaps. Sylvia kept the

uncharitable thought to herself. The two fulfilled the roles of cook, housekeeper, butler, and estate steward, though they should have been pensioned off long ago, and she was glad of their company.

Galen let out a sigh. "One shouldn't speak ill of the dead, but if I'd known what a mess Hubert would leave us all in, I'd have tanned his hide with my strop a few more times while he was still a lad. He should be dealing with the likes of Ruford, not you."

Sylvia finished her tea. "If Hubert were still here, we'd have no need of Ruford, because Hubert had his own ship." And if her husband hadn't let the insurance lapse on his sleek, fast cutter, she and Jimmy wouldn't be in the dire straits in which he'd left them. With a settlement from Lloyd's of London in hand, she might have been able to talk Jimmy and the villagers out of resuming the smuggling runs, and give herself more time to come up with another viable, *legal* source of income.

And if wishes were horses, as her papa used to say, beggars would ride.

She pointed at the buckets of water lined up before the hearth. "Think they're warm yet?"

"Aye. Been setting there since before supper."

Sylvia peeled off her clothes while Galen hauled the tub out from the corner, brought it close to the hearth, and poured in the buckets of steaming water.

Once upon a time, they'd had enough servants in the household to heat the water and take it up to her bedchamber. But for the last year or so, after having to let go most of the other servants, she hadn't the heart to ask that of Galen or Gerald.

However infrequently Sylvia indulged in a bath instead of making do with washing up at the basin in her bedchamber, Galen didn't question her need to immerse herself up to her neck in warm soapy water after dealing with Ruford.

Galen emptied the last bucket. "Before I forget, my lady, stay out of the gold salon upstairs. More of the ceiling came down this afternoon. We moved the rest of the furniture into the rose salon."

Ah, the lovely ground-floor rose salon, where Hubert had proposed. The room where he'd convinced her Uncle Walcott that he could provide for his bride. The only room in the manor that did not have peeling wallpaper or a collapsing ceiling.

Sylvia stepped into the tub. "Good place for it. If the summer doesn't go well, we'll all be sleeping in there when the rains come and the weather turns cold." She sank into the water up to her chin.

Galen gave her a playful slap to the top of her head. "Buck up, missy. We're off to a good start." Her confident expression faltered. "Aren't we?"

Sylvia suppressed a sigh. "Yes. Yes, we are."

"Of course we are. Everyone's garden is starting to produce. They'll all be fat as lords in no time, you'll see." After setting the washcloth and soap within Sylvia's reach, Galen gathered up the tea things and began cleaning up.

Sylvia washed quickly, trying not to picture the

roofless cottages in the village, the families crowded together in the remaining sound structures. Two widows, with seven children between them, had resorted to combining their households into one after the shipwreck last year. Three families had given up altogether after the last storm, and emigrated to Canada.

They needed an entire summer's worth of profitable shipments to repair the winter's damage. If things kept getting worse, more people would leave until the village was abandoned altogether, and she'd have no choice but to return to her uncle's home and his squalling brats. She wouldn't allow that to happen.

She finished her bath, dried off, and slipped into the night rail and wrapper Galen had kept warming by the fire. Leaving the servant to tidy up the kitchen, Sylvia climbed the stairs to her room, and felt her way along in the darkness rather than waste burning a candle.

At this stage in her life, she had expected to have a child or two, perhaps another on the way. A husband who treated her with respect, if not actual affection. Supervising the housekeeper and deciding how to best stretch her household budget should have been her biggest worries.

Instead she was consorting with smugglers, fending off the advances of a deceitful, stinking lothario, had no children nor hope of any, and her husband had turned out to be a first-rate liar before inconveniently dying. She was left with the burden of an entire village with crumbling cottages and a population decimated by the losses from the shipwreck last spring and the war with Napoleon.

Finding another husband would solve many of her problems. But she'd looked over her options among the villagers, and the men she'd met in the nearby towns when there had been enough money to attend the occasional rout at assembly rooms. Between war casualties and the lost ship, most of the eligible men were gone. She was better off here, making the best of things with Jimmy and Galen and Gerald.

She climbed into bed, sighing as she sank into the lavender-scented mattress and pillow.

A moment later, soft footsteps padded across the floor, the bed dipped, and a fluffy tail fell across her face. "Lie down, Macbeth," she muttered, pushing the tail aside.

The cat kneaded her pillow and turned, first by her right ear, then by her left shoulder, before settling in the middle of Sylvia's chest.

Luckily the lavender that grew in such abundance locally kept the vermin at bay. Galen had withdrawn her objections to a beast in the house after Sylvia had convinced her that a cat who was regularly bathed in lavender water would not only *not* bring in vermin, but would keep the mice out of her pantry. Macbeth performed his duties with great zeal and diligence.

She buried her fingers in his luxurious fur, rubbed under his ear. His rhythmic purring and soft warm body soon had her boneless, her eyelids drooping. If Macbeth's tiny body generated this much heat, perhaps she should get a dog before winter. A big, warm, furry dog who wouldn't mind sharing bed space with a cat.

A big, warm, furry dog . . . with big teeth and a taste for smelly sea captains.

Chapter 2

London
June 1816

"**D**o you plan to regain consciousness any time soon?"

Tony buried his head farther under the pillow, trying to shut out his older brother's booming voice.

"Mama was quite worried about you when you didn't come home yesterday. Do you know how much time I had to spend with her, reassuring her you were not floating facedown in the Thames with a knife stuck in your back? Time I could have spent with my *wife*?"

Ben not only didn't go away, but plopped down on the edge of the mattress. The bed and Tony groaned in unison.

He hadn't really had that much to drink, had he? Just a few glasses at the faro table. And one while on board Nick's ship, but that one didn't count, since the tide had come in and Tony had heaved his guts out over the railing. And of course there had been the glass or three at his brother's wedding breakfast, just before he . . .

Oh. Just before he kissed his new sister-in-law. Soundly. With his brother standing less than three feet away.

Not his brightest move. Tony pushed the pillow aside and risked opening one eye to glance at his brother sitting on the edge of the bed. He squinted, trying to block out most of the light stabbing his eyeball.

Ben looked back at him, his head cocked to the side, one eyebrow raised. No sign of a weapon in his hands, or murder in his eye. Maybe he'd already forgiven Tony for the liberty he'd taken with Jo. A charming lass, his new sister-in-law.

"Are you in there?" Ben poked him in the shoulder.

Pain exploded in his shoulder and upper back. Tony hissed and rolled onto his side, away from the finger. His head throbbed anew, the room dipped and swayed, and the contents of his stomach threatened to make a return appearance. "Kill me now." He squeezed his eyes shut.

"Not just yet." The bed shifted as Ben stood up.

Tony lost his balance and started to roll onto his back, only to hiss in pain again as his shoulder made contact with the mattress. What the . . . ? He swung his legs over the side and slowly sat up, examining the backs of his hands. Knuckles were fine, no bruising or scratches. If he'd been in a fight, as his body felt, he hadn't defended himself very well.

A mug was shoved under his nose. Tony looked up, trying to see the expression on his brother's face, but Ben was tall enough, and Tony's head hurt enough, that just now he couldn't see that high.

Ben grabbed Tony's hand and wrapped it around the mug. "Thompson promises this will get rid of the worst of your hangover."

"Your footman? What's he know about . . . Never mind." He sniffed, took a sip. Nothing he'd ever order at a pub, but if it would stop the incessant pounding and settle his stomach . . . He gulped it down.

"You can ask him for the recipe later, when you thank him for putting you to bed last night."

Tony choked.

Ben patted him on the back, and Tony jumped up, away from the pain. Every touch hurt, and Ben wasn't even trying.

When the floor and walls settled, Tony took stock. He was still fully dressed, minus his coat and boots, in the same garments he'd worn to the wedding breakfast. A few new stains since then, though. But he had no recollection of Ben's giant blond footman helping him to bed.

"Alistair brought you home, then Thompson carried you up the stairs. Had to pause on the landing while you . . ." Ben made a rolling gesture with his hand, and Tony's stomach lurched in response. "I believe you owe the maids a generous vail, by the way."

"I'll do that." He reached for the bell pull.

"Don't bother." Ben leaned against the bedpost, his arms folded. "Already ordered a bath to be brought up, as well as a light breakfast. Even though it's past two."

"Your servants can handle two requests at once now?" He must still have too much alcohol in his system to be baiting his brother like this. "Oh, right, Jo's in charge again. Got them working like clockwork, she does."

Ben straightened to his full height, standing several inches taller and wider than Tony. He spoke softly, his low voice filled with menace. "That's Lady Sinclair, to you."

"Of course. My apologies." Tony held his hands to his temples, which were throbbing even harder under his brother's glare.

They both turned at a knock on the door. "Enter," they called in unison.

A parade of servants marched in, and within moments they had set up a tub with steaming buckets of water before the fire, a tray with food and tea on the desk, and bowed and curtsied on the way out.

"Not a moment too soon," Ben said as the door closed behind them. "You reek of Blue Ruin and cheap perfume, and I don't want to know what those other scents are."

"Sorry to offend your olfactory senses." Tony struggled out of his waistcoat and shirt, wincing as he caught a whiff of himself. "But this *is* my bedchamber." He dropped the clothes in a heap. "Unless you're kicking me out?"

Ben pushed Tony onto the bed before he fell to the floor, as balancing on one foot to peel off his stockings seemed beyond his abilities at the moment. "You can take up bachelor quarters if you want, though I think Mama would prefer you stay here for a while, now that you're finally done with school. She's concerned."

Stockings dealt with, Tony stood up and struggled to remove his breeches. What, had someone stitched the buttons closed while he slept?

"I confess to being a tad concerned, myself," Ben continued. "I know it wasn't easy for you, putting off school so long and finishing well after your chums, but your behavior lately . . . at the wedding breakfast—"

"One is supposed to kiss the bride."

"One is supposed to keep his tongue in his own damn mouth!"

Tony covered his ears and winced at the reverberating boom bouncing around inside his skull. "Sorry," he said when the echoes finally died down.

The buttons still wouldn't release. Tony grasped the material and yanked. Buttons flew across the room and bounced on the hardwood floor. Ah, much better. He let the breeches puddle at his feet, and struggled with the tapes on his drawers.

"And then you went off carousing with your friends for two days—"

Tony jerked his head up. Two days? "This isn't Wednesday?"

"Thursday. Afternoon."

Hmm. There was something happening on Thursday. Something he was supposed to do. But his brain hurt too much to dredge up the details at the moment.

"Mama thinks you're trying to become a rake like Nick, with a mistress in every port . . ."

Tony let the words wash over him as Ben continued his rant. Mama worried too much. And Nick only had one mistress. The knot undone, Tony shucked off his drawers and headed for the tub before the water cooled.

"And then you—Good Lord, what have you done to yourself?"

Tony stopped. He'd grown up, is what he'd done. Since his brother had last seen him au naturel, Tony had studied with fencing masters and boxing instructors, men who saw rules and laws more as guidelines than rigid codes. He may not have inherited Papa's height and title, but he was no longer a scrawny little schoolboy, favorite target of bullies. Not anymore.

"No wonder you flinched when I touched your shoulder. Whatever possessed you to do that?"

"Flinching is a perfectly reasonable response to pain." Tony started for the tub again.

Ben leaped off the bed, caught up to him. "No, I meant, what possessed you to do *this*?" He spun him around and pushed Tony's chin over his shoulder so he could see his back in the mirror.

Tony shoved the dark brown hair out of his bloodshot eyes and focused his gaze. Good Lord, what *had* he done to himself? Dried blood had congealed on a fresh wound just above his right shoulder blade, with colorful bruises radiating out from it, down his back and over his shoulder. He flexed his muscles. Bad idea. The floor started swaying again.

Ben grabbed him by the elbows and gave an exasperated shake of his head. "Only sailors and convicts have tattoos. Which do you intend to be?"

Tattoo? He'd had enough to drink that he'd let Nick talk him into getting a tattoo? Had to have been Nick—Alistair might sketch the image, but would never embed it on his skin. Nick, however, had come back from his last voyage to New Guinea with some tribal design wrapped around his bicep. Tony would pound him. Just as soon as his head stopped pounding.

Ben cocked his head to one side. "What is it?"

"You just said it's a tattoo."

Ben thwacked him on his uninjured shoulder. "A tattoo of *what*? What image did you admire so much that you had to get it permanently etched onto your skin?"

Good question. Tony didn't even remember visiting a tattoo artist. Come to think on it, there were a lot of gaps in his memory, between the outraged roar from Ben after Tony had kissed Jo, just before he departed with his friends, to waking up this morning. Afternoon. Whatever.

"It defies description. You'll have to wait until the swelling goes down." Tony perched on the edge of the tub, his head hanging down, as he allowed Ben to tend to his shoulder.

They'd done this as children—Ben would push aside their nurse or governess to take care of Tony's scraped knees and bloody nose himself, especially if

Ben had been the one to inflict the injuries in the first place. Never with malicious intent, of course—the bumps and bruises were just a consequence of Tony tagging along after a brother five years older and so much bigger.

But they were adults now, and Ben had other responsibilities. "Not that I don't appreciate being awakened from a sound sleep for no apparent reason, but shouldn't you be with your bride?"

"She's sleeping."

Tony looked up at the unexpectedly gentle tone in Ben's voice. Was that a blush staining his brother's cheeks? He drew breath for a teasing comment about newlyweds, then remembered he was in a rather vulnerable position at the moment. Ben gave him a wry grin that said he knew exactly what Tony had been thinking. "Perhaps she's awake by now."

Ben's grin widened. "Perhaps." He dunked the washcloth in the tub and plopped it over Tony's head. "I'll just go see."

Tony shoved the dripping cloth out of his eyes and watched his brother head for the door.

Once again Ben walked with the self-assured posture of a soldier, his limp barely noticeable. "When you're decent and can think straight, come see me. I have a proposition for you." Ben shut the door behind him.

When Tony had left for school last fall, Ben still needed crutches. Doctors said it was a miracle he hadn't lost his leg altogether in that blasted battle at Waterloo. Mama had said in her letters that Ben worked hard to be rid of even a cane. Tony was convinced a certain managing female was responsible for Ben's recovery. An auburn-haired beauty who smelled of lemons, whom he had better, apparently, address as Lady Sinclair.

Tony allowed himself to fall over the edge into the tepid water, splashing all over the floor. Careful of his aching shoulder, he washed and shaved. He now had the funds to hire a valet—perhaps he should finally get one.

When Jo, now Lady Sinclair, had come to work for Ben, she'd shifted their investments and increased their worth considerably, in spite of the embezzling secretary that had preceded her. Even Tony's modest inheritance from his maternal grandmother had been doubled.

And they'd been hiring servants at every turn the last few months—what was one more? The love match between Ben's aging butler and housekeeper had infected the rest of the staff. He'd lost track of how many servants had paired up and run off and had to be replaced.

Tony heaved his aching body out of the tub and got dressed.

He had made do without a manservant while at school by having his clothes tailored so that he didn't require assistance. Good thing they were loose over his aching shoulder. The New Guinea tattoo artists must be more skilled than those at the London docks, because he couldn't imagine Nick putting up with this much discomfort.

Whether it was the hangover remedy or bath and

clean clothes, he was starting to feel human again. Recovered enough, in fact, to feel a smidgeon of curiosity about Ben's proposition.

He made his way downstairs to the library. All was quiet within. He debated whether to knock, but Ben had told him to come down as soon as he was ready. He opened the door and stepped in.

Behind the massive oak desk, Ben was seated in his big leather chair, account ledgers spread across the desk, with his wife sideways on his lap. Jo had a pencil in one hand and was moving balls on the abacus, or at least attempting to do so, with her other hand. Her progress was impeded by Ben's nuzzling of her ear.

Tony stood motionless, frozen. He should leave them their privacy, but found himself unable to look away. His breathing hitched and an unfamiliar emotion crept over him.

Envy.

Not specifically for his brother's wife, attractive though she was, but for their relationship. Happiness and contentment seemed to ooze from their every pore. Ben was at peace, because of the laughing woman on his lap.

Could Tony ever find a similar joy and peace for himself? Or was that also reserved solely for the eldest son, along with the title and family wealth?

"Pull up a chair."

Tony looked up with a guilty start at his brother's command.

"I'll leave you two to your chat." Lady Sinclair struggled to get up, her cheeks flooded with color. She had faced down menacing merchants and towering servants in her role as "Mister Quincy," but was still embarrassed to be caught on her husband's lap. Charming. Or perhaps she just couldn't bear to look at him after the liberty he'd taken with her the other day. He wouldn't blame her.

Ben's arms tightened around her waist. "You don't have to leave just yet," he murmured.

"Yes, no need to leave on my account," Tony felt compelled to add as he sat down. He must have a death wish. Judging by the narrowed expression on his brother's face, Ben would gladly help make that wish come true.

Lady Sinclair peeled Ben's arm from her waist and slid to the floor, adjusting her gown as she straightened. "Will you be staying in for dinner tonight?"

Tony wasn't aware he was grinning until Ben scowled at him. "Yes, Jo, um, Lady Sinclair. I wouldn't miss it."

"Until tonight, then." With a last blush, she swept from the room.

"Now then." Ben pushed aside the abacus and account books.

Tony sat up. Before his eyes, the jolly newlywed disappeared, replaced by the Earl of Sinclair, head of the family.

"How's your head?"

"Much better. Thompson's cure is quite effective."

"Yes, I know." Ben picked up a pencil, then set it down again. "As I said earlier, Mama is concerned by your recent behavior. As am I. I know it can't have been easy, holding things together while I was . . . away."

Five years of away, five years of uncertainty, where the younger son had to put a good face on the disaster their family had become, the scandal fodder after Papa's suicide. Five years of delaying his schooling, not knowing if he'd ever return to complete the remaining year.

Now Ben was back, recovered from his injuries, married, getting on with his life.

Mama was out of mourning, being courted by both a viscount and a marquess, getting on with her life.

And Tony . . . He hadn't a clue what to do with his life.

Ben was still speaking. Tony reluctantly brought his thoughts back to their surroundings. ". . . job at the Home Office. Dunwood wants a clerk he can rely on, and I told him you'd be well suited. You're not a green lad just out of Cambridge. You have skills and experience that will stand both of you in good stead." Ben leaned forward, palms flat on the desk. "It will do you good—the salary will make you independent of any allowance, enable you to leave Grandmama's inheritance untouched. You can let bachelor quarters without worrying about the expense. Mama will still worry about you, of course, but you won't have to be present for it."

Work as a clerk for Lord Dunwood? Tony leaned back in his chair. A respectable position, an independent income, a regular schedule.

Predictable. Subject to a supervisor's whims.

Boring.

"So? Will you meet with him?"

Tony sighed. He really didn't have much of a choice. "Yes."

Ben stood, clapped his hands together once. "Splendid. He's expecting you tomorrow at ten. You can discuss specifics, come to an amicable agreement." Ben glanced at the door, then back at Tony.

"Go to her, you randy, besotted fool."

With a grin, Ben slapped him on his good shoulder and strode from the room.

Tony slumped in his chair. Ben's joy permeated the place, inescapable. He had to get out of the house. Go beat his former best friend to a pulp.

He suddenly remembered what was happening on Thursday, and leaped out of his chair.

Less than an hour later, Tony stepped out of a hansom cab, took a deep whiff of salty air tinged with day-old fish, and coughed. He threaded his way through the doxies and costermongers on the docks, to the slip where Nick's brig was moored.

"What the hell did you do to me?" he shouted when Nick waved at him from the deck.

"Do? Old chum, I did nothing to you. Come aboard." Nick gestured for Tony to walk up the plank.

"You must think me daft. I have no intention of setting foot on that blighted dinghy ever again."

Nick threw his head back, let out a far too hearty laugh, and swaggered down the plank. "Keep loading, swabbies," he shouted up to the deck.

"Aye, Captain," came the chorus of replies. His

crew continued to swarm over the deck and dock, loading casks and barrels.

Tony eyed the stack of provisions. "Still leaving on the evening tide?"

"Sure I can't persuade you to join me?" Nick threw his arm around Tony's shoulder, leading him to a nearby coffeehouse. "Jonesy has another brew he'd like you to try, certain to cure your green gills."

"The last cure nearly killed me." Tony shrugged off the arm, which was putting pressure on his injured shoulder.

"Don't be sore. Oh, that's it, you *are* sore." Nick gave another hearty laugh.

"It's your fault." Tony pointed at his damaged shoulder. "I would never have done this if you hadn't gotten me foxed."

"What could I do? You were admiring the tattoo on Jonesy's arm. Seemed only right to let you get one of your own."

What could possibly have been on the first mate's arm that prompted him to get one like it? Nothing; Nick was still joshing him. Nick had pulled more than his share of pranks—years ago, they'd met in the headmaster's outer office because of his penchant for pranks. This was just one more. Only this time, there would be no scrubbing off the whitewash.

Tony drew breath to argue, but was cut off by Nick's shout of "Alistair!" and enthusiastic wave.

Standing head and shoulders above the unwashed crowd, their friend changed direction and headed toward them in front of the coffeehouse. "Thought the plan was to see you off at the dock," Alistair said as he drew abreast of them.

"Tony needed coffee."

"Still hung over? Didn't think you'd had all that much to drink."

Tony opened the coffeehouse door and stepped through first. "Nick wants to flirt with the serving wench one last time before he goes to sea."

"Good lord, man, it's only a two-week voyage." Alistair pushed his coattails aside as he took a seat at their favorite table. Nick and Tony followed suit.

"Two weeks—an entire fortnight during which I shall have to abstain from sweet curves, long hair, gentle voices, and soft skin." Nick trailed a finger down the hand of the serving wench who came to take their order. She giggled and blushed, and left with their request for coffee and biscuits.

"Perhaps you should hire a better-looking crew," Tony suggested.

"I don't know that's necessary." Alistair appeared to give the matter grave consideration. "Jonesy wears his hair in a long queue, and your bosun's voice has been soft ever since his throat was crushed in a fight. Where was that, Barbados?"

Nick laughed. "Le Havre, actually."

They reminisced about some of Nick's past adventures, then switched to the trip he was about to depart on, a counterclockwise sail around the coast of England, until their order arrived.

The serving wench flirted outrageously with Nick after she set down the plate of biscuits and gave him his cup, staring at his black hair tied back in a queue, mesmerized by his gold earring and dark blue eyes.

She finally tore her gaze away to set a cup in front of Alistair. He brushed the light brown hair from his eyes and smiled his thanks at her. One, two, three . . . there it was—the hitch in her breathing as she stared into his blue eyes and angelic face. The wench smiled back, ready to melt in a puddle at his feet. Or his lap. "Anything else you gents be wanting?"

Tony cleared his throat and pointed at the third cup, still in her hand.

"Oh, right, so sorry, sir."

Tony gave her a wry grin. She blushed and gave a slight shrug. No, of course she couldn't help herself. After facing the full force of Nick's allure and Alistair's unconscious charm, one right after the other, any woman would be flustered. Tony, with his brown hair, brown eyes, and smaller frame, seemed almost innocuous in comparison.

Almost.

Nick dunked a biscuit in his cup, splashing coffee. "Are you still leaving tomorrow?"

Alistair nodded. "Traveling on foot, I'll have just enough time to see a few sights and take a roundabout way to William Herschel's."

Tony stirred sugar into his coffee. "Tell me again why you finagled an invitation to visit him. What's so special about his forty-foot telescope?"

Alistair spoke slowly. "It's forty feet."

"So you're saying size really does matter?" Nick sat up and puffed out his chest.

Alistair took another bite of biscuit. "So, Nick's sailing in a few hours, I'm leaving on a walking tour in the morning . . . what are *you* up to?"

"Has your brother called you out?"

"No." Only two biscuits left. Tony grabbed one.

Alistair snatched the last biscuit from Nick's fingers. "Then you lead a charmed life."

"Ben doesn't get angry—he finds *solutions*." Tony told them about the offer with Lord Dunwood.

"A nice, steady position sounds just the thing. You'll always know what to expect of tomorrow." Nick brushed the crumbs from his cravat.

Tony snorted. "This, from the man who can't wait for tomorrow and has to sail toward the horizon to bring it closer?" He turned to Alistair. "How would you like to know what you're going to do every day? The same thing, day after day?"

Alistair shuddered.

"Exactly."

"A living death, to be sure." Nick drained his cup. "So, you're going to take the job, right?"

Tony sighed. "Probably." He could turn it down with a clear conscience if he had an alternate plan. Any plan.

"I do know what I'm going to be doing fourteen days from now," Nick announced. "Getting reacquainted with the fair Esmeralda at the Duck and Drake Inn at Weymouth."

"You're still seeing her after, what, three years now?" Alistair's brows rose. "I must meet this paragon of womanhood. I'll see you in Weymouth in two weeks."

"You can meet her, but her heart is already spoken for." Nick held his hand over his chest.

Alistair snorted.

Soon after, they walked Nick back to his ship and saw him off. Alistair left to finish packing for his journey, and Tony was left to contemplate the fact that he was about to accept a boring job instead of setting off on an adventure of his own.

"Elliott will be waiting out front to drive you to the City," Ben said as Tony lingered over a cup of tea with three sugars at breakfast the next morning.

His appetite suddenly gone, Tony set the cup down. "Right, no sense me hiring a hansom cab when you have no need of the coach yourself." He doubted Ben had set foot out of doors since the wedding, though he was certainly still getting his exercise.

Ben's only reply was a waggle of the eyebrows. He reached for his wife's hand, and the two left the dining room, disappearing up the stairs.

"I do hope you and Lord Dunwood get along well," Mama said, interrupting Tony's thoughts.

"I'm sure we shall." Tony tossed his napkin on the table. "I can get along with anyone." He bussed his mother on the cheek, and stepped out the front door.

Soon, Elliott set the horses in motion and eased the coach into traffic, joining the throngs of carts and hacks that filled the street. Tony leaned back against the velvet squabs and closed his eyes, trying to shut out the din of vendors hawking their wares.

Alistair was leaving for a walking tour of the countryside, was on the road south out of town even now.

Nick had set sail on last night's tide, off on his own adventure, even if it was just a routine trip around the English coastline.

Tony was on his way to a job, in an office, in the crowded, noisy, dirty City.

He rapped on the roof. "Elliott!"

"Yes, sir?"

"Head south. We're not going to the City. We're going to catch up to Alistair."

Chapter 3

"You've gone stark raving mad," Alistair muttered as they watched the coach head back to town.

"Entirely possible," Tony said with a grin. He slapped Alistair on the back and they set off walking in silence, save for the chirp of birds, the crunch of their boots on the road, the occasional coach or cart rumbling past them.

Tony breathed deeply. Not the miasma of London, but the fresh clean scent of tilled earth. Blue sky above, not four walls and a ceiling. Fields stretched in every direction. Already, London was just a memory.

His decision to join Alistair was precipitous, yes, but the right one.

He wasn't completely unprepared for the journey.

Perhaps he'd made his decision as he'd dressed that morning, without realizing it. He'd placed the entire remainder of his quarter's allowance in his purse, much more money than he normally carried. Since he refused to sacrifice comfort for the sake of fashion, his boots and clothes should hold up well. He could always buy toiletries and a change of linen when they stopped for the night. And he'd asked the coachman to relay his request to Ben to have bank drafts waiting at points along Alistair's planned route, just in case he ran short of funds.

"How do you think your brother will react when he learns you've rejected Lord Dunwood's offer?"

Tony reluctantly gave up his contemplation of the clouds. In a fair fight, Ben could probably still pound him into the floor. Which wasn't much incentive to fight fair, or to go home again.

"Perhaps his real intent all along was simply to goad you into doing something, just as you did. Force you to do something with your life."

"You think Ben is that calculating?"

Alistair shrugged. "I'm just saying I know how difficult the last five years have been. If you want to play truant and explore England with me for a while, that's fine. Maybe you'll find your life's calling along the way."

Find his life's calling. Good one.

The day passed quickly, the miles eaten up beneath their boots. It was nearing dusk when hunger finally made them stop at an inn.

"This evening's special, whatever it is, and a mug of ale for each of us, please," Alistair said to the serving wench when she approached their table. He immediately turned his attention back to Tony and their interrupted conversation, teasing him about running away from home.

The young woman lingered long enough to witness Alistair's smile, and Tony knew she was a goner. She stared at Alistair over her shoulder as she returned to the kitchen.

Tony pointed his finger at his friend. "You still have no clue of the effect you have on them, do you?"

"What effect, on who?"

"Never mind." They chatted until she returned and set their platters down. Tony couldn't resist a spot of mischief. He lowered his chin and looked up at her through his lashes, the way he'd often seen his friend do it, and kept his voice low. "Would you mind terribly bringing us more ale, miss?"

She melted before him. "My pleasure, Brown Eyes." She was back in less than a minute with full tankards. "Anything else you fancy?" She leaned over, offering Tony a peek down her gown, almost to her navel.

That was just too easy. Or she was. Tony cleared his throat. "Um, thank you, no, we're good."

"I'm sure you are, ducks." She walked away, her hips swaying provocatively.

"If you're that desperate for company, I'll make myself scarce." Alistair dug into his food.

"What? Her? Oh, good heavens, no. Just, no." Tony certainly didn't mind a little company now and then, but he did mind being one among many. "I was

just conducting a little experiment. And it worked."
They ate the indifferent stew the wench had brought.
"Actually, she did remind me of something Ben said
yesterday."

Alistair pushed his empty platter aside. "Oh?"

Tony pushed his platter aside, as well. "Accused me
of becoming a rakehell."

Alistair coughed. "You?"

"You needn't look so shocked. I did kiss the new
countess." He wiped his mouth with a napkin. "Perhaps that's my life's calling."

"You got away with kissing her once, but your
brother will certainly call you out if you try that again."
Alistair took a deep drink, emptying his tankard.

"No, you dolt. I meant, perhaps my life's calling is
to become a rakehell."

Alistair spewed ale.

"It's not that far-fetched. I'm fairly good-looking. I
may not have your extraneous height and fallen-angel
looks, but some women like a more compact package.
She certainly did." He pointed at the wench, who
winked at him as she served another table.

"Not that I'm disagreeing in the slightest with your
appeal to the fairer sex—"

"However . . ."

"However, I think if one has to make the conscious
decision to become a rake, one is not *really* a rake, but
merely a poseur."

Hmm. Perhaps Alistair had a point.

"Sleep on it. Maybe your calling will come to you
in your dreams."

* * *

Later that night, dreams stayed just beyond his reach as Tony as fidgeted on the lumpy mattress, trying to find a spot that didn't aggravate his sore shoulder.

Nick had served his country with his ship, and Alistair was trying to prove something important in the field of astronomy. Was there any subject that stoked his own fire?

Giving up on sleep, he pulled on his breeches and shirt and climbed out the window, up to the peak of the roof where Alistair sat, silhouetted against the starry sky, telescope raised to one eye.

"If only I had a more powerful scope," Alistair said softly. "I could measure the seas on the moon, unlock the secrets of the universe."

"What is it you're trying to do, again?"

That was all the encouragement he needed. Give him a willing audience, and the scholar could wax poetic about celestial bodies for hours on end. Nick could go on just as long, speaking in awed tones about the lines of his ship.

Tony encouraged his friends, admired and supported them, just as they would support his avocation . . . if he had one.

He'd had one, temporarily, when he'd acted in the earl's place. Coordinating the efforts of their estate managers, overseeing the family's investments, supervising the running of the household—he'd been consumed every waking moment with his new duties. Willingly, gladly.

With his father barely cold in his grave, Ben off to

fight Napoleon amidst gossip that he'd killed their father's rival, and Mama plunged into deep mourning, a recluse, it had been left to Tony to pull them through. He'd left school and stepped into the role thrust upon him, and done a damn fine job under the circumstances.

But Ben was back, life had attained a new normal, and Tony was left adrift. He'd finished school, of course, but now that he was done, what was he supposed to *do*?

So far, the most intriguing idea was to become a rake. The family finances were in excellent condition. Tony didn't *need* to work, unless he found something he wanted to do, a cause to take up.

As Alistair talked about perturbations of planetary orbits, Tony's head began to swim. So, astronomy was out of the question. The mere thought of getting on a boat again unsettled his stomach, so his calling would clearly have nothing to do with ships or the sea.

His brother's passionate interest, aside from his bride, was helping soldiers. Too many had come home from the war to find no way to support their families. The new Lady Sinclair had been hiring ex-soldiers right and left, but Ben had taken it one step further— buying inns, and putting men to work running them. Ben's solicitor was kept busy investigating potential properties for Ben to purchase.

Perhaps Tony should involve himself in his brother's endeavor. Alistair's walk about the countryside was going to take them to a great many inns. Tony could evaluate the inns and send reports back to Ben.

As lifelong passions went, it wasn't much, but it did give him something to do in the short term. Some purpose, while he tried on the role of rake.

His immediate future settled, he realized his teeth were chattering. Alistair had donned boots and coat before climbing up, but Tony's bare feet felt like blocks of ice. Whatever cause he eventually took up, it would not require him to shiver outdoors in the middle of the night, or climb up on roofs. "I'm going back in, where it's warm."

"You've no stamina at all." Alistair grinned as he looked through his telescope.

One week after leaving London, they stopped at the Happy Jack Inn on the Dorset coast early one afternoon. Tony had scrutinized each inn they passed as a potential purchase for Ben, and sent his notes home in the penny-post, hoping his steady flow of correspondence would allay his family's fears and annoyance. Alistair observed the stars each night, but repeated rain showers and cloudy skies had left him in a funk—observations would be impossible tonight. Tony just wanted a hot meal, and to get dry.

A serving maid came out of the kitchen, bringing them the evening's special. Obviously the innkeeper's daughter, with the same red hair and strong chin as the stout older man who'd brought their bread and ale a few minutes before. "Can I get you gentlemen anything else?" Her voice was breathy, but her dress was cut high enough her abundant charms were not on display. She flashed a crooked but innocent smile.

Tony was reminded he hadn't done much yet to further his career as a rake. He smiled up at her. He'd never been with a redhead before. Would *all* her hair . . .

Her father appeared, filling the kitchen doorway, glowering at Tony.

On second thought, perhaps the innkeeper's daughter was not the best idea for his first conquest as a rake. "Thank you, but this is enough." He kept his smile pleasant but neutral.

"As you wish, sir." She walked back to the kitchen, hardly any sway to her hips at all.

Tony returned to his rapidly cooling stew, and glanced around again at the deserted taproom. The place was clean, aside from soot-stained walls and ceiling that swallowed up most of the daylight. They'd seen no employees save the innkeeper and his daughter. An older woman, who must be the innkeeper's wife, had emerged from the kitchen doorway long enough to hand the girl the bowls of stew.

"This might be the most promising inn for Ben I've seen so far."

Alistair glanced around. "Certainly could benefit from a new investor. I don't think it's been painted in this century."

The outer door opened and slammed against the wall, caught by a gust of wind. A woman stepped through and struggled to close it again. A widow, given her unadorned straw bonnet and half-mourning gown of gray. Tony was about to jump up and offer assistance when she shoved the door closed. She gave an embarrassed smile when she saw the two men sitting at the corner table.

Tony's heart lodged in his throat.

In London, he probably wouldn't have given her a second glance. But here in the wilds of Dorset, there was something utterly perfect about her reddened cheeks and full lips, her windblown dark blonde curls peeking out from the gray ribbons of her bonnet. Her husband must have been monumentally unfortunate or criminally stupid to have widowed her at such a young age.

She blushed as Tony continued to stare, and hid her green eyes by glancing down at the basket on her arm.

She was a widow. He wanted to be a rake.

Perfect.

He scooted his chair back. Before he could rise, she strode across the taproom and disappeared into the kitchen.

"I'll just pay our shot, and we can be off." Alistair threw his napkin on the table.

"What? Why?"

Alistair followed Tony's gaze, which was still locked on the kitchen doorway. "You just saw her for the first time, haven't even spoken with her yet. You can't be serious."

"Oh, but I can. I think I'm in love."

"You're in lust."

Tony shrugged. "Same thing."

The innkeeper's daughter came out, and Alistair settled the bill. After she left, he pulled out the dog-eared map from his pocket. "I want to head inland for a while. We can be in Wool by tonight, and in Shaftesbury the following night. I have a friend with a five-foot telescope there, built by Herschel himself. One of his earlier models."

The widow came out of the kitchen just then, now juggling two baskets on her arm. The ribbons of her bonnet had become tangled with the handles. Tony was across the room and at her side before Alistair had even finished his sentence. "Allow me to give you a hand." Tony rested his hand on hers, where she gripped the basket handle.

Her eyes widened in surprise. "No, thank you, sir, it's quite all right."

Tony untangled the ribbons and smoothed the worn gray satin between his fingertips. "No trouble at all," he murmured. While her hands were occupied with the baskets, he took the liberty of tying the ribbons into a neat bow beneath her chin. He also took the liberty of touching his bare fingers to the underside of her chin in the process, and brushed her bare neck just above her unbuttoned pelisse.

Her soft skin was chilled from the storm outside. The fichu tucked into her neckline had been tugged loose on one side by the wind, revealing a small strip of creamy flesh above her bosom. Tony wanted to brush his fingers there, too.

By the time he finished tying the bow, instead of a maidenly blush coloring her cheeks, there was a decided glint in her green eyes. Outrage? Defiance? Her pulse fluttered at her throat.

Alistair strolled to their side. "Please forgive my forward friend, madam. He seems to have left his manners behind in London."

She forced a polite smile, baring a few teeth. White and straight. Lovely. "No harm done."

Tony drew breath to protest Alistair's insult. Alistair continued, with the smile and smooth-as-honey voice that made women want to toss their skirts for him. "Alistair, Viscount Moncreiffe, at your service, madam." He gave an elegant bow. "May I assist you with your burden?"

Her smile was genuine now, drat Alistair. "Thank you, but that won't be necessary. Good day, gentlemen." And with that, she hurried out of the taproom before Tony could utter another syllable.

"So, shall we head north?"

Tony stared out the window, watching the widow's retreating form, her steps confident. The wind hugged her dress to her curves, which were just the right size, perfectly proportioned. He waved at his friend. "You go on ahead. I think I'll stay here a while."

Alistair slowly nodded. "This wouldn't have anything to do with the new career you mentioned, would it?"

He let his smile speak for itself.

Alistair stroked his chin. "I suppose she was pretty, in a rugged, rural sort of way." He folded the map and tucked it back in his pocket. "You know, we don't really have to go to Shaftesbury. We have an entire week before we're supposed to meet up with Nick in Weymouth. We could stay right here."

We? "No, no, you go on ahead. I'll meet up with you in a week or so."

"You want to stay here, by yourself, in this quaint little village where you don't know a soul? Do you know what you're getting yourself into?"

"You mean, besides the lady's bed?"

Alistair slapped his shoulder. "I'll give you this, my friend. You have excellent taste. She seemed charming. Too bad she wouldn't give you the time of day."

"That will change. Trust me."

Alistair hefted his haversack over his shoulder. "Are you sure you don't want to come with me? That telescope is five feet long." He held his hands outstretched to demonstrate the size.

"Did y'see the pretty widow?"

Alistair set his haversack down. "You know, she really was pretty. Perhaps I should stay."

Ignoring the tease in Alistair's tone, Tony picked up the haversack and put it back on Alistair's shoulder. "I wouldn't want to be the cause of you missing out on that five-foot telescope." He gave Alistair a shove toward the door.

"All right, all right. I can take a hint." Alistair stepped outside. The wind had calmed and the rain had stopped, at least for the moment.

"See you in a week. Or thereabouts."

Alistair shook his head, laughing, as he strode across the inn yard. "Happy hunting!"

Tony grabbed his own haversack and went to book a room for the night at the Happy Jack, formulating his plan for wooing the widow.

First, though, he had to find her again.

Late that evening, Tony once more sat at the corner table in the taproom, eating mutton and cheese. Mrs. Spencer, the innkeeper's wife, and her daughter had been less than forthcoming regarding the widow's identity. Even though he'd followed the same direction she had taken when she'd left, questioning villagers regarding her identity had proven equally frustrating and fruitless. Between the war against Napoleon and a shipwreck last spring, the village had more than its share of widows. Finding the right one could prove problematic.

The pouring rain and blustery wind had made him give up his search for the evening. After a good night's sleep, tomorrow he'd begin again. Until then, tonight was the perfect opportunity to gather more information for his brother about the inn.

"Why do you want to know?" Mrs. Spencer stood beside Tony's table, her fists on her hips.

"Just curious how many employees it takes to operate a fine establishment such as this, one that is not on the post road and doesn't appear to have much local custom, never mind travelers." Tony smiled at her.

Mrs. Spencer harrumphed, filled his tankard, and left without answering his question.

Perhaps the inclement weather was keeping the locals at home. Even the blazing fire in the hearth could not dispel the gloom, with the tallow candles adding to the dreary atmosphere rather than dispelling it.

Tony almost dropped his fork when the door blew open and two men walked in. They wrestled the door shut against the wind, then turned and tripped over themselves when they spotted Tony in the corner.

"Good evening," he called.

"Aye," the younger of the two newcomers replied, straightening his threadbare coat. With stooped shoulders and weather-roughened cheeks, he looked sixty if a day.

His companion grunted as he removed his cap and ran gnarled fingers through his short hair, before jamming the cap back on over the silver spikes. They moved to one of the rickety benches before the fire and sat down.

Spencer came out of the kitchen, a stained towel over one shoulder, and scowled at Tony.

"Spencer, bring us a pint of your best," the elder of the newcomers called.

"And keep them coming. 'Twill be a long night," the other added. His companion elbowed him in the ribs and cast a look over his shoulder at the table in the corner.

Tony pretended not to see, as he was busy draining his tankard of ale. The food was indifferent, but the drink was exceptional.

"Keep yer shirts on," Spencer grumbled, and left the room, wiping his hands on the towel.

The door blew open again with another gust of wind and rain, and more men ambled in, congregating near the fire. All seemed to be of an age with the two already present, and all gave Tony much more than a cursory glance. They conversed in hushed voices, the words lost before they reached Tony's ears.

Tony raised his empty tankard as Mrs. Spencer made the rounds with a large pitcher. She obliged, not spilling a drop.

"Thought the rain would keep everyone at home tonight." He pointed at the men by the hearth.

Mrs. Spencer whirled back toward him, pitcher held high. "What did you say?"

Tony set down his tankard. "Just that I thought the taproom was empty earlier because everyone was staying home, out of the rain."

"Right. Home. Rain." She bobbed her chin and hurried toward the kitchen, throwing him a glance over her shoulder before ducking through the doorway.

He'd heard people in rural counties were a bit eccentric. He was beginning to believe that the rumors, at least in this case, had merit.

The door opened again, and this time there were boys with the old men coming indoors, in their mid- to late teens guessing by their posturing and strutting.

If Tony were prone to paranoia, he might think the looks thrown his way were suspicious. Perhaps the men had heard of Tony's inquiries about the widow, divined his intentions, and were simply being protective of her.

Some of the men filed out, including the two who had entered first. The wind had calmed, and no rain blew in while the door was open. The half dozen remaining stayed by the fire, their backs to Tony. If he were in London, he'd think he was being given the cut direct.

With the break in the storm, Tony decided to take a quick walk down to the beach before turning in. He pulled his coat tighter about his shoulders and stepped outdoors. He could almost feel the clouds above, hanging low over the land. Precious little light spilled from the inn's windows, leaving the courtyard almost solid black. Odd. There should at least be a lantern in the stables. He had definitely heard horses earlier.

He'd gone a few steps in what he thought was the correct direction when he heard a harsh *"Now!"*

What little light there'd been disappeared as a not-quite-empty flour sack was thrust over his head, choking and blinding him.

Hands grabbed at him. Tony swung, caught nothing. He coughed, tried to call out, but the sound was cut off by a fist punching him in the stomach. He bent over, gasping for air, struggling to tug the suffocating cloth from his face. More hands were on him, holding the flour sack in place, pinning his arms.

He'd spent countless hours at the London docks among the dregs of humanity with nothing worse happening to him than bruising his knuckles, only to be attacked and bested here, in a tiny, remote village on the picturesque coast. How utterly humiliating.

But he wasn't down yet.

He kicked. Connected. Someone grunted in pain, one hand loosened from his neck. Encouraged, Tony kicked backward, found another shin. Another grunt.

He was able to pull his right arm free, tried again to rip off the blinding sack.

"Stubborn one, ain't he?"

Tony had just enough time to register the fact that the speaker was next to his ear before they whacked him on the back of his head. Stars flared before his eyes. He staggered, multiple hands still holding him upright. He swung his fist toward the speaker. Another fist struck him, this time on his sore right shoulder, right over the tattoo. Pain exploded in his back, and gravity seemed to disappear.

"About time," was the last thing he heard before his knees buckled and the darkness claimed him.

Chapter 4

Sylvia sat at the dressing table in her bedchamber, staring at the flame of the single lit candle. Her meeting with Captain Ruford was only a few hours away. Cold dread settled in the pit of her stomach.

There was one way to avoid meeting with Ruford ever again. She fingered the tattered letter that lay among the hairpins and ribbons on her dressing table. Now that her year of mourning was over, Uncle Walcott had invited her to come back and live with him. His wife was busy with the new baby—their tenth—and their governess had left without giving notice. She was the fifth to depart in as many months. Walcott was confident Sylvia would prefer his well-maintained house in Manchester to Jimmy's decaying manor in the wilds of Dorset.

Unpaid servant, or smuggler. Surely there had to be more options?

She tossed the letter into a drawer and slammed it shut.

She picked up her hairbrush and ran it through her unruly curls, preparing for her meeting on the beach. Realizing her fingers were trembling, she balled them into fists in her lap. She would not allow Captain Ruford to unnerve her like this.

How would she fend him off this time? She must find some way to deter his advances, and curtail his cheating them, without putting their business relationship in jeopardy. Her men, and their families, were relying on her to keep some small amount of money coming into their pockets for food on their tables, thatch on their roofs.

There had to be a way. She would have to look beyond her upbringing as a genteel young lady, her education in how to be a dutiful wife, mother, and run a household. Those traditional skills had proven useless when it came to hiding casks of brandy, transporting the goods to their customers past the noses of the Revenue agents, or finding customers in the first place. Her less conventional skills, like knowing how to stop the bleeding of a dagger wound, had proved invaluable of late. She would have to go further, be even more unorthodox.

She would have to think like a smuggler. Act more like a smuggler.

What did a smuggler do that she did not?

She glanced out her window. The crescent moon

was hidden by clouds, with enough rain and wind blowing to make even the most determined Revenue agent prefer to stay by his own hearth. A perfect night for landing illicit cargo.

Right about now, her men would be gathering in the taproom of the Happy Jack for a pint before setting out for their vigil on the beach in the storm, waiting for the signal, when the real work would begin.

She'd join them. A half-pint might settle her nerves. They might be surprised at first to see her, but she had no doubt they'd try to make her feel welcome.

She grabbed her bonnet and left her room.

She paused outside the door to Montgomery's bedchamber. After a moment's hesitation, she entered and felt her way to the desk near the window, and opened the top drawer. There, just where she'd put it after his funeral, was the short dagger he'd always kept tucked inside his boot.

The steel was cold in her hands. Heavy. She'd never concealed a knife on her person before. Had never so much as gutted a fish. But in the thirteen months since Montgomery's death, she'd had to do a lot of things she'd never thought she would. Like lead a group of smugglers.

Her men all carried a knife or two, as well as a pistol.

She tucked the knife into her half-boot. After a cautious step, and an adjustment to make sure she wasn't going to cut her own ankle, she strode determinedly down the stairs.

Galen was in the front hall, preparing to leave for her weekly cribbage game with Mrs. Spencer. Three of her men were there as well, waiting to escort Sylvia down to the beach.

"Evening, my lady." Monroe tipped his hat as she came down the stairs, and stepped back so that his bulk didn't block the hall. Trent and Corwin also doffed their hats.

"Slight change in plans," she called as she joined them. "I feel like going down for a half-pint."

"Beg pardon, missy?" Only Trent called her that.

Galen harrumphed.

"Excellent suggestion, m'lady." Monroe tugged his hat down around his ears. "I could do with a pint meself on a night like this."

Sylvia grabbed her basket, already loaded with her pistol, bandages and other medical supplies, and they headed out into the night.

The group split up when they reached the Happy Jack. The men entered the taproom, while Galen went around to the kitchen door. Sylvia followed, to learn from Mrs. Spencer what the reaction of the inn's patrons had been to the cheese Sylvia had traded in exchange for other supplies this afternoon. The cupboard had been frightfully empty. As she stepped indoors, memories of her encounter with the two strange gentlemen came flooding back.

The one who'd introduced himself, the viscount, was obviously a gentleman in every sense of the word. His companion was something else entirely. Her cheeks heated at the memory of how the rogue had touched her. He'd managed to take something as innocuous as tying the ribbons of her bonnet and turn it into an attempt at seduction. She might have been flattered by his attentions, had he not made her feel as though she were being stripped bare by his eyes.

His soulful brown eyes . . .

The inn's kitchen was warm chaos, as usual. Spencer and his daughter hurried to fill orders for the villagers in the taproom, and Mrs. Spencer caught Galen up on the latest gossip. Sylvia took off her bonnet, torn between listening to the ladies and joining her men in the taproom.

"You can't be none too careful these days." Mrs. Spencer wagged her finger. "Them city fellows think they can get away with anything. Got no right harassing good country folk." She had to raise her voice at the end, to be heard over a sudden commotion outside. "Time to put my feet up for a spell." Mrs. Spencer gestured for Galen and Sylvia to follow her to the private parlor, with an invitation for a nip of sherry.

Before they had taken a step, the kitchen door burst open and slammed against the wall, quivering on its rusty hinges. Four men clustered on the stoop, a large cloth bundle at their feet.

Hayden kept the door from swinging shut again. "I caught one, my lady!"

"What do you mean, you caught him? *I* caught him!" Doyle poked Hayden in the chest. " 'Twas my blow that knocked him out."

"We all caught him, you twits." Baxter, ever the voice of reason, gave both men a shove backward.

Sawyer stepped up into the space vacated by Doyle and Hayden. With his stooped shoulders, Sylvia hadn't seen him at first. "What would you like us to do with the bugger, my lady?"

"Him, who?" Sylvia looked from one weathered face to another. She shared a glance with Galen, who looked just as puzzled.

"A Revenue agent, my lady." Doyle gave the lump at their feet a jab with his toe.

"He's been sniffing around all afternoon, asking all sorts o' questions." Sawyer took off his cap, ran gnarled fingers through his short silver spikes, and slipped his cap back on.

Monroe came to the taproom doorway, tankard in his hand, saw the bundle, and called for Trent and Corwin.

Sylvia clutched her bonnet, her knuckles white. They'd had a few close calls with the local Revenue agent, but so far no confrontations. Their operation was too small to pay any attention to when there were much larger, more dangerous gangs to contend with. Last month a Revenue man had been found facedown in Worbarrow Bay, a knife in his neck.

"Didn't want this one interfering tonight." Baxter gave the lump another kick. "Sawyer wanted to slit his throat and dump him in the bay."

"Did not. Wanted to tie him on his horse, point him at the cliff, and slap the mount's flank."

"That's not very nice to the horse," Doyle muttered.

"He didn't come on no horse," Hayden interrupted. "Spencer said so."

"We could still take him up to Worbarrow," Corwin suggested.

"Gentlemen!" Sylvia shouted. All the men were instantly still, their full attention on her.

In the sudden quiet, they heard a low groan emanate from the bundle of cloth at their feet.

Sylvia set her bonnet on the table. "We may be desperate, but we are not the Worbarrow Bay gang. No blood will be shed, do you understand?"

All seven men clutched their hat or cap to their chest, nodding. A chorus of reluctant "Yes, my lady," and "Aye, milady," echoed through the kitchen.

Sylvia nodded. "Take him into the parlor, and we'll see how badly he's injured. Then we'll decide what to do with him." She turned to Mrs. Spencer. "If you don't mind?"

"Not at all. Haul 'im to the parlor, lads!"

The seven men, each old enough to be her father or even grandfather, picked up part of the flour-dusted bundle and scuttled through the doorway, down the back hall, and into the parlor. Mrs. Spencer hurried ahead to toss a sheet over the sofa before they set down their dirty burden. The men grumbled and pushed each other, and Sylvia heard more than one muttered curse as they untied the knots.

Finally they all stepped back, ropes and various flour sacks in their hands, and Sylvia had her first look at the man on the sofa.

Blast. She should have known. It was the rogue who'd accosted her this afternoon.

Before today, she'd almost forgotten what a handsome, healthy young man could look like. Well, perhaps not so healthy anymore. Better see what damage, if any, her men had done to him.

On his left side, knees drawn up, wrists still together though no longer bound, his body just fit between the arms at the ends of the sofa. The dusting of flour made him look like a statue, hard and cold as marble. She clucked with impatience, fished a handkerchief out of her reticule and dampened it with water from the vase on a side table, and began to wipe his face. His long lashes brushed his cheeks, hiding the eyes that had distracted her so much during their first encounter.

"Careful, my lady, he's a wily one." Doyle rubbed his shin.

"I'm sure we can subdue him again if necessary." Sylvia watched the stranger's chest rise and fall to confirm he was still breathing. He wore an embroidered waistcoat and fine linen cravat, and his shoulders were encased in finest wool, an elegant dark brown before it had been defaced by the flour.

She knelt beside the sofa and returned to cleaning his face. Strong jaw, chiseled nose, high cheekbones, full lips set in a mouth that looked like it smiled often. She remembered how he'd smiled at her this afternoon, remembered how her stomach had fluttered.

He was in need of a shave, but aside from the stubble his skin was smooth, not lined by weather or time. He appeared to be only a couple years older than she, at least a decade younger than her husband had been. Montgomery had smelled of the ocean, of salty air and hemp ropes. The only scent emanating from the stranger, aside from the flour, was a hint of sandal-wood soap.

She tipped more water onto the handkerchief and smoothed the hair near his brow, revealing a rich chestnut brown. Not a single thread of gray marred his temple.

All the Revenue men she'd seen or heard of were much older than this. Sylvia slid her gaze down the rest of his body. Light brown breeches hugged his well-formed legs, the fabric equally as fine as his coat, both with perfectly neat stitching. His boots, with the tops turned down, showed some wear but had recently been well polished. Sylvia recognized the same style and material of footgear that Montgomery had once bought in London, at a cost that would have fed the fully staffed household for a month.

No government agent earned enough to dress this well.

"Blast," she whispered, sitting back on her heels. Her men had meant well, but they'd assaulted and kidnapped a gentleman. The man might be a rake, but he was innocent in their match of wits with the Revenue men.

"My lady?"

"Something wrong?"

"Is the bugger dead, then?"

She held up one hand, halting the flood of questions from the men clustered around her. "He's not dead. He's also not a Revenue agent."

"How can you be sure?"

"Sounded like one to me, asking so many bloody questions."

"It ain't a coincidence he showed up the same night a shipment is due."

She ignored them all, and set about discovering why he hadn't moved or made any sound since the moan on the doorstep. She ran her hands down his limbs, checking for broken bones. He gave a slight twitch as she passed her hand over his right shoulder blade, but she felt nothing give where it shouldn't. Even in his relaxed state, she could feel sleek muscles. His hands were callused. Not those of a man who performed harsh labor, but neither was he an idle gentleman of leisure. He must have been unconscious before they tied him, fortunately, because there were only the faintest of marks from the rope on his wrists.

The irony of the situation was not lost on her. Earlier, she'd been irked by his attempted liberties, merely touching her chin unnecessarily while tying her bonnet without her permission, and now she was running her hands all over his body.

Satisfied there were no broken bones, she slid her fingers through his hair, which was just a little longer than was fashionable, ignoring its silky softness as she searched for a lump or soft spot. There, on the back of his head. Not the mushy give of a broken skull, thankfully, but her fingertips came away covered in a sticky mix of blood and flour.

His left hand shot out and grabbed her wrist. Sylvia gasped. She looked beyond her fingers, past his strong grip, to his eyes. Wide open, the color of rich chocolate, they stared at her unblinking.

"What the hell are you doing?" His voice was low and intense, the rich timbre even smoother than she remembered. The cultured accent confirmed his social status as gentleman.

"Checking that they didn't accidentally bash your skull in." Knowing the men were still clustered around her, Sylvia was able to keep her voice steady. He was young and strong, but they had him outnumbered eight to one. Ten, if Galen and Mrs. Spencer joined in. Both hovered near the doorway, ready to call for assistance if needed. The tiny parlor was already crammed full of people.

Still gripping her wrist, the stranger slowly sat up and swung his legs over the sofa. He glanced at the men. "Step back, or I'll snap her like a twig."

She heard their intake of breath, felt their indecision. "You'll do no such thing." She swung her free hand to the side of his head and shoved him back down to the sofa. Being a gentleman, he hesitated to use his strength to retaliate against a woman. She used that hesitation to jump up to her feet and plop down on his chest.

Who knew that years of minding her rambunctious cousins would come in so handy? The fact that he was undoubtedly still woozy was also in her favor. She'd once kept her fifteen-year-old cousin down like this for five minutes, until he'd promised to stop trying to kiss the upstairs maid.

Conscious of his hand around her wrist, she forced a smile and met the stranger's shocked gaze. "No one is going to hurt you, sir, and you are not going to hurt anyone, either. Am I clear?"

He gave a brief nod, and glanced at the men.

She glanced at them also, though the stranger shifted beneath her, and she felt his free hand touching her lower back. Quite low. Her stomach gave a slight flutter. His silent message was a warning that he could unseat her if he chose. "Am I clear?" She stared at them until all had nodded in agreement. She looked back at the stranger. "You see? No one means any harm. This was all a terrible misunderstanding."

"Can't breathe," he wheezed.

Sylvia hopped to her feet. Only then did he release his grip on her wrist. She turned sideways, her gaze darting between her men and the stranger as he slowly sat up again.

Tony filled his lungs with air and took in his surroundings. The woman hadn't been that heavy, and he'd rather enjoyed the unusual perspective, but he didn't like being at such a disadvantage.

After a moment of being upright, he stopped seeing two of everything. He eyed the people gathered before him—seven old men plus the young woman in gray. He blinked. They must have hit him rather hard that it took him this long to recognize the pretty widow from this afternoon, the one he'd been searching for. The one he'd stayed behind to pursue. The very same one who'd been sitting on his chest just moments ago.

What a wasted opportunity.

She still wore half-mourning, a plain gray gown that had seen better days, with no ornamentation whatsoever. The men surrounding her, however, were ornamented with pistols and daggers, and even a cutlass or two.

"You're smugglers." He shook his head, and regretted it immediately as his vision blurred for a moment. "How could I have been so stupid? Dark and stormy night, deserted inn on the coast . . . what else could be going on?" He held his fingers to his temples, hoping to ease the throbbing.

"What are we going to do with him, my lady?"

The voice was hushed, but Tony recognized the stoop-shouldered speaker as one of the first men who had come into the taproom earlier. Tony looked the group over again, and realized all of them had been in there.

The widow addressed him. "I'm afraid they mistook you for someone else, sir. How is your head?"

"Rather have another hangover than this." He touched the back of his head, found the lump, and winced. His fingertips were now as bloody as hers.

"Scalp wounds have a tendency to bleed dreadfully," she said, as though she dealt with them on a regular basis. "Galen, please bring my basket. Mrs. Spencer, could I trouble you for some warm water?"

Tony followed her gaze in time to see the only other females in the room, the innkeeper's wife and an ancient matron in the black and white bombazine of a housekeeper, turn and leave. The ruffians in the room shifted, blocking the exit. Though could one call this group "ruffians," at their advanced age?

He stood up, his knees threatening to buckle. Only a group of ruffians could have knocked him about so easily. The old codgers did have the advantage of surprise, and had blinded him at the start.

It was a poor sop to his ego.

The widow darted forward, her hand under his elbow to steady him. He rested his clean hand on her shoulder while the floor danced a jig.

Once the floor settled, and the contents of his stomach seemed willing to stay put, he tried speaking again. "Since you say this was a mistake, I'll just go up to my room if you all don't mind. We are still at the Happy Jack Inn, are we not?"

He felt her stiffen, but she didn't reply.

"Afraid we can't let you do that." The men each took a step closer, forming a semicircle around Tony and the woman.

"Hayden's right." The young woman turned her troubled gaze on Tony. She stood close enough for him to inhale her soft lavender scent, and see flecks of gold in her green eyes. "You'll need to stay here, at least for a few hours, until we're, um, finished."

"And then what?" Perhaps he'd rather not know.

She flinched. He felt it. The hair stood up on the back of his neck.

"Can't have no witnesses, my lady." Tony didn't recognize the low voice.

She stiffened again, raised her chin. "I said we shall have no bloodshed."

Tony looked over at the men, noticing again the abundance of weapons on their persons, thrust into boot tops and belts or sashes at their waist. Harmless old codgers, indeed. "I have no interest in your affairs, good sirs, legal or otherwise. If you are in any danger, it is not from me."

No one relaxed. At least three of the men rested their hands on a knife handle or butt of a pistol stuck through their belt. Oh, hell. How was he going to get himself out of this one?

The woman at his side spoke up. "We'll leave him here, and Mr. Spencer will make certain he doesn't go anywhere while we're . . . busy, and then he can return to his room." A low murmur went up, and a few more men reached for their knives. She noticed, too. "And tomorrow he'll be on his way, out of our village, never to return." She looked up at him. "Isn't that right, sir?"

"Perfectly agreeable plan. I have no objection to waiting here. The sofa was quite comfy." His smile felt a bit forced, but his skull was pounding, and the men still looked ready to use their knives. "Tomorrow I'll be on my way toward Weymouth." The floor was threatening to tilt again. Tony kept his hand on the woman's shoulder.

Noticing his wobble, she reached out a hand to his waist, probably with the ridiculous notion she could help keep him from sinking to the floor.

Noise from the doorway made the men turn.

"I thought you were going to join us for—" The speaker, a lad of about eighteen, cut himself off at the sight of Tony and the woman. He, too, had a pistol thrust through his belt, and a cutlass at his waist. A black scarf almost covered his bright red hair. "What are you doing to Sylvia?"

Ah, the woman had a name. Strong, yet feminine. Suited her. "I am doing nothing to her. She, however, is keeping me from pitching face-first to the floor."

The lad looked ready to continue his interrogation, his brows drawn together, but the two women returned just then, bringing a basket and basin of water to Sylvia.

"Please sit down, sir." Sylvia urged Tony back to the sofa.

He allowed himself to be maneuvered down. Perhaps from this angle he would seem less of a threat to the men. Mrs. Spencer shoved aside a vase on the small table to make room for the supplies.

Sylvia used both hands on the side of his face to point his chin toward the floor. Her hands were warm, her voice soft and steady. "This will only take a moment."

"The lad needs a restorative cup of tea, he does," the housekeeper announced. She patted him on the knee. "Be right back."

The men rearranged themselves again after her departure, their boots just visible in a ring around the sofa as Tony stared at the floor. Better than watchdogs. He closed his eyes to concentrate on Sylvia's ministrations.

Her touch was gentle, working a damp cloth through the hair at the back of his head, washing away the blood. He'd noticed the gold band on her third finger. Had he been mistaken about her status as widow, and this lot simply guarding her in her husband's absence?

"What is this, straw?"

Tony looked up, but Sylvia pushed his head down again. She was slowly carding her fingers through his hair. Might have been pleasant, soothing even, under other circumstances.

"Good heavens, what did you hit him with?"

He heard the irritation in her voice, and silently seconded it.

"'Twas a pitchfork."

"From Spencer's stables."

"He wouldn't go down, elsewise."

Tony raised his head. "I would have responded to a simple request." Sylvia pushed him down again.

"Be glad it wasn't the fork they use for muckin' out the stalls." Laughter rang out.

"Hush, all of you." Sylvia patted his shoulder. "What's done is done. Mrs. Spencer, I need to borrow a pair of scissors. There are still buttons on the bandage."

Tony tried to look over his shoulder. "You're not cutting up a shirt on my behalf, are you?"

Sylvia touched his jaw, pushing him back into position. "What better use for Montgomery's shirts, hmm?"

"Who is Montgomery?"

"My late husband."

Mrs. Spencer briefly stepped into his line of sight

as she retrieved scissors from a mending basket. Just what he needed, more sharp blades in the room.

A few snips, one button bounced on the floor and was retrieved by a guard dog, then Tony smelled something other than lavender wafting from Sylvia, an earthy and medicinal scent. Moments later she pressed against the back of his head and began winding a cloth around his skull.

"A bandage isn't necessary, madam. I've had worse injuries that healed just fine."

"Quiet, laddie, and let the lady tend."

Sylvia finished winding the bandage and tied it off, but he still felt her hand on the back of his skull, pressing on the bandage, though she finally let him raise his head. "You needn't wear it for long. Just a little while, to let the herbs do their work." She leaned forward as she spoke, her words soft against his ear. Warmth began to spread through him, radiating from her hand on his head.

Tony stiffened. Here he was on a sofa, a beautiful woman putting her hands all over him. What would a real rake do under these circumstances?

A real rake would never be surrounded by seven old codgers. He sighed.

The housekeeper came back, handed him a full teacup, and sat on the sofa beside him. "So, are you married?"

He paused, the cup halfway to his mouth. "No."

"Promised to anyone? Drink up, lad, drink up." She urged the cup toward his mouth.

Tony swallowed. And coughed. "There's tea in your brandy."

"That's the restorative part. Anyone you're about to be promised to?"

"Galen, no." Sylvia had removed her hand but stayed close to the sofa. He felt her increased tension.

"My lady, yes. Here's the perfect solution, dropped on our doorstep, practically in your lap."

Their positions were entirely wrong for him to be in anyone's lap, but the suggestion certainly piqued his interest. As long as the lap was the lovely Sylvia's.

He downed another swallow of the tea-laced alcohol. He'd swiped enough from his brother's cellar to recognize fine French brandy. Made perfect sense, since he was among smugglers.

"What harebrained idea are you getting at, you old fool?" The eldest of the codgers took another step forward.

The housekeeper turned her steely gaze on the men in the room. "That good-for-nothing captain has been wanting to lift my lady's skirts, but even the likes of him wouldn't dare poach on another man's property."

Tony heard the gasp from Sylvia behind him, could practically feel the embarrassment radiating from her. This time the room didn't tilt when he moved his head. He wasn't sure whether it was the brandy, the herbs on the bandage, or simply the passage of time, but he was feeling much better. Better than she felt, at any rate, given her troubled expression.

"Galen, just what are you suggesting?" The red-headed interrogator took a step closer.

"The captain *has* been getting a might fresh," one of the men said. Others nodded.

"Damned insulting, what he does."

"I'd call the bugger out if I were a few years younger."

"If it were up to me, I'd just take my knife and cut off his b—"

"Gentlemen, please!" In her agitation, Sylvia had rested her free hand on the back of the sofa, her fingers gripping the upholstery.

Without conscious thought, Tony reached up and patted her hand. At his action, the housekeeper's eyes widened. She smacked his knee, practically chortling with glee. He resisted the urge to rub his stinging flesh. "I'm not sure I understand what it is you have in mind, madam."

"Simple, laddie. You're going to help protect our lady from that nasty piece of work captain by pretending to be her new husband."

Chapter 5

Husband?

    There was a buzzing in Tony's ears, or was it just the men talking amongst themselves? A few hours ago he'd been trying in vain to learn the widow's identity, and now they wanted him to pretend to be her husband. A broad, satisfied grin right now would probably not be wise. He bit the inside of his lip.

"This is insane," Sylvia said. "We don't have any idea who this man is. We don't even know his name."

"Well then, lad, what's your name?" one of the watchdogs said.

"It doesn't matter," the eldest codger interrupted. "Have you gone daft, woman?"

"You're not thinking this through, you old fart." The housekeeper leaned forward. "If he goes down to the beach with you tonight, pretending to be my lady's new husband, the captain won't touch her. And if this lad is the one handing over the purse, he can't exactly bear witness against us, now can he?"

"She has a good point." The redheaded lad stroked his chin.

"Would it hold up with the magistrate, if it came to that?"

"Don't matter, we can't trust him."

"Might be worth a try."

"I say we cut off his ears and gouge out his eyes. Won't see nothing, won't hear nothing."

Tony's head began to swim again as all the men continued to talk at once.

"What's your name, lad?"

"Who's your family?"

"Where are you from?"

Tony looked at the housekeeper in exasperation.

"Shut yer clacks!" she shouted.

The sudden silence was deafening.

Sylvia rested her hands on her hips, though she hadn't moved away.

He took a fortifying breath, inhaling more of her sweet lavender scent. "My name is Tony Sinclair, and I come from a respectable old line but, alas, am the younger son. If we were to perpetrate this hoax, madam, you would become simply Mrs. Sinclair." He tried to gauge her reaction. She gave him the same look she might to yesterday's fish.

He turned back to her watchdogs. "I have no desire to be a smuggler, but I am rather partial to my features in their current arrangement. I would be willing to assist in your endeavors—tonight—if that would assure you that I have no intention of informing the authorities of your activities." Though he did have every intention of using the opportunity to woo the widow. She was melting toward him. Now she looked more intrigued than affronted.

Someone moved, his cutlass blade glinting in the candlelight. Had he really just agreed to act as a smuggler? It couldn't be much more dangerous than climbing about on rooftops with Alistair. Though one couldn't be hung for doing what Alistair did.

The men grumbled and mumbled. Galen and Mrs. Spencer beamed. Sylvia furrowed her brow.

Tony glanced at each of the men. "Do we have an agreement, gentlemen? Tonight we work together, and tomorrow we each go our separate ways. Unmolested." Well, he'd separate from the men, but he planned to have Sylvia begging him to stay.

"It's up to Lady Montgomery."

Her brow still furrowed, she sat on the arm of the sofa. The men also seated themselves, rearranging the various chairs and sofas so they could see her and still keep an eye on Tony. She raised her hand to her temple.

For his part, he would have no trouble whatsoever pretending to be married to the comely young widow. Gentleman's honor practically demanded it of him, if the housekeeper's assessment was accurate. It meant he would have to stay close by Sylvia's side, tuck her dainty hand in the crook of his arm. Look longingly into her green eyes. Smooth a dark blond curl, the color of wet sand. Kiss that delightful rosebud mouth.

And later, when they were alone, remind her how much physical pleasure was to be had between husband and wife.

He would have no trouble playing the role of doting husband, with the lovely Sylvia as his wife.

Sylvia stared at the stranger, her mind racing. An hour ago she'd simply wanted to go have a drink with her men. Half an hour ago her men had wanted to kill the stranger. And now she was supposed to pretend to be married to him?

He gazed back at her, the smoldering heat in his brown eyes making her feel flushed. She remembered the touch of his bare hand on her throat when he'd tied her bonnet, his fingers hot against her chilled skin.

Perhaps she should move farther from the fire—the room was getting too warm.

She shifted her thoughts to her coming meeting with the captain. Mr. Sinclair's scent was not offensive. True, he had tried to take liberties with her person, but nothing like what Ruford aimed for. Sinclair's hand had been on her lower back only because she'd been sitting on his chest.

She remembered the feel of his muscles. He had strength, vitality, intelligence. And yes, drat him, charm. "Mr. Sinclair, have you ever dealt with a nefarious person before?"

"One of my chums has his own ship. While Nick may be a gentleman, his crewmen are not. I assure you, I can handle your smuggling captain."

So he was comfortable around ships? That had to be in their favor.

"My lady, this is the best way to be rid of the captain's advances." Galen patted Mr. Sinclair's knee again. "The lad's willing, and the men will keep an eye on you both."

There was a chorus in the affirmative. Her men sat straighter, their hands once again going to their weapons.

Her men would keep her safe, as they had always done. They may have lost some of the spring in their step, but with so many of them, what could go wrong?

Mr. Sinclair would be the one to deal with the captain, with Ruford's malodorous person and putrid breath, his roaming hands and leering gaze. Not her. She almost sagged with relief.

Was it wrong to use Mr. Sinclair as a shield? He didn't seem averse to the idea. Indeed, he was staring at her as a starving man would a buffet.

The important men in her life—father, uncle, husband—had all let her down at a crucial time. Could she trust Mr. Sinclair to hold up his end of their bargain? He certainly seemed eager to hold *her,* at any rate.

Well, it was only for tonight, and tomorrow Mr. Sinclair would be on his way. The captain would mind his manners in the future if he thought she had remarried.

"You'll need different clothes." Sylvia stood up. "Those fine garments you're wearing will only make the captain want to charge us even more for each load."

"He only brought but one little bag with him," Mrs. Spencer volunteered.

"Traveling light." Mr. Sinclair brushed some flour from his sleeve. "I didn't expect to be taking part in a theatrical production."

"I could fetch some of my husband's things." Mrs. Spencer pointed over her shoulder.

Aside from the incredible difference in size and build between the two men—Mr. Sinclair's trim frame would be adrift in Spencer's tent-sized shirt—the innkeeper's coarse working-class clothes wouldn't suit their charade. "Thank you, but I don't wish to inconvenience you any more than we already have," Sylvia said. "I think Hubert's clothes might be a closer fit for the role."

The smug look on Mr. Sinclair's face acknowledged that she'd taken note of his person. Would he be so self-satisfied if he knew she'd not only looked her fill, but felt along his limbs, as well? Her hands burned.

The clock on the mantel chimed the hour.

"We best be getting up to the manor house, then," Trent said. "Ain't enough time to go fetch clothes, bring 'em back here, and still get down to the beach." He turned to Mr. Sinclair. "Can ye walk, lad, or did the boys hit you too hard?"

Mr. Sinclair stood up to his full height, shoulders back. "Lead the way."

"Good luck, my lady!" Mrs. Spencer called as everyone headed out.

The seven men surrounded Mr. Sinclair as they walked up the hill to the manor, with Jimmy and Galen on either side of Sylvia.

"We'll be right beside you the whole time." Jimmy

patted the hilt of his cutlass. "We won't let the bugger get away with anything."

Sylvia wasn't sure which bugger he was referring to, but it didn't really matter.

Gerald opened the front door when they arrived, his white hair sticking up in tufts around his nightcap. He clutched his dressing gown closed. "I suppose there's no point asking how the cribbage game went." He looked only vaguely surprised to see so many people on the doorstep.

"Let us in, you sleepy twit." Galen shouldered her husband aside and entered the house first.

The men swarmed in behind her and headed for the staircase. Galen reached between them and snagged Mr. Sinclair's sleeve. "If you want to pull off this charade, you'll need rings. Give me your hand, lad."

"But I thought Lady Montgomery was to be my pretend wife, not you." He winked.

The housekeeper cuffed his shoulder. "Don't sass me, lad." Her tone was gruff, but Sylvia could swear she saw the housekeeper blush before she ducked her chin to note Mr. Sinclair's ring size.

Within minutes, all seven men accompanied Mr. Sinclair to an upstairs bedchamber, dressed him in Montgomery's plain clothing, and returned him to the foyer. Galen left when they did as well, and had just returned before Mr. Sinclair and his entourage descended the staircase.

"I don't wish to alarm you, my dear," Mr. Sinclair said, still adjusting the slightly too large shirt and breeches, "but if your watchdogs continue to follow my every move, I may not be able to perform at my best on our wedding night." He drew out the last two words.

Sylvia felt her cheeks heat, but before she could reply, Galen cuffed him on the shoulder again.

"Mind your manners, laddie. Hold out your hands, both of you, please."

Sylvia twisted the narrow gold band on her finger. "But I'm already wearing a ring."

"New husband, new ring. Off it comes." Galen held out her hand.

Sylvia stared at the ring that Montgomery had placed on her finger just over four years ago. She hadn't taken it off since. She'd been tempted, especially after she found out how badly she and her uncle had been misled about Montgomery's finances. There had been seven little screaming horrors in her charge before she married, but the roof at her uncle's home did not leak.

Now Uncle Walcott had ten children.

Sylvia yanked off the ring and handed it to Galen. She received a heavy gold band in exchange.

Galen placed a smaller ring on Mr. Sinclair's palm. "They belonged to my parents," she said. "I'll want them back when you're done." She cleared her throat. "Go on. Exchange rings."

Mr. Sinclair gave a rakish smile. "A pretend wedding for a pretend marriage." He held her hand and gently slid the ring onto her third finger. "With this ring, I thee temporarily wed."

Sylvia stared at the wide band, with an engraved pattern worn smooth in places. Anything to keep from staring at his hand holding hers. She remembered what had happened just hours after the last time a man had slid a ring on her finger. Mr. Sinclair's hands were strong, but not roughened from years at sea. Rakes were supposed to be highly skilled in the bedroom. Against her will, her breath quickened.

Well, she wouldn't be finding out how skilled he was. She wasn't going to fall prey to a handsome face and charming smile. Men had caused her nothing but grief.

She looked up—and was hit dead center with the full force of said charming smile. Mr. Sinclair—should she call him Tony now?—was holding out his left hand, waiting. She reluctantly entered into the game. "With this ring, I thee temporarily wed."

"Finally!" Jimmy stepped forward. "If we don't leave now we'll miss the signal, and all this will have been for nothing."

"Ceremony isn't over yet. The bride hasn't been kissed." Before anyone could protest, Mr. Sinclair leaned forward. Sylvia braced herself, torn between annoyance and curiosity. Very mild curiosity.

He curled his fingers around hers, raised her hand, and turned it over. With a smoldering look in his eyes, he dropped a kiss on the inside of her bare wrist.

Sylvia tried to breathe normally, not wanting her fluttering pulse to betray her reaction. No one had ever kissed her there before. It was just his mouth on her wrist. No reason his warm lips against her bare skin should send a tingle up her arm that spread down to her toes.

He let go slowly, his fingers trailing across her hand. "Now we're ready." He held out his arm, his eyes betraying his satisfaction, reveling in the reaction he'd provoked in her. "Shall we?"

Sylvia raised her chin. He wouldn't have that effect on her again. She rested her hand in the crook of his arm, and led the way out the door and into the black night. Her men followed at their heels, while Galen and Gerald called out well wishes.

Tony tried to concentrate on the feel of Lady Montgomery's hand resting on his forearm, rather than the apprehension winding through his gut. What had he involved himself in? He hadn't felt this mix of dread and excitement since he'd followed Nick into a midnight prank against the headmaster. If this went wrong, there would be far worse consequences than a caning and stern lecture.

As they stood at the top of the cliff, buffeted by the wind, he swiped the bandage from his head and stuffed it in a pocket. With his free hand, he checked that he was no longer bleeding. His fingers encountered something gritty, coarser than dried blood. Sylvia's herbal concoction? Couldn't tell in the dark, but the scent was pleasant.

Soon, signal lights were exchanged, and he was standing on the beach with Sylvia, her seven watchdogs, and six more men who'd come from the inn. Small boats appeared out of the inky blackness and slid with a hiss and a rasp onto the fine pebble beach. Sailors spilled out of the boats and mingled with Lady Montgomery's men, who formed lines and began passing small casks from the beach, disappearing into the darkness by the base of the cliff. Much as he was curious about the details of the operation, it wasn't worth the risk to ask. The less he knew, the more likely her men were to let him go as agreed.

One man separated from the group and came toward them, taking off his feathered tricorne hat and sweeping into a bow.

Assailed by the stench of sweat, Tony took a step backward, then recovered his lapse. Through the thickness of his borrowed shirt and coat, Sylvia's fingers dug into his arm. He gave her hand a reassuring pat. When he saw the flare of annoyance in the stranger's eyes, he stroked her hand with a proprietary air.

"Good evening, Lady Montgomery." The stranger reached for her free hand, but she evaded contact by locking her fingers together over Tony's arm.

"Good evening, Captain Ruford, but I'm Mrs. Sinclair now."

"Mrs. . . . What?"

"You're interrupting our honeymoon, so we'd like to get on with the business at hand," Tony said.

"Married? When? You said nothing last time we met."

Tony wasn't sure if the captain was angry or just shocked.

"There are a great many things I have never discussed with you, Captain."

The captain's eyes narrowed. "How long have you known one another?"

Tony opened his mouth to speak, but the lady beat him to it.

"We met at an assembly in Weymouth. Two years ago."

"I fell in love at first sight," Tony jumped in. "But alas, the lady was already taken. I thought I would perish of unrequited love." He felt Sylvia's gaze on him. Remembering the look on his brother's face whenever Ben spoke of or glanced at his wife, Tony tried to effect the same besotted expression as he looked upon Sylvia now.

With only the pitiful light of a lantern at their feet, he felt more than saw her breathing hitch, her expression change. He wrapped his arm around her waist, pulling her even closer to his side. Her curves fit against him perfectly, just as he'd known they would.

The captain turned his head to spit out a stream of tobacco. "Montgomery's been dead thirteen months. What kept you?"

"And an agonizing thirteen months it has been. I wanted to wait the appropriate interval. I want no one to cast aspersions on my lovely Sylvia." Tony leaned over with the intention of dropping a chaste but loving kiss on her cheek, strictly for the benefit of their audience. But she turned at the same time, so his kiss landed directly on her mouth. They both froze for an instant.

Remembering their audience, Tony brought his hand up to cup her cheek, still kissing her. She leaned into his touch. Under other circumstances, he would have taken it further, tasted her. The captain loudly cleared his throat.

Tony pulled back. He had to grasp Sylvia's elbow to steady her. He took pride in the fact it took her several seconds to open her eyes again. Tony suddenly realized the sailors had slowed down in their unloading of the boats, and Sylvia's men were staring at him. Only when she flashed a look of reassurance at them did they resume their movements.

"I see you were serious about interrupting your honeymoon." The captain spat again. "I would be just as anxious to be getting beneath her skirts. Shall we get to business, then?"

Tony took a half-step forward, putting Sylvia half behind him. How dare this piece of scum even look upon her? He felt pressure against the small of his back. He reached around, and felt a weighted cloth thrust into his hand. The purse.

"Yes, Captain, let's finish as quickly as possible, shall we? I've much more important business to attend to once we get home." Tony dropped the purse into Ruford's outstretched hand.

"Them government lads continue to dog me," Ruford said, hefting the purse. "I'll need more—"

"We've had our own problems," Tony interrupted before Ruford could get going. "The Revenue agents have been sniffing around the village. We aren't going to give you any more than the original agreed-upon price, for the original number of casks. If anything, we should be paying you less to cover *our* increased expenses."

By now the men had finished unloading the boats, and Sylvia's watchdogs had gathered at the base of the cliff. Ruford's men stood between them and the boats. The redheaded lad pushed his way to the front of the group until he stood on the other side of Sylvia. Except for the slap of waves on the shore, silence reigned for a moment.

Tony saw one of the sailors and two of the watchdogs reach for weapons at their waist. The hair on the back of his neck prickled.

"I am feeling generous," Ruford said at last. "Consider it a wedding gift." He waved to his men, and they began piling into the boats and heading back out to the bay.

Tony almost allowed himself to relax. A few more minutes, and this charade would be at an end. Sylvia's men would let him go, and she'd be eager to show her appreciation for his help. He was about to become much better acquainted with Sylvia and her eminently kissable lips.

"It appears you chose your champion well, my lady." Ruford gave her another bow, then turned his attention back to Tony. "As enjoyable as transactions with her ladyship have been, I'm relieved to be dealing with a man again. It will be much easier to conduct business with you. We understand each other, I think."

Tony found himself calmly nodding in agreement, though he felt anything but.

Ruford leaned closer. Tony barely heard him over the stench. "Don't know how much longer I would have continued. Can't do business with a chit or a cub. Just ain't right."

Tony heard the outraged inhale from the redheaded lad at Sylvia's other side. She forestalled his protest with an elbow to his ribs.

"Until next time, Sinclair," Ruford said, and strode off to the waiting boat.

"But Captain—"

Ruford ignored Sylvia's call. "Enjoy your honeymoon!" As they rowed out to the bay, the men in his boat joined in with crude suggestions of how to pass the night.

Tony wished he could cover her ears. Though he had designs on her person, a lady shouldn't be subjected to such coarse comments.

When the darkness had swallowed up the last boat, she turned to her waiting men. "We'll go up to the house and let Mr. Sinclair collect his things. The rest of you go back to the inn, as usual."

There were murmured replies, and within moments Tony was hiking back up the cliff path, accompanied by Sylvia and her watchdogs. No one attempted conversation until they were on level ground, traversing a gravel path flanked by clumps of fragrant lavender, the single lantern casting menacing shadows over the wildly overgrown shrubs.

"Thank you for your assistance this evening, Mr. Sinclair."

Tony grinned at her businesslike tone. He could pretend nothing had happened between them, too. "Your watchd— your men will follow our agreement?" He glanced at the black sky above, the stars hidden by rain clouds.

"Of course they will."

Soon after, Tony changed back into his own clothes and hurried down to the brightly lit hall. Despite the pack of watchdogs that hounded his every movement, a true rake would find a way to take advantage of the situation, not to mention the widow. With her husband dead more than a year, she must be lonely for company by now. Lonely for more youthful companionship, at any rate. And her reactions to his advances so far had proven she was receptive. Amenable. Dare he say eager?

"Since Ruford now believes there's another man involved, he should mind his manners. Once again, thank you." She held her hand out, but it wasn't for him to kiss.

Tony would rather kiss than shake hands on their gentleman's agreement, but he'd take what he could get, for the moment. Her grip was just like her, firm and unhesitant. Would the watchdogs clout him over the head again if he tugged her close and kissed her? "You're sure you can handle Ruford from here on out?" As disagreeable as their brief meeting had been, Tony couldn't imagine a lady having to face the scoundrel on a regular basis.

The front door burst open. "We've got a problem, Syl." The redheaded youth shouldered his way through the mass of men clustered in the hall, shooting daggers at Tony when he got close. "Ruford's first mate and another crewman are down at the Happy Jack, drinking ale."

"There's nothing unusual about that, Jimmy." She turned to Tony. "You'll need to stay here a while longer. As soon as they've gone, you can go back to your room at the inn, as we planned."

Jimmy shook his head. "They got rooms for the night."

Tony felt a sense of foreboding. "I take it that *is* unusual for them?"

"Not to worry," Sylvia said, a little too brightly. "They've stayed the night at least once before, and been gone in the morning. Sometimes the ship needs provisions and can't wait until they reach the next harbor. That's all."

"Not this time, Syl. We heard the mate talking to Spencer. The captain sent him to find out what sort of wedding gift would be most appropriate for you and the gent." Jimmy turned a meaningful gaze on Tony. "Even if it takes a while."

So much for simple plans.

Sylvia tucked a curl behind her ear. Tony itched to do it for her. "And what did Spencer say?"

"He suggested a silver candelabra for the dining table." Jimmy folded his arms. "And thanks to Mrs. Spencer, by dawn the whole village will know about your fake marriage." Jimmy turned to Tony so they were standing toe to toe. "Looks like you aren't leaving anytime soon."

Sylvia made a small sound and sat on the footman's bench with a thud.

Tony joined her. Several of the men began talking,

their disjointed conversations washing over him as he sorted through the consequence of this little snag in their plans.

"What if we just told the captain it was a lie?"

"Are you daft?"

"The gent just has to stay here a few days. They'll go away, and my lady will get a nice candelabra."

"But the captain will expect to see the gent again. He'll have to stay."

"Only until the next delivery. Then we'll just say he's gone."

"Gone where?"

"Dead, gone. He fell off the cliff."

"No, we could say he drowned."

"Even better, we could say he died from—"

"Excuse me?" Talk of his untimely death jerked Tony from his thoughts. The men continued talking. "Gentlemen!" At last the conversation died down. "It's late, and we're all tired. May I suggest we examine this problem in the morning? Until then, I'm sure you know a back way so I can get to my room without the first mate seeing me." Tony looked at the group expectantly.

"No." He almost missed the quiet statement from the lady at his side. "We can't risk it." She turned to him. "You'll have to stay here." She stood, seemingly stronger than she had been just a moment ago. "Galen, what do we have available?"

The housekeeper stood on the stairs to be seen above the crowd in the hall. All eyes turned toward her. "I'm afraid the only other upstairs room fit for human occupation is the master's, my lady."

"My lady, you can't be serious!"

"We can't trust the bugger."

Sylvia held up her hand, and the men quieted again. "Galen, please prepare the room for our guest." The housekeeper bobbed a curtsy and went upstairs. "Doyle, please retrieve Mr. Sinclair's luggage from the inn."

"Aye, my lady." One of the watchdogs detached from the crowd and exited the front door.

Tony exchanged glances with Sylvia—hers expressing trepidation—and reconciled himself to spending the night, alone, with a comely widow sleeping in the adjoining bedchamber.

Alone, except for three watchdogs, who produced pillows and blankets and sprawled in the doorway to his room, the doorway to her room, and on a cot in the dressing room that connected the two bedchambers.

Even a seasoned rake would have trouble getting past such a challenge.

But wasn't the pursuit just as much a part of being a rake as the having? The chase could be almost as much fun as the catch.

Once everyone was finally settled for the night, Sylvia closed the door to her bedchamber, sat on the edge of the bed, and stared at the lit candle on the bedside table. Such indulgence, all the candles they'd had to light tonight.

She'd begun the evening wanting to act more like a smuggler, to think beyond the boundaries of her upbringing, and now she had a seductive stranger sleeping in the next room. Uncle Walcott would be aghast.

This situation certainly hadn't been covered by her education as a genteel young lady.

Sleeping just next door was a handsome, charming man, not related to or acquainted with anyone she knew. A man with smoldering brown eyes and a warm smile that made her want to melt in his arms. She was too mature to indulge in such nonsense. Besides, he probably behaved that way with all women. She was not going to succumb to the charms of a rake.

But she owed him some measure of gratitude, because Mr. Sinclair had solved part of her problem in that Ruford's crude advances had been completely circumvented. At least for now.

Murmured conversation from the adjoining chamber had her looking toward the dressing room door. She couldn't make out the words, but knew Mr. Sinclair was probably speaking with Sawyer, who had appointed himself guardian of her virtue, and claimed the valet's cot in the dressing room for the night.

It was sweet, if a tad overprotective, for some of the men to stay the night to make certain the stranger caused her no harm. There was no real need for protection. A man like Mr. Sinclair might break her heart, if she gave him the chance—which she wouldn't—but she knew instinctively that he would never physically hurt her.

On the other hand, her instincts had also persuaded her to accept Montgomery's suit, and look how well *that* had turned out. She tiptoed to the hall door and opened it.

"Do you need something, my lady?" Corwin rose up on one elbow from his pallet in her doorway.

"Just making sure the candles were all out," she whispered.

"Like old times, isn't it, my lady?" A dark shape farther down the hall shifted, and Sylvia recognized Monroe, sprawled in front of the adjoining bedchamber's doorway. He and his wife and their five children had slept in the rose salon most of February after a storm had ripped away their roof.

"Fewer people in the house this time, though." Hearing his answering chuckle, Sylvia wished both men a good night and closed her door again.

No one was going to get past Corwin or Monroe. From either direction.

She swiftly changed into her night rail and huddled under the blankets, suddenly chilled. Where was a warm male body when she needed it? "Macbeth!" she called softly. No answer. With so many people in the house, the cat was likely staying on the upper floors, away from strangers and nearer to the mice. Sylvia wrapped her arms around her knees, drawn up to her chest.

Most nights after landing a cargo, she fell asleep soon after getting into bed, exhausted. Tonight her thoughts were as relentless as the waves, tossing her one way and then another.

Not counting Ruford's previous attempts, she had been subjected to more advances today than in the past year or more. She had been caught off guard when Mr. Sinclair tied her bonnet this afternoon, distracted when he kissed her wrist, and shocked breathless when he kissed her on the beach.

His lips on hers had been warm and yielding, and heaven help her, she'd wanted to yield to him. Touch him. Good thing there had been an audience present, or she might have lost her senses altogether.

She'd never lost her senses with Montgomery. Kisses from her husband had been rare. When he'd bothered, he tasted of tobacco, or fish. His lips were rough, chapped from long hours at sea. Like his hands. When he came to her, it was usually late at night for a hasty coupling, and then he'd go right back to his own room. Demonstrations of affection were limited to a gruff "Mind yourself," said jointly to her and Jimmy, as he left for another voyage.

Mr. Sinclair had already proven himself to be a demonstrative man, and if given half a chance, she had no doubt he would happily demonstrate much, much more.

But Mr. Sinclair did not hold her in any *true* affection. As soon as he realized she was not receptive to his advances, he would be on his way, forgetting all about her. In fact, he was probably annoyed, rightfully so, at being dragged into their mess, and was undoubtedly devising a way even now of escaping their company. He'd leave, and her heart would be safe from his onslaught.

Sylvia flopped down on the bed, pulling the blankets up to her chin. Where was that blasted cat? She needed something warm to hold on to.

Chapter 6

Tony awoke in a strange room, morning light streaming through the window. Nothing unusual about that—he'd spent the night in a different bed, a different inn, every night for the last week. What was unusual was having a cat on his chest.

It faced him, its length running from Tony's collarbone to hip bone.

"Good morning," he whispered.

The black cat flipped its fluffy tail and blinked gold eyes at him, but left its chin resting on Tony's chest.

"I don't recall inviting you into my bed." Cautiously, he raised one hand and stroked the cat. He was rewarded with a low rumbling purr. The cat looked at ease, but its position was more of a crouch than repose. At any moment, its claws could dig into all sorts of vulnerable flesh.

The cat blinked again. Tony continued stroking it, plunging his fingers into the thick, soft fur. Purring reverberated through his torso. When he paused, the cat nudged him with its head.

"So, I take it you're in charge around here?" The cat stretched a paw to Tony's chin, its claws sheathed. For now. "Less talking, more petting. Understood, sir. Or is it madam?" Tony resumed petting the cat.

Footsteps in the hall caught their attention. Both swiveled their gaze to the door. Without warning, the cat leaped from the bed and disappeared behind the faded armchair near the fireplace. The footsteps retreated, but the cat did not reappear.

Tony sat up, aching all over. His shoulder throbbed, and his kidneys must be bruised. He swore he'd never underestimate the strength of determined old men.

He scratched his beard stubble and looked around. Faded blue and white striped curtains let in the light, and a glimpse of the Channel in the distance. He swung his legs over the side of the bed, pushing the bed curtains out of the way. Dust motes swirled in the sunbeam. He sneezed. Standing barefoot on a threadbare rug, Tony assessed the antique furniture, the faded upholstery. Broad daylight was less flattering than the single candle last night. His reflection in the mirror had gaps where the silver had bubbled and peeled. "I'm guessing the money ran out about a generation ago, Lady Montgomery."

He hadn't heard anyone enter since he'd been escorted in here last night and Sawyer had disappeared into the dressing room that separated the two chambers, his hand resting suggestively on the pistol tucked into his belt. But Tony's haversack was slung over the back of the dressing table's chair, and a pitcher of fresh water sat in the cracked basin. "I suppose hot water and breakfast on a tray would be too much to expect, eh, kitty?"

The cat did not deign to reply. Tony peeked behind the chair, but there was no sign of the cat. The furnishings were sparse enough that he should have been able to spot the fluffy tail if the cat was still in the room. He shrugged, then washed, shaved, and changed into his only other clothes. Should he fold those he'd slept in and pack them into his haversack, or hang them up in the wardrobe? The watchdogs had agreed he could leave, but that was before the smuggling captain had expressed his preference for doing business with Tony, and left men behind at the inn.

He dropped onto the chair. Yesterday morning, his biggest concern had been how far he and Alistair would travel in the day, and whether they would reach an inn before getting thoroughly soaked in the rain. Today, he was a smuggler.

His brother Ben would be so proud.

Tony snorted. He tugged on his boots, straightened his cravat, and opened the dressing room door.

No one was there. The blanket had been neatly folded on the cot, which in turn had been tucked out of the way. Nonplussed, Tony stood still. There was no sound or movement in the other bedchamber, either.

He stepped out of the dressing room, then opened the door again and stuck his head inside. The master's side still had several garments hanging, including the clothing he'd borrowed last night. But the lady's side, which should have been overflowing with colorful gowns, held only a half dozen or so, in faded shades of gray and black.

At least one of the watchdogs had left. Was that because they had locked him in the room? Sylvia may not intend to keep him prisoner, but her watchdogs might. Well, he'd climbed up and down his share of drainpipes before. Nothing to it. But just in case, he tried the doorknob first.

The door swung open.

"Morning." Doyle leaned against the railing, arms folded. "We thought you might sleep 'til noon."

"Not generally." Tony stepped into the hall. "Unless there was a great deal of alcohol involved the night before. Alcohol that was consumed, that is."

Doyle gave a bark of laughter. "Follow me, and we'll find you something to eat." He led the way to the stairs. "Mind the third and fifth steps." Since Doyle avoided those steps entirely, Tony skipped them as well.

Downstairs, Doyle led him to the dining room, whose wallpaper had water stains around the window, and kept going straight on through to the servant's hall and down to the kitchen.

The housekeeper looked up from the pot she stirred at the hearth. "Told you he'd still be here come morning." She held her hand out.

Doyle dug in his coat pocket and handed over a penny. "Lucky guess," he grumbled.

"Never bet against me, chum." Tony wasn't sure if he should sit or go back to the dining room.

"Sit you down, lad." The housekeeper pointed at the rough oak table with the wooden ladle in her hand. Tony obeyed. The housekeeper was also the cook, it appeared, as she scooped watery gruel into a bowl and set it before Tony. Soon he also had one scone of indeterminate flavor, with butter but no preserves, and weak tea with milk but no sugar. A request for other accompaniments was met with a shake of the cook's head.

"Won't have more until tomorrow, and that's only if the boys get the load handled right and tight today."

Tony nodded and dug into the paltry meal. All the excitement from last night had only increased his normally hearty appetite. This would have to do until he could get back to the inn for a real meal.

Ignored by the housekeeper, Doyle retrieved another cup from the drainboard and poured tea for himself. "Bloody hell, woman, didn't you put any tea leaves in the pot?"

Galen cuffed him. "Soon as the lad is done eating, take him to see my lady, and then get your arse down and help with the load."

Since it had taken only a few bites to consume the meager breakfast, Tony stood. "Ready."

Doyle poured his untouched drink back into the teapot. "Until tomorrow, my fair Galen," he said. He bent down to kiss the cook's cheek.

"Get going," she snapped, and thwacked him on the backside with the flat of her spoon. Despite the gruff tone, Tony noticed a hint of a grin stealing across the old gel's cheeks.

Doyle led the way back upstairs, and down one hall to another until they went through a door and stepped into another world.

Unlike the water-stained and ancient wallpaper that covered the other walls, here daylight streamed in through clear glass walls and ceiling. He was assaulted by the rich, earthy scent of young plants and exotic trees. In the midst of the dense foliage he spotted Sylvia, draped in a faded gray gown and dirt-stained apron, working at a potting bench. She looked up at their arrival, and dropped a hand spade onto the bench and came toward them, wiping her hands on the apron.

"Good morning, Mr. Sinclair," she called to him.

"Lady Montgomery." Conscious of Doyle standing just behind him, Tony took her proffered hand and kissed her knuckles. He held her a little longer than necessary, relishing the feel of her warm, bare skin, noting the slight calluses, delighting in the appearance of her short blunt nails, complete with dirt beneath. Several sandy blond curls had come loose from the ribbon at her nape and danced around her cheeks. She pushed one out of the way with her forearm. The desire to tuck it behind her ear was so strong, Tony had to force his arm to remain at his side.

Doyle cleared his throat. Tony released Sylvia's hand, and both took a step back.

"Thank you for showing our guest the way, Doyle." Sylvia smiled up at him. "I'm sure we don't want to detain you any longer."

Doyle returned her smile with a grin of his own. "She says it a might nicer than old Galen, eh?" He gave Tony a nudge with his elbow. "I'll just be down at the livery, my lady. Monroe and Corwin are still here, helping Gerald with the gold salon."

Tony watched the silent message pass—Doyle and his brawn may be leaving, but help was still just a shout away. Now Tony knew the names of the watch-dogs who'd slept outside his door, though he was still uncertain which was which.

Doyle left, and Sylvia returned to the potting bench, gesturing for Tony to follow.

"Trent and Baxter have been down to the inn this morning." She resumed transplanting a tray of seedlings into small pots, not looking at Tony. "Captain Ruford's first mate plans to stay here until the next cargo." She finally looked up. Despite the bright sunlight flooding the room, he couldn't read her expression. "A week from today."

She seemed to expect a reply, but Tony didn't know how to respond.

"His other crewman is staying, as well. They'll both report back to Captain Ruford about, ah, the goings-on in the village."

Tony filled the next pot with soil from the bucket, just as Sylvia had been doing. "Goings-on, such as our honeymoon?"

Her cheeks flushed a delightful shade of pink. "If

you wanted to, I'm sure you could evade my men, and go back to the inn and talk to Ruford's people. Or you could be on your way to wherever you were headed before you were detained—"

"Kidnapped."

"—and not give us another thought." She paused, as though the next words exacted a great toll on her. "But I ask that you not do that."

Tony slid the filled pot across the bench top and picked up the next. "Why?"

Sylvia pulled the pot closer, made a well with her finger, plopped a seedling inside, and tucked the dirt around it. "Ruford was the only supplier who would even talk to me and Jimmy about doing business. Without the cargo Ruford delivers, there is no other way to bring income into the village before winter." She gave the seedling another pat. "This is all we have."

She accepted the next filled pot from him. "I don't expect you to stay all season. I'm only asking that you stay until the next cargo is landed. A week at the most." Despite her words, she looked pained by the thought of him remaining even an hour.

Their hands brushed as they moved the pots. Tony trailed his fingers over hers. "And what will you tell your captain after next week?"

Sylvia glanced up, her chin held high. "I will think of something by then." She gathered up the potted seedlings into a crate.

"Let me see if I understand what you're asking. You

want me to go on pretending to be your new husband, at least for the next week. And we're a family of smugglers?" He stepped closer to his "wife," his breeches brushing the folds of her skirt.

Sylvia stepped back. "Yes." Her eyebrows rose as he wiped his hands on her apron.

Hands now clean again, Tony tucked one of her curls behind her ear. His voice was husky when he spoke again. "And just how far do we carry this charade?" He brushed his thumb across her silky cheek.

Her breath caught, and released in a rush. "The whole village knows of our ruse by now. We just need to pretend for the sake of Ruford's first mate and sailor." She spun on her heel and carried the crate of seedlings to a row of shelves staggered against the south wall. "You'll need to stay here rather than at the inn, of course. Sawyer, Doyle, and the others have already offered to take turns, ah . . ."

"Guarding your virtue from me?"

She blushed, a delightful pink that tinted her cheeks and neck, down to her collar. He wondered how far down the blush continued. "They're very protective, and have been a tremendous help since Lord Montgomery passed, but sometimes . . ."

"They smother you?"

"I never said that." She quickly transferred the pots to an open, sunny section on the middle shelf. She retrieved a pair of shears from the potting bench and began pruning a row of larger plants. "The accommodations may not be what you're used to, but I can promise you clean sheets, meals at regular times, and one glass of the finest brandy every night, if you want it."

Tony scooped up the leaves and stalks that fell. "Is the bed companion included in your offer?"

She dropped her shears. "Excuse me?"

He paused at her shocked expression, and barely suppressed a grin. "The black cat. It was on my chest when I woke up."

"Macbeth was with you last night? Why, that—"

"Traitor?" Tony retrieved the shears. "He seemed quite at his ease on the bed, but disappeared as soon as we heard footsteps in the hall."

"He knows he's not supposed to be in Mont— that bedchamber. He usually sleeps with me."

Tony held up the shears. Sylvia plucked them from his hand, careful not to touch him in the process. "And his disappearing act? There were no doors or windows open."

She resumed pruning. "It's a very old house. There's rumored to be a priest's hole somewhere, and any number of secret tunnels and corridors."

Tony followed her, picking up the pruning debris. "Secret tunnels? How quaint."

"Montgomery said it was all hogwash, but Macbeth seems to get into just about any room he wants, regardless of the state of the doors and windows. And the house is practically mouse-free."

By now Tony's hands were full. Lady Montgomery pointed out the compost bin just beyond the door to the outside.

He came back into the conservatory, now noting the

orange trees with small fruit, strawberry plants heavy with green berries, and several other plants with young fruit. One row of pots he recognized as containing herbs. Everything growing under Sylvia's care was either edible or useful in the stillroom. Everything had a practical purpose.

"So you're willing to provide me with food and shelter, and all you ask in return is that I stay and maintain our charade?"

Sylvia rested her fists on her hips. "Well, on a property this size, there are always more tasks than workers."

"And you have such a youthful staff."

Her expression clouded. "Many of the young men from the village went off to fight Napoleon."

"And didn't come back." Tony picked up another fallen leaf. "My elder brother nearly lost his leg, and his life, at Waterloo."

Sylvia nodded slowly. "And most of the crew on Montgomery's ship was from the village, as well. All hands perished when they wrecked last spring."

"And so you have a crew and staff of tottering elders."

Sylvia wiped the blades of her shears on her apron. "Galen and Gerald should have been pensioned off years ago, but the dear hearts won't leave us. They've been here since before Jimmy was born."

Tony raised his eyebrows. "The young redhead who was none too happy to see me last night?"

"He can be a trifle impatient at times, but he means well. He is also rather—"

"Protective?"

She nodded.

"With so many vigilant defenders around, you have nothing to fear from me." Except her own reactions, of course. She was weakening toward him. He could tell.

"You'll stay, then?" She looked as though she hadn't quite let herself believe it until then.

Even if he hadn't already decided to stay in order to pursue the pretty widow, the vulnerability hiding behind her bravado would have decided the issue for him. He had no pressing plans, no reason he couldn't delay meeting up with Alistair.

Until then, Tony would live in a house, almost alone, with a charming and beautiful widow. "I will stay, on one condition."

It was her turn to raise her eyebrows, as Tony moved nearer, close enough to catch her lavender scent, watch the pupils flare in her expressive green eyes.

"I want you"—he tucked another wayward curl behind her ear—"to call me Tony."

Her breathing hitched. "All right. Tony. You should probably address me as Sylvia, then. Montgomery and I were more formal, but—"

"I am not a formal man, Sylvia. My brother got the title, not me. He got the family fortune, too. All I inherited"—he leaned a little closer and tilted his chin down so that he was looking at her through his eyelashes—"was the fair face."

Her tongue darted out to lick her lips, and he bent closer, intent on kissing her. Her sudden burst of laughter jolted him backward.

Damn. That trick always worked for Alistair, even when the dolt did it unconsciously.

She wagged her finger at him. "You're trying to charm me, Mr. Sin— Tony. That won't work." She allowed another bubble of laughter to escape. "So, we have an agreement?" She held out her hand to shake on it.

"We do." Tony shook her hand, then slowly, deliberately, raised her hand to his lips. Holding her gaze, he kissed the tender flesh on her inner wrist, his lips lingering on her fluttering pulse. The scent of earth and growing things, sweeter than any French perfume, washed over him. "Madam wife. Temporarily."

That earned him another blush. She cleared her throat. "Right." She coughed again. "As to the 'having more work than workers' part, Gerald is upstairs in the gold salon, where part of the ceiling collapsed. Perhaps you could lend a hand?"

"But a husband needs to spend time alone with his wife." Tony draped his arm around Sylvia's waist.

She froze for a heartbeat, then took a step sideways, out of reach. "*Pretend* husband." She brandished her pruning shears. "And there is no one present now for whom we need to pretend."

"Ah, but we do need to practice." Tony followed Sylvia down the aisle. "We must be comfortable in each other's presence if we are to succeed in this charade." He lowered his voice. "Comfortable with each other's touch."

She shook her head. "Montgomery and I almost

never touched . . . in public. Nothing more than my taking his arm as we walked down High Street, or his handing me in or out of the carriage."

"But as you said, Montgomery was more formal. I, however, am a tactile man. I need to touch things that belong to me, however temporary the arrangement."

Her chin came up again. "I do not belong to you, even less than I belonged to Montgomery."

"An independent spirit. Forgive me, madam. I was under the impression you needed my cooperation for your scheme to succeed."

He began walking toward the door, silently counting.

"Wait."

He had barely reached three. Knowing it would be unwise to smile just now, he kept his expression neutral as he pivoted to face Sylvia.

"I thought you said you had only one condition."

"One condition that you didn't know about. After our kiss last night, surely you expected a little . . . physical contact? I have just embarked on a criminal career, at your behest. You had to know I'd expect some benefit."

"Benefit?" Sylvia gaped at him. "Why, you pompous, arrogant, conceited popinjay! You, you *libertine*!"

As Sylvia blustered, Tony thought of all the fun they were going to have in the coming week.

She picked up a glass carafe from the shelf above the potting bench, intent on lobbing it at his head, no doubt, when she suddenly quieted. She stared at the carafe, and the assorted other containers on the shelf.

Choosing a better missile? Perhaps he should ease up a tad, get her more accustomed to his presence. "Something wrong?"

She sighed. "I have to go down to the inn. Jimmy was supposed to take these with him when he went to help with the casks."

A chance to learn more about the smuggling operation, and walk about with his "wife" on his arm. Tony opened the door. "Shall we go, then?"

Chapter 7

Within minutes, Tony was striding down a winding path along the cliff to the Happy Jack Inn, Sylvia's hand tucked in the crook of his arm. Her ever-present basket was slung over her free arm, the contents covered by a green-checked cloth. She'd refused his offer to carry it. Gray clouds still hovered above, but kept the rain to themselves.

"Are we moving the casks to a new hiding place?"

They took several steps before she replied. "Not exactly."

Tony didn't blame her for her reticence, though couldn't help wishing she'd be a little more forthcoming with the details of the illegal operation in which he'd become involved. He'd never before done anything more

106

illicit than help dismantle the headmaster's carriage, and reassemble it inside the gent's sitting room.

The cliff path eventually joined a road, and soon they were strolling down High Street in the middle of the village. They passed cottages with broken windows and missing thatch, and more than one whose bare rafters left the upper floors open to the sky. Viewed in the unforgiving light of day, the entire village had obviously been lacking funds for quite some time. What were they spending their smuggling profits on? Certainly not paint or lumber.

But the streets were uncluttered and free of offal, unlike London. Here, the air was swept clean by the near constant breeze fresh off the Channel. A man could breathe deeply here and not choke.

Even the most run-down cottages had well-tended gardens, though, with a profusion of vegetable patches and the occasional flower. Tony recalled that his brother's cook occasionally served those particular blooms as edible garnish. Seemed the entire village shared Sylvia's penchant for the practical over the ornamental.

Other pedestrians called out cheery greetings to Sylvia as they walked, and gave Tony the once-over. A preponderance of the women they passed were dressed in the gray or lavender of half-mourning. To the few who paused, Sylvia introduced him simply as "Mr. Sinclair" with no hint of the nature of their relationship.

Her grip on his sleeve tightened when a mounted rider in an outdated coat and breeches slowed to their pace, and tipped his hat. "Lady Montgomery," the man drawled.

"Mr. Tipton," Sylvia returned, her nose in the air, though her face had gone pale.

The rider stared pointedly at Tony.

Sylvia coughed. "Tipton, Mr. Sinclair. He and I were recently, er, married."

Tipton's eyebrows rose, disappearing above his hat brim. "Really? I don't recall the banns having been read."

"Special license," Tony jumped in. "As soon as she consented to make me the happiest of men, I didn't want to waste a single day."

"Certainly understand your point of view." Tipton cocked his head to one side. "But why would she give up the title to marry a plain mister, eh?"

"A title without a fortune is of little use."

"You don't say." Tipton's gaze grew more calculating, blatantly studying Tony's well-tailored garments.

He let the confirmation of his wealth speak for itself. Sylvia's knuckles were white where she gripped his sleeve, as Tipton continued to stare. Tony covered her hand with his own. He wished she had let him carry the basket—she was trembling, making the glass containers inside clank against each other. Must be an interesting story behind her acquaintance with Tipton.

Sylvia cleared her throat. "We don't wish to keep you from your rounds any further. Good day, Mr. Tipton." Sylvia gave a slight push on Tony's arm, urging him forward.

The two resumed their walk, and Tipton nudged his horse into a trot.

"What was that about?" Tony said as soon as Tipton was out of earshot. "I thought everyone in the village was in on our charade."

"That doesn't include the Revenue agent." Sylvia's face was now flushed with color.

"That was a Revenue agent?" Tony stared after the figure disappearing around a bend. A man whose job it was to catch them at their illegal nighttime activities, and who would gladly see them hung for it. He could have happily gone his entire life without actually meeting one.

And here Sylvia stood, carrying paraphernalia in her basket necessary to the smuggling business. No wonder she had trembled.

Perhaps Tony hadn't fully thought through the potentially negative aspects of pretending to be the lovely Sylvia's new husband, before agreeing to the scheme. But unlike his decision to travel with Alistair, this time he could at least blame his rash decision on the blow to the head he'd received.

"What is he doing about in the day? Thought Revenuers only tried to catch smugglers at night, when they're landing their cargo."

"The cargo has to be moved sometime. Tipton is probably dead certain one was brought in last night."

Tony couldn't help wincing at her choice of the words "dead certain." He cleared his throat. "So, what are we doing today?"

Sylvia entered the yard of the Happy Jack. "We're just a couple out to have lunch at the local pub."

Tony shrugged, and opened the door for her. At the inkeeper's request, they took a table in the corner, the same that he had occupied with Alistair. Had that been only twenty-four hours ago? Once again his life had taken a dramatic turn in a short span.

From his father's suicide, to Ben suddenly joining the army and leaving Tony as temporary head of the family, to setting out on tour with Alistair in order to avoid a boring job, Tony had become adept at adjusting quickly. Surely that too was a requisite skill for a successful career as a rake?

They had barely pulled their chairs up to the table when Spencer came over with one tankard and a pitcher, and poured less than a finger's worth.

"Baxter says he knows what he's doing, my lady, but I think you should lend a hand just the same." Spencer set the tankard down in front of Sylvia.

Tony watched as she took a sniff from the tankard, then a sip—and delicately spat it back. She cleared her throat. "Baxter never could get the ratio right." Sylvia pushed her chair back and stood, gesturing for Tony to do the same. "You might as well come along. In for a penny."

Spencer finally gave his attention to Tony. "Sorry about the misunderstanding last night. No hard feelings, eh?"

"How could I say yes?"

The innkeeper laughed and gave Tony a hearty slap on his sore shoulder that made him stagger the first few steps as he followed Sylvia. She was headed for the kitchen, and he caught up just as she went down into the cellar.

Tony was glad of his coat as the temperature dropped significantly by the time they wended their way past sacks, barrels, and crates of supplies. Sylvia opened a door that Tony didn't at first recognize was even there, it blended into the wall so well.

Inside was another room, with small casks stacked to the low ceiling, lining two walls. A worktable sat in the middle, surrounded by open barrels, and topped with glass carafes and other vessels of various sizes, as well as several packets of what looked and smelled like burnt sugar. Three men that Tony recognized from last night were arguing, but broke off when they saw the newcomers. Jimmy was nowhere in sight.

"Gentlemen," Sylvia said.

In perfect unison, all three pulled off their caps and chorused, "My lady."

"You're just in the nick of time," the eldest of them said.

"I thought we was doing right fine," a second said.

"Not if the pitcher abovestairs is any indication," Sylvia said.

The second man jutted his chin, preparing a protest.

"If you make it too weak, Baxter, we'll have to find new buyers for each batch."

Baxter lowered his chin. "Aye, m'lady."

"Told you you was putting in too much water." The third man finally spoke up.

"And you was putting in too much sugar, Corwin."

Baxter gave Corwin a light punch in the arm, which Corwin returned, with more force. Baxter swung his fist back, but before he could strike, it was caught by the eldest of the three.

"Knock it off before I plant you both a facer," the old man growled. He had to be seventy if a day, but Tony didn't doubt he could hit both men. Baxter and Corwin also apparently believed, as they straightened their coats and looked away, grumbling under their breath.

"Thank you, Trent. Where's Jimmy?" Sylvia pushed the containers on the table out of the way, and set down her basket.

"He said none of these was right, and went back up to fetch the proper one. Is that it, then?" Trent pointed at the glass Sylvia had just retrieved from her basket.

Before Sylvia could respond, they heard the grind of wood on stone. Daylight and a gust of fresh sea air poured in through an opening in the wall. Jimmy stepped through, then leaned his shoulder against the door to push it closed.

"There you are, Syl. Did you bring it?"

Sylvia held out the carafe. "If you'd taken the street instead of the tunnel, our paths would have crossed, and I could have saved you the trip back to the house."

Tony folded his arms. "I thought you said the secret tunnels and corridors were hogwash."

"*Montgomery* said the tunnels were hogwash." She untied the strings on her bonnet and hung it on a peg near the door. "Two carafes full to each cask, and one of these." She pulled a spoon and salt cellar out of her basket and handed them to Corwin.

As Tony watched, Baxter picked up one of the half-ankers of brandy they'd unloaded from the boats last night, and tipped the contents into a larger barrel, while Jimmy filled Sylvia's carafe with water from a bucket, and tipped that into the barrel, too. Corwin, meanwhile, spooned burnt sugar into the salt cellar, leveled it off, and emptied the contents into the barrel.

"Isn't that sacrilege?" The intoxicating, rich scent of brandy and sugar permeated the air.

"The distillery ships out their product in concentrated form," Sylvia explained. "Drinking it as it comes straight from the cask can be dangerous."

"Just ask Corwin," Trent said, dumping in another carafe of water.

"Sick as a dog, he was," Baxter added.

"Shaddup," Corwin growled. He tipped the barrel back and forth, stirring the contents.

Jimmy dipped a clean glass in and held the contents up to the lamplight. "Looks about right, don't it, Sylvia?"

"Let's check it in the daylight."

Jimmy opened the door. A fresh sea breeze swept through the room, clearing Tony's head of the brandy fumes. He followed Sylvia and Jimmy outside. Weak sunlight broke through a few of the clouds. The path leading up to the door was barely visible, just a tiny break in the tall grasses whispering in the wind, clinging to the hillside that rolled away, down to the shore.

Off in the distance was the ever-present sound of crashing surf.

"Well, Mister— Tony? What do you think?"

Tony brought his gaze from the distant sea to Sylvia's green eyes, the same color as the ocean in a spring storm. "What?"

She waved the glass under his nose. "What do you think?"

I think I could drown in your eyes. He kept his mouth shut, and took the glass from her, brushing her fingers. He held it up to the sun, squinting.

"Did we add enough burnt sugar? Too much?" Jimmy shifted his weight from one foot to the other.

"Wish I could have had some in my tea this morning, burnt or not." Tony swirled the amber liquid, then held the glass under his nose. "Looks right. Smells right." He tasted, let it slide down his throat. Sighed. "My brother would be proud to have this in his London cellar."

"Excellent." Sylvia took the glass from him before he could even think about drinking the rest, and went back inside and poured it into the barrel. "This first barrel is for Spencer, as usual, then start loading the cart as soon as Doyle finishes repairing it. The Seven Feathers Inn at Wool is expecting a delivery from us today. And make sure all of the barrels have a stamp— Tiplon is out riding."

"Aye, m'lady," the men said. Jimmy joined them, and the four settled into a routine of reconstituting the brandy and sealing it in larger barrels, complete with tax stamps.

Tony watched them for a bit, Sylvia at his side. "If I

didn't know better," he said, leaning over to whisper in her ear, "I'd think you actually paid customs on those barrels."

"We did, once. Or rather, Mr. Spencer did. He buys legal provisions for his inn, including brandy."

"Illegal mixed in with the legal. Brilliant, my lady."

"Thank you." Her smile lit up the room as though the outside door had been opened. "Now that we have set aside payment for Mr. Spencer, let's go upstairs and have some provisions sent up to Galen. This afternoon you shall have sugar for your tea." She put her bonnet back on, grabbed her basket, and led the way upstairs.

They exchanged greetings with Mrs. Spencer and her daughter, baking pies in the kitchen. "The package you're expecting is here," Sylvia told her.

"I'll let everyone know, my lady. Thank you." Mrs. Spencer accepted a slip of paper from Sylvia and glanced at it before tucking it in her apron pocket. "I'll have one of the lads deliver these later."

"Shopping list?" Tony teased.

"Since we don't have a grocer in the village, we buy many of our supplies through the inn." Sylvia turned back to Mrs. Spencer. "May I see the list again? I don't remember if I wrote down everything Galen wanted."

The women chatted about groceries. Tony stepped toward the door. "I'm just going to get a bit of air." Sylvia waved at him and continued discussing with Mrs. Spencer the merits of black currant versus blackberry preserves.

Tony had taken only a few steps outside when a girl peeked around the corner of the stables. "Mister!" she whispered, gesturing for him to come.

He glanced around the yard, seeing if anyone else was about.

"Mr. Sinclair!" the girl whispered again, gesturing. Still in pigtails, she couldn't be more than eight or ten.

Tony walked over to the stables, but she disappeared by the time he turned the corner. Before he realized what had happened, an old woman grabbed him by the lapels and pushed him up against the wall. Six other women gathered in a semicircle, blocking him in. All were old enough to be his mother or grandmother, and each held a knife, knitting needles, rolling pin, or other implement he couldn't identify but did recognize as capable of inflicting pain. Two of the women were those who had exchanged pleasantries with Sylvia on their way to the inn.

"Ladies," he managed after the initial moment of shock. The first woman had let go, but a tiny old woman still pushed on him, her palms flat against his chest. She looked like she would break in two if he so much as breathed on her. "To what do I owe the pleasure?"

"We know what you're up to, laddie, and it won't work." The old lady in dark blue pointed her rolling pin at him in emphasis.

"Up to?"

"Trying to get under Lady Montgomery's skirts. Didn't work for that nasty captain, won't work for you, neither."

"You tell him, Edith." This came from the stoutest and youngest of the bunch, at least forty, who had first grabbed him.

Edith nodded, shaking her rolling pin.

"I assure you, good ladies, I have the most honorable of intentions—"

"We know you kissed her last night." The speaker pointed her knife at him. A very large, sharp-looking knife that looked quite capable of gutting a pig. Or a rake.

"Right, Mildred. That weren't honorable, no how. You can pretend to be her new husband, but that don't give you a husband's rights." This speaker backed up her point with a long, pointed meat fork, aimed at Tony's throat.

He swallowed. "Perhaps not, under normal circumstances, but it did accomplish the goal of fending off the captain. If anyone was going to kiss the lady, wouldn't you prefer it was me rather than him?" He flashed his best, most charming smile.

"Wouldn't mind a kiss for meself." The words were almost lost in Tony's waistcoat, mumbled by the little woman still trying to press him against the wall.

"Hush, Marge." The fork wavered between Tony and the little old lady attached to his shirt.

Marge glanced up at the fork-wielder. "You're just jealous, Bernice. Look at that mouth of his. Made for kissing, it was." Good thing Tony was a grown man, not a green lad, too mature to blush. "And he's all nice and hard, in all the right spots." She squeezed his chest for emphasis.

A hole should open up in the ground right now, and he'd sink blissfully from sight.

"That don't change nothing." Edith waved her rolling pin. "We ain't going to let you hurt our lady." The other three women, silent until now, murmured in agreement.

"If you do," Bernice said, stepping closer until her long-handled fork touched the knot in Tony's cravat, "you'll soon be singing a different tune." The sharp tines glinted in the sunlight.

Mildred took a step closer as well, both her voice and knife dipping low. "And you'll be singing it soprano."

Tony gulped. "I'm touched, as I never have been before"—he glanced down at Marge, still clinging to his shirt—"by how much you all care for Lady Montgomery. I can only assure you I have no intention of hurting her, and merely want to help her through this difficult time."

"Out o' the goodness of yer heart, laddie?" Edith scoffed. She hadn't lowered her rolling pin, but at least it wasn't pointed directly at him.

"What little boy doesn't dream of becoming a pirate? But most boys grow up to be upstanding citizens. Smuggling isn't quite piracy, but still has an element of risk, a dash of danger. And I'm only doing it for a short while." The ladies weren't backing away. Time for the truth, or at least a version thereof. "And yes, I admit, Lady Montgomery is delightful and easy on the eye. What man wouldn't want to spend time in her company?"

The weapons lowered a bit at his confession.

A door opened and closed in the inn yard. Tony turned his head at the sound of Sylvia calling his name. "Just a moment," he shouted. He looked at the ladies expectantly.

"Don't forget what we said." Edith shook her rolling pin at him.

"You keep your word, or we'll keep ours." Mildred tapped his shoulder with the flat of her knife.

Marge flashed a grin missing several teeth, and gave his chest a last little two-handed pat before she followed the others down a path that quickly disappeared among the tall grasses headed toward the beach.

Tony chuckled as he watched the ladies disappear. "What champions you have, Sylvia," he whispered, before heading back to the inn yard.

He doubted any London rake had to contend with such defenders.

Chapter 8

Tony went inside, where he found Sylvia seated at the corner table in the taproom, lunch for two spread before her. "Miss me?"

She gave him a forced smile, and gestured with her chin toward the fireplace. One of Ruford's sailors lounged on a bench near the fire.

Tony leaned down to give her a kiss on the cheek before taking his seat, and moved his chair to the side. The new position enabled him to better watch the sailor, as well as cozy up to Sylvia. He dug into the crab, mackerel, cheese, and fresh vegetables. After the dreadful breakfast this morning and indifferent fare he'd been eating the last week while traveling, he almost moaned with pleasure. He could hardly wait to taste the apple tart for dessert.

"Like it?" Sylvia paused in her eating.

"I've died and gone to heaven." He took another bite of crab puff, savoring the delicate flavor. "After the stew they served yesterday, I didn't think the Spencers could cook like this."

"For strangers, no."

"So this is another benefit to being married?" The word rolled off his tongue as easily as the fine food slid down his throat. "I could become accustomed to this." He grinned at her after swallowing a mouthful of savory fish.

Sylvia's smile froze.

Tony glanced over his shoulder, following her gaze. The first mate had returned to the taproom, followed by a man Tony had never seen before.

Though of average height, the stranger seemed to leach the light from the room, and not just because his broad build blocked much of the doorway as he entered. He sat down at the far table, across from the first mate, and they rested their elbows on the table, deep in quiet conversation.

"That's Teague," Sylvia whispered. "Leader of the Worbarrow Bay gang. Why is he talking to Crowther?"

"Ruford's first mate?"

Sylvia nodded. "It's bad enough they want Jimmy's beach to land their cargo, but now they want our cargo, as well?"

"You have an on-going disagreement with a smuggling gang? An actual gang?" As sweet and vulnerable as Sylvia was, the most hazardous disagreement she should be involved in should concern the accuracy of a shopkeeper's scale.

Her eyes narrowed. "We're in a dangerous business. I thought you understood that."

"Yes, but all your men are—" He cleared his throat, before he could stick his foot down it. "I just didn't think of you and your men as being a gang."

"What else would we be?" Her hand tightened on her fork, its sharp tines pointing upward.

He eyed her fork's proximity to his thigh. "This fish is delicious. Have you tasted yours yet?"

Sylvia gave him another narrow stare, but let the matter drop and dug in to her own meal. They continued to eat in silence. He kept an eye on the men conversing in the corner. Just as he polished off his apple tart, the two men stood and shook hands.

"That can't be good," Sylvia muttered.

Crowther headed over to the fireplace, while Teague started for the door. He tipped his head toward Sylvia. "Lady Montgomery," he said without breaking stride, looking smug.

"Mrs. Sinclair," Tony corrected.

Teague stopped. "What?"

Tony pushed back his chair and stood, his hand resting on Sylvia's shoulder. "My wife is properly addressed as Mrs. Sinclair." He watched Crowther join the other sailor, but neither of them said a word as they shamelessly eavesdropped.

Teague stepped closer. "Wife?" He was only a couple of inches taller than Tony, but nearly twice as wide. His coat seams strained over his chest and biceps, as though he spent his nights tossing casks of brandy as easily as other men tossed chunks of coal. "Felicitations, my lady. May I take it you've, ah, retired?"

He felt Sylvia tense. "Nothing of the sort, old chum," Tony interrupted. "I was happy to join the family business." He refused to back away, even as the brute across from him flexed his muscles, making his coat even tighter.

"Mr. Teague owns the Stone's Throw Inn near Tyneham, Mr. Sinclair," Sylvia said.

Tony gave her a fatuous smile, before turning his attention back to Teague. "Oh? Interested in selling, by chance? My brother is always looking to buy another inn."

"Actually, I'm planning to *expand* my interests." Teague glanced at Crowther.

Tony gave Sylvia's shoulder a light squeeze of reassurance. "So what brings you to our little cove?"

"Opportunity." Teague folded his arms over his barrel chest.

Mrs. Spencer came out of the kitchen just then to clear the dishes from the table. When neither Tony nor Teague stepped aside, she spun around and headed back, hands empty.

"I'd wager young Lord Montgomery is none too happy, having another man about the house."

"You'd lose." Tony folded his arms, mirroring Teague's cocky stance. "James is quite happy to have

someone else to help shoulder the responsibilities."
Tony kept his tone level, but couldn't resist a little
muscle-flexing himself.

Sylvia was suddenly at his side, tucking her hand in
the crook of his arm. "We don't wish to keep you from
your business, Mr. Teague," she said sweetly.

Teague gave a small nod, acknowledging his dis-
missal. "Good afternoon, then. I'm sure we'll run into
each other again, Sinclair."

"Count on it."

Together they watched Teague exit, and a few moments later heard hoofbeats as he rode out of the yard.
Sylvia picked up her basket beside her chair and gave
a tug on Tony's arm, pulling him out the door.

"Such an eager bride," he murmured, just loud
enough for Crowther to hear. Sylvia's cheeks turned
red but her steps didn't falter.

"We can't let Teague take over Ruford's shipments," she said once they were on the curving High
Street, headed uphill and inland, away from the inn.

"Why not? Wouldn't you rather do business with
someone, *anyone*, other than that stinking lothario?"

"Of course I would." Sylvia let out a deep breath.
"But no one else would do business with *us*. Jimmy
and I, that is. Few captains would even speak with us,
and most of those held the meeting just so they could
have a laugh at our expense."

"But now it's not just you and Jimmy." Tony
stopped in the street and turned her, his hands on her
shoulders so he could look into her sea-green eyes, let
her see the sincerity in his. He'd promised to stay a

week at least, but now he was seriously considering staying beyond that. And not merely because he'd just had his first decent meal since leaving London.

He'd been looking for a direction, an avocation, a cause to take up. In the short time he'd been here, the people of this tiny village, and their struggle to survive, had made an impression on him. They needed help. Tony's help. At least through the next few shipments. He gave Sylvia a gentle squeeze. "You have me now."

Sylvia's heart pounded in her chest. She wanted to believe him, believe *in* him. But he was from a different world, belonged elsewhere. He'd soon grow tired of their scrabbling existence and move on. He'd let her down, just as the other men in her life had let her down. "You can't stay here indefinitely. I'm sure you have obligations. What about the friend you were traveling with? And won't your family be concerned with your prolonged absence?"

Tony shook his head. "Alistair is on a pilgrimage to study big telescopes, my mother is surrounded with suitors these days, and my brother just married his secretary."

"He— I beg your pardon?" Sylvia thought of her father's secretary, back when she was in pigtails—Papa and Mr. Driden had both been bald and wore spectacles.

Tony held out his arm, and they began walking again. "The new Lady Sinclair had disguised herself as a young man in order to get the job with Ben. It's a long story, but ends well. They're nauseatingly happy with each other."

Sylvia couldn't imagine trying to pretend to be a young man. "She wore breeches, in public?" What a shocking creature Tony's sister-in-law must be.

On second thought . . . what a brilliant idea. How much simpler would it be to conduct business but not have to fend off unwanted advances from the likes of Ruford? She glanced down at herself, trying to picture her figure in breeches and tailcoat.

When she looked up, Tony was staring at her with a speculative gleam in his eyes, as though he too were picturing her in breeches. She coughed. He raised his gaze to her face, the picture of innocence.

Thinking of Tony's family reminded her of one of his earlier comments. "What did you mean, your brother is looking to buy inns?"

Tony shrugged. "Call it a hobby of his."

"Hobby?" Sylvia's mind raced with the implications. Tony's brother was wealthy enough to buy inns, plural, for a hobby? She looked down at her threadbare dress, remembering the condition of the house he'd seen, the wretched breakfast Galen had undoubtedly fed him this morning.

Her cheeks burned with mortification. What must he think of her? Of Jimmy, Doyle, Baxter, and the others. She had become accustomed to the village and its poverty since she had taken up residence four years ago. It was just the way things were.

She glanced at Tony's fine attire. His coat alone must have cost more than all the gowns in her dressing room combined.

Why was he willing to play along with their charade?

Was this all just a lark to him? A rake pursuing another conquest? The rich, idle aristocrat amusing himself at their expense?

She thought of his hands when she'd touched him last night, checking his injuries. She'd felt his calluses. Sensed the coiled strength in his muscles, all over his powerful body. Aristocrat, yes, but not an idle one.

She gave herself a mental shake. She couldn't allow herself to be distracted by the attractive package. His presence was a gift that would only be taken away again, and she would not become attached to it.

They reached the turnoff from the main road, the manor house visible on the bluff. The day had grown dark again, clouds obscuring the sun, concealing the manor's peeling paint, shadows filling in the missing mortar between bricks, hiding decades of damage from winter storms and blustery winds.

"What a grand house."

Sylvia followed Tony's gaze, staring at the manor. "Grand?" A falling piece of the ceiling in the gold salon had almost knocked her senseless last week.

"It was once, and could be again. Notice the intricacy of the frontispiece, the pedimented windows?" Still facing the house, he wrapped an arm around her shoulders, tilted his head close to hers and gestured with one hand, his voice low. "Picture it with fresh paint on the portico columns. An army of gardeners trimming back the ivy. A phaeton tooling along the graveled drive, pulled by a matching set of bays. Do you see it, Sylvia?"

Almost. What was clearer to her was his thumb

stroking the bare skin at the hollow between her neck and shoulder. He had shifted closer so their bodies touched, hip to hip, thigh to thigh. She turned her head to face him, a rebuke on her lips, but he was still staring straight ahead at the house, his focus a hundred years away. His gaze flicked to her, then back to the house so quickly, it might have been her imagination.

His strong arm around her was thrilling, his faint scent—sandalwood soap and *him*—intoxicating. The heat from his body scorched her skin. If she tilted her chin, she could kiss his smooth-shaven cheek. If he turned his head, their lips would meet.

What was she doing? She had no business thinking about kissing him. "You're right, it probably was grand, a generation or two ago. Now, though, I think the dairy cattle have better shelter than we do." She shrugged out of his loose embrace, and veered off the path toward the barns, taking a shortcut across the field.

"But the stables don't have pedimented windows." Tony stayed at her side, stepping carefully in order to keep his boots out of the cow patties.

"Farleigh, are you in here?" she called as soon as they entered the cool, dim interior of the barn.

"Back here, my lady."

She walked past the rows of stalls and milking stanchions, breathing in the sweet scents of milk and straw, with the slight undertone of fresh manure, to the workbench at the back. She dug two small jars of ointment out of her basket and set them on the bench next to the leather collar he was repairing. "One is udder balm, the other is for your stump."

Farleigh gave her a gap-toothed grin. "Thankee, my lady." He picked up the collar, the bell clanking, and limped over to the cow waiting for it in the nearest stall. "But which is which?"

"Your choice, sir. They both work equally well."

Tony glanced at Farleigh's wooden leg. "A casualty of the war?" he asked softly.

Sylvia nodded, then continued on to the workroom connected to the barn. Miss Atwood was at work preparing the cheese, while Mrs. Brewer churned butter and her children played at helping. Both women looked expectantly between Tony and Sylvia.

"You've heard about Mr. Sinclair, no doubt."

Miss Atwood finished pouring the milk and wiped her hands on her apron. "Aye, my lady. It appears everything we've heard is true." She beamed at Tony.

He gave an exaggerated, elegant bow to each in turn. "Charmed, ladies."

Miss Atwood giggled, and even staid Mrs. Brewer simpered.

Both ladies were Tony's age or older, and it should not bother Sylvia that he was smiling at them. All rakes flirted outrageously, with all females. She had no special claim on him.

Sylvia gritted her teeth. Before the women could make cakes of themselves over him any further, she handed them each their jar of hand cream and collected the day's butter, and headed back toward the manor house. To her surprise, Tony stayed right beside her, giving the ladies only a farewell wave as he exited the barn.

It wasn't his fault that so many of the local women

were starved for male companionship. Though he certainly didn't seem to mind offering it.

They had crossed the pasture and were back on the road before he spoke again. "Have you always been the village apothecary?"

His soft-spoken question surprised her, and she carefully considered her answer before she replied. "Many of the local ladies were not exactly overjoyed four years ago when Montgomery searched for a wife farther afield. They didn't realize he was simply marrying the niece of a business acquaintance."

"They didn't welcome you into their midst." There was no condemnation in his voice, only understanding.

"I probably would have reacted the same way in their position. When Montgomery and I paid our monthly visits, I learned that many of them worked outdoors just as hard as the men, and noticed their hands were just as painfully chapped in the winter. So I started bringing them jars of balm I'd made. Ointments to help injuries heal. Soon after, while he was away at sea, they started inviting me to tea, and to their sewing parties."

"Social entrée made possible by jars of hand cream." Tony nodded his approval. "London ladies should be so enterprising."

"Would London ladies gather together to dye their gowns black after a shipwreck?"

He rested his hand on her shoulder. "Probably not."

Enough examining the past. The present was far more interesting. "Why are you here?"

"I'm accompanying you back home so Crowther doesn't doubt our story."

Sylvia stopped, the roofless shell of the gatehouse behind her, and leaned against the post where a gate once hung so she could watch Tony's expression. "No, I mean why are you here in Lulworth? I can understand why you stayed last night—the lads can be intimidating at times. But why didn't you leave this morning? No one could have stopped you."

"Truly?" He plucked a tall grass stem and stuck the end between his teeth. "I like Marge."

"Marge— Mrs. Miggins? You're staying because you like Mrs. Miggins? She's eighty-nine and claims to have been a mistress to King George."

Tony tilted his head. "She does seem fond of men."

Sylvia closed her eyes briefly. "She didn't pinch you, did she?"

"She pinches, too?"

Sylvia began walking toward the house again, Tony falling into step beside her. She would *not* think about what it would be like to pinch the handsome man at her side, and forced her mind to more practical matters. She made a mental note to cut back the rhododendrons that lined the drive now that they'd finished blooming—there was no longer room for a carriage to pass in some places. They may lack funds to replace things, but the pruning shears were still serviceable. "How did you meet Mrs. Miggins?"

Tony shifted the grass stem to the other corner of his mouth, and took entirely too long to answer such a simple question. "She and a few of her friends said hello to me while we were at the Happy Jack this morning."

"When? I didn't—"

"You were inside chatting with Mrs. Spencer. It was just me and seven lovely ladies, all of whom brandished a rolling pin or some other weapon."

Sylvia paused mid-stride. "Weapon?"

Tony tugged on her elbow, helping her over a wheel rut in the path. "After our kiss last night, they just wanted to make sure my intentions toward you are honorable. Your men are gossips, it would seem."

And they had the gall to call Mrs. Spencer a busybody?

If not for the audience that had been present, she might have been able to truly enjoy the kiss. Perhaps next time.

Next time? There should never be a next time. Last night had just been a fluke, a mistake. Never to be repeated.

Unless it was necessary for their charade, of course.

She looked at Tony sideways, studying his full mouth, sensual lips. No hardship there, should they have to kiss. For appearance's sake, for their charade. After all, husband and wife would do far more intimate things with each other. And as a widow, didn't society grant her a little more leeway, as long as she was discreet?

Jimmy hailed them just then, as he emerged from the rhododendrons that hid the shortcut to the cliff path.

"All done?" she called, grateful for the interruption before her imagination could embarrass her any further. Tony was a rake, having a bit of a lark. Of course he'd be interested in kissing her, if she was willing. Trouble was, a rake would want much more than a chaste kiss, and she had no intention of being one among his undoubtedly many conquests.

Jimmy checked that the last branch went back into position, concealing the path, and brushed at the leaves and dirt on his clothes. "All right and tight, all the usual arrangements made for the deliveries, so I was just going up to see what can be done with the gold salon. Trent says another so'westerly is going to blow through soon."

As the three of them continued toward the manor, Sylvia couldn't restrain a sigh. Trent's knee was never wrong. The last so'westerly had been less than a week ago, and they'd used most of their lumber to shore up the salon. But it was too little, too late, and the sodden ceiling had collapsed anyway.

Was that the distant rumble of thunder already? Sylvia scanned the horizon, and then breathed another sigh, this one of relief. She stepped to the side, out of the way of Doyle and his wagon loaded with supplies. She'd almost forgotten today was the farrier's monthly visit.

Doyle tipped his hat as he rolled past, headed for the back door. "Mrs. Spencer sends her compliments, my lady."

"Thank you. I'm sure Galen will be delighted to see you."

"She always is." Doyle gave a cheeky grin and flicked the whip above his horse's ears.

Jimmy opened the front door for Sylvia, then headed up the stairs.

Sylvia hung her bonnet on a hook and continued down the hall. Tony stayed at her side. Her steps faltered. "Where are you going?"

"Wherever you're going."

Oh. "I have work waiting for me in the stillroom."

"Then I'll help." He lowered his voice. "I can be very handy."

She could imagine all too well what he might be able to do with his hands. The stillroom was at the back, isolated from the rest of the house. And small. Tony would be able to stay quite close to her, the whole time. Work his charm on her with no one around to interrupt. She gulped. "W-what if you helped Jimmy instead? He and Gerald have had a difficult time making any progress with the gold salon."

Tony glanced at the staircase. "If you're sure that's what you want?"

No, but that's what she needed for peace of mind. "I'm sure."

"Very well, my lady." He turned for the stairs, and she hurried down the hall before he caught her staring, watching him take the steps two at a time.

Once in the stillroom, Sylvia found it difficult to concentrate on her work. She had never before spent time with a rake. Was not entirely sure she'd even met one before Tony. There certainly weren't any here in Lulworth Cove, and her uncle had strictly limited her circle of acquaintances in Manchester. Tony, with that smile, those eyes, must be quite successful at it.

Not all the local ladies were ready to succumb to his charms, though. She wished she could have witnessed the circle of women threatening him with rolling pins.

Hours later, she got up from her bench in the still-room, stretching her back, trying to work out the stiffness from mixing several new batches. She caught a whiff of a new scent—dinner cooking—and her stomach growled.

She made her way to the kitchen and picked up Macbeth, who was milling around the cook's ankles, mewling for a tidbit.

"Just stop that whining now, because you ain't getting none," Galen growled, waving her spoon for emphasis.

"Stop what?" She hadn't even asked for a taste yet.

The cook spun around. "Oh, my lady, I didn't see you come in. That blasted cat's been begging for hours. Told him to go catch his own supper."

"I'll see what I can do to distract him." Sylvia settled the cat in his favorite position, seated in the crook of her arm with his front paws hugging her shoulder.

"Ready to eat in less than an hour," Galen said, reaching for her knife and chopping board.

"I'll go see what the men have been up to, then." As soon as Galen had her back turned, Sylvia snagged a piece of fish off the platter and fed it to Macbeth on the way out the door. "Good thing I left my work apron on," she whispered. The cat purred his appreciation. "Fish breath." He washed his paws while Sylvia climbed the stairs, following the sound of loud thuds emanating from the gold salon.

She opened the salon door and stopped, her mouth agape.

The windows were flung wide open, a fire roaring in the grate, and Tony and Jimmy had stripped to their shirts, sleeves rolled up. Both were barely recognizable, covered in detritus, dust, and sweat, each with a kerchief covering the lower half of his face and a scarf tied around his head. Dust motes danced in the air.

The last of the furniture had been removed after the ceiling fell, but several pairs of chairs had been brought back in, along with planks of lumber. Tony stood on the makeshift scaffolding, swinging a hammer and pry bar. Chunks of damp plaster fell with each powerful blow, landing on the curtains laid on the floor beneath.

Sweat glistened as it slid down his neck, and made his hair stand out in spikes at the edges of his scarf. Soaked with perspiration, Tony's shirt clung to him, the white lawn rendered nearly sheer. It revealed a birthmark on the back of his broad shoulder, and highlighted his impressive musculature. She'd already known he was strong, having felt along his limbs last night while he had been unconscious. But watching him in action, seeing his muscles bunch and shift as he worked . . . Her mouth suddenly went dry.

"Beg pardon, my lady." Gerald suddenly stood behind her, trying to get into the room. He, too, was covered with dust.

Hoping none of her attraction was revealed on her face, she stepped aside to let him in with his burden, a tray with glasses and a pitcher, plus more cloths draped over one arm.

"Your timing is perfect, my good man." Breathing heavily, Tony dropped his tools and sat down on the scaffold, his feet swinging free, and accepted a glass of water.

"As always," Jimmy added between pants, reaching for a glass.

Sylvia stepped through the doorway. "You two have certainly been industrious." Even Tony's lashes were coated with white plaster dust.

He tugged the kerchief down so he could drink, and raised his glass to her in a toast. He tipped the glass back, his throat working as he swallowed the entire glassful in one go, his neck exposed because his cravat was gone and his top two shirt buttons undone. Her breath hitched at the sight. Seeing a man's chest apparently had the same effect on her that a glimpse of a woman's ankle had on men.

A glimpse of Tony's chest, at any rate.

A little water escaped the side of his mouth, and trailed down his jaw and throat, disappearing inside his collar.

Sylvia licked her lips. That sound had to be the cat purring, not her.

Jimmy tried to drink his entire glass down as well, and choked.

Tony thumped Jimmy on the back, and winked at Sylvia.

She stiffened her spine. The man was a peacock, showing off for her.

Ah, but what a show. And when was the last time an attractive man, someone past adolescence but not yet into his dotage, had showed off for her? No reason she couldn't enjoy it. She relaxed her posture. Slightly. "I came up to warn you that dinner should be ready in an hour or so. Much as I appreciate what you're doing, you can't come to table like this."

"Yes, my lady." Grinning, Tony held out his glass so Gerald could refill it.

Sylvia glanced around the room again, definitely not watching Tony drink, or the rise and fall of his chest as he caught his breath. There were ladders and various tools scattered all over, in addition to the debris-strewn drapes that had once been gold velvet. Well, she'd planned to replace them anyway. Someday. "What is it you're doing, by the way?"

"Sylvia, isn't this great? Tony says he knows how we can fix the roof, and the ceiling, and the walls. We just have to get all the wet stuff out of the way and dry out the wood." Jimmy swung his feet, in perfect rhythm with Tony's.

"It appears the dry rot isn't too extensive yet." Tony set his empty glass on the tray. "You'll need to replace the missing and damaged roof tiles, and buy a few other supplies. Will that be a problem?"

So much for buying fabric for new dresses, even though her year of mourning had ended a month ago. How long could one wear nothing but gray or black, and retain one's sanity? But the house was more important than her wardrobe. "No, of course not. Monroe is going to West Lulworth tomorrow, to make a delivery and pick up supplies—we'll ask if he has room in his wagon."

"I'll prepare a list, then."

Sylvia left after they promised to wash up in time for dinner. Sounds of hammering, and the thumps of plaster falling, followed her down the stairs.

Within an hour they were all seated around the table, Jimmy freshly scrubbed. Tony was too, and Sylvia was surprised to recognize his fine coat, shirt, and breeches, all perfectly clean.

"Earlier I took the liberty of borrowing work clothes from your husband's wardrobe," he said, accepting a filled plate from Gerald. "I hope you don't mind."

Caught staring at him, Sylvia felt heat rise in her cheeks. "Not at all. In fact, use whatever you want of his. Hubert won't mind."

Tony smiled. "I'll take you at your word."

Was it just her imagination, or did his words carry other meaning? What rakish interpretation could he have given her innocent offer? And his eyes seemed to sparkle with mischief. Perhaps it was just the candle-light playing tricks.

They ate in near silence for several minutes. If Sylvia had worked up an appetite in the stillroom, Jimmy and Tony must be nearly starving after their exertions. She waited until Gerald served the third, and final, course before voicing a question she had wondered since her visit to the salon.

"How is it that you know about dry rot, plaster, and such?"

Tony cracked a walnut in half, offered it to her, and

cracked another. "When we were in school, Alistair, Nick, and I would often go to one another's homes for holiday. One winter, a big storm damaged part of Nick's house. We made such a nuisance of ourselves asking the workmen endless questions, they put us to work."

"Nick's parents allowed this?" Sylvia nibbled on the walnut half.

"Nick's father was *delighted*. Free laborers."

"A real pinchpenny, eh?" Jimmy stuck his walnut halves onto a hunk of cheese and ate the whole thing in one huge bite.

Sylvia frowned at him. Really, sometimes he behaved as if he were eight instead of eighteen.

"Wha'?" he mumbled, his mouth still full.

"So, I may not be a journeyman roofer or plasterer, but I think I can help young Lord Montgomery here get the house weatherproofed again. And if we work quickly, perhaps we can even do so before the next so'westerly undoes all our efforts."

"Capital!" Jimmy reached for another wedge of cheese, but this time cut it into small pieces and ate them with his fork.

"Yes, capital, indeed." She should sound more enthusiastic, but she worried what Tony might ask for as payment in exchange. Even with the profit from last night's shipment, there was still so little money, so many expenses.

"Since I've agreed to stay, I might as well keep busy while we wait for the next cargo." Tony drained his wineglass, which had been filled with water. "As you said, a property this size has more tasks than workers."

Sylvia could have kissed him, right then and there. Except for the niggling concern about what compensation he'd expect. He'd probably want more than a simple kiss.

"Of course, you're welcome to come watch." He'd lowered his chin, looking at her through his lashes.

"Why would she want to watch us get all dirty and sweaty?" Oblivious to Sylvia's sudden intake of breath, Jimmy scooted his chair back from the table. "I'm still hungry. I'm going to see if Galen baked any tarts. Coming?" He looked at Tony.

"No, I think I'll stay here. But do bring one back if there are any to spare."

Sylvia wiped her mouth with her napkin as Jimmy dashed from the room.

"Now that the cub's gone . . ." Tony slid his hand across the table and tapped Sylvia's fingers. "I believe you owe me something."

"Beg pardon?" She hoped he hadn't noticed the squeak in her voice.

Tony slowly traced a figure on the back of her hand. "Part of our bargain." His voice had dropped, low and soft and slow, almost as much of a caress as his hand, which was still stroking hers. "You promised something if I wanted it, and I find I do want it."

Chapter 9

She couldn't breathe. "I did? You do?"

He nodded. "One glass of the finest brandy, every night." He sat back and held up his empty glass. "There was no wine with dinner, and I've never cared for port, but I wouldn't mind a glass of brandy just now."

The rotter. He was winding her up on purpose, just like one of her cousins' toys. Wind it up, pull the string, and watch the top spin like crazy.

Well, she wasn't letting Tony pull her string.

She got up from the table with as much dignity as she could muster and retrieved the decanter from the sideboard. "Here, pour for yourself. I don't want to take the chance of spilling it. Might land on your head."

He grinned unabashedly, acknowledging her threat, yet unfazed. After he filled his own glass, his hand hovered near hers. "Care to join me?"

She paused. What was the harm? "Just a finger's worth."

He poured the requested amount, and handed back the decanter. He waited until she was seated again, and held his glass up in a toast. "To what shall we drink?"

That was easy. "To no more leaks."

"To no more leaks." They drank, and Tony closed his eyes, presumably in appreciation. He leaned back in his chair, the wineglass held between his fingers like a brandy snifter, and slowly swirled the liquid. "Are there many more of them?"

"Too many. The one on the southwest corner is the largest. That's where the roof is missing the most tiles." She took another sip of her brandy, and then it was gone. Drat. Perhaps she should have allowed herself a tad more.

"How long has it been this bad?"

"Well, there was the storm last week, plus—"

"I wasn't referring to the roof."

Oh.

"Was it like this when you married him?"

She folded her napkin and smoothed the edges. "Let's just say marriage to Montgomery was better than the alternative."

Tony raised his eyebrows but didn't press the issue. That was a point in his favor.

He'd hear the story at some point anyway, seeing as how all her men were gossips. Apparently. "Montgomery's father was not skilled when it came to money, other than spending it, and not on the estate. Hubert tried, but the blockade with France for so many years hurt his shipping business. Two years ago, after several business ventures went badly, he turned to his grandfather's trade. Smuggling. Things started getting better. Then last spring, a gale blew across the Channel. His ship was battered against the rocks, and all hands perished."

Tony said not a word, but leaned across the table and poured half his brandy into her glass.

She didn't need it, though she appreciated the gesture. She'd made peace long ago with what life had thrown at her.

Jimmy bounded back into the room just then, a smear of jam at the corner of his mouth. "I saved one," he announced, setting the tart on the cheese plate between them. "There would have been more, but Macbeth caught a mole this afternoon and left it on the kitchen doorstep and scared the bej—Scared Galen. I think he does it just to annoy her. She had to calm her nerves with a dose or two of spirits, barely got dinner ready."

Jimmy paused, and they all turned toward the sound of voices in the hall and the front door closing. "That will be Corwin. Smashing. Now he and I can finish our chess game before you two turn in." Jimmy went around the table, heading for the hall.

"I thought it was Sawyer we were waiting for." Tony took another sip of brandy.

Jimmy looked back over his shoulder. "No, I'm sure it's Corwin's turn tonight." And with that, he was gone.

Sylvia stared at Tony.

He drew slow circles on the back of her hand with his fingertip. "You think I forgot about your guard dogs planning to take turns sleeping in the dressing room that separates us?" His voice had turned low and soft again. "I assure you, there's no need for them. Your virtue is safe with me." He covered her hand with his own. "As safe as you'd like it to be."

She snatched her hand back. The smoldering look in his eyes was back.

She was having trouble breathing again. Perhaps she should step outdoors. Fresh air would clear her head.

Tony stood, offered his hand, and pulled her up. Instead of letting go and stepping back once she was on her feet, he tugged her closer, the toes of his boots disappearing beneath the edge of her skirt, close enough for her to feel the heat radiating from his body, and inhale his scent of sandalwood soap and musk.

Her mouth went dry. Her dress felt too small, the bodice too tight.

He leaned in, closer still, his breath warm on her cheek. His lashes swept down, hiding his eyes, just before his lips met hers in a simple kiss.

There was no audience present, no witnesses for whom to playact. He still held her hand, his fingers wrapped around hers. Electrifying, almost overwhelming. His free hand came up and cupped her jaw, his thumb caressing her cheek. Heat blossomed within her, threatened to burn her from the inside out. He touched her, stroked her, but he did not demand entrance.

She was tempted to part her lips, but knew there would be no going back if she let him in. It might already be too late.

What felt like hours later, he pulled back a fraction. His lips brushed her ear as he whispered, "I suggest we go join the others now, before I do something for which you'll never forgive me." He tucked her hand in the crook of his elbow. "Shall we, sweetheart?"

Too dazed to speak, she merely nodded.

He patted her hand, as though aware he'd rattled her, and led the way to the rose salon.

Corwin was there, playing chess with Jimmy, while Monroe sat before the fire, smoking his pipe, commenting on each player's move. Gerald was lighting two more candles, and Galen entered with a tea tray. Tony escorted Sylvia to the sofa by the fire, then sat next to Monroe and the two began discussing the trip to West Lulworth in the morning. Macbeth trotted in, glared at Jimmy, and leaped up into Sylvia's lap.

It was all so . . . normal.

She declined the offer to play cards when the chess match was over. Turned out Jimmy had only offered out of politeness, since he immediately demanded a rematch with Corwin. While they set up the board and began again, she stroked Macbeth, sneaking the occasional glance at Tony.

He was the picture of innocence, the epitome of propriety. Corwin and Monroe would never suspect the outrageous things he'd done and said when he'd been alone with her.

That was the idea, wasn't it? To lull them all into a

false sense of security, get them to lower their defenses, before he . . . Before he what? Ravished her?

She choked on her tea.

"Everything all right, Syl?"

"Fine, Jimmy."

Monroe got up to refill his teacup, and Tony sent her a glance heated enough to singe her eyebrows.

To hide her flaming cheeks, she bent her face to look at Macbeth, but his eyes were closed, his tail slowly flipping in the way that signaled for her to keep petting him. Typical male, only wanting one thing.

Her hand froze. That was it, wasn't it?

Tony didn't necessarily want *her*, he just wanted. She was a widow, the youngest in Lulworth Cove, and at the risk of being arrogant, the most appealing. She still had all of her own teeth.

The handsome, rich aristocrat, amusing himself by taking part in their little drama, simply wanted female companionship. And she was the pick of the litter.

That was all. He'd probably had a female companion in every town he'd stopped in on his way from London while traveling with his friend. Just look at how he'd accosted her, a complete stranger, at the inn during their first encounter. If she were a different type of woman, they might have spent that afternoon in his room. Or the hayloft.

Well, she wouldn't fall for his tricks. She might enjoy his attention—after all, he was charming and she was only human—but it would go no further. Once their crisis with Ruford was handled, Tony would be on his way, no doubt to another female . . . companion . . . in another town. There was nothing to keep him in Lulworth Cove. She refused to be just one of his many conquests.

She would enjoy, but not succumb.

Monroe wandered over to watch the chess match. Tony settled on the sofa beside Sylvia, his arm stretched along the back, not quite brushing her shoulders, and turned toward her. Her breath caught.

"Mind if I pet your . . . cat?" His hand hovered above Macbeth, still curled up on Sylvia's lap.

"Go ahead, if you dare. He doesn't like most men." Macbeth continued to slowly flip his tail.

Moving very slowly, Tony stroked the cat from just above his eyes, between his shoulders, down his back, all the way to the tip of his tail. Macbeth purred even louder. Tony did it again.

This time, Sylvia felt Tony's fingertips stroking her neck above her collar, underneath her hair, at the same time he stroked the cat. His expression did not change, Macbeth did not move, and no one else in the room paid them any attention.

She struggled to breathe normally. The pressure of his fingers increased, massaging away the knots of tension at the base of her skull. She should tell him to stop. She felt like purring.

Amazing. His fingers were strong on her neck, easing the tension, yet feather light on Macbeth, as he continued the cat's favorite stroke. She let Macbeth purr for both of them.

"There is a dainty little woman in Singapore who would do you a world of good."

Tony was leaning so close, she felt his warm breath against her cheek. She remembered the feel of his lips against hers. "Excuse me?"

"My friend Nick found her on one of his voyages. He'd lie on his stomach, then she'd take off her shoes and walk up and down his back. Releases all the tension. He swears by it."

If she was tense, it was Tony's fault. He hadn't moved back, yet no one else in the salon seemed to notice.

Macbeth stretched and yawned, baring his teeth, then climbed over to Tony's lap.

Sylvia could only stare.

The cat turned in a circle before settling himself, with one paw on Tony's stomach, and looked up expectantly.

"You're a harsh taskmaster, Sir Macbeth." Tony rubbed his finger under the cat's chin, who resumed his loud purring.

"Now that's something I thought I'd never see." Jimmy perched on the arm of the sofa next to Sylvia. "I didn't think the cat liked anyone but Syl."

Tony eased his hand away from Sylvia's neck. She should feel relieved, but already missed the contact. She berated herself.

"Felines are notoriously discriminating." Tony ruffled the cat's ears. "Aren't you, kitty?"

Sylvia cleared her throat. Good thing she wasn't relying on Jimmy to protect her virtue. Tony probably could have had his hand down the back of her dress, and Jimmy wouldn't notice. "Finished your chess game already?"

"Checkmated in only six moves. I think I'd better turn in for the night."

Sylvia caught Monroe stifling a yawn. "Excellent idea." And it was one sure way to prevent herself from succumbing. She'd have more willpower after a good night's sleep.

Soon the household settled in for the night, Corwin on the cot in the dressing room, Monroe on a pallet out in the hall.

She waited for Macbeth to jump up onto the bed and join her. And waited. Everyone had sought their own bed, Monroe already snoring in the hall, when she heard a quiet voice. Tony. Judging by the silences between, a one-sided conversation. Talking to her cat.

The little traitor was spending the night with Tony. Again.

Sylvia rolled over, punched her pillow, and waited for sleep to claim her.

When she awoke, it was well past her usual time to be up and about. Normally she would take an afternoon nap the day after landing a cargo, to catch up on the sleep she'd missed, but having Tony in the house had thrown off her routine yesterday. She was surprised Galen hadn't come in to wake her already.

The house was quiet. No thumps from the gold salon.

She threw the covers back, startling Macbeth, who had been curled up at the foot of the bed. "So you came in after all." She rubbed behind his silky ears, earning a purr for her efforts. It didn't take long to mollify the cat after his rude awakening, and she soon got ready for the day and went downstairs.

"He went with Monroe," Galen announced as she set breakfast in front of Sylvia, answering her unasked question. "He grabbed a scone hot out of the pan and ran out the door to catch up with the wagon. Said he wanted to pick out the supplies personal like."

Sylvia poured herself a cup of tea, made with new leaves. Ahh, heaven. "I didn't know any gentleman from London had ever seen the sunrise, except by staying up for it."

Galen chuckled and set a jar of preserves on the table, along with the scones.

Sylvia grabbed two before Galen could take the platter away, and smeared them with fresh butter and preserves. Mmm. Was she really so easy to please, just a little fresh food? She'd wager Tony's other female conquests wouldn't be so easy.

Perhaps he'd already tired of pursuing her? Her hand froze with the teacup at her mouth. That's why he'd run out so quickly this morning—anything to get away from the boring little backwater burg and the country turnips in it.

As if sensing the direction of her thoughts, Galen sat down with her own cup of tea. "Gerald freshened up the suite this morning." She stirred a drop of honey into her cup. "The mister's haversack and other set of clothes is still there, and his razor and whatnots are on the dressing table."

Sylvia let out a shaky breath. "This is ridiculous. Two days ago we didn't even know he existed."

Galen patted Sylvia's shoulder, then quickly drained her cup and went back to work.

"It's only that we need him for dealing with Ruford," Sylvia said.

"Yes, that's it."

"And it will be nice to no longer have changing weather conditions inside the house."

"Whatever you say, my lady."

Sylvia quickly ate the rest of her breakfast in silence. She had a lot of work to do, too.

She went about her chores determinedly not thinking about Tony, what he was doing, or when he would return. There was no point in doing her usual cleaning, since Jimmy and Gerald were doing their best to fling about as much dust as possible in removing the debris from the gold salon. Eventually they settled on tossing it directly out the window down onto the lawn, but not until after they'd tracked plaster dust down the stairs and all the connecting halls.

Sylvia mixed and delivered a tonic for Mrs. Doyle's colicky baby, and had just sat down for the household's midday meal in the kitchen when the wagon rumbled up the drive. Her stew forgotten, she dashed outside, but slowed to a more decorous pace once out in the drive. The others were only a few steps behind her.

Tony was driving Monroe's wagon, loaded high with slate tiles, lumber, and other supplies she couldn't even name. Monroe lay stretched out on top of the whole, snoring.

"Whoa," Tony called to the old nag in the traces. The wagon creaked to a halt. He flashed a grin at Sylvia as he set the brake. "Miss me?"

Her stomach fluttered. Must be more hungry than she thought. "We just sat down to eat."

"Ah, then my timing is perfect."

Monroe snorted and sat up, wiping the corner of his mouth. "Someone mention food?"

"S'pose I can set another place," Galen said. "Bring your lazy arse inside."

Gerald released the horse into the pasture to graze while the humans went indoors.

After the worst of their hunger had been appeased, Jimmy excitedly quizzed Tony about the supplies he'd bought and plans to use them. Much of the discussion included terms unfamiliar to Sylvia, but she wasn't listening to the words, she was watching the speaker.

Tony's brown eyes were bright, his features animated. When hand gestures weren't sufficient to explain his ideas, he resorted to drawing with slate and chalk, plans for the roof and walls and ceiling, plans that would soon have the entire southwest side habitable again, on all floors. Simple plans for him, but impossible for ancient Gerald and young Jimmy to implement on their own.

And impossibly beyond their reach, financially. But one had to have dreams.

"Of course, only if that's the way you want to do it."

Tony set the chalk down. "I'm merely making suggestions. It's entirely up to you."

"No, no, I like this." Jimmy leaned on his elbows, studying the slate. "We'll put the roof tiles on so no more rain comes in, then really get going." He stabbed the slate with his index finger. "This is exactly what we'll do."

Sylvia couldn't contain a smile at Tony's tact. He acknowledged her thanks, but quickly lowered his eyes, almost as though he were being modest.

Galen gave a huff and got up to clear the dishes. "Them roof tiles ain't going to nail themselves in place. The rain's a'coming, lads."

"I best get going, too." Monroe stood and scratched his stomach. "My barn is fixin' to blow down with the next stiff breeze, otherwise." He gave Galen a peck on the cheek. "Delicious as always," he said, then made his farewells and was out the door. Jimmy and Tony left as well, to unload their supplies from Monroe's cart.

Sylvia had her own work to do, but that didn't prevent her from taking a break to check on the men's progress. Until she discovered that their work required lengths of rope, and Tony balancing near the very edge of the roof, four stories up.

He gave her a jaunty wave from his lofty perch.

It was enough to lodge her heart in her throat. She waved back, safe on the lawn, standing near their scattered building materials, and quickly retreated to her conservatory. It wasn't so much that she couldn't bear to watch. She was more concerned that his peacock streak would emerge again, and he'd hurt himself while showing off.

Yes, that was it.

Tony heaved a sigh of relief as he watched Sylvia disappear from view. If he was going to slip and fall, which he'd nearly done several times already, he'd rather not have her witness him dangling from a rope forty feet above the ground. Or, heaven forfend the ancient rope should break. Falling prostrate at the widow's feet was not part of his seduction plan.

He pounded in another nail, securing another tile, ensuring another six square inches of roof wouldn't leak. And then another, and another. Gerald kept him supplied from the stack they'd hoisted up to the roof, and watched over their safety ropes tied around the chimney. Jimmy worked just ahead of Tony, wrenching the ruined tiles free and tossing them over the side. Though the roof might be new, the lawn would never be the same. But the lawn couldn't keep rain out of the house.

Less than a quarter done, and his back ached, his knees were on fire. Fiery red streaked his palm, forerunner to blisters. Why was he doing this, again?

Seduction plan. Right.

Sylvia was skittish. Instead of sailing straight ahead, he'd have to tack back and forth for a while. He'd devised the perfect plan to win her over. He would woo her with his labor. What woman could resist the gift of a weatherproofed house?

The men around her had been trying to take care of her, but youth or old age prevented them from being truly effective. Not to mention a serious shortage of funds. Tony had strength and something none of Sylvia's other men had—the experience of having run a healthy earldom for five years. He knew things about carpentry and crop rotation, plaster and poultry. He could give her something far better than flowers, more practical than writing an ode to her beauty. He had the means to improve her day-to-day life.

Plus, he was slightly better off in the funding department, though it had taken nearly all of his own blunt this morning to buy just what was needed for the most urgent of repairs. The purse Jimmy had given him last night had barely covered the cost of nails.

He had kept enough coins for a different kind of gift for Sylvia, though, an item he'd purchased this morning. He'd hold it in reserve until the opportune moment.

"Think we'll finish before the storm hits?"

Tony glanced at Jimmy, at the currently cloud-free horizon, and the vast expanse of naked roof. "I'm willing to try if you are."

Jimmy grinned, and cut another tile to size.

From up here, the view of the rolling countryside and sea was incredible. The steady breeze dried the perspiration before it could soak his shirt, and the air was fresh and clean. But as he stood and stretched, and got a dizzying look over the edge at the broken tiles on the ground below, he decided he'd much rather be knocking down wet plaster. Indoors.

He surveyed the progress he'd made so far, calculated

how long it had taken, how much was left to go, and realized at this rate they'd finish . . . in about four days.

The wind picked up. Tony muttered a curse, and bent back to work. He didn't look up until he heard a shout, hours later.

"Lady Montgomery says you should come down for dinner," Baxter said, letting down the bag he'd carried over his shoulder. Sawyer stood beside him, dusted with flour, as always.

"Don't have time." Tony set another tile in place.

"She said you'd say that." Sawyer handed Tony a small cloth-wrapped bundle of cheese, bread, and cold mutton, while Baxter handed over a wineskin from his bag.

"Out of our way, laddie." Baxter made shooing motions with his hands, and both men began setting tile. Judging by their appearance, they had already done their own day's work, and had still come to help Sylvia.

Tony stepped out of their way, closer to Jimmy. "What about you?" He took a bite of the cheese. Delicious.

"I, ah, went down a while ago and ate." Jimmy handed Tony two fabric bundles, and tied on his own set. "Sylvia's idea," he said with an embarrassed shrug. "She uses these when she's on her knees in the garden all day."

Something that had been tied around Sylvia's bare flesh? Tony held the cloths close to his chest as he retreated to the roof peak. The precious bundle turned out to be two lengths of muslin, each wrapped around a pad of straw and wool. Where were these six hours ago, before his knees had needles sticking in them? But they were Sylvia's, and she had sent them for him. That was all that mattered.

Tony sat against a chimney stack to rest his back, and stretched out his legs with a groan. The scent of food teased him, stronger than the sea breeze, and he smiled. Sylvia was feeding him. His seduction plan was working.

Perhaps he'd bring her up here when the work was done, with a blanket and a bottle of wine. Together they'd watch the sun dip below the horizon, stare at the waves lapping at the beaches, until the stars came out. He'd put his arm around her shoulders, she'd lean into him, he'd kiss her, and taste her, and then . . . His butt was going numb.

On second thought, the hard, cold slate roof was not the place he wanted to make love with Sylvia the first time. The blanket, wine, and sunset idea had merit—it just needed a more comfortable venue.

He quickly finished eating and returned to work.

Thanks to the added efforts of Baxter and Sawyer, by the time daylight disappeared, nearly half the roof was done. Perhaps they would beat the storm, after all. Or perhaps Trent's knee was wrong.

They climbed down and staggered into the house, drunk with exhaustion. Tony waved to Sylvia from the rose salon doorway, taking care to stay downwind of her, then stumbled to his room, stripped, washed up with the cold water in the basin, and fell into bed. He dreamed of holding Sylvia in his arms.

He awoke with her cat curled against his side.

Dawn barely streaked the sky. Tony stretched, tight muscles screaming in protest, grabbed another pair of ill-fitting breeches and shirt from the previous Lord Montgomery's wardrobe, and dressed in the gloom. He glanced at last night's dirty water in the basin, decided there was really no point in shaving, and headed up to the roof.

Sylvia climbed up every few hours, bringing a basket filled with food and drink. They sat on a blanket she spread beside the chimney stack, far from the edge, and he ate while she pointed out spots of interest on the Lulworth coastline, visible from their elevated position. Her accent was slightly different from that of Jimmy and the other locals, but he couldn't quite place it. Somewhere farther north. Inland.

". . . of course, Middle Beach is only accessible from the sea. Spencer has a skiff we can borrow, so we can put in at Durdle Door Beach, and row out to have our picnic there after the storm passes."

So caught up in listening to her lilting voice, Tony had missed some of the content. She wanted him to row out onto the Channel, in order for them to have a picnic on a beach? He gaped at her. A little boat? Out on the sea?

He remembered the last time he'd been out on the water—on Nick's big ship, which had even been tied up at the dock, and still Tony had found himself heaving his guts out over the side. Much of the images from that day and night were blurry, but he clearly recalled his white-knuckled grip on the railing as his dinner spewed into the Thames. His stomach churned.

"It's the only beach I haven't been to, in the four years I've lived here."

He winced at her wistful tone. "Montgomery never took you?"

"My husband didn't like to eat al fresco. Said he had enough of that sort when he was at sea, no need to do it on the land."

On Sylvia's far side, Jimmy snorted. "Hubert was always up himself."

"Jimmy!"

"Ain't like I never told him that to his face," Jimmy mumbled into the wineskin.

Tony hid a grin. Yes, indeed, older brothers could be full of themselves at times.

And he might not be Sylvia's husband in truth, but there were definitely things he could do that Montgomery never had. A secluded beach on a warm summer day, a blanket, a bottle of wine, and Sylvia . . . Might be worth the risk of going out on the water. The beach would definitely be a more comfortable venue than the roof. If he survived getting there.

By the time she brought a mid-afternoon snack, Tony couldn't hold something as small as a fork—the blister on his palm had burst, and his fist refused to close. It didn't hurt, though, or at least not that he could tell, what with his back, shoulders, and knees being on fire.

But they were nearing their goal of covering the roof. It was going to be close—storm clouds were crowding the horizon. Whitecaps littered the Channel, and the surf crashing on the beach was audible even over the wind whipping at their clothes.

Sweat dripped onto Tony's nose. Another drop fell, then another. He looked up.

Roiling black clouds were flying toward them, letting loose a curtain of rain so thick he could no longer see the Channel. Lightning flashed, followed by the booming crash of thunder.

"Close enough!" He had to repeat his shout before Jimmy heard him. Tony pointed at the storm almost upon them. Jimmy's jaw dropped. "Grab everything that isn't nailed down, or it will be in the next county by morning."

Chapter 10

⚬⚬⚬

They were soaked to the skin by the time they cleared their work materials from the roof, now slick with rain, and hurried down to gather the debris being flung about on the lawn. He wasn't going to let his efforts go to waste—what good was keeping the weather out from the roof, only to let it come in through broken windows?

Sylvia and Galen must have had the same thoughts, as they had the task nearly completed by the time the three men reached the lawn. Within minutes the property was as secure as they could make it. Everyone collected in the entry hall, breathing hard, dripping wet. Tony leaned against the closed door, listening to the wind and rain buffet the house. Jimmy shook his head like a dog, spraying water on them all.

"Jimmy!" Sylvia admonished.

"What?" He tried for an innocent expression, but a grin broke out.

Tony met her gaze, her dismay giving way to good humor. Her curls were in a riot from the wind, her cheeks flushed from wind and exertion. Her lips were set in a gentle smile, glistening and rosy. If he kissed her, would she taste of the sea breeze, fresh and clean with a hint of salt?

"Off with ye, then," Galen said, gesturing for them all to move. "You're all filthy and dripping on my floors. Get yourselves dry, and I'll scare up something to warm yer bones."

"Yes, ma'am." With a last grin shared with Sylvia, Tony and the others all trooped upstairs to their respective rooms to change.

He stripped off his sodden clothes and dropped them in the basket at the bottom of the wardrobe. Sylvia was in her room, just a connecting dressing room away, doing the same thing. She had been almost as wet as he. Did she now stand naked in her room, too? With no lady's maid, did she need assistance unbuttoning her gown? He almost knocked on the door to offer his assistance, then realized he should probably put some clothes on before offering to help Sylvia remove hers. Shriveled with cold did not reveal him at his best.

He toweled off and dressed as quickly as his shivering allowed, in his only clean clothes. He'd have to ask Galen about washing his other set. He debated between knocking on the adjoining door, or out in the hall. The sound of the hall door opening made the decision for him, and he darted out.

Damn. She was already dressed. In yet another drab gray gown.

"May I escort you down?" He held out his arm.

"Actually, I was going to check on the gold salon first."

"To see how my repairs are holding up?"

"To see if the rain is staying outside." She turned, without taking his arm.

He followed her down the hall and up the stairs, admiring the view the whole way. Not the wallpaper, which was dreadfully faded, but Sylvia's derriere. The gentle sway of her hips was mesmerizing in the half-light of the darkened hall, her gown swishing from side to side with each step, revealing the tempting hint of a curve. His hand itched to trace it, to explore the curve.

Come to think of it, his hand really did itch. Sting. Burn, even.

Damn blisters. He concentrated on watching Sylvia's backside. Much better.

The fire had been kept going in the salon to help dry things out, as he'd requested, though it had burned low and cast a soft glow across the room. Sylvia stepped over the debris, moving along the wall, toward the window.

Tony reluctantly stopped staring at her and examined the walls and ceiling around the window. So far, all the moisture appeared to be staying outside.

"Your workmanship appears to be holding up, sir."

Sylvia glanced at him before taking a seat on the scaffolding before the window, which faced the oncoming storm. Windblown rain slapped at the glass, smearing the view entirely before dripping down, leaving a distorted view of the storm before the next gust blew more water onto the panes.

He sat beside her, close enough to feel her warmth, to hear her breathing, to inhale her delicate lavender scent. "We'll see how it is by morning, if this onslaught keeps up." He couldn't resist resting his right hand on her shoulder. Tried to give it a reassuring squeeze, but pain shot through his hand.

Lightning flashed and thunder shook the house, rumbling almost directly overhead. Sylvia jumped. Tony wrapped his arm around her. She stiffened, but then relaxed her posture after a moment, and didn't shrug off his contact.

"I used to love thunderstorms, as long as I was someplace safe and dry."

Tony was more than happy to keep her safe in his embrace. He tightened his arm around her. "Used to?"

"Before I understood how powerful they are, how destructive they can be. At home in Manchester, storms were just a spectacle, something exhilarating to watch. But here on the coast, they can destroy people's homes. I've seen it happen all too often lately."

"But you're safe here. And dry."

Sylvia murmured agreement, a sound that sent sparks shooting through him. She nestled closer, tucking herself in the hollow of his shoulder. Tony hardly dared breathe.

They remained in place for several minutes, Sylvia mesmerized by the storm, a look of awe and wonder on her face, Tony not wanting to do anything that would make her move away from his embrace.

Perhaps her men would all stay away tonight, safe and snug in their own homes while the storm howled outside. No guard dogs sleeping outside Sylvia's door, no one to prevent him from crossing into her bedchamber. His heart beat a little faster.

After the hard day everyone had had, surely they'd all seek their beds soon? He wound one of her curls around his left forefinger. Later tonight, he could put that same look of awe and wonder in her eyes, regardless of the storm outside.

A sudden harsh gust rattled the window, and startled Sylvia. She wrapped her arms around him. He steadied her with his blister-free hand, and gave her a reassuring smile. Her answering smile froze before it fully formed. Good thing he wasn't playing cards— his expression must be conveying his intent. She looked torn between acquiescence and reluctance.

Given half a chance, a little more time alone with her, he could erase any indecision, any hesitancy, to the point she would be the one to initiate their intimacy. He doubted anyone had made her feel desirable since before her husband's death. Perhaps even longer.

He could fix that, too, even better than he had the roof.

The dinner bell rang, startling them both.

Sylvia slowly sat up. "We, ah, should go. Downstairs, that is." She ran her fingers through her hair, the curls flattened where she'd leaned against him.

Tony ran a curl between his fingers. "Wouldn't want Galen to come searching for us. She wields that big wooden spoon like a weapon."

Sylvia smiled at his jest, her equilibrium restored, at least for the moment. She took his arm, and they went down to dinner.

Galen had prepared a thick hot stew, and warm bread with butter. Tony discovered he was famished and ate two helpings, still not keeping up with Jimmy's three. He was also hampered by his stiff right hand, which forced him to eat left-handed. He passed up Sylvia's offer of the nightly glass of brandy—he wanted nothing to fog his mind later on. He wanted to be able to remember every detail with crystal clarity.

The three of them moved to the rose salon while Galen and Gerald cleaned up. Tony had claimed Sylvia's arm as escort, and she tugged him down beside her on the sofa nearest the fireplace.

"Jimmy, please fetch my bag."

Tony would have moved to a more decorous distance. Having Sylvia know about his plans was quite sufficient—no need to let anyone else in on it. But she held him in place.

Jimmy simply shrugged and left without comment.

"I thought ladies always kept their needlework or whatever in a basket by their chair, not in a bag."

"I do." She pointed to a wicker basket next to the armchair, overflowing with stockings and other items waiting to be mended.

"Then . . . ?"

"Give me your hand, please."

He held his hand out.

"No, I want the hand that's too sore to hold a spoon."

Oh. He thought she wouldn't have noticed. He did give her his hand, by first wrapping his arm around her shoulder and dangling his hand inches from her delicate chin. It was risky—they were alone for the moment, but wouldn't be for long. But it was worth it. Sylvia fit perfectly against him, just as before. Strong, but soft in all the right places.

"Very amusing, sir." Sylvia grabbed his wrist and pulled his arm over her head, and held it, palm up. The hand seemed permanently curved, as though still holding the hammer or tile cutter.

He inhaled a hiss as she spread his fingers open.

"Hurt?"

"Not so you'd notice." He gave her his best cocky grin, the effect of which was ruined when she flattened his fingers and he gasped.

Jimmy returned, and dropped a small, ancient portmanteau at Sylvia's side. He leaned over them, staring at Tony's red palm and oozing blisters. "She's going to make you cry."

"Oh, I doubt that."

Sylvia didn't comment, but pulled several jars and cloths from her bag, while still holding Tony's wrist. Jimmy settled in the armchair by the fire, and watched the proceedings through heavy-lidded eyes. The storm continued to howl and rumble outside, occasionally rattling the windows.

Sylvia paid no heed, absorbed in her work, and Tony was absorbed in watching her. From a small flask, she pulled the cork out with her teeth. Before an erotic image regarding her mouth could fully form, she poured the alcohol on his palm.

"Holy sh—!" Tony squeezed his eyes against the sudden searing pain.

"Told you." Jimmy slouched farther in his chair, long legs stretched out in front of him.

Much to Tony's embarrassment, there was indeed moisture at the corners of his eyes. He glanced at Sylvia, but her brow was furrowed as she worked, paying no attention to him whatsoever, other than keeping his fingers open, palm flat.

He hurriedly wiped his eyes with his cuff. "Why don't you have blisters? You worked just as hard and almost as long as I did."

Jimmy wiggled his fingers. "Ripping off old tiles doesn't require the same finesse as setting new ones in place. I switched back and forth, used both hands."

Tony would have harrumphed, but Sylvia tugged his hand closer, her fingers wrapped around his wrist. His arm brushed her waist with her every breath, and nearly touched the underside of her breast. He could prevent the improper contact if he edged forward on the sofa, and straightened his arm. He didn't. He could increase the contact if he scooted back, or raised his shoulder. With Jimmy only a few feet away, he didn't do that, either.

Once Sylvia was satisfied his palm was clean, she slathered it with a thick, sweet-smelling ointment, and wrapped a bandage around his hand. Quiet snores came from Jimmy by the time she finished.

"That should help speed the healing process." She rested his hand on his thigh. "Try to keep it clean and dry, and use it, but gently, or it will stiffen up."

While Sylvia put her things away, Tony inspected the neat bandage and flexed his hand. Too late—it was already painfully stiff. Though it had been stiff and sore since yesterday, so he probably couldn't blame that on Sylvia's handiwork. "Two nights ago, you treated the cut on the back of my head. Tonight, my hand. Is this a habit we've formed, my lady? Every other night you minister to my wounds?"

"Perhaps you should try to not get wounded." Her green eyes sparkled with humor.

Galen entered with a tea tray, and poured each of them a cup.

"New leaves this time?" he asked.

"They was new just this morning." She winked and headed for the door.

"You're not staying?" Sylvia picked up her cup.

"Beg pardon, my lady, but Gerald is nearly passed out back in the kitchen. I'm going to put him to bed, and join him."

"Good night, then."

One chaperone gone, though they still had Jimmy, snoring in his chair.

The storm pounded against the house. Fire crackled in the grate. All but two candles were snuffed out. Perfect night for a seduction.

He sipped his tea, to moisten his suddenly dry

throat. After he set the cup down, he leaned back, his arm casually draped along the back edge of the sofa, mere inches from Sylvia's bare skin above the top of her gown. Should he stroke his thumb down her soft, smooth neck first? Or kiss her hand, work his way up her arm and shoulder, her strong jaw, delicate cheek, and finally to her delectable mouth? Whisper his desire in her ear?

She leaned back, within reach of his hand. Slowly, he brought his arm around her.

"You must be exhausted," she said softly. "You were up there working before dawn." She stroked the back of his hand where it draped over her shoulder.

Tony watched her touch him, enjoying the feel of her hand on him almost as much as what it represented. Other than for medicinal purposes, this was the first time she'd taken the initiative in touching him. Excellent progress.

"I still have some energy left." He'd be more than happy to expend said energy with her. All night long.

He felt her breathing quicken, saw her bosom rise and fall.

Could she hear his heart pounding? He wrapped his other arm around her, too, his thumb caressing the small expanse of smooth, bare skin above the neckline of her gown. Her soft lavender scent wafted up to him. He wanted to comb his fingers through her curls, caress her cheek. He wanted to kiss her. Everywhere.

Jimmy snored.

He wanted to move this upstairs.

"You've had a rather long day as well, I imagine."

Rubbing his hand down her back wasn't quite as satisfying as it could have been, what with the bandage blocking much of his sensation. He ran the backs of his fingers down her soft-as-down cheek, intending to tilt her face up for his kiss, whisper his invitation to go upstairs.

He jerked his head at a sudden noise. The storm still wailed outside, but not as strongly, as it blew itself out heading inland.

The noise came again. Blast. Someone was pounding on the front door.

Sylvia sat up and edged away from him, taking a moment longer to recognize the source of the noise. Jimmy snorted and shifted, but didn't waken.

"You have visitors." Tony couldn't believe his luck. Whoever was out there better have a damn good reason for interrupting.

The door knocker sounded, three loud raps, and Sylvia hurried to answer, Tony at her heels with a candle.

"So sorry to intrude, my lady," Hayden said, shivering on the doorstep. At least a dozen adults and children were huddled behind him in the rain. "Lightning struck the old oak on High Street, and it smashed two cottages. Wind ripped the roofs clean off three others. The Happy Jack and the church are already packed to the rafters. We've nowhere else to go."

Chapter 11

Sylvia stepped back, gesturing. "Come in, all of you. We'll find room."

Tony lit the wall sconces as people streamed into the hall, filling the space with bodies and the scent of mud and rain blowing in after them.

Hayden's wife, Mildred, entered, her arm around their fifteen-year-old daughter, Betsy. "So sorry I haven't been able to come help with the cleaning yet this week, my lady." Betsy sniffed back tears.

Sylvia patted the girl's shoulder. "Don't worry about it. You can help later."

Betsy started to move forward, but grabbed her mother's shawl. "Look, mum, there he is!" she said in a hoarse whisper. "You didn't tell me he was handsome. How could you threaten to cut off his ballocks?"

173

Blushing furiously, Mrs. Hayden bent to whisper in her daughter's ear, pushing her forward, as Sylvia choked back a laugh. Busy with the sconces, Tony either didn't hear or pretended not to. A moment later, though, she caught his glance. He betrayed no emotion, just raised one eyebrow a bit, his chin lowered, as he stared at her for several heartbeats.

Mr. Hayden herded his twin boys in just then, who ran along the hall, shouting for "Lord Monty."

Jimmy had finally awakened and come to investigate the noise. Grabbing one boy under each arm, he swung them up until they squealed. "Hullo, what's this?"

Hayden explained as Sylvia ushered in Mrs. Doyle, arms full of squalling baby, with three more children clinging to her skirts. Doyle was helping Mrs. Pitsnoggle negotiate the steps. The widow had stayed with them since her own cottage had been damaged in a storm last winter. Behind them was Baxter, helping his aunt, Mrs. Miggins, shake out and fold her pink parasol.

"Lord have mercy!"

Sylvia shut the door in time to hear Galen's exclamation. The housekeeper stood by the stairs in her wrapper, Gerald behind her, white tufts of hair sticking out from beneath his nightcap.

Yes, indeed. However were they to deal with all this? Children were crying, Jimmy had the Hayden twins shrieking with laughter, and the colicky baby paused her screaming only long enough to inhale another breath. The adults were talking among themselves, discussing the storm, the damage, and whatever were they to do now?

Well, they couldn't stay in the hall all night. Sylvia clapped her hands. "May I have your attention, please?" No one seemed to hear. She drew breath to shout again, when Tony pierced the air with a two-fingered whistle.

"Lady Montgomery has something to say," he said into the sudden silence.

All eyes turned to her. She gave him a nod of thanks. "Betsy, you know where the towels and blankets are—let's get everyone dried off. Galen, please find something to warm everyone from the inside. Gerald, the fire in the rose salon has burned down. Everyone, that's the warmest room at the moment." She gestured for them to go into the salon.

Mrs. Hayden went to help Galen in the kitchen, Betsy darted up the stairs, and everyone else headed into the salon. Sylvia helped Mrs. Pitsnoggle hang up her wet cloak and escorted her to a sofa near the fire. The same sofa where Sylvia had been snuggled up within Tony's arms, just minutes ago. Warmth spread from her chest down to her toes. In the circle of his embrace, she'd felt safe and secure, and wanted. Tony made her feel wanted, desired, in a way Hubert never had.

But it was only for the moment. Soon he'd be moving on, to another town, another woman.

Bemoaning that fact would accomplish nothing.

She wouldn't waste her energy on things she had no control over. Once Mrs. Pitsnoggle was settled, Sylvia checked to see what else needed to be done, and smiled at the sight of Mrs. Doyle comforting her two toddlers. She glanced around, looking for the baby who had finally—thank heavens—stopped crying.

Tony was pacing before the doorway, the baby balanced on his hip. She was trying to poke her tiny fingers into his mouth while he talked to her. He returned the favor, tapping her bottom lip with his index finger, and they settled a truce with her fists clutching his fingers.

Sylvia's heart constricted. She found herself blinking back a tear, and quickly wiped it away so she wouldn't miss a gesture, a single change of expression. She could have watched all night, until Mrs. Pitsnoggle intruded on her thoughts. "Damn fine man you snagged yourself."

She cleared her throat. "He's only here temporarily, to help us out."

Mrs. Pitsnoggle snorted.

Betsy took the infant from Tony, and he began talking with Baxter, Hayden, and Doyle.

Soon, the hall was filled with dripping garments hung up to dry, everyone had something hot to eat or drink, and children began nodding off on their parents' laps. Sylvia's eyes were gritty with fatigue. Time to get everyone settled for what was left of the night.

Most of the extra beds were gone, sold off long ago, and the bedchambers were uninhabitable, anyway. Last winter, Monroe's family had simply slept on pallets in here until their roof was fixed. But the salon wasn't big enough to hold all the refugees from this storm.

Betsy could stay with her, and the Hayden twins would be overjoyed to sleep on the valet's unused cot in Jimmy's room. But everyone else?

Her gaze swept the room. Tony stood just inside the door again, talking with Doyle, this time . . . oh, dear heaven, this time with his packed haversack slung over one shoulder.

Sylvia staggered back a step, her heart pounding. No, he couldn't. Not yet.

Doyle slapped Tony on the back and went to whisper in his wife's ear.

Sylvia walked over to Tony on leaden feet. "Aren't—" She cleared her throat, tried again. "Aren't you at least going to wait until the storm lets up? I mean, I know all this isn't what you bargained for, but—"

Tony cupped her cheek with his uninjured hand. "Sweetheart, I'm not going anywhere. I promised I'd stay and help you deal with Ruford. Sinclair men always keep their word."

Too choked up to speak, she pointed to his haversack.

He tossed it to the floor, over by the door. "That's an awfully big bed in the master's chamber. Doyle has a big family. I thought it made sense for me to bunk down here, and let them sleep up there."

She started breathing again.

He leaned forward and dropped a kiss on her cheek. "Still my second choice for sleeping arrangements, however," he whispered. "We have unfinished business, you and I." He stepped aside, guiding Sylvia to do the same, as the Doyles walked past, carrying their sleeping children.

"Thank you, Mr. Sinclair," Mrs. Doyle said.

"My pleasure, madam."

Mrs. Miggins came back into the room with an armful of blankets. Tony jumped as she passed close by. "Marge!" he said sternly. "I thought we had an agreement."

"*You* had an agreement, laddie. *I* got me a handful." She snickered and made pinching motions with her thumb and forefinger. She dropped her burden, and she and Mrs. Pitsnoggle made their beds for the night, each taking a sofa.

Sylvia tried not to laugh. She was so tired and her emotions so raw at this point, she feared if she started, she might not be able to stop. She could offer to rub Tony's abused flesh, but the rogue would probably say yes.

Hayden and his wife had bedded down on a pallet near the fire. Jimmy took the twins upstairs, and Betsy leaned against the doorjamb, yawning. Baxter had pulled chairs together, propped his stocking feet up, and was already fast asleep.

As Sylvia turned to go, Tony dropped another kiss on her cheek. "Sweet dreams, sweetheart." He pulled the cushions from several chairs, lined them up on the floor, and lay down with a sigh.

Sylvia blew out the last candle, caught Betsy by the elbow, and tugged her up the stairs. At least now she wouldn't have to worry about resisting Tony's advances. With this many chaperones, he wouldn't be able to do much. Her equilibrium was safe.

By the time Galen shook Sylvia awake the next morning, the men had all left, including Jimmy and Tony, to inspect the storm damage and begin repairs. The kitchen was chaotic, as Mrs. Doyle and Mrs. Hayden disagreed on the food to be prepared. Galen had abandoned them in favor of tackling the mud and dirt tracked in last night, and overseeing Betsy with the overwhelming laundry. Mrs. Pitsnoggle and Mrs. Miggins were left to deal with the children, who were running rampant through the halls. At least the tonic had finally worked, and baby Claire had ceased her constant crying.

Sylvia went down to the barns to check on Farleigh and the other dairy workers. Everyone, including the cows, had been safe inside during the storm. Only minor damage had been sustained, which included a new leak in the roof. At least it dripped over an empty stall, and not into the feed or workroom. She might tackle that repair herself, before the leak got worse.

She spent the rest of the day in her stillroom, treating a near-constant flow of villagers with assorted injuries from the storm and its debris. Each told a different tale about the storm's destruction, describing the damage to their homes and gardens.

If they'd just had a chance to finish repairs from the previous storm, it wouldn't have been so bad. How many more families would give up, abandon the village, this time?

It was well past dark before the men dragged themselves to the doorstep, exhausted and filthy. Galen ordered them to wash up outside before she'd allow them indoors. Grumbling, they stripped to the waist and washed at the pump.

Sylvia lingered near the window, watching Tony sluice water over his naked torso, his sleek muscles glistening in the lamplight. He wasn't as tall as Baxter, nor as brawny as Doyle, but his compact frame was perfectly proportioned, with a flat abdomen and deeply muscled chest that she longed to explore with her hands. She wanted to offer him a soapy washcloth, but only if she could run it over his skin herself. And with no one else around.

She winced. What had happened to her vow not to succumb?

Perhaps she could look—she just wouldn't touch.

After everyone had a hot meal, Sylvia debated joining Mrs. Pitsnoggle and Mrs. Miggins in the salon, but they'd brought their mending out. Hayden and Doyle, each with their wife, lingered at the table across from Baxter, Jimmy, and Tony, discussing how best to repair the storm's damage. She paid no heed to their conversation, was instead watching Tony, until she heard his name repeatedly brought up. He quietly acknowledged their thanks for his help, but didn't preen, as she expected.

As they discussed implementing his ideas, she realized how much of an impact he was making on the village, how he was weaving himself into the fabric of their lives.

She wouldn't be the only one to come unraveled when he left.

The next morning, Mrs. Doyle and Mrs. Hayden headed out with the men, to salvage belongings and food supplies from their homes. Good thing, since the week's stores at the manor house were sadly depleted by the unexpected guests. Sylvia wondered if Tony had grumbled about having no sugar for his tea, or if it didn't really matter, since today it was hardly more than hot water anyway.

She spent the day with Galen and the older children, clearing the storm debris on the estate grounds, stacking the broken branches for firewood. Thankfully, all of the new roof tiles appeared to have survived the storm.

When the men dragged in after dark, Sylvia brought out her bag in the dining room, and treated Baxter for a gash from broken glass, and Hayden for several cuts and scratches.

Jimmy sat down next, and pointed out a splinter in his thumb. "Next year we're going to plant mangel-wurzels in the north field instead of wheat," he announced.

Sylvia moved the candle closer, to better see the sliver. "Oh?"

"Tony says we'll get better yields if we rotate which crop is planted in which field every year."

"Tony says." She adjusted her grip on the tweezers, and tried again. "How does he come by this knowledge? I didn't know he was an estate manager."

"While his brother was off fighting Napoleon, Tony

was in charge for five years. Of course, he had stewards and managers working for him, but he was responsible for overseeing the estates."

Estates, plural?

"Ow!"

"Got it." Sylvia held the tweezers over the candle flame until the splinter sizzled out of existence.

Jimmy declined her offer of liniment, preferring to dab it on himself, and left to challenge Hayden to a game of checkers before they turned in.

Tony sat down, his hand on the table before her, palm up. "Afraid your bandage is a little worse for wear."

She cut off the bandage and inspected the damage. His blisters were still red, but no sign of infection yet. And still sore, judging by his hiss as she cleaned his palm. "Jimmy says you ran your brother's estates."

"For a while. I seem to have a habit of stepping in temporarily."

He flashed a smile, but all she could hear was the word "temporary." As if she needed reminding. More reason to keep her vow.

She smoothed the ointment on, trying to be efficient and impersonal, but her gaze kept straying to the exposed V of flesh visible below the hollow of his throat. He'd changed into another of Hubert's clean but too-large breeches and shirts, open at the neck. After seeing Tony shirtless at the pump, she knew about the planes and muscular curves hidden beneath his clothing. Her fingers itched to map them.

As she applied a fresh bandage, she couldn't help

admiring his long, strong fingers. Couldn't help remembering how they had felt as he trailed them down her cheek, along her neckline, massaged her neck.

The band of gold on his left hand glinted in the candlelight. She touched the gold ring, reminding herself it was all part of the subterfuge, nothing more. Tony turned his hand over and curled his fingers around hers.

Startled, she met his gaze. She hadn't thought about how he'd construe her action. They were alone in the dining room, alone for the first time in two days. She'd have to save her from herself, since there was no one around to do it for her.

She bent his fingers flat, pretending an examination had been her intent all along. She traced the softer skin in the middle of his palm, felt the calluses surrounding it. It was red, with hot spots where he'd soon have more blisters. New cuts and scratches adorned both hands. "If you keep abusing your hands like this—sawing, hammering, and whatnot all day— however do you expect them to heal?"

"Plenty of time for whatnot after our chaperones go back to their own homes."

She stared down at the table, until she felt the sudden bloom of heat leave her cheeks. She should come right out and tell him she didn't want to be one of his many conquests. Then he'd stop teasing her, flirting with her. "I think you should know—"

"Yes?"

Words died in her throat as she spotted dried blood at the corner of his left eye. Without the candle pulled close, she would have missed it, as half of it was hidden under the hair fallen over his brow. "How did this happen?"

He reached questing fingers to the area she indicated. "Ah. Just a scratch. Nasty, uncooperative branch. You extracted a fragment of it from Jimmy's thumb, I believe."

"Lean forward, and let me clean it properly."

"Yes, ma'am." He gave a slow smile, the one that melted her insides. With his elbows on the table, he propped his chin in his left palm and closed his eyes, his expression one of complete trust and innocence.

Beneath the table, his thigh brushed hers. The contact could have been coincidental, but Tony shifted in his chair until more of his leg touched hers, and the pressure increased. She refused to acknowledge it. But she didn't move away, either.

She dabbed alcohol on a cloth. She paused, staring at his sensuous lips curved in a small smile, his sculpted cheekbones highlighted by the flickering light, long thick lashes against his cheeks. He was saved from perfection by the slight crook in his nose. She traced it with her finger.

His eyes opened.

"How did that happen? It looks like your nose was broken."

"An upperclassman at school accused me of being pretty."

"And he broke your nose?"

"Only because I broke his first."

She couldn't resist a glance at his hands, pictured

them curled into fists. She shook her head, and reached to brush his hair out of the way. The dark brown strands slid through her fingers like silk, thick and healthy, with a tendency to curl where it was still wet. Hubert's hair had been thin on top when she'd met him, and continued to fall out. He'd hated it if she tried to touch what was left during their twice-monthly lovemaking.

Tony's eyes narrowed. "Is it bad?"

Oh, very bad, indeed. "I don't want to get this in your eyes. Close them."

He did. She would *not* wince at how close he had come to damaging his gorgeous brown eyes. "It might heal faster if I put sticking plaster on it."

"No need. Save that for something more serious."

She nodded. "It runs so close to your eyebrow, there shouldn't be much of a scar. Though if there is one, it might give you a rather rakish look."

That made him grin.

Her ministrations complete, they stood up at the same time, but neither moved away. With their proximity, Sylvia realized that Tony was just a few inches taller than she. If she stretched up on her toes, she could kiss him on his mouth, even if he didn't bend down. Hubert had been tall enough that he had to co-operate in order for her to kiss him. He didn't, and she soon stopped trying.

Tony was only three years older than her twenty-two summers, probably far too young to think of getting married. Besides, most aristocrats waited until they were thirty or so, and worried about heirs, before they gave a thought to marriage. Tony had no succession to secure. He could go on for years, flitting from one female companion to another, with no thought to the consequences or the future.

Marriage to Hubert had not been the relationship she'd hoped it would be, but she still wanted to try again. She enjoyed the sense of belonging that the people of Lulworth gave her, but yearned for something more—the companionship of marriage, the intimacy of belonging to one man, and him to her.

She did not want another seafaring man who would be gone for weeks or months at a time. Neither did she want a man who went from one female's bed to another's, or who kept a mistress. She was selfish enough to want him all to herself.

She wanted someone who would be there to sit before the fire each night and play chess before bed, or watch the storms with her, his arm protectively about her shoulders, sheltering her in the comfort of his embrace.

"Something troubling you, Sylvia?" Tony tipped her chin up with one finger.

She blinked. "How much longer, do you think, before the Doyles can move back to their home?"

Tony ran his fingers through his hair. "Tomorrow night, perhaps, or the next day for certain. Our goal is to get them home before Ruford returns, and we have to work through the night."

Only two more nights until the next shipment was due. How could she have nearly forgotten something so important?

Tony continued. "They've already discussed it amongst themselves, and decided the Doyles can squeeze in Mrs. Miggins, as well as Mrs. Pitsnoggle, until Baxter has a chance to rebuild later."

"But what about Baxter?"

Tony grinned. "He intends to sleep on the cot in the dressing room between us."

Chapter 12

The next two days passed in an exhausting blur, with everyone working frantically to get homes repaired and habitable. The men were gone by dawn and didn't return to the manor until well past dusk.

To her relief—or disappointment, she wasn't certain which—Sylvia hardly had a moment alone with Tony, what with Baxter on the cot in the dressing room between them at night, and houseguests and their children surrounding them during the evening. Mrs. Miggins made an excuse to walk past Tony often enough that he must have a black and blue spot. When he threatened to retaliate in kind, she beamed and increased her efforts to pinch him.

After lunch the second day, Sylvia decided she had

better tackle the leak in the barn roof before the rains came again.

Farleigh maneuvered the ladder into place for her. "Are you sure you be wanting to do this, my lady?"

"The other men have more important things to do, but we can't let that leak get any worse. And don't offer to go up yourself—we both know what might happen with your wooden leg on the ladder." She checked that the tools and supplies were in the carpenter's apron around her waist, gathered up her skirts, and climbed up to the roof.

The view was not as good from up here as it was on the roof of the manor house, but the distance to the ground was not dizzying, either. She located the damaged area, got down on her hands and knees, and set to work.

Within a few moments, she found a new reason to marvel at Tony's skill. How had he made this look so easy? The nails bent over, refusing to go in straight for her, and she narrowly avoided smashing her fingers with the hammer.

"Trying to put me out of work?"

Startled on the upswing, she almost let the hammer fly out of her hand. She sat back on her heels and stared at Tony, who was making his way across the roof toward her. "I thought you were working down in the village."

He dropped down beside her, and folded his legs. "We stopped for lunch. Would you believe there was a waiting line for the privy?"

She smiled. "No."

He tucked a curl behind her ear. "Then would you believe I lament not having a moment alone with you since your house was invaded by refugees?"

Her stomach fluttered, but she firmly tamped it down. She would not give in to his seductive smile, those smoldering eyes. Tony was just like the summer storm, sweeping through and stirring everything up, and would be gone just as quickly, leaving destruction and heartbreak in his wake. But not *her* heart. She cleared her throat.

"Farleigh is quite agitated, having you up here. What repairs couldn't wait?"

Sylvia pointed them out. "I didn't want to let the problem get out of hand."

Tony solemnly nodded. "Very wise. As long as I'm up here, how about we make a trade?" He tugged the hammer from her hand, and replaced it with a small parcel he pulled from his pocket.

She fingered the string tied around the brown wrapping paper. She couldn't remember the last time she'd received a gift. "What's this for?"

"Just . . . something I thought you should have." He hammered the patch in place, driving in the nails—straight—with powerful blows.

Sylvia tore her eyes away from him and ripped open the paper. Inside was a spool of green ribbon.

Tony lifted the spool up to her cheek. "I was right," he said softly. "The green matches your eyes perfectly."

Her heart beat erratically.

"Since your year of mourning is up, you'll be wanting to add a little color back to your wardrobe. You should have emeralds, but I thought you might prefer something more practical."

She nodded. "There are few occasions to wear emeralds in Lulworth, but ribbon is always useful." They shared a wry grin. "Thank you."

"You're welcome." He continued to gaze at her, his smoldering brown eyes melting her insides like chocolate.

His expression, his intent, was certainly that of a rake. But this ribbon was not the gift of a rake. It was pretty yet practical. Thoughtful, but unlikely to draw attention or arouse any speculation. It did not flaunt his wealth, and was inexpensive enough she could keep it without feeling obligated to return it.

He did not gamble or drink excessively. To her knowledge, he had not bedded any women during his stay. Not even Mrs. Hamlin, a voluptuous widow of hearty sexual appetites still considered a beauty in her early thirties. According to Galen, who heard it from Mrs. Spencer, Mrs. Hamlin had caught Tony alone while he was working on Doyle's house and offered herself up to him, but he'd sent her on her way with a pat on her shoulder. And would a rake really tile a roof in order to impress his intended conquest?

Perhaps she had misjudged Tony, misconstrued his intent.

"Everything all right up there?" Farleigh had stepped far enough away from the barn to see up onto the roof, and stood looking up at them, his hand shielding his eyes from the sun.

Tony muttered a curse, and gathered up the few

supplies Sylvia had brought out. She tucked the spool of ribbon in her apron pocket. "Just about done," she called.

Tony offered her a hand up, and moments later they stood on solid ground. Farleigh asked about the new patch, and Tony called farewell as he headed back to the village. Sylvia watched him walk away, her stomach in the vicinity of her boots. She fingered the ribbon in her pocket. At least she'd have something tangible to remember him by after he left.

That night, Sylvia stood next to Trent on the chalk cliffs overlooking the cove, watching for the signal light below. He may have lost the ability to make out newsprint, but he could identify the prey in a falcon's claws when she barely saw the falcon in the sky. Tony was pacing behind them, wearing a long cape that swirled about his ankles with each turn. He stopped beside Sylvia.

"I don't like it," he growled.

"I know." She didn't like it, either, but what could they do? There was no way to contact Ruford and put off tonight's meeting.

"Crowther and McCutcheon looked entirely too pleased with themselves this afternoon."

"I know."

"And Teague . . . shouldn't he still have been at the Stone's Throw? His inn should have sustained enough damage from the storm to keep him there a while longer, instead of sniffing around at the Happy Jack."

"I know." Sylvia restrained the urge to sigh. Since returning home at dusk, Tony and Jimmy had talked of nothing else but the scene at the inn this afternoon.

The most urgent repairs completed and the last of their houseguests restored to their own homes, or at least to their temporary homes, Doyle, Hayden, Baxter, Jimmy and Tony had gone to the inn for a celebratory mug of ale. And walked in on Ruford's first mate accepting a purse from Teague.

Conversation at dinner had centered on speculation of what Teague was paying Crowther for, and whether it would affect their business dealings with Ruford. Sylvia had a sinking feeling it did.

"And then there's—" Tony stopped, his head tilted to one side.

"What?"

Trent shifted uneasily. Sylvia glanced from him back to Tony. Now she heard it, too. Hoofbeats. A horse walking near the cliffs this late at night could only mean one thing.

"Is there a—"

"Hiding place?" Trent pointed over the edge. "About ten feet down, a hollow in the chalk big enough to hide two, should anyone peer over the edge. Beyond that, not much until you reach the bottom."

"You take it." Tony grabbed Sylvia's hand and the lantern, and headed higher, toward the peak of the cliff, swiftly striding through the coarse grass.

"What's your plan?" Sylvia whispered. His hand squeezed hers, not letting go.

Tony stopped as the ground started to fall away on the other side of the chalk down. "Lovely view, isn't it?" The quarter moon was barely bright enough to allow them to see the Channel as an expanse darker than the land. "You wouldn't happen to have a blanket with you, I suppose?"

She made a show of patting her skirt. "Must have left it in my other gown."

He took off his cape and spread it on the ground, sat, and tugged her down beside him.

"What are we doing?" Under other circumstances she might enjoy sitting with Tony at her side and gazing at the stars, but the hoofbeats were getting louder, closer.

"We're hiding in the open."

She arranged her skirts, aware Tony had edged closer to her, his muscular thigh resting along the length of hers. He pulled a white cravat out from his dark shirt and tied it on as though dressing for dinner. The stark white linen must be visible for miles.

"Whatever are you doing?"

"Is it straight?" He fidgeted with the knot.

"Almost." She adjusted the folds, her fingers brushing his chin, and noted that he needed to shave.

"Probably better if it's a tad crooked, anyway." Before she could object, he'd untied the new green ribbons of her bonnet and set it on the grass, and his fingers were suddenly at the top button of her pelisse.

Since the evening was mild, she had almost left it at home. But for meeting with Ruford, she wanted all the barriers possible between herself and the captain's lecherous gaze.

Tony's finger stroked her exposed skin above her collar. "Trust me?"

To stay? No. But here on the cliff, in the dark? She nodded, her heart in her throat.

He unbuttoned her pelisse and slipped it off one shoulder. She started to shrug out of it completely, but he shook his head, his hand on her shoulder to stop her. Her heart was beating so loudly, she could barely hear the approaching hoofbeats. Her breath hitched as she suddenly felt cool air on her shoulder, and Tony slipped her gown even farther down her arm, his touch feather light on her bare skin.

"That should do it," he murmured. His bandaged hand held her at her waist, while his other threaded through her curls, holding the back of her head.

He leaned in, close enough for her to inhale his scent, feel his warmth, closer still until she felt the prickly stubble on his chin brush hers, felt the softness of his lips in a glancing kiss to her cheek, then nuzzling her neck.

She wrapped her arms around him, lest she lose her balance and fall. Feeling the coiled strength in his back and shoulders, the warmth of his embrace, she suddenly wanted more. Why was he kissing her neck, when she wanted his lips on hers? She buried her fingers in his thick hair, intent on guiding him into proper position. The tip of his tongue flicked the underside of her ear. She trembled.

"You like?" he murmured against her neck, one hand roaming her rib cage, fingers massaging her scalp.

Almost panting now from his continued ministrations, speech beyond her capability at the moment, she nodded. He held her so close, the movement made his stubble rasp against her neck. Combined with the light touch of his roaming fingers and the slight huff of breath in her ear, she couldn't help herself. A giggle escaped.

"You're ticklish," he whispered, his lips brushing her ear.

"Am not."

His fingers dancing on her ribs, he gently blew in her ear.

Another giggle escaped, and suddenly she was on her back, Tony all around her, tickling her ribs, kissing and nipping her neck, making her laugh. She tried to tickle him, but he grabbed for her hands, and the wrestling match was on. Their arms and legs tangled, hands seeking, fingers touching, shielded from the rough grass by the cape's silk lining.

His hand brushed her breast. He suddenly went still.

All trace of laughter gone, Sylvia stayed motionless, not wanting to dislodge his hand. His touch seemed to burn through her dress and chemise, scorching her skin. How much better would it feel if there was no barrier at all?

He cupped her gently, his thumb caressing. "Sylvia," he groaned. He slid his hand up to her bare throat and slowly back down again, until his fingertips dipped below the neckline of her gown. Yes, yes, so close, just a little more, a little farther . . .

"Hullo, what have we here?"

Tony abruptly sat up, pulling Sylvia with him. The

hoofbeats had stopped because the rider had arrived. She hid her face against his shoulder, mortified. "Devil take the hindmost," Tony muttered, pulling her sleeve back up on her shoulder. He wrapped his arms around her back, holding her close, shielding her from prying eyes. "Can't a man find a moment alone with his wife *anywhere*?"

The horseback rider raised his lantern. "Sinclair, isn't it? And Lady Montgomery?"

"Mrs. Sinclair," Tony corrected.

"Good evening, Mr. Tipton." Unable to look the Revenue agent in the eye, Sylvia kept her face hidden against Tony's shoulder, her head tucked under his chin. Her cheeks must be glowing red in the darkness.

"Ma'am. Waiting for a signal?"

Sylvia sucked in a breath.

Tony tightened his hand on her back. "What signal would that be?" His tone was a perfect cross between innocent and annoyed.

Tipton harrumphed. "A bit late for honest folks to be out and about, don't you think?"

"Not when honest folks have had a houseful of nosy, prying guests for a week," Tony growled.

"Ah, yes, the refugees from the storm. Interrupt your honeymoon, did they?"

"Damn right."

"It was our Christian duty to take them in," Sylvia said. With Tony rubbing small circles on her back, her breathing had almost returned to normal. Her heart still pounded in her chest, though.

"Well, I don't wish to interrupt the course of true

love," Tipton said. With his face shrouded in darkness, she couldn't tell if he was sincere or sarcastic. Had they allayed his suspicions, or increased them? "Do carry on." He nudged his horse and moved away.

Tony held his finger to her lips. "The thicket of rhododendrons behind the stables might offer more privacy." His voice was just loud enough to carry. "Or is there hay in the loft?"

He moved his finger as she began to smile. "Yes, there's hay."

"Excellent." He helped her to her feet, shook out his cape and put it back on, then grabbed her hand and strode toward the manor house.

They had only gone about twenty paces when Tony slowed, then stopped, his head tilted, listening. She could no longer distinguish the sound of hoofbeats from the crashing surf.

"Well, that was interesting." Tony's teeth flashed in the darkness in a grin before he untied his cravat and stuffed it back inside his shirt.

Sylvia attempted to straighten her clothing, as well. Her fingers shaking, she had trouble with the buttons on her pelisse.

"I didn't hurt you, did I?"

Her fingers gripping the closure, she looked up at the concern in his voice. "No, of course not." No man had ever touched her the way he just had, trying to make her laugh. Then again, she'd never had a man pretend to make love to her in order to distract a Revenue agent.

Hubert had always focused solely on completing

the act, never on giving her goose bumps or tickling her. He'd accidentally tickled her once, and had not been amused by her mirthful reaction.

Tony nudged her hands aside. "Allow me." His touch was deft and sure as he did up the buttons. He trailed his fingertips along her jaw before his hands dropped to his side. Warmth shot through her at his touch.

They quickly retraced their steps and Sylvia picked up the shuttered lantern. She almost held it aloft, to search for her bonnet, but Tony ran a few steps and caught the bonnet as it was being tumbled by the wind. He returned to her side and perched it on her head, then tied the ribbons beneath her chin.

"Thank you." Standing so close, she was trying not to stare at his chest, the pale patch of exposed skin at his throat, his supple lips as he smiled.

"Any time you have need of the services of a lady's maid, I am more than happy to oblige." He held his arm out. "I'm even better at removing clothing than restoring it."

Speechless at the images that flashed through her mind of him undressing her, she took his arm, and they headed back to their previous lookout spot at the cliff's edge.

Still thinking of the feel of Tony's fingers on her bare skin, Sylvia nearly jumped when Trent poked his head up over the edge.

"Any trouble?"

"None," Tony whispered back. "Any sign yet?"

"None."

Sylvia busied herself checking the lantern, until her thoughts were under control, and back on the task at hand.

Hands . . .

About to give her inconvenient carnal nature a stern talking-to, Sylvia was vastly relieved to see the signal light, blinking down at the mouth of the cove.

"Is Tipton likely to ride back this way?" As Tony followed her down the steep path in the darkness a few moments later, he kept one hand on her shoulder, the other on the cliff face.

Sylvia shook her head. "That was already his second pass tonight. He doesn't usually make a third."

He squeezed her shoulder. "Then we have nothing to worry about, do we?"

She almost laughed at his wry assurance.

Within minutes, Jimmy and her men were unloading casks from the small boats, and Captain Ruford stood before her, the purse already counted and tucked into his cloak pocket. Crowther stood a few feet away, looking smug as McCutcheon joined the chain of men unloading. The sense of foreboding returned, settling in the pit of her stomach.

"I have found a new supplier," Ruford announced. "He can give me twice the number of payloads I now carry across the Channel. Can you handle more frequent cargoes?"

"Not bloody likely," Crowther interrupted.

"And how would you know?" Tony took a step toward the first mate. "Are you privy to all the details of our operation?"

"Anyone can see these doddering old fools and cripples of yours couldn't handle one more cask, let alone twice as many loads per month."

"What rot!" Sylvia jabbed her finger toward Crowther. "You saw how quickly they were able to repair the damage from the storm this week." She faced Ruford. "Don't listen to what he says. We can handle whatever number of cargoes you can safely land."

Ruford scratched his chin. "Well, see now, then we have a bit of a dilemma. The other gent says he can handle 'em all, and he'll pay me a farthing more per cask, to boot."

"I'll give you the boot," Tony muttered.

"What other gent?" Neither Ruford nor Crowther seemed inclined to respond. She was about to ask again when another figure appeared out of the darkness, his boots grating on the pebbles beneath their feet.

Teague.

Her gut twisted.

"Don't take it personally, Lady Mon— Mrs. Sinclair. It's just business." Teague's teeth flashed in the darkness in a travesty of a smile. "Business between men."

Sylvia wanted to kick his teeth in.

"Well, then, let's talk business. Man to man." Tony took a step toward Teague.

"It's already been settled." Teague stepped closer to Tony. "The captain's mate has accepted my coin, and agreed to sell their extra cargo to me. Will sell all of their cargoes to me, in fact. He has no wish to continue his association with a strumpet the likes of her." He jutted his chin toward Sylvia.

She gasped.

Tony took another step toward Teague. "She is a *lady*. Even a bottom feeder like you should be able to recognize members of the upper class."

She heard a retort from Teague, but was too shocked to make out his words. She forced herself to remember this was business, even if Teague was trying to make it personal. All those people of the village relying on her . . . She balled her fists but kept her tone sweet. "Captain, we had an agreement."

"Yes, my dear lady, we did." He glanced over his shoulder. "Crowther, never tell me you have made arrangements that undermine our existing agreements with this enchanting person." Sylvia breathed through her nose as the captain stayed by her side, his unwashed scent wafting over her.

Crowther stepped around Teague and Tony, who were deep in heated conversation, and came to his captain's side. "I was only thinking of the profit for the crew, sir, as well as the profit for us."

"Mm, profit, yes. I'm sorry, my dear, but—"

"But, Captain." Sylvia gave him her brightest, most beguiling smile. "There are other considerations beside pure profit."

Ruford sidled closer, his putrid breath fanning her cheek. "Yes, my dear?"

Sylvia swallowed the bile in her throat. Without the income from smuggling this summer, the coming winter was going to be harsh, indeed. "Allow us to make a counteroffer. I believe that is the way business works?"

"It can. What do you have in mind?" His finger trailed a path down her cheek, to the collar of her pelisse.

She willed herself not to shudder. She had to raise her voice to be heard above the argument between Tony and Teague. "Let me discuss it with the men, and consult our account books. Perhaps we can come up with an offer that suits you better than Teague's."

"I'm eager to hear your offer." His hand slid away from her pelisse, brushing her shoulder as it did so. "Tomorrow, at the Stone's Throw Inn?"

"I hardly think so. We'll meet you at the Happy Jack."

Whatever the captain replied was lost as Teague roared and swung his massive fist at Tony.

Tony ducked. Teague swung again, and Tony rammed his shoulder into Teague's midriff, and shoved him against the cliff wall. Teague slid down, gasping for breath. "I warned you once," Tony said, stepping back and straightening his waistcoat.

"Aye, that you did." Teague stood and dusted off the seat of his breeches. "You skinny little runt." He lunged for Tony, caught him about the waist, swung him up, his cape flaring out, and slammed him into the ground. Sylvia cringed at the sound of pebbles grinding, hoping none of the sounds were broken bones. After a moment of hushed silence, Tony sat up but didn't immediately stand. Teague wore a self-satisfied smirk.

The men had stopped moving the casks and gathered in a loose circle. Bets were being taken, with

Teague the odds-on favorite. He stood only two or three inches taller than Tony, but outweighed him by at least four stone.

Ruford took Sylvia's elbow and guided her a few steps up the cliff path, out of the way, chuckling.

"There is no humor in this!" She wasn't sure if she was angered by Tony's fighting, or worried that Teague would injure him. Or worse. She'd heard stories about Teague, his deft skill with knife and pistol, and the cruel pleasure he took in using both. But so far neither had used any weapons but words and fists.

Tony picked himself up, shook his head, and wiped his palms on his breeches. He glanced over his shoulder, at the black water rolling up the beach to the stones just behind him, then back to Teague. "Come on, you fat and greasy innkeeper."

Teague gave another roar and charged. Tony bent his knees, leaning forward. He buried his shoulder in Teague's stomach again, then straightened, lifting Teague up and over. Teague landed with a splat on his back.

Another wave rolled in, soaking Teague's legs. His chest heaved with outrage, and his fists clenched at his sides, but he didn't get up.

Money changed hands among the spectators, with excited whisperings, descriptions, and exclamations as they quickly resumed unloading the boats.

Tony straightened, his hand on the small of his back, as he stared at Teague for a moment, who looked like a beached whale, his lower legs lapped by the waves. With a satisfied nod, Tony sauntered over to Sylvia's side and draped one arm around her waist. "Everything all right, sweetheart?"

He wasn't even breathing hard.

Thrilled by his strength and cunning, Sylvia was torn between the desire to kiss him and hug him and make certain he was uninjured, and being offended by his display of schoolboy antics. "Captain Ruford has agreed to meet us tomorrow to discuss our counteroffer." She was pleased her voice betrayed no emotion.

"Until tomorrow, then." Tony nodded farewell to the captain, who climbed into the last boat with his men and pushed off from the beach.

Teague rolled to his side and slowly got to his feet. "This isn't the end," he growled. Sylvia's men each took a step toward him. Teague held up one hand to forestall them, and walked to the path on the far side of the cove, toward his home in Tyneham.

Tony took Sylvia's hand, and headed up the cliff path.

They had reached the rhododendron-lined path before Sylvia dared speak. "I can't believe what I just saw. Two grown men, going at each other like crazed animals."

Tony shrugged. "He insulted you, and he doesn't seem the type inclined to meet at dawn. I think I may have lost an inch, though. Lifting him must have compressed my spine."

Sylvia opened her mouth, but no words came out. He had been in a fight because another man insulted her?

Warmth tingled through her, all the way to her toes.

Jimmy caught up to them. "Here you go." He dropped several coins into Tony's hand. "Your share of the winnings. Most of our men placed a bet."

"My share? No, give it back. They need it more than I."

Jimmy jogged ahead of them, out of Tony's reach. "You don't understand. We all bet on you—those coins are from Ruford's crew."

"Ah, well, in that case . . ." Tony slipped the jingling coins into his waistcoat pocket.

Jimmy slowed until they caught up to him. "We can't let Teague take our loads, Syl. What are we going to do?"

"Make Ruford a counteroffer. That's why we're meeting him tomorrow night."

"An offer of what, though?"

Sylvia sighed. "We'll think of something by then."

Moments later they reached the manor house. The blessedly quiet house with only five people in residence—all the others were finally back in their own home or staying with friends. Exhausted from the excitement and extra work since the storm, Galen and Gerald had already turned in, and left no candles burning.

Jimmy headed down the hall to his room, yawning loudly in the darkness.

Tony followed Sylvia to her door, close at her heels. She put her hand to his chest, pushing him back. Much as she might be tempted to finish what they'd started on the cliff before Tipton rode up, they couldn't. "Baxter will be up here any moment," she whispered.

Tony dropped his chin to his chest. After a moment he heaved a great sigh. "Then I wish you good night." He took her hand, but instead of raising it, he leaned in and kissed her on the cheek.

"Good night." She slipped into her room and sank onto the edge of her bed, listening to his steps fade away. She should move, wash up, go to sleep. But today, tonight, all week in fact, had just been too tumultuous.

Macbeth jumped up, and she sank her fingers into his soft fur. After a few minutes of stroking him, listening to his soothing purr in the darkness, she felt calmer.

She stripped off her garments, remembering the feel of Tony sliding her gown down her shoulder. He had been playful yet tender, considerate but oh so tempting. The things he did with his hands, his mouth . . .

She splashed cold water on her face. She had other, more important things to worry about than her growing weakness for the charming rogue. Teague was trying to take away their business, and Ruford was willing to let him. She couldn't allow that to happen.

She poured more water into the basin to wash. How could they change Ruford's mind, make him an offer he couldn't refuse, without having to include herself in the negotiation? Ruford could probably be talked into giving them his cargo for less than they paid now, if she were part of the payment.

She needed a bath. Not just a quick washup, but a

drag out the tub from the kitchen corner, hot water up to her neck, soak in the tub.

She poked her head out the door into the hall. All was quiet, no one about. She'd heard Baxter's muffled knock on Tony's door several minutes ago, and the rustle in the dressing room as he settled for the night. She pulled on her wrapper, not bothering to put on anything else, and tiptoed down the back stairs.

Tony tugged the ancient copper tub closer to the hearth, checked the temperature of the buckets set before the blaze, and dumped the water into the tub.

He straightened and bit back a groan. Every bone and muscle in his body screamed in protest at the abuse he'd heaped on them tonight. For that matter, the abuse from all this week. He yanked his shirt off over his head, shucked his breeches, and sank into the hot water. Ahh.

Baxter had sneaked into the kitchen for a snack before coming upstairs, and mentioned the buckets of water warming by the fire before he'd turned in. Since everyone was in their own room, it seemed a crime to let the heated water go to waste. Tony was never wasteful.

With some of his soreness relaxed away, he washed his hair, an awkward task using only one hand. He was trying to keep his right hand dry, as Sylvia instructed. The blisters did seem to finally be healing. Since he'd seen her to her room, he'd have to change the bandage himself.

Ah, sweet Sylvia. She'd been heaven in his arms.

Had it not been for the approaching Revenuer on horseback, he could have taken her right then and there on the windswept cliff top, the pounding surf a backdrop to their lovemaking. He'd made her moan and sigh, and laugh. She didn't laugh nearly enough. And her sensuous sighs when he'd found her sensitive spots . . .

He dipped the pitcher in the water and poured it over his head.

She was willing. He'd bet his last farthing on it. Heaven knew he wanted her. It was just a matter of timing, and location. And getting rid of their blasted chaperones.

Finished washing, he draped the cloth over the edge and leaned back, his head resting on the back ledge, and stared at the flames, his eyelids growing heavy.

Sylvia had asked for his help in dealing with Ruford, but now it seemed Teague was the bigger problem. Could they outbid the behemoth, and continue to get their cargoes from Ruford? And what made Teague so confident he could handle all of the loads? Even if he had more men in his gang—young and healthy men—there were still the patrolling Revenue agents to consider.

Hearing a soft gasp at the doorway, Tony opened one eye.

Sylvia stood there, barefoot, clutching a thin cotton wrapper closed at her throat, her curls tousled, her mouth open in a silent "oh." The way the soft cotton hugged her form, she couldn't have anything on beneath it. He licked his lips.

After thoroughly enjoying the sight for a moment, he realized she wouldn't have known he was down here, in the tub. Stupid, selfish idiot. He'd used her hot water. "Give me a moment, and I'll set more water on for you." He sat up.

She held her hand out to stop him. "No, no, I just came down for, um, I was a bit hungry. Yes, I came down for some cheese and a cup of tea."

"Tea." He leaned back again, water sloshing. It was warm rather than hot now, but still pleasant. As was the company.

"And cheese."

She still stood in the doorway, ready to scurry away. "Well, don't mind me." Tony closed his eyes.

There was a long pause, then he heard movement. Soft footsteps across the flagstone floor, the rustle of her wrapper. The clatter of dishes. More rustling.

"Would you, um, do you want anything?"

Leaping out of the tub and having his way with her on the kitchen table would probably be considered poor manners. "Whatever you're having." Now that he thought about it, he *was* hungry.

He heard the scrape of wood on the floor, and opened his eyes. Sylvia had pushed a chair next to the tub, and placed a plate with cheese on the seat. She was bent over at the hearth, pouring tea into two cups. The firelight rendered her wrapper sheer. He was right—not a stitch on underneath. He longed to map her curves with his hands, his mouth, kiss her sweet flesh. Their escapade on the cliff earlier that night had left him wanting more, much more.

Once she'd eaten, he'd repeat his offer to fix her bath. Offer to wash her back. Maybe wash her hair, as well. He imagined Sylvia relaxed and naked in the tub, leaning back as he ran his fingers through her silky curls and caressed her bare skin, slick and glistening from the warm water. He'd lift her out and dry her with the towel warming by the hearth, caressing every inch of her soft skin. There'd be no barriers between them, not people, not clothing, nothing to stop them.

Galen would never know, as long as they remembered to put the salt cellar and pepper grinder back on the table afterward.

Sylvia caught him staring, and blushed. She quickly set one cup on the chair, and sat down on the floor, her back against the side of the tub. If she'd sat in a chair, she'd be high enough to see into the tub, and see his growing interest in her presence. But this way, she was close enough for him to touch her.

They ate in silence for a few moments, Sylvia studying the depths of her cup between delicate bites, Tony studying Sylvia. He recognized the moment she began to feel at ease again. Soon after, she turned to face him.

"Why are you doing this?"

His left hand had crept along the edge of the tub, just a fingertip away from stroking her bare neck. But she hadn't paid any attention to his wandering hand. "Because a pitcher of cold water didn't seem adequate tonight."

Her lips curved, almost a smile. "No. The roof, Doyle's cottage, Ruford and Teague . . ." She waved her hand, encompassing the house and its inhabitants, perhaps even the village and environs.

"I'm trying to impress you. Is it working?"

She gave him a sideways look, her chin lowered. "Why are you doing this?"

He sighed. His hand was covered in blisters; he'd cheated death by working on the edge of a slick roof forty feet above the earth where sane men stayed; he'd pretended to be a smuggler, knowing the government would see it as no pretense if he was caught; worked himself to exhaustion helping near strangers repair their homes; and just tonight had fought a man twice his size in defense of a woman he'd known only a week. A woman who had become his acquaintance because members of her gang had abducted him and knocked him unconscious.

Why, indeed?

Sylvia was on her knees now, leaning closer, intent on his answer, her green gaze focused on his face, her lips slightly parted.

He sat forward, cupped her cheek with his left hand, and kissed her. She stayed perfectly still, allowing him to brush his lips against hers, to caress her cheek with his thumb. He pulled back a fraction, giving her a chance to escape should she want it.

She followed him, not allowing a break in contact. Fire coursed through his veins as their breath mingled, and she kept her lips pressed against his. Someone moaned.

They separated a hair's breadth. "Good answer," Sylvia whispered.

Chapter 13

Tony licked his bottom lip, tasting Sylvia, wanting more. His heart beat faster, watching Sylvia watch him, her gaze riveted on his mouth. She grabbed him, her delicate hands holding his head, fingers plunged into his hair, and pulled him close, her kiss demanding, exploring.

He opened, wondering how she'd react. She stroked the tip of her tongue along his lip, shocking a moan out of him, before she slipped inside and deepened the kiss. She was tentative, barely touching his tongue before she retreated.

Apparently her first husband had a lot to answer for, as there was much in her education left incomplete. Tony was happy to teach such a willing pupil.

With one hand still cupping her cheek, he brought

his free hand up to her neck, lightly caressing the sensitive flesh, as he claimed another kiss. He delved deep into her mouth, thrusting in and out, mimicking the motion he had every intention of making, very soon.

Raising her mouth from his, gasping for breath, her fingers still tangled in his hair, she gazed into his eyes. "Now I understand."

He dropped a kiss at the corner of her mouth, and worked his way up to her ear. "Understand what?"

"Why you didn't . . . kiss me . . . like that . . . before."

He smiled against her cheek. "Because I knew that once I tasted you, I wouldn't be satisfied until I held you, made you writhe in pleasure, and buried myself deep inside you?"

"Oh." With her lips parted, he kissed her again. He let his left hand drift down from her cheek, along the smooth column of her neck, down to the swell of her breast. It fit his hand perfectly, as he knew it would. He dipped his hand in the water and then cupped her again, dampening the thin cotton, revealing a dusky circle.

She drew her shoulders back, giving him better access. He swept his thumb back and forth, eliciting a soft moan from Sylvia. He almost didn't hear it over the thudding of his pulse. Blood pounded through his veins, quickening his breathing.

She returned the favor, trailing her fingers across his chest, dipping her hand below the water, coming agonizingly close to discovering just how much he wanted her. He forced himself to be still and allowed her to explore him, her fingers getting bolder, tracing a damp path from his throat, down his shoulder, across his chest, circling the little nub that hardened under her touch.

Just as he was going to drag her into the tub on top of him, she looked up at him, her eyes dark with desire, the green irises almost gone, eclipsed by her dilated pupils. She licked her lips. "Perhaps we should—"

Footsteps in the hall.

Blast.

Sylvia's eyes widened. She glanced at the doorway, back at Tony, then was up and dashing out the door, a flash of bare leg as she turned the corner.

His heart still racing, Tony leaned his head back, and barely refrained from banging it on the edge of the tub. Good thing he was sitting in tepid water. Cold would be even better. Icy.

Galen entered a few seconds later, yawning. "Well, isn't this a fine sight to greet the morning." She barely paused before she tied on her apron and set to work. "Come down to breakfast a might early, did you?"

"Haven't been to bed yet." And oh, the plans he'd had for bed . . .

The tub was in front of the hearth, where Galen needed to cook. She stood beside the tub, feet spread, arms folded over her chest. "Hungry, were you?"

The plate, littered with crumbly bits of cheese, was on the chair seat, as was his cup. Had she noticed the second cup on the floor?

He sighed and closed his eyes briefly. She hadn't moved. "Would you be so kind?" He pointed at the towel folded on the edge of the hearth.

She shook it out and held it open, but didn't let it go. Well, fine.

Tony stood up in the tub and took the towel from her, and wrapped it around his waist. Only then did Galen busy herself with pots and pans. He stepped out, dried off, and pulled his breeches back on, but didn't bother with his shirt.

He was almost done putting the tub away when Galen spoke again.

"My lady probably has something for those bruises."

He couldn't help glancing over his shoulder, but of course he couldn't see his back. It probably had the outline of every rock he'd landed on when Teague had thrown him down like a child's doll, not to mention the almost-healed tattoo. "They're fine."

Galen grunted. "Men." A moment later she tossed him one of yesterday's scones. "You haven't been to Australia, have you, laddie?"

He didn't dare ask her for butter, so he ate the scone dry. "I have never set foot off this benighted island." Being on Nick's ship didn't count, since they had still been tied up at the dock. She grunted, but did not continue the conversation.

After a last look to make sure he'd cleaned up his mess, Tony grabbed his shirt and trudged upstairs to bed. Outside in the pale dawn light, birds were cheerfully chirping.

Too bad he didn't have a gun.

Sylvia awoke with a start as the clock struck noon. Galen had brought her a cup of tea, now cold on the bedside table, but let her sleep. Had Galen witnessed her cowardly flight up the back stairs? She flung the covers back and got up to dress.

There was no need for her wrapper—her cheeks heated at the memory of last night. She imagined she could still see the damp imprint of his palm on the wrapper, directly over her breast, as she'd fled up the stairs. She seemed to be in a perpetual state of embarrassment since Tony had arrived. And in a perpetual state of hunger, that no food she knew of could satisfy.

It had never been like this with her husband. She'd done her duty with Hubert, and really, that's all it had been. Duty. He'd never made her heart pound, her blood race, or taken her breath away—in a good way, that is. Never before had she felt this need to constantly be near a man, to touch him, have him touch her. Hear his voice, see his smile.

But Tony was only here temporarily. Developing feelings for him could only end badly for her when he left. Even worse, since he had revealed a wanton side of her that she would now have to acknowledge, finding a husband would be even more difficult. She wouldn't be easily satisfied. Only a man who could rouse her to breathless excitement would do. So far, she'd only encountered one, and he wasn't husband material.

Disgruntled, she dressed without washing and went straight to the stillroom, not bothering to detour through the kitchen for a quick meal. She pulled the account book from its hiding place, grabbed the writing slate and chalk, and sat on the bench at her worktable.

Minutes later, she realized she had drawn nothing

but nonsensical images on the slate, and hadn't thought of a single useful thing. Other than the memory of Tony's kisses last night. How he'd looked in the tub, clean and wet, with water glistening on his golden skin, soap bubbles hiding the most interesting parts . . .

Jimmy sauntered in, yawning and scratching his jaw. He was old enough that he now needed to shave almost twice a week. Thinking of beard stubble made her think of the whisker burn on her neck, not to mention how it got there. Heat rose in her cheeks, and she hurriedly wiped the slate clean.

"So, what's our counteroffer?" Jimmy leaned his palms on the table beside her, peering over her shoulder at the slate.

Sylvia cleared her throat. "I'm not sure we can make one that's acceptable to all parties."

"We don't need to make Teague happy, just Ruford." He swung one leg over the bench and sat down. "*Can* we pay the captain more than Teague has offered him?"

She glanced over the account book. "Money is so tight already. Perhaps Spencer would accept a smaller percentage? And we could look for more ways to economize. I could wear my gray gowns another year." The thought made her cringe inwardly. She could always try dyeing the fabrics again. That wouldn't cost much.

Jimmy entered into the spirit. "We don't really need sugar for our tea, or preserves for the scones. And mackerel is always easy to catch—we'll eat more fish. Will that be enough?"

"Perhaps. We still have to finish repairs from the storm's damage. We didn't count on those expenses."

"Well, maybe there's something other than money, something we can offer Ruford that Teague can't. Other than you, of course."

They discussed possibilities, none of which seemed likely to succeed.

She refused to give in to desperation, but was about to throw down her chalk in disgust at their lack of progress when Tony walked in. Her heart skipped a beat, then settled into its normal rhythm, albeit a tad faster.

The mischievous glint in Tony's eyes faded somewhat at the sight of Jimmy. "When you get a moment, if you wouldn't mind . . ." He held up his right palm to her, with the dirty bandage.

"Now is fine."

Jimmy got up to retrieve fresh bandages from a cabinet. "That was a first-rate show last night."

Sylvia coughed. She thought it had been Galen's step she heard last night heading toward the kitchen. Tony glanced at her, then at Jimmy, his expression giving nothing away.

"When Teague dropped you like a sack of potatoes on the beach, I thought you were done for."

Sylvia started breathing again. Jimmy handed her the bandages, then rummaged in the cupboard for the correct jar of ointment. He was slow in the task, as he kept looking over his shoulder at Tony, his voice betraying his growing excitement.

"And then when you taunted him, and he charged

like a bull, and you sent him sailing up and over, like he was . . . was . . ."

"A sack of potatoes?"

"Exactly!" Jimmy shouted. "Can you teach me that trick?"

Sylvia plucked the jar from Jimmy's wildly waving hand before *it* went sailing.

"It's no trick, just a simple equation involving momentum and leverage, but yes, I can show you." Tony sat down and rested his hand on the table in front of Sylvia. She cut the old bandage off, holding his wrist to keep his hand steady.

"That would be capital!" Jimmy slapped him on the shoulder.

Tony flinched. His face betrayed no emotion, but since she was holding his wrist, Sylvia had felt his involuntary reaction. Pain.

Jimmy declared his intention of raiding the kitchen, and Tony waved him out the door.

"You're hurt." She inspected his palm, saw no sign of infection, and slathered it with ointment.

"No, it's feeling much better." He closed and opened his hand several times. "See?"

"I meant your back. Your shoulder."

"I'm fine. Perhaps a little stiff from lying on the beach last night."

Sylvia shook her head as she wrapped the new bandage around his hand. "Betsy told me about the blood."

He went still. "Beg pardon?"

"When she was doing laundry, Betsy noticed dried blood on your shirt. Inside. Near the shoulder."

"Oh. That. 'Tis nothing." He gave her his cocky grin.

"Then you won't mind letting me have a look. Take off your shirt."

"Ah, I understand. You just want to see me half-naked." His grin had become a comical leer.

She almost smiled back. "I saw you . . . last night. But not your back."

He heaved a dramatic sigh. "If you insist."

"I do."

He swiveled around on the bench, facing away, and tugged his shirt off over his head.

Sylvia gasped. His back was ablaze in color, covered with bruises of varying sizes, some fresh in livid blue and purple, others fading green and yellow. There were irregular marks from last night's fight, where he'd impacted on the rocks of the beach. Fist-sized marks from last week, when her men had mistaken him for a Revenue agent.

Most intriguing was the palm-sized discoloration on his right shoulder blade—what she'd thought was a birthmark. Parts of old scabs remained, and there was still some swelling amidst the marks. But there was a distinct pattern.

"A tattoo? You have a tattoo of—" She traced the lines, the points. "A mariner's compass?" She looked at Tony in a new light. She'd never known any gentleman who had a tattoo. Then again, she didn't know all that many gentlemen. Smugglers, rogues, and other scalawags made up most of her circle of acquaintances lately.

She'd seen a tattoo only once before, on the forearm of one of Hubert's crewmen, who had told amazing but farfetched tales of sailing to the South Seas.

He grunted. "Been wondering what the hell it was."

"You didn't know?" If she remembered the man's story, it had taken over an hour of painful pricking to render the pattern.

"I, um, wasn't exactly conscious at the time of application."

Well, if the process was as painful as she'd heard, perhaps that was for the best.

"My friend Nick had me try a seasick remedy while we were on board his ship, and after the wine we drank at Ben's wedding breakfast . . ."

"You were drunk."

"And sick." He snorted. "A compass. Of all the—"

"You didn't choose the design?"

He shook his head. "Must have been Nick. He was always trying to watch out for me when we were in school."

"I don't see how—"

"Much of that day is fuzzy, but I do remember mumbling something about having no direction in my life." He smiled at her over his shoulder. "Nick apparently took it to heart."

"Direction." Sylvia closed her eyes. He could stop in their village, stay a while and play smuggler, because he had nowhere else to be. No direction, no agenda, no plan. She was frantically planning for the winter, and he probably didn't even have a plan beyond next week. Further proof of how wrong he was for her.

Still, she could enjoy the view. Like admiring a work of art in a museum—didn't necessarily mean she wanted to take the art home and keep it.

She patted his left shoulder, the one not bruised. "Stay here. I have some liniment that will help the soreness."

"Galen said you would. That's who came into the kitchen after you left, by the way."

It shouldn't matter—she was a grown woman, a widow, and Galen was not her mother. If Sylvia wanted to have a tryst with a handsome, charming man, then it was nobody's business but her own. Still, she felt heat bloom in her cheeks.

She retrieved the bottle from the cupboard. "Rest your arms on the table, and lay your head down." Tony complied. She rubbed the liniment into his warm, smooth skin, feeling his every bone and muscle.

The strength and vitality she'd sensed in him that first night, when he'd been unconscious on the sofa, was nothing compared to this, being able to rub her hands on him, no clothing as a barrier, no crowd of observers. She was not caressing him—this was a medical necessity.

"That stuff smells like you."

She looked up.

"Lavender, I think." Tony leaned back, tugged her toward him and . . . sniffed her hair. His exhale warmed her ear and sent tingles down her spine. "Definitely lavender."

"It's useful in a lot of preparations." She stood up before Jimmy came back and caught her in a compromising position. "I modified Doyle's horse liniment recipe, added a few things. Lavender reduces inflammation, helps prevent infection."

"You don't say." Tony slid his hand down from her wrist, tangling his fingers in hers.

She took a deep breath, trying to calm her heart, which was beating much too fast. One would think she'd never held hands with a half-dressed man before. "And chamomile seems to help wounds heal faster."

"I don't smell chamomile. Just the lavender. Your scent."

She swallowed. "I bathe Macbeth in lavender water. Keeps the fleas away. And—"

"I didn't think you could bathe a cat." He tilted her hand back and forth. "Hmm, no scars."

"You can if you start bathing them when they're too small to put up much of a protest. After a while they realize it's for their own good. He actually looks forward to it."

Tony's brows rose in disbelief.

"Well, he at least doesn't try to jump out of the tub. He knows I won't let him on my bed if he has fleas."

Tony stroked his thumb over her wrist. "I imagine he'd put up with almost anything, to be allowed into your bed."

The heated look in his eyes was making her insides

jump and quiver. If he kept this up, she'd throw him down on the table and have her wicked way with him.

That was probably his plan. The only plans he seemed to make were for getting her into his arms, into his bed.

Sylvia tugged her hand free, and pushed his undamaged shoulder back down. "Let me finish," she said brusquely. She dribbled more liniment down his back.

He closed eyes, resting his cheek on his forearm. Suddenly he chuckled. "We seem unable to break our habit." She paused, her hand at the base of his spine. "You, ministering to my injuries."

"Perhaps you should break your habit of getting injured." There was a bruise just above his hip, at the waistband of his breeches. It disappeared below. Dare she?

Medical necessity. She dribbled more liniment on her fingers and worked it into his skin. His breathing hitched as her contact became more personal. She followed the contours of the bruise, dipping her fingers just inside his breeches.

"Careful." His eyes remained closed, though he reached around to loosely grasp her wrist. "Don't start something we can't finish right now."

Right. She had been getting carried away again by the sight, and feel, of all his lovely bare skin.

He let go, and she slid her hand up along his spine, proving that she'd had no ulterior motives whatsoever, and capped the bottle.

"Is that what I think it is?" Jimmy bounded into the room, staring at Tony's back.

Sylvia busied herself putting the bottle away and wiping her hands, hoping no one else noticed their slight tremble.

Jimmy leaned over Tony, staring at the tattoo. Crumbs from the tart in his hand fell onto the bare skin.

"Did you bring enough for everyone in class, young man?" Tony hadn't opened his eyes yet.

"I, um . . ."

"Thought not." Tony sat up, but made no move to put his shirt back on. He held it bunched on his lap. "Yes, it's what you think, and I don't recommend getting one. Hurt like the devil for over a week. Not to mention making a bloody mess of my shirts."

"Syl, do you remember old Preston? He had a tattoo like that, only it wound around his entire forearm." Jimmy straddled the bench and sat down. "Said some tribal savages held him down while they pricked his skin with really sharp ivory sticks, over and over and—"

"Enough." Tony shook out his shirt and pulled it on. "I prefer to remain blissfully ignorant of the details, if you please." He stepped away from the table, tucking his shirt into his breeches.

Sylvia was sorry to see all that bare skin covered up, but it was probably for the best. She had apparently used up all her willpower when it came to Tony.

He sat down again and dragged the account book closer. "Now that my injuries have been treated and my survival ensured for at least another day, we have a problem to deal with. Any suggestions?"

We.

Sylvia's heart swelled. She sat down, on the opposite side of the table. Really, perhaps she needed to get more rest if she was going to get so emotional over someone taking on their problems and making them his.

This was dangerous. She couldn't allow them to rely on Tony. He was here temporarily. Things would only be that much harder after he left if she let herself rely on him.

She sighed. "If we had our own ship again, we wouldn't need Ruford. And smuggling was much more profitable that way, even after paying a crew to sail it."

"Yes, well, Hubert took care of that, didn't he?" Jimmy clenched his fist on the table. "Bloody idiot couldn't navigate his way across a duck pond. If he hadn't wrecked on Mupe Rocks we'd be papering the gold salon in pound notes by now."

"He managed to find his way between Liverpool around to London and back several dozen times." She laid her hand on his. "It was a storm, Jimmy. How many ships have wrecked on Mupe Rocks in your lifetime alone?"

He stared down at the table, and traced the grain of the wood with his thumbnail. Suddenly he looked up. "If we eliminate Teague as a customer, Ruford won't have anyone to sell to but us."

Tony stared at Jimmy. "Eliminate?"

Jimmy shrugged. "You asked for suggestions."

"We are not the Worbarrow Bay gang," Sylvia said. "How many times do I have to say, we will have no bloodshed?"

Jimmy mumbled under his breath.

"Let's see if we can come up with something a tad less bloodthirsty." Tony closed the account book. "I imagine simply offering more money is not an option." At her nod, he continued. "Perhaps we can barter with him."

Jimmy took a cloth-wrapped bundle out of his pocket. "Well, Syl has all sorts of remedies. Most of the villagers come to her instead of the apothecary in East Lulworth."

Sylvia cringed at the thought of treating Ruford or any of his men. "I'm sure he has his own surgeon on board."

Tony helped himself to a chunk of Jimmy's cheese. "Ruford and his crew are not going to come anywhere *near* Sylvia."

"Mackerel? With Sawyer and Baxter going fishing every day, we always have plenty of fish."

Sylvia shook her head. "The crew can drop a line over the side anytime, and catch all the fish they need to on their own."

Tony had started to pop the cheese in his mouth, but pulled his hand back. "Cheese." He gazed at the chunk as though he'd never seen it before.

"That's certainly something we have plenty of." Jimmy made gagging motions. "Sometimes I get so sick of it, I never want to see cheese or fish again in my life."

True enough. Which was why she'd started experimenting with the traditional local cheese recipe, despite Mrs. Brewer's protests in the dairy workroom. Sylvia and Miss Atwood had started adding different herbs to the mix, and letting it ripen in different locations. "Fortunately we've only lost a few of the cattle to disease or other disasters that have plagued the village in the last few years. We skim the milk first, to use the cream for butter, and let the cheese ripen up to six months."

Jimmy snorted. "Any longer than that, and the rinds get so hard, Doyle threatens to use them instead of wheels on the carts."

Tony grinned. "There you are, then. What captain would turn down fresh rations for his crew?"

Could it be that simple? The answer to all their problems was . . . cheese?

The three of them walked down to the Happy Jack at dusk, and settled at a table in the corner, their backs to the wall, watching the door. Mrs. Spencer brought them each a mug of cider and bustled away again after squeezing Sylvia's hand and whispering "Good luck."

Several of her men were gathered on the benches before the fire, all looking as though they had nothing better to do of an evening but drink at the local alehouse. At least, that's what Sylvia hoped Ruford would think. Even Baxter was there with his aunt, Mrs. Miggins, eating at another table.

Just as her nerves were stretched to the breaking point, Ruford entered. He peered through the dimness of the gloomy interior for a moment, noting every person present, before he strode to their table.

"My lady, may I say how nice it is to see you again." He raised her hand for a sloppy kiss. Sylvia struggled to keep the smile on her face. "Gentlemen." Jimmy and Tony exchanged nods with him, and Ruford sat down. He eased his chair to one side so that he too had a view of the door. Sylvia nudged her chair closer to Tony, trying to get upwind of the captain.

Tony waved, and Mrs. Spencer brought out another mug of cider. After a few excruciating minutes of drinking and idle chitchat, Jimmy set the purse on the table with a thud.

Blast. He was supposed to save that as a last resort. That money was needed to finish rebuilding after the storm. Sylvia reached into the basket at her feet and brought up a sizable chunk of cheese wrapped in cloth, and set that on the table, blocking the money from the captain's sight.

"I'm eager to hear what you have to offer, my lady." Ruford patted her knee under the table.

The captain wouldn't touch her if she was sitting on Tony's lap, would he? Tony wouldn't mind if she moved there, she was sure.

Tony rapped his knuckles on the table. Ruford finally dragged his gaze from Sylvia to Tony. "You have to buy rations for your crew with the money you make. We're offering to save you that step. Have you tried the Dorset blue vinny?" He pulled the knife from his boot, cut off a chunk, and offered it.

"Cheese?"

At least Ruford hadn't laughed outright.

"It's very nutritious. It will keep your men strong, and able to work hard." Sylvia tried not to look too eager.

"And it's tasty." Tony popped a bit in his mouth.

"Cheese is cheese. We can get all we need when we dock in Swanage, along with our other provisions." Ruford sat back, arms folded across his chest.

Sylvia took the chunk off Tony's knife and held it out to the captain. "At least taste it. It's my own variation on the traditional recipe."

"Yours? Very well. For you, my dear lady." He took the chunk, brushing his fingers along hers.

Tony wiped his knife blade and stuck it back in his boot. Sylvia reached down to pat her half-boots, checking that her own knife was still in place. She'd grown so accustomed to carrying it, now she hardly left the manor without it.

The inn door slammed open, and Ruford dropped his cheese.

Sylvia's relief at the newcomer not being Teague was short-lived as she recognized Tipton's tall, spare frame. The Revenue agent's gaze swept the room.

Sylvia grabbed the purse from the tabletop and bent over to hide it in her basket.

But the basket had been kicked to the far side of the table.

She tucked the purse under her skirt, between her knees, trying to muffle the clink of the coins. A shadow fell across the table just as she arranged her skirt again.

"Good evening, Lord Montgomery, Mrs. Sinclair." Tipton doffed his hat. "I didn't know you were acquainted with the captain."

"We're trying to reach an agreement on terms for a

business arrangement. Do go away." Tony took a sip of his cider.

Sylvia felt the color drain from her face.

Tipton leaned on the table. "What business arrangements would you need to make involving a sea captain, pray tell?"

She pressed her knees together to prevent them from shaking. And clinking.

"Cheese, of course. We've had an excellent year, and need a more efficient method of transporting it to market." Tony gestured at the round of cheese on the table.

"Ah, yes, Lulworth Cove's delicious secret recipe Dorset blue vinny. Even the folks up in Shaftesbury have heard of it."

"They have?" Jimmy sounded even more surprised than Sylvia felt.

"So the goods you have need of transporting are . . . cheese?"

Tony cut off another bit and offered it to Tipton. "What else could there possibly be?"

Tipton popped the bit into his mouth. "I bid you good evening." He sketched the slightest of bows toward Sylvia, and claimed the only free table in the taproom. Mrs. Spencer hurried over to take his order. Moments later she brought him a platter and a tankard, and he dug into his meal.

The outer door opened and another man walked in, headed straight for Tipton's table.

Jimmy leaned around Tony and whispered. "What's Danielson doing here?"

Sylvia shook her head. "Tipton's not supposed to report to him for another three days."

"That's Mr. Tipton's superior?" Tony murmured.

Sylvia nodded. "All of the riding officers who patrol the Lulworth coast report to Danielson—but they usually report to him at the office in Weymouth."

Tony scratched his jaw. "I wonder what brings him our way?"

"This can't be good," Jimmy muttered.

"I need to get back to my ship before the tide turns," Ruford suddenly announced.

His ship was anchored in the cove—she'd seen the masts when she'd walked to the inn. It didn't matter what the tide was doing. "But—"

"However, I plan to take a walk on the beach in the morning."

"The view is particularly lovely at about nine," Tony said.

Moments later he was gone. Danielson summoned Mrs. Spencer over. Tipton lifted his tankard in salute. Jimmy and Tony nodded back. Sylvia couldn't move.

Move. Oh, no. She tugged on Tony's sleeve, and he bent close so she could whisper in his ear. "Hayden, Monroe, and several others are supposed to move the brandy tonight, from the caves up to the inn's cellars. We have to stop them."

Tony drained his mug of cider, then leaned over to whisper to Jimmy. Seconds later, Jimmy had taken his mug and joined Trent and Corwin on a bench by the fire. Tony pushed back from the table and stood, leaning his forearm on the back of Sylvia's chair. "Newly-weds, right?" he whispered in her ear.

She shivered down to her toes. "Yes."

With one arm under her knees and one behind her shoulders, he scooped her up. She couldn't help a startled yelp, which drew attention. She looped her arms around his neck to keep from falling, and hid her face against Tony's chest as he settled her more securely in his grip and strode, not for the door, but for the staircase.

She heard the chuckles and whispers, didn't need to open her eyes to see the knowing grins. Tony was halfway up the flight when she heard Mrs. Miggins shout "Give 'im a kiss for me, lass!" Laughter covered the sound of her mortified groan.

Tony kissed her forehead and kept climbing. He didn't stop until he reached the bedchamber at the far end of the hall. "Can you turn the knob?"

"Put me down. I'm too heavy for you to be hauling about."

"Just turn the knob."

Sylvia reached down and opened the door. Tony strode through, made sure the room was unoccupied, and kicked the door shut with a resounding thud. The sound must have been audible all the way to the tap-room.

Sylvia felt his heartbeat solid and steady beneath her cheek. His breathing was only slightly labored, his breath coming in gentle huffs against her hair. She could smell him, the clean scent of his sandalwood soap, a hint of lavender from the liniment she'd rubbed into his back, and something subtle underneath, uniquely Tony. When he spoke, she could feel his words as much as hear them, a comforting rumble.

This was entirely too pleasant. And . . . exhilarating. Really, she should insist he put her down. She couldn't remember anyone ever carrying her like this. She'd never sprained her ankle. Certainly Hubert had never picked her up. "What now?"

He took a few more steps into the room, closer to the bed. The very large, very comfortable-looking bed. "Well, what would newlyweds do in a situation like this?"

Chapter 14

Her jaw worked, but no words came out. Images came to mind, though.

He chuckled, and set her feet down but kept his arm around her shoulders. The purse fell to the floor with a *clunk,* barely missing her toes. "Trust me?"

Him, yes, but not her voice. She nodded.

He cupped her cheeks with both hands, strong yet gentle, his fingertips stirring her hair, and emotions deep within her. Yearning, desire, a wish for impossible things.

"Then believe me when I say I would like nothing more right now than to do what newlyweds would." He kissed her, long and thoroughly, until her toes curled and she locked her arms around his waist, drawing him even closer, surrounding herself in his warmth and strength. Much, much too soon he pulled back. "But we have to make sure your men aren't caught by Tipton and Danielson," he whispered against her cheek. "No telling how long they'll stay in the taproom."

Of course, her men. They were the reason for this little display. How could she forget about them? While she struggled to regain her poise, Tony tucked the purse into his waistcoat pocket. He flung open the window, looked out, then climbed through and leaned back in, holding out his hand.

"You can't be serious. On the roof, in the dark?"

"Perfectly safe. I'll keep you steady."

Before she could think twice, Tony had grasped her under the arms and pulled her outside, then grabbed her hand and led the way across the slate tiles.

"You've spent entirely too much time on roofs."

"Undoubtedly. And when you're traipsing about on rooftops, it's always good to know more than one way to reach the ground." They worked their way down from one gable to another until Tony stepped down onto the roof of the privy and jumped to the ground. He held his hands up, his expression clearly confident that she would leap into his arms.

Sylvia sat down and swung her legs over the edge, judging how far she still had to go. She really liked the fact that she'd never sprained her ankle.

Tony patted her foot, which dangled next to his shoulder. "Jump, sweetheart. I'll catch you." Again he held his arms up.

She'd already admitted that she trusted him. With

her physical safety, at least. Her heart was another matter. She jumped. He caught her as promised, though he did stagger backward a few steps. He squeezed her in an entirely-too-brief hug. "That's my girl. Now, where do we find Hayden and Monroe?"

She led the way down the sunken lane to the cove where her band of smugglers were working, her steps confident despite the darkness, Tony holding her hand.

He'd called her sweetheart again. When no one else was around to hear.

Probably just a habit he'd formed from their subterfuge. It meant nothing.

Why did she wish it meant something to him? She'd known from the beginning that he was here only temporarily.

The men should be along here. The moonlight was too faint to see more than vague shapes looming in the darkness. She stopped to listen. Tony bumped into her, let go her hand to wrap his arms around her, and kept them around her waist even after he'd steadied them both.

"What is it?" he whispered. He rested his chin on her shoulder, his warm breath against her ear sending delicious shivers down her spine. She rested her hands on top of his, held snug against her belly. Strong and secure. She could get used to this.

She shook herself. "Monroe!" she called softly, as loud as she dared.

One of the shadows separated from the others, and moved toward her. "My lady?"

Other shadows moved, shapes shifted, and soon

more of her men were there on the path beside them. Sylvia started to explain about Tipton and Danielson, but footsteps on the path had everyone diving for cover. Tony held her close, wrapping his black cape around them both to better conceal them.

Her heart pounded. Much as she enjoyed the closeness, they could not be caught. They could not use the same subterfuge they had the other night on the cliff. There was no logical, *legal* reason for them to have left their room with its big soft bed, and come outdoors for a tryst.

Footsteps drew closer. "Syl?"

Sylvia stood, breathing a sigh of relief. "Jimmy!" Everyone else came back to the path as well, brushing themselves off.

Jimmy pointed over his shoulder, toward the inn. "Trent is spinning a yarn for everyone in the taproom, including Danielson and Tipton. Should keep them occupied for a bit. Corwin left after I did—he'll be along shortly."

"Right here, my lord. Figured the lads could use a hand."

With the Revenue agents occupied and their whereabouts confirmed, it was too good an opportunity to pass up. The men quickly re-formed their brigade for moving the half-ankers of brandy up from the caves. Tony joined the formation, and handled the casks with ease and grace. "Might as well help while I'm here," he said when she glanced at him.

Sylvia tore herself away from watching him long enough to enter the back door of the kitchen, and confirm with Mrs. Spencer that the Revenue agents were indeed still in the taproom. They arranged for a signal in case the agents left.

They had just moved the last casks from one of the caves, and stowed them in the regular storage places—the inn's cellar and the church's rafters—when the signal came. Jimmy and Baxter accompanied Tony and Sylvia up to the manor house on the sunken path, while the rest of the men scattered to their own homes.

The next morning, Sylvia stood between Jimmy and Tony on the cliff overlooking the beach well in advance of the scheduled meeting time. Ruford's ship, the *Polly Anne,* bobbed on the gentle waves out in the cove, her sails furled. Gulls and plovers dipped and soared in the air above them. She envied their carefree existence.

"As a last resort, Jimmy. The money was supposed to be offered only as a last resort. I thought you understood what that meant." She fidgeted with the fichu tucked into her neckline. It was too warm for a pelisse, but she wasn't going to let Ruford see any more skin than necessary.

"I know, I know. How many times do I have to say I'm sorry?" Jimmy threw a rock over the cliff's edge.

Tony lowered the spyglass from where he'd been staring off to the east, and let out a frustrated sigh. "I still don't see any sign of him." He handed her the spyglass, and she tucked it into the pocket sewn into her skirt for it.

"The captain? He's probably still snoring be-lowdecks." Jimmy tossed another rock.

"Not Ruford. Teague."

Sylvia froze. "Why do you expect to see Teague?"

"If I were in his shoes, I'd want to make sure no one mucked up the deal I'd made with Ruford."

Jimmy hefted another rock but didn't throw it. "You'd be around to counter the counteroffer?"

"Precisely. And he wasn't at the inn last night."

Baxter arrived then, out of breath from running. "Here's the cheese you asked for, my lady."

Sylvia checked the cloth in the basket he'd brought, the basket she'd had to leave behind last night. "This isn't the same round we left on the table."

"No, that one, um, got eaten." He gave an apologetic shrug. "I took this one from the batch that's ripening in the cave by Stair Hole."

Several of the caves in the Portland stone cliffs around the cove were too small to hide more than a few tubs, but were just right for keeping the cheese in a cool, dark place while they ripened. She was also interested to see—and taste—the effect of their proximity to the sea, and the constant cool temperature. She'd planned to let this batch go another month, but the immature blue vinny was still good, if a bit crumbly.

"There's Ruford's skiff," Tony said, pointing to the cove. Four sailors were pulling on oars, bringing the captain ashore.

Baxter headed inland, presumably back to the inn where everyone anxiously waited for news, while the three of them went down to the beach.

Sylvia struggled to maintain her composure during the obligatory greetings and posturing by the three men. How could Tony joke and smile at a time like this? The fate of the village hung in the balance of whether or not Ruford liked her cheese.

They were prepared to offer smoked mackerel, and a bit more coin. Everyone had agreed to take a smaller percentage of the profits if necessary. Something was better than nothing. But they were all counting on the cheese to sway the captain to their side.

At last Ruford took the chunk Tony offered, and placed it in his mouth.

Sylvia held her breath.

Ruford spat it out, his face wrinkled with disgust. "What the hell kind of bilge waste are you offering?" He spit a few more times and wiped his mouth on his sleeve. "That's the most vile—I wouldn't feed that to my dog, if I had one! It tastes like the bottom of the harbor at low tide!"

"What?" Tony cut another chunk and took a bite. And immediately spat it out. He fought to keep his features from twisting. "All right, *that* batch didn't turn out so well, but you heard what Tipton said last night about—"

"I'm very sorry, my dear." Ruford lifted her hand for a kiss. "But I cannot accept your counteroffer. Our agreement is at an end." He almost ran for the skiff waiting at the water's edge. "I wish you the best of luck in finding another captain. You shouldn't have any trouble now, with your new husband to act on your behalf." The last line was practically shouted, as they were already several feet from shore, his men pulling the oars with powerful strokes.

"But . . ." It was useless. Ruford had his back to her, and the wind carried her words in the wrong direction.

"He didn't even give us a chance to offer the fish!" Jimmy went on to describe the captain's dubious parentage.

How could it all go so terribly wrong, so fast? How could they get another captain in time? It had taken months of searching filthy, smoke-filled dockside taverns to find Ruford. She couldn't go through that again.

Ruford had implied that Tony would act on their behalf, make it easier this time to find other ships, other captains. But Tony would never stay. He'd given his word he'd help her deal with Ruford, and the lecherous captain no longer presented a problem. At least, not the problem Tony had agreed to help with. And since she had no intention of giving in to his charms and falling into his bed, he'd probably be on his way soon.

Today, even.

She shivered, suddenly cold to her bones.

Tony was about to leave, and Ruford's skiff was receding from view, a small dot in the distance, just as their chances of survival were fading.

Suddenly Tony's arms were around her shoulders, drawing her in close. She buried her face against his cravat, feeling the hot prick of tears. She refused to let them fall.

"Here, sweetheart." He kissed her temple and ran his hands up and down her back in a vain attempt to soothe her. She clutched his lapels, holding on for dear life.

"What do we do now?" Jimmy sounded as young and forlorn as when he'd received news of the shipwreck and Hubert's death.

"It will be all right," Tony whispered.

It was not all right. Things would never be all right again.

"Well, I suppose that's that. I might as well join my cousin in Canada." Sawyer was the first to break the stunned silence in the crowded taproom after Jimmy had relayed the news.

Sylvia sat on one of the benches before the cold, empty fireplace, Tony next to her, his arm wrapped around her shoulders. He hadn't broken physical contact since their hug on the beach.

"My nevvy's been after me to move in with him and his passel of brats," Mrs. Pitsnoggle said. "He says Dorchester will be better for me health than living by the sea, but I knows he just wants someone else to help look after them ankle-biters."

There were a few other mutterings in a similar vein. After the storm in April, a few villagers had moved away rather than try to rebuild. Several had left last year, after the shipwreck. Those who stayed had done so because of the promise of reward from smuggling. A chance to rebuild their lives, their homes, their village.

And now that hope was gone.

Uncle Walcott had written again last week, renewing his offer to let her come live with him in Manchester. Practically insisted. And if she was staying out of loyalty to Jimmy, he could take care of that—as Jimmy's guardian, he could force the boy to move to Manchester, as well.

Sylvia gazed out the window at the rolling sea, the windswept cliffs, the twisting High Street lined with rhododendrons, neat little cottages and their gardens. Even the roofless cottages had a stark beauty.

She'd left Manchester on a cold November day. A dense yellow fog had hung low over the city, shrouding the smoke-belching cotton factories the coach rolled past on her way to the port. She had struggled to grow anything in the tiny garden of Walcott's town house. She'd missed her parents' cozy home in the Cotswolds, where she and her mother had grown all the herbs they needed without any difficulty. All except the herbs that would save them from the smallpox epidemic that had swept through.

A few years later, marrying Uncle Walcott's business partner and moving to the remote Dorset coast, leaving behind the houseful of rambunctious cousins and crowded, dirty city, had seemed like a godsend.

Now her husband was gone, and their method of supporting the remaining villagers seemed to be gone, as well. But she would not allow Jimmy to be torn from his ancestral home, crumbling edifice that it was. The two fishing boats could bring in enough fish to keep them all from starving. She would find out what went wrong with the cheese, and go back to the boring traditional methods of production.

Life was about moving forward. She was not going back.

She would find a way to survive. Here.

Tony slipped out of the taproom and headed down to the beach. The villagers were all so busy crying into their ale, he doubted anyone would miss him. Even Sylvia could barely look at anything but her fists clenched in her lap.

Something had been wrong this morning, and not just the briny cheese. Ruford had scurried back to his ship like a frightened rat.

Had Teague already made his counter to their counteroffer? The man seemed awfully certain he could move as much cargo as he wanted, whenever he wanted to move it. Tony would bet his last penny Ruford was actually afraid to sell his illicit cargo to anyone but Teague now.

He needed to know why. He needed to make Sylvia smile again, to lift the weight of defeat from her slender shoulders.

Ruford was on his ship, anchored out in the cove, unlikely to come ashore again anytime soon. Tony heard the first mate shout the order to weigh anchor.

Their last hope was about to sail out to sea.

Did he need to do this badly enough to row out there in a little boat, tossed about on the merciless waves? He could swim to the ship. Nick had tried to drown him when they were twelve, but succeeded in teaching him to swim instead.

But once out there he'd still have to climb aboard

the cutter, which was bobbing on the waves, back and forth. In constant motion.

The anchor clanged up and locked in place. There wasn't enough time to swim. He fought down the nausea.

He grabbed a skiff leaning up against the cliff and dragged it between the fishing boats to the water's edge, then ran back for the oars. Before he could talk himself out of it, he pushed off and started rowing.

Sylvia realized Tony had disappeared while she'd been lost in her thoughts. She missed his comforting presence at her side. She'd have to get used to that. She blinked back a tear, refusing to let it fall.

She interrupted Corwin, who'd been discussing possible employment opportunities at the Swanage docks. "You are not moving to Swanage." She pointed to Sawyer. "You are not emigrating to Canada. And you"—she pointed at Mrs. Pitsnoggle—"are not going to become an unpaid governess to your nephew's children. We are all staying right here. Baxter, please show me which cave you got the cheese from this morning."

Baxter closed his mouth with a snap, then jumped up from his chair. "Yes, my lady."

She followed him out, her back straight, knowing every eye in the room was on her. They were all counting on her. She wouldn't let them down. Again.

"Ahoy!" Tony called as he neared the cutter.

After some grumbling from the men above, a rope ladder was rolled over the side, and Tony climbed up.

"Don't worry, I didn't bring any cheese," he said once he'd been led to Ruford on the aft deck.

"You shouldn't be here." Ruford's gaze darted between Tony and the companionway hatch.

"I just came to find out why you refuse to sell us your cargo. It's as if it didn't matter what we offered as counter to Teague—your mind was made up. Why is that, I wonder?"

"Because that's the way it is." Teague emerged from the companionway near the wheel.

Oh, hell. This did not bode well for Sylvia and her men.

Ruford stepped back, as though in deference to Teague.

Tony kept his expression carefully neutral. "Are you going to let him bully you on your own ship?"

Ruford seemed to locate part of his spine, and stood a little taller. "It is simply good business. I'm selling to the highest bidder for the highest profit."

The wind shifted, and Tony was caught downwind of the captain. That, combined with the constant rocking motion of the deck, made him really wish he'd skipped breakfast. He swallowed down the bile and turned to Teague. "What makes you so certain you can safely move the extra loads? Have you bought off all the Revenue agents and excisemen in the area?"

"Just the important ones." Teague rocked back on his heels.

"Why, thank you for the compliment."

Tony stared at the man standing in the shadow of the mainmast. "Tipton?"

"Good morning, Mr. Sinclair." Tipton moved out of the shadows. "You really should have stayed in bed with your wife."

"You should have stayed in bed too, Tipton." Danielson had just climbed the ladder from belowdecks, and stood beside Teague. Ruford took a step to the side, looking as if he wished everyone would just get off his ship. His crew stood around, murmuring, seeming as uneasy as Tony felt.

"You're a busy man, Captain," Tony said to Ruford. "Three appointments in one morning?"

"No appointments," Ruford grumbled. "They just showed up. One after another."

"Sir?" At the sight of Danielson, the color drained from Tipton's face. "I—I don't understand."

Teague sneered. "Did you really think you could take my coin and then turn me in?"

Tipton ignored Teague, and spoke to Danielson. "I told you about the plan. We could have charged him with bribery as well as smuggling, and be certain he hung for it!"

"Yes, but your plan interferes with mine. You may be happy with the pittance we're paid, but I am not. Mr. Teague is making it worth my while to look the other way."

"But you can't! That's—"

"Shut up!" Tony hissed. Tipton demonstrated the self-preservation instincts of a lemming, and continued to sputter his moral outrage at his supervisor. Teague was caressing the two pistols stuck in his belt, sending a chill down Tony's spine.

"I believe Mr. Tipton is going to pose a problem," Danielson said.

"No trouble at all." Teague drew one of his pistols.

Bloody hell. On a moving deck, he was just as likely to hit Tony as Tipton.

Tipton was still babbling, his attention focused on Danielson, completely oblivious to his mortal danger from Teague and shushing motions from Tony.

Teague raised his arm and cocked the pistol.

Sylvia picked her way among the rocks and tide pools at the water's edge, following Baxter to the caves. The first two were large and deep, used for temporarily storing the brandy, though the first was empty at the moment.

The third cave was wide but too shallow, and filled up at high tide, which was just coming in. They'd have to hurry, or end up swimming back. The fourth and fifth were deep enough but too narrow for more than one person, and so usually weren't used. With lots of outcroppings as natural shelves and a near-constant temperature, though, they had seemed an ideal place in which to ripen the cheese.

Baxter finally stopped at the fifth cave. Sylvia ducked past him and entered the cool, damp interior. Instead of being neatly stacked at the far end where she had placed them, cheese rounds were carelessly heaped on the nearer, lower outcroppings—below the high tide watermark.

"Baxter!" Sylvia took a deep breath as her shout

echoed off the cave walls, and forced her fists to un-clench.

"Yes, my lady?"

"Someone moved the cheese. Do you know any-thing about it?" She was proud that none of her anger slipped into her voice.

He ducked his head and peered into the entrance. "I think it might have been moved last month, or maybe after the first load of tubs we landed. Yes, that's it—we needed to put some tubs back there." He pointed.

She squinted into the darkness at the back of the cave. Now that she looked closer, there were a couple of tubs, forgotten on the farthest, highest shelf.

"Guess we forgot to move the cheese back when there was room to move the tubs to the other caves."

She wanted to pound her head against the cave wall. Well, pound someone's head against the wall. A wave washed in, soaking her skirt to the knees. A cheese round bumped against her shin, floating on the incom-ing tide. How many had washed away altogether?

At least now she knew why the cheese had tasted like low tide.

There were still at least a dozen ripening rounds, to-tally useless. Well, maybe they could let them ripen a few months longer and use them as spare cart wheels.

She marched out into the bright light. There were several dozen other rounds ripening in her stillroom, the cellar, and other places. Safe places. All was not lost. Though she doubted she could ever convince Ru-ford to try another taste.

She started to pick her way back to the beach when she glanced at the *Polly Anne*. Men on deck were shouting and running, climbing the rigging, setting the sails. She pulled out her spyglass and trained it on the ship.

Ruford was at the helm, but Teague was there, too, pointing a gun at Tipton, and . . . Oh, dear heaven, what was Tony doing on the ship?

Before Teague could fire, Tony lunged for Tipton, intending to shove him over the side and follow him into the water. But one of the sailors stepped in the way, and knocked Tony and Tipton to the deck.

"I knew it," Ruford muttered. "A bloody hero. The damsel in distress wasn't enough, you have to try to save the idiot as well."

Tony sat up, but with the sailor looming over him, didn't try to stand. "Even an idiot has the right to live."

"Hey!" the idiot objected.

"Meddling amateurs," Teague said. "I'll see to it they don't interfere anymore. Them and all their cohorts. Captain, get under way. We'll dispose of these two out in the Channel, and let the tide take care of the bodies."

"Fine, fine, just don't get any blood on my deck." Ruford gave the order to Crowther, who shouted commands to the crew.

Most of the crew sprang into action, but not the brute standing behind Tony. Several other men also loitered nearby. Neither Ruford nor Crowther seemed to mind. Tony swept his gaze up and down the man standing over him.

Boots. The loitering men were all wearing boots. The crewmen heaving on the ropes to hoist the sails were all barefoot, as were those who'd climbed the rigging.

No wonder Teague was so confident, with members of his gang on board.

The wind caught the billowing canvas with a snap, and the ship lurched. So did Tony's stomach.

"Just where do y'think you're going?" The brute grabbed the back of Tony's collar as he got to his knees.

"If the captain doesn't want any blood on his deck, I doubt he wants—" Tony lurched for the railing and leaned over the side, heaving his guts out. The grip on his collar prevented him from jumping overboard.

His stomach empty, seeing the waves crash against the ship's side made Tony's head spin. He stood up on shaky legs, one hand on the brute's shoulder to keep from falling. "Thanks, chum."

"S'are'right." The brute was a good six inches taller and twice as wide as Tony, with hands like hams. Said hands were pulling Tony away from the railing, his feet barely touching the deck.

"Tie them up," Teague shouted.

"Aye, boss," the brute said, and started to push Tony down.

"If you would be so kind," Tony said. The man

grunted in surprise, and paused in his shoving. "I became ill while I was down on the deck. If you let me, say, sit on that locker at the stern so that I might see the cliffs, perhaps we can avoid a nasty repeat of the experience, and keep the good captain's deck clean?"

The brute thought that through, shrugged, and shoved Tony down onto the locker. While he tied Tony's hands behind his back, another of Teague's men tied his ankles together. Two others did the same to Tipton, and shoved him onto the locker beside Tony.

"I knew you was up to no good," Tipton said. "Newlywed, my arse."

"In case you've forgotten, I just saved your sorry arse a minute ago."

Tipton opened his mouth to retort, but one of the brutes held up a kerchief. "He didn't say I had to gag you, but I will iff'n you both don't shut up."

"Mum's the word," Tony said. The brutes glared at Tony and Tipton for a moment, then the one put his kerchief away.

The four stayed close by, though their attention wandered. Teague and Danielson conferred near the wheel, where Ruford was steering the ship out of the cove, headed for open sea. The cliffs at their back were already receding as the ship picked up speed.

The increased motion made Tony light-headed. The meager contents of his stomach sloshed around, threatening to come up again at any moment.

"You're looking a might green there, chum." At least the brute didn't laugh.

"Thanks ever so much for pointing that out," Tony groused.

What an ignominious end. If he'd lunged right instead of left, he could have jumped overboard while Teague shot Tipton, and swum to safety in the calm waters of the cove. Instead he'd merely bought a little time, perhaps only minutes.

And Sylvia . . . He swallowed a lump in his throat that had nothing to do with the ship's movement. He'd known he'd leave her soon, but not like this. Not like this.

Well, they weren't dead yet.

Their guards stared out as the ship sailed past the mouth of the cove, the rocks disconcertingly close. Tony scooted closer to Tipton and stretched his arms. His fingers scrabbled on the man's sleeve, until Tipton finally understood what was going on and moved closer. A little more, a little . . . there. Tony got his fingers on the rope around Tipton's wrists and worked at the knot. Sweat broke out on his brow and upper lip, slid down the small of his back, and made his fingers slick.

The brutes were still staring at the receding cove. Now out on the open water, the ship's bow lifted high on a wave, dipped low into the trough. Tony fought to keep from heaving, concentrating on the knot. Just the knot.

It broke free. Tony twisted and stretched his wrists out so Tipton could return the favor.

Tipton jumped up, struck the brute nearest him, and wrested the pistol from the man's belt as he fell.

Tony stood and hobbled to the side, out of the way of the falling man, but his hands and ankles were still tied. The other brutes swung at Tipton. He fired the pistol. Another man fell.

"Shoot them!" Teague roared, and raised his own pistol.

Tipton swung his spent pistol at another of the brutes. Teague cursed.

With a deafening blast, another pistol fired near Tony. He blinked as blood splattered him. Tipton fell backward, over the railing.

Teague raised his pistol, aimed between Tony's eyes.

The ship rose on a wave, as did the bile in Tony's throat. He lurched to the left, ready to heave.

Teague fired.

Pain exploded in Tony's right temple just before he sailed through the air, and then slammed into the water. He sank into its cold depths.

Chapter 15

◇◯◇

With her spyglass still trained on the receding ship, Sylvia heard the pistol fire, saw Tipton fall over the railing. A heartbeat later, there was another pistol shot. Tony flew backward over the side. "No!"

The *Polly Anne* kept going as though Sylvia's world hadn't just ended.

"Bloody hell!" Baxter shouted, echoing her thoughts. "I don't believe it. I saw it with me own eyes, but I don't bloody believe it." He slumped down on one of the rocks. "I'm right sorry, my lady," he murmured a moment later, his hand on her sleeve.

No. Perhaps . . . Perhaps the shots had missed. A moving deck, a poor marksman . . . No pistol fired true—how many times had Hubert complained of that?

"We have to go get them," Sylvia said, shoving the

spyglass in her pocket and scrambling over the rocks. "We have to get them before they drown."

"But, my lady . . ." Baxter trailed off at the glare she gave him. "Yes, my lady. We'll go get them."

Agonizing minutes later they had a skiff in the water, Baxter rowing toward the mouth of the cove as Sylvia searched the water ahead. "Faster, row faster!"

"Going as fast . . . as I can," Baxter wheezed.

Sylvia shielded her eyes with one hand, scanning the surface, then groaned in frustration and pulled out the spyglass again. Speeding along on the west-southwesterly wind, the *Polly Anne* was now too far away for her to see the men on deck. Probably headed for Worbarrow Bay. She hoped they wrecked on Mupe Rocks.

She lowered her gaze to the water's surface, trying to scan every inch at once. If Tony couldn't swim, he'd already be drowning. They had to find him, fast. The skiff rose and fell on the waves. "I think I see something. A little to your right, to the right!" She stood up to get a better look. "Pull, man, pull!"

They drew alongside the dark object floating in the water. Sylvia dropped to her knees, reached out, grabbed his shoulder, and yanked.

Tipton rolled over in the water, staring up at the sky with sightless eyes. The sea had washed away the blood from the gaping hole in his forehead.

Sylvia let go with a gasp. No, no, no . . .

Baxter rested the oars in the locks. "Keep the boat steady, my lady." He grabbed Tipton and hauled him up and in, to the bottom of the boat, while Sylvia kept them from tipping over.

If Tony had suffered the same fate . . .

It was all her fault. He had become mixed up in their dangerous affairs because of her. He had put his life at risk, for her.

But what had he been doing out on Ruford's ship, with Teague, putting himself in such danger?

Tony better not be dead, because she was going to wring his neck.

She glanced at Tipton's lifeless body, and shuddered. She'd never again see Tony's brown eyes sparkle with mischief or smolder with desire. Hear his husky voice whisper outrageous suggestions just to get a rise out of her. Feel the beat of his heart beneath her cheek. Taste his kiss.

He'd made her come alive, and now he was dead.

"My lady."

She looked up at Baxter's touch on her hand. She couldn't bear to see the anguish in his face, which must mirror that of her own. She cleared her throat and stared out at the waves. They still needed to retrieve Tony's body.

Something bobbed near the surface a few yards away. "Up ahead—" Her voice broke. She coughed, tried again. "Up ahead, to your left."

Baxter pulled on the oars with grim determination. Soon they reached what had caught Sylvia's eye. Like Tipton, he was floating facedown, but with his hands tied behind his back. Motionless.

Sylvia swallowed. She would not cry. Not here, not now.

Later. When she was alone. Just as she would be alone for the rest of her life.

She took a deep, fortifying breath, and reached for Tony.

Just as her hand touched his cold shoulder, he popped up, head and shoulders above the water, gulping for air.

Sylvia shrieked. A heartbeat later, she grabbed him, crying out his name. She was overbalanced, his weight too much to bear, threatening to pull her into the water. She was too happy to care.

"'Bout bloody time," Tony gasped, and started to sink. Water ran down his face, his dark hair plastered to his head, dripping into his eyes.

Baxter caught Tony's collar before his chin slid below the water.

"Permission to come aboard." He shook his head, water spraying everywhere. Blood oozed from a wound on his temple.

Baxter chuckled. "Aye, matey." He leaned over to grab Tony more securely.

The boat tilted, the side dipping almost to the water's edge. Sylvia leaned the other way while Baxter hauled Tony into the skiff. Both men were gasping for breath by the time Tony lay sprawled on the bottom of the boat. He quickly rolled to the side, away from Tipton, and struggled to his knees.

"Miss me?" Water still dripped into his eyes, which sparkled with humor.

Sylvia gave a watery chuckle. She touched his cheek, his shoulders, and slid her hand down to his chest, over his heart, which beat as fast and hard as her own.

"If you'd be so kind," Tony said over his shoulder. "I can't feel my hands."

Baxter fumbled at the wet knot, cursing.

Sylvia pushed aside her damp skirt and retrieved her knife from her half-boot, her hands shaking. It was the first time she'd ever needed to use the blade. Now she was delighted she'd taken up the habit of carrying it.

"No offense, sweetheart, but I like my appendages the way they are."

She nodded and passed the knife to Baxter, who made short work of the ropes binding Tony's hands and ankles.

Tony rubbed his raw, red wrists. "Ah, much be—"

Sylvia kissed him. His lips were cold and wet but soon warmed, soft and welcoming. He threaded his fingers in her hair and she shivered at his cold touch, reminded how close he had come to the coldness of death. She threw her arms around him and pulled him closer, not caring the rest of her dress was getting soaked.

There it was—his heartbeat, next to hers. Tears began to fall, rolling unchecked, hot against her cheeks.

"Shh, sweetheart, it's all right," he whispered. "Takes more than a pistol shot to do me in."

She laughed, a shaky sound, and sniffed. Baxter handed her a kerchief. She wiped her eyes.

"Here you go, my lady." Baxter gave the knife back to Sylvia.

Tony moved to the bench beside Sylvia while she tucked her knife away. Baxter started rowing for the beach, and the crowd of onlookers who'd gathered. Sylvia wrapped her arms around Tony, not caring who saw, or that she was getting even more wet. She was never going to let go of him. He pressed a kiss to her temple.

"You're one lucky bast—bugger, sir."

That wasn't the half of it, Sylvia agreed silently. Her throat was too clogged to try to speak. Tipton at their feet was too close a reminder of what could have happened. She tightened her grip on Tony's waist, and felt him shiver. She let go, reluctantly, while he shrugged out of his coat and laid it over Tipton, then clamped on again when Tony straightened.

He reached up to brush something from his eye, and she realized he was still bleeding. She untucked her fichu, folded it into a narrow strip, and wound it around his head. It would have to do until she got him home.

"How did you possibly manage to hold your breath that long?" Baxter pulled on the oars, every stroke bringing them closer to safety.

"I didn't." Tony rubbed his hand down her back. "One of the benefits of having friends who tried to do me in on a regular basis when we were lads at school was learning all sorts of interesting tricks. Won many a wager with that one. Never thought I'd have to use it for real, though."

Tony suddenly realized he was in a boat out on the

waves, and did not feel sick. Might have something to
do with the woman clinging to his side. Or the after-
math of nearly dying.

He started to shake. Nerves or cold, he couldn't really tell. His head pounded. Sylvia tightened her arms
around him, and he wrapped her more securely in his
embrace. When he'd been sinking into the cold water,
he'd thought he'd never hold her again. He brushed
another kiss to her temple, drinking in her clean scent,
the hint of herbs, feeling her silky hair.

Soon he heard the crunch of gravel as the skiff
grounded on the beach. They were surrounded by people who had watched his rescue from the sea, and were
now excitedly chattering away nineteen to the dozen,
pulling him out of the boat and away from the beach.

He answered their questions as best he could as
they led him up the path and to a cart that carried them
to the manor house. Sylvia stayed at his side until they
reached the hall outside their bedchambers. Mrs. Hayden pulled her along to her room, clucking about the
state of her wet gown, while Baxter and Gerald gave
Tony a push into his room.

With their assistance, he was soon toweled off and
into clean clothes, his wet garments hung up to dry.
His boots, alas, would never be the same.

"My Galen is warming something up in the
kitchen," Gerald said, giving him a tug toward the
door, "and there's a nice fire going in the rose salon."

"And there's brandy down there, too." Baxter took
him by the other arm, and they helped him down the
stairs.

Tony went along for the ride, feeling a bit dazed. He'd nearly died today. At least twice. The man beside him *had* died, his blood splattering all over. Tony looked down at his hands, his chest. No sign. The sea had washed Tipton's blood away, as if the killing had never happened. As if Tipton had never lived, let alone died a violent death.

Was there any sign remaining that he had passed time on earth? Had he left behind any legacy besides failure?

What was happening to Tipton's body? Tony didn't realize he'd spoken the words aloud until Baxter answered.

"Doyle and Corwin are taking care of 'im. Don't you worry none, sir."

The chattering crowd from the beach had moved into the rose salon, but they parted to make a path to the sofa near the fireplace. "Here you go, laddie." Mrs. Miggins tucked a knitted throw around his shoulders.

He clutched it close, surprised to see that his hands trembled, even more surprised she hadn't tried to pinch him as he'd passed. "Th-thank you, Marge."

She smiled and tenderly patted his cheek, then bellowed over her shoulder, "Where's that gel with her bag?"

"I got the bag, Syl," Jimmy shouted from the hallway.

Someone thrust a glass of brandy into Tony's hand, urged it toward his mouth. He took a swallow and felt it burn down his throat, to his empty stomach. He took another drink, feeling the warmth spread through him, and then another.

Sylvia hurried into the room, clutching a shawl around her shoulders. She'd been in such a hurry to change, she hadn't bothered with shoes. Bare toes peeked from beneath her gray gown. She sat beside him on the sofa, opened the bag Jimmy held for her, and pulled out her supplies.

"Make a hole, people, make a hole," Galen shouted at the crowd, entering the room with a tray held high over her head. The bodies parted like the Red Sea.

Galen set the tray down on the nearest table, and plucked the brandy from his hand. "Put something solid in your stomach to go with those spirits, lad." She replaced the glass with a chunk of cheese.

Tony saw what she had given him, and chuckled. The chuckle gave way to laughter. He couldn't stop. Tears squeezed from the corners of his eyes.

Sylvia took the cheese from him and closed his fingers around a fresh scone, still warm from the oven.

As soon as he'd taken a bite, she tilted his head back and dabbed a cloth at the wound on his temple. When had someone taken away the scarf she'd wrapped around his head out in the boat? He wanted to keep that.

"It just grazed you," Sylvia murmured.

Her touch was wonderful but whatever was on the cloth stung, and made his eyes water again. Stung so much it made her eyes water, too.

"Good thing we saved the sticking plaster for something more serious, eh?" She gave a watery chuckle.

He brushed her tear away with his thumb. "Yes," he whispered.

The sticking plaster applied, she turned her attention to his wrists, rubbing liniment where the rope had left raw marks.

Sawyer thumped him on the shoulder. "Good thing ye've a hard head, laddie."

"Yes," Tony murmured. He glanced up at the room full of people, all faces and names he should know but couldn't quite connect one to the other at the moment. They didn't seem to mind, as they continued to talk amongst themselves, occasionally glancing his way, pointing at him, gesturing, retelling the tale of the morning's adventure.

His hands had almost stopped shaking. Seemed it was contagious, though, as Sylvia was now trembling. He lifted his arm and wrapped her next to him, pulling the throw over her. He half expected someone to object, but Mrs. Miggins tucked the throw around them both and shooed everyone away.

Sylvia snuggled against his side and locked her arms around his waist, banishing the chill from the Channel that had lingered in his bones. Her warm breath puffed against his neck.

The crowd lingered, reluctant to leave, and he realized he was looking at Sylvia's legacy. Her courage, hard work, and ingenuity had kept this community together through difficult times. If she died, she would be remembered, missed. Could the same be said of Tony?

He thought back to that first night out of London, when he'd shivered on a rooftop while Alistair had gazed at the stars. Tony had been looking for a cause to take up, something to do. Well, there was plenty to do here in Lulworth Cove. And it involved ships, after all.

His search for direction had led him straight here to Sylvia. Here he could have purpose, make a difference. Make a life for himself that had meaning.

He sighed in contentment. This was where he belonged. Where Sylvia belonged. Here, in his arms, close to his heart. "Sweet, sweet Sylvia," he murmured, stroking her soft curls.

Tony opened his eyes. Didn't remember closing them, but he must have, else why would he be staring up at the ceiling, his head resting on the sofa back?

Sylvia was still cuddled up against him, under the throw. Her feet were up on the sofa, tucked under the edge of her gown. Her eyes were closed, her breathing deep and steady.

Mrs. Miggins was stretched out on the other sofa, snoring. Jimmy leaned against the chair opposite, slouched on the floor.

"At least we still 'ave the fishing boats, so's no one will go hungry," Baxter was saying. He was sitting on the floor, his back against the sofa near Sylvia's feet, a glass in his hand. He reached for the nearly empty decanter on the floor beside him, and saw Tony.

"Hey, he's back wi' us." Baxter kicked Jimmy's foot.

"Eh? What?" Jimmy smacked his lips and reached for his glass, knocking it over in the process. Good thing it was empty.

"Think you've had enough, cub." Tony kept his

voice low, not wanting to wake Sylvia. The rest of the crowd had apparently left while Tony rested his eyes, leaving just the five of them in the salon. Mrs. Miggins snorted and rolled over in her sleep, presenting her back.

Baxter chuckled. "D'you know, there never was a Mr. Miggins."

"What? No!" Jimmy muffled his snort of laughter.

"S'true." Baxter gave a solemn nod. "She was working at the seaside in Weymouth when Farmer George came for a visit. He took a fancy to her."

"The king?" Jimmy's jaw gaped.

"None other. Insisted she attend him at his bathing machine. Even had her taken up to Lon'n when Parliament went back into session. She stayed there for years, a maid at the palace."

Tony tried to picture a younger Marge pinching His Majesty's arse.

"Hey." Baxter slapped Tony's shin. "You was goin' tell us how you kept from drowning."

"Ah." He cleared his throat. Baxter handed him a full glass. The brandy slid down his throat, warm and soothing. Or maybe it was having Sylvia in his arms that was warm and soothing. "Your instinct is to struggle against the ropes, to break free of the knot so you can swim. But the water makes the knot tighter, and while you struggle, you sink."

Jimmy folded his legs, leaning toward Tony to catch every word. "So what do you do?"

"Put your nose between your knees."

Baxter bent forward, his nose nowhere near the vicinity of his knees. "Then what?"

"Then you wait until you feel your back break the water's surface."

Jimmy's brows shot up. "What? Don't you sink? How can you float?"

Tony put his finger to his lips, then pointed at Sylvia. Jimmy clapped his hand over his mouth.

"Then what, mate?" Baxter was still straining to reach his knees with his nose.

"When your back breaks the surface, you breathe out, and pop up like a jack-in-the-box."

Baxter popped up with such force he hit his head on the sofa cushion.

Tony grinned. "Just like that. You take a breath before you sink, then bend over and do it all again."

"Cor blimey, what a trick!" Jimmy giggled.

"Take his drink away, would you?" Tony nudged Baxter with his toe.

Gerald appeared in the doorway. "Dinner will be served in ten minutes." He clicked his heels, bowed, and left.

Jimmy tilted his head to one side. "I forgot he used to be just the butler." He scratched his chin. "Everybody has to do so many jobs these days."

Sylvia sat up, blinking and rubbing her eyes. She peered down at her bare toes and tried to cover them with her skirt.

"No one noticed, sweetheart," Tony whispered.

Sylvia turned her sleepy green gaze on him, and

something in his chest tightened. He pictured how she'd look after lovemaking, sated and drowsy. His breathing quickened.

"How's your head?" She reached to check the bandage, smoothing his hair out of the way.

He leaned into her touch. "Probably feel even better after a meal."

Her eyes widened. "Oh, my goodness. Galen will never let me live it down if I come to the table barefoot." She dashed from the room.

Tony watched her retreat, grinning. After nearly dying, it felt good to think of something as mundane as proper dinner attire.

"Aye, he's a goner," Baxter said, climbing to his feet. "Knew it from the moment she sat on 'im and he put his hand on her a—"

"I—what?" Tony stood up, a little too fast.

Baxter steadied him, then reached a hand to pull Jimmy up. "Come along, Auntie," he called. He shook Marge's shoulder. "Time to eat."

She sat up. "What's that? Someone mention food?"

They soon had Mrs. Miggins on her feet and moving toward the dining room. She insisted on taking Tony's arm, which he didn't mind, since that should keep him safe from her penchant for pinching. Baxter kept a hand on his other elbow, as he was still a bit wobbly on his feet. With Jimmy alongside, it was an interesting shuffle to get the four of them through the doorway.

"Marge!"

* * *

After the dishes were cleared, they all stayed at the table, discussing inconsequential topics. No one wanted to bring up the subject of Tony nearly dying, but neither did they seem willing to let him out of their sight. Sylvia kept a close eye on him, looking for any signs of slurred speech, blurry vision, or other problems stemming from his injuries this morning.

It had been too close. It was a miracle he had survived when Tipton did not. She just wasn't that lucky. Someone must have been watching over him for her.

It was Tony who finally broached the topic. "Did you know that Danielson is crooked as a corkscrew?" He took a sip of his tea, one of Galen's "restorative" cups. "Bought and paid for."

"Tipton's boss?" Baxter poured himself a second glass of brandy, and offered some to Sylvia.

She declined. "That explains why Teague thinks he can move his cargoes at will."

"That rat bastard." Jimmy slammed his fist on the table.

Mrs. Miggins chortled and pointed a bony finger at Jimmy. "What he said."

"Easy, lad." Baxter patted Jimmy's arm.

"We're still left with the problem of whom to buy our cargoes from, since Ruford is afraid to sell to anyone but Teague." Sylvia sighed.

"In good weather, maybe we could just sail the fishing boats over to Cherbourg and fetch the brandy ourselves." Jimmy turned to Baxter. "Would it be safe taking the boats that far?"

Baxter furrowed his brow. "Aye, we could certainly

sail across the Channel. It would be coming back, loaded down with casks, that would be risky. And our fishing smacks would have no chance of outrunning any Revenue cutters."

"Stop talking about nonsensical things," Mrs. Miggins said. "Let's be practical. It was kind of the Doyles to take me in, but their ankle-biters is getting on me nerves. When are you going to fix it so I can move back into me own cottage?"

Tony brought up several ideas he'd had for rebuilding the house, which had been smashed in the storm by a falling oak. He soon became frustrated drawing with slate and chalk, so Sylvia fetched paper and pencil. She propped her chin on her hand, her elbow on the table, and watched in fascination as he drew, making a three-dimensional object come to life on a flat piece of paper.

It was good to have plans, to have dreams, but how could they possibly rebuild Baxter's cottage now? Until they found another captain, another ship, there would be no money for rebuilding. She kept her concerns to herself, not wanting to spoil everyone's evening.

"Put more windows in there, lad. I need lots of light for my sewing."

"Yes, ma'am." He added a few more lines here, moved them there, then pushed the paper in front of Mrs. Miggins. "How's that?"

She harrumphed her approval.

"How do you know how to do this?" Jimmy mirrored Sylvia's position, chin in his hand, following Tony's every move.

"What, draw?" He added a few more touches to the sketch. "A legacy of my misspent youth. I was often scribbling when I should have been paying attention to my tutors."

"But how do you know how to draw a cottage, as opposed to, say, a bird?"

Tony flipped the paper over. Within a few strokes, Sylvia recognized a gull taking shape. He pushed it in front of Jimmy, who duly admired it.

Sylvia flipped the paper back over. "But this is not merely a sketch of a cottage—it's more like a building plan."

He shrugged. "We had to rebuild several shepherd's huts on my family's estate a few years back. I wanted to make sure we replaced them with something that would last, so I did a little research, hired an architect." He tapped the drawing. "This should withstand any storm the Channel blows our way, for many years to come."

There was that word again—"our." Was it just a figure of speech for him, or was he actually thinking of himself as one of them, planning to stay?

She never wanted him to leave. If she'd had any doubts about the depth of her feelings, this morning's dramatic events had put them to rest. In spectacular fashion.

Baxter folded up the drawing and tucked it into his shirt, "Thank ye kindly, sir. Now I must get Auntie to bed. I'm going to help the lads fill a few barrels tonight, my lady. I'll see you in the morning."

She wasn't sure, but she thought Baxter winked at

Tony as Mrs. Miggins said her good-byes. Tony didn't actually blush, but he did duck his chin as Baxter gathered Mrs. Miggins and headed out.

Soon after their guests departed, the household settled in for the night. It felt odd not having someone sleeping in the dressing room. Jimmy followed Tony to his door, asking more pointed questions, wanting all the gory details of what it was like to be shot.

Horrified by the reminder, Sylvia shut out their conversation, and went through her usual routine and climbed into bed. But when she closed her eyes, she saw again Tony falling over the railing into the sea. Saw Tipton's lifeless body.

Petting Macbeth didn't calm her as it normally did. The cat jumped down from the bed after a few minutes and walked off in a huff, his tail quivering.

Perhaps some chamomile tea would calm her. Sylvia pulled on her wrapper and tiptoed down the back stairs.

Galen sat at the kitchen table in her nightclothes, sipping a cup of warm milk. "Can't get to sleep after your nap in the salon this afternoon, my lady?"

Sylvia refused to be embarrassed. It was perfectly normal for one to sleep for a time after one had been a trifle overset, as she had. She set the herbs to brewing. "I could ask why you aren't asleep."

"Gerald fell asleep first. Snoring fit to wake the dead." She took a sip. "Someone was watching over that young man of yours today."

Sylvia paused in the act of reaching for a cup. "He's not *my* young man."

"Someone watching over you, too, to send him your way."

It *had* seemed providential for Tony to arrive in their tiny village just when he was needed. Other travelers stopped through now and then, but few stayed.

Then again, no one had ever before been abducted by her band of smugglers.

"It's not easy, seeing your first corpse what ain't laid out in his coffin."

Sylvia's cup clattered as she set it on the table. "I keep seeing Tipton's face after we pulled him out of the water. And seeing Tony facedown . . ." Her hands shook as she strained her tea.

"Reminded me how fragile life is, and to spend all the time with my loved ones I can—you never know how long you've got. Which is why I'm going to wrap my arms around Gerald, though he be snoring louder than a pig in the sun." Galen patted her hand, then gave an exaggerated yawn. "I'll just toddle off to bed now, in case you want that bath you didn't get the other night."

Sylvia forced herself to meet Galen's knowing grin, and calmly sipped her chamomile tea.

"Tony may not be as tall as Hubert, God rest his soul," Galen said from the doorway, "but he ain't smaller."

Sylvia choked.

"Good night, my lady." Galen shuffled off in the direction of her quarters.

Sylvia forced herself to breathe.

She actually could be resentful, or at least a bit jealous. Galen had seen enough to make comparisons between the two men. Since she had rubbed liniment on Tony's bare back, Sylvia realized she had seen more of him than she ever had of her husband.

In four years of marriage, Hubert had never once appeared unclothed in her presence. Even when he visited her bedchamber, he had raised his nightshirt and her night rail rather than remove their garments. And he had always come to her in the dark of night. If she'd had a candle still lit, he blew it out.

Tony was upstairs now, in bed. She should check on him. He'd seemed fine at dinner, with no aftereffects of his brush with death, his gait steady and straight as they climbed the stairs and walked the hall. But sometimes injuries didn't manifest themselves right away. A cousin who'd been kicked in the head by his horse one morning had seemed fine that afternoon, but didn't wake up the next morning.

Tony had to wake up tomorrow. If he didn't, there'd be no point in the sun rising.

Chapter 16

Sylvia paused in the hall outside Tony's door and listened. Light spilled from under Jimmy's closed door farther up. She heard the usual creaks and groans as the house settled, but no sound came from within Tony's room. Was that good, or bad? She didn't even know if he snored.

She didn't want Jimmy to catch her in the hall, so she returned to her room and silently closed the door. Tonight she wouldn't hear Tony talking to her cat, because Macbeth had entered while she was gone and claimed her pillow. "Is His Majesty comfortable on his throne?" she whispered. He flipped his tail in greeting.

Sylvia stroked behind his ears, then tiptoed through the dressing room and put her ear against the other door.

Still no sound. She opened the door and peered inside.

Tony didn't snore.

Or perhaps he wasn't asleep yet?

Perhaps he made no sound because . . . No, she refused to complete that thought. "Oh, this is ridiculous," she muttered under her breath. She marched across the room to the hulking shadow of the bed, and stopped there to let her eyes adjust to the darkness. The fire had not been lit, and no moonlight shone through the open window.

She moved closer, to the head of the bed, and peered down at Tony's head on the pillow. His face was a pale blur against the bed linens, but she still couldn't tell if he was breathing.

She didn't want to disturb his slumber, but it would really disturb hers if she couldn't assure herself he was indeed fine. She reached out, intending to place her palm on his chest.

His hand shot out and grabbed her wrist.

She squeaked.

"Sylvia?" His low, husky voice washed over her like a caress. Without letting go of her, he sat up. The blankets slid down to his lap.

He wasn't wearing a nightshirt.

She licked suddenly dry lips. "I, ah, just wanted to check on you once more before I turned in. Head injuries can be unpredictable." There. That sounded plausible.

"Well then, let's be thorough, shall we?" He swung his legs over the side, clutching the blankets to his lap, and reached for the flint on the bedside table.

The candle flared to life, and Sylvia gasped.

Tony's bare upper torso gleamed in the candlelight. Her fingers itched to trace the strong planes and muscular curves, the slight smattering of dark, curly hair on his chest. He tilted his face up to her, arms at his sides, shoulders back. "Well?"

She swallowed. "Everything looks, um, fine."

He tilted his head to the side, eyeing her from beneath his lashes. "Really." He drawled the word out.

He was questioning her motives, her experience as a healer? She reserved that privilege for herself. To take a better look at his bandage, she shuffled a bit closer to the bed, her wrapper brushing his knee.

His *bare* knee.

Judging by the amount of flesh peeking out at the blanket's edge, which Tony held at his hip, *all* of him was bare.

She'd never before spoken to a naked man.

She forced herself to continue to breathe. After a few deep breaths, while he continued to watch her in silence, his lips curved in a slight smile, she reached out to conduct her examination. Her hands hardly shook at all as she checked his bandage. She ran her fingers through his silky hair, probing his skull for any knots or soft spots or other problems, just in case he'd hit rocks beneath the water's surface. His previous scalp wound, where Doyle had whacked him with a pitchfork, had completely healed.

Reluctantly, she stopped touching him and brought the candle close to his face. She bent her knees and peered into his eyes. With the light closer, his pupils contracted, revealing more of the rich brown irises. Delicate veins in the whites still appeared tiny, just as they ought. His eyes were crinkling at the corners.

She was not going to give in to his amusement. The memories of today's events were just too vivid, too frightening. She straightened, putting a little distance between them. "Your eyes appear to be normal, which is a good sign there's no damage to your brain. And there isn't any fresh blood on your bandage, which is also good. You'll probably have more of a scar here from the pistol shot than—" Her voice broke.

Someone had pointed a pistol at his head today, and fired. Tears welled in her eyes, choked her throat.

"Than what?" His voice low and husky, Tony rested his hands on her hips and slowly pulled her closer until she stood between his legs.

"Than from the tree branch that scratched you." She traced the line above his eyebrow, where the barely visible scratch was healing. His skin was warm. He was alive. She sobbed.

With her eyes squeezed shut against the tears, she felt herself being tugged and pushed until she sat on the bed beside Tony, her legs draped over his, his arms wrapped around her, enveloping her in his warmth and comfort.

She buried her face in the hollow between his shoulder and chest, and let the tears fall unchecked.

He held her tighter, one hand rubbing soothing circles on her back. He pressed a kiss to the top of her head. "Shh, sweetheart, it's all right."

The sound penetrated through the fog of her sobbing. There it was again, that endearment, when no one else was around to hear his playacting. She'd give almost anything for him to mean it, to truly be his sweetheart.

Her tears easing, she hiccupped. He kissed the top of her head again. Now she could think a little more clearly. Enfolded in his embrace, she inhaled his scent—a little lavender from the liniment, his own musk, a hint of the sea.

She sniffed, and he handed her a kerchief. She dried her eyes and sat up, pulling back slightly. Reflected by the candlelight, her wet tears glistened on his naked chest and ran in a rivulet down his flat stomach, stopping only at the blanket bunched in his lap. She swabbed the kerchief against his chest, drying her tears. She ran the soft linen over his bare skin, down his stomach and across his chest. His breath came faster. His curly chest hair sprang back after her touch, surprisingly crisp and coarse and utterly intriguing.

He groaned.

She jerked the kerchief away. "Did I hurt you?"

His head was tilted back, eyes closed. "Not in the way you think." He grabbed her hand that held the kerchief, and raised it to his lips for a kiss. "We started something at the bathtub the other night," he whispered, and kissed a trail up her arm to her neck, stopping just beneath her ear. With a sigh, he dropped his hands to the bed. "Unless you want to finish it, you have to leave. Now." He patted her knee. "A naked man with a beautiful woman on his lap cannot be held accountable for his actions."

She pulled back in surprise.

"What, you didn't know I was naked under here?"

She laughed. She felt giddy and light-headed. And she had to be with him, to touch him everywhere, re-assure herself in the most elemental way that he really was whole and healthy.

And to be brutally honest, she wasn't going to deny herself any longer. She wanted to succumb.

She grabbed his face for a kiss, leaning toward him until they toppled backward on the bed. They kissed, long and lingering, hands everywhere, touching, ca-ressing. "I really did just want to make sure you were all right," she said as he kissed his way along her jaw. "I didn't intend to wake you."

"I'm quite happy to be awake," he whispered in her ear. "Parts of me are *very* awake." The blankets had shifted as they kissed, uncovering Tony. He guided her hand down his chest, past his belly, lower, until she grasped him, and he wrapped her fingers around him.

"Oh, my." She explored his size and shape, stroking the warm velvet skin.

He groaned.

"Did that hurt?"

"It's torture." He thrust into her hand. "Do it again."

She did. Again and again.

His hands fell to the sides, clutching the sheets. His eyes were closed, head arched back as he lay beside her. The candle was still lit. Feeling quite bold, Sylvia rolled more to her side and raised up on one elbow, so she could see better. The healthy, aroused adult male, revealed in all his glory. Allowing, nay, *asking* for her touch. She was happy to oblige. She continued to explore, drinking in the sight laid out before her like a feast. She touched his chest, the planes and curves that had so intrigued her when she caught only glimpses of it, dipped her fingertips in the hollow of his throat, watched his Adam's apple move as he swallowed.

She tried not to be distracted by his fingers in the hair beside her ear, his thumb caressing her cheek. She concentrated on his reactions—his every sigh, moan, and sharply indrawn breath as she mapped the contours of his body, catalogued the differences between his and her own. Found more of the crisp, curly hair.

She glanced up, startled to see his eyes were open now, watching her every move. How long had he been staring while she behaved like a wanton? Mortified, she felt heat suffuse her cheeks. She clenched her hand, forgetting what she'd been holding just then.

Suddenly he rolled her onto her back, and leaned over her. "I want this to last," he whispered. "And it won't if you keep doing that."

He untied the belt at her waist and pulled her wrapper open, revealing her night rail. "So you do have at least one gown that isn't black or gray," he murmured. She glanced down at the thin pale blue cotton, the one she had worn for almost a decade. On their wedding night, Hubert had presented her with a heavy, long-sleeved, high-necked white night rail with a long row of tiny buttons. After his death, she'd cut it up to use for bandages. "This suits you," Tony continued, his fingers at her neckline drawstring. "You should always wear blue. Sky blue, to go with your sea-green eyes and sandy blonde hair." He untied the bow and slipped it open, baring her chest.

She gulped. "If you like it so much, why are you trying to remove it?"

"Because I like what's underneath even better." He leaned up on one elbow, tugging her gown open farther, off to one side, until it gaped and exposed her shoulder and breast. "Oh yes, much better."

She wanted to squeeze her eyes shut, to cover herself, to blow the candle out. But he had allowed her to look at him. It was only fair she let him do the same. Just, please hurry up about it.

But he didn't hurry. And he didn't just look.

He touched. He kissed her again, then trailed his fingertips from her lips, down her neck, along her chest, circled her breast. She braced herself, but instead of grabbing a fistful of flesh, Tony continued to circle with his fingertips, his touch feather light. He drew circles on her breast, ever smaller, maddening, until he suddenly bent down and kissed the peak.

She stopped breathing.

His lips were soft and gentle, his beard stubble slightly rough. His tongue darted out and circled the nipple, now a hardened nub. Fire shot down her spine, out her toes.

"Breathe, Sylvia."

She exhaled.

He lowered his head again, drew her nipple into his mouth. And gently suckled.

She gasped and arched her back. She tingled in

places she didn't know she had places. Her breath raced in and out. Her fingers curled at her side, clenching the sheets. She couldn't stand much more of this. She never wanted him to stop.

He lifted his head, grinning. "No one's ever done that for you before?"

She could only shake her head.

"Let's see what other new experiences we can give you."

He caressed her skin, his hand working across to her other breast, sliding underneath her cotton gown. "This has to go," he growled. He gathered the fabric at the hem and slid it up her legs, his hands slithering from side to side, stroking her calf, her knee, her inner thigh, higher still. She lifted her hips, and he brushed his hands over her bottom.

She gasped.

"Sweet, sweet Sylvia," he murmured. He urged her to sit up, grasped the hem of her gown, now bunched at her waist, and lifted.

"Wha—what are you doing?" She pushed down on his hands, leaving the gown at her waist.

He knelt beside her, resting his weight on his palms. He opened his mouth to speak, but closed it after emitting only a small sigh. He cradled her face in his hands. "I want to see you. I want to touch you. All of you." He kissed her mouth, each eyelid, even the tip of her nose. "I want to feel your soft, warm skin next to mine. Will you let me do that?"

He was asking permission? Her mouth fell open. He stayed motionless, his eyes on her face, waiting for her answer. He would let her say no. She grabbed her gown and yanked it up, over her head, and tossed it to the floor.

The look of open admiration on his face was worth the embarrassment of appearing nude before his gaze.

He claimed her mouth in a searing kiss, his hands roving, searching, caressing her body. They both lay back, her head on his pillow, as he continued to look his fill, touching her in ways and in places she had never been touched before. Overwhelmed with sensation, she stopped being self-conscious—he had made just as much, if not more noise than she. She'd had no idea that having her neck kissed and suckled could be so pleasurable.

"Like that, do you?" He chuckled, his warm breath whispering over her, his lips brushing her sensitive skin.

"Mmm." She threaded her fingers through his thick hair, careful not to dislodge the bandage, and held his head in place. He was free to move on to do whatever he wanted to, just . . . not yet. She felt his teeth gently nip her, in the curve between her neck and shoulder. The pleasure was almost painful. "Do that again," she gasped.

He did. And repeated the action on the other side of her neck. Then he slid down, rubbing his hard body against hers, until his mouth was level with her breast. He lavished it with attention, while his hand wandered lower.

Concentrating on the sensations created by his mouth, she was unaware of what he was doing with his hand until she felt him part her. Down there. Slowly he ran his fingers up and down, in and out. "Wha— Oh."

"Another first?" She felt the vibration of his voice against her chest as much as heard it.

She nodded. She opened her eyes again—when had she closed them?—and locked gazes with Tony. There was heat in his expression she had never seen there before, an intensity that shook her. His fingers moved, touching her, slow, fast, and slow again. Sparks shot through her.

She froze. Didn't even breathe.

"Relax," he whispered. "Let it happen."

"Let—" She took a breath. "Let what happen?"

Tony looked puzzled. Then his expression cleared. "No one's ever touched you like this? Never made you feel like, ah . . . like you're going to explode?"

Explode? "Good heavens, why would anyone want to do that?"

He coughed, but she could have sworn he was covering up a laugh. At her expense. She let her breath out in a huff, and rolled over to reach for her night rail, pooled on the floor.

"Oh, very nice," he murmured. He cupped her derriere.

She jumped.

He stilled her with one arm reassuringly over her, his hand caressing her breast, and pressed a kiss to the back of her neck. She gasped. The nape was just as sensitive as the side. He stayed close enough that she felt his lips brush her skin as he spoke, his chest against her back.

"I can't do it justice with words—no one can—but let me show you why you'd want to, ah, explode."

His touch was soothing, exciting, eliciting moans, and soon her heart was pounding again, her breath coming in gasps. "Let's go back to something you're no doubt more familiar with." He scooted over, urging her onto her back, and raised himself over her.

She settled amongst the pillows and blankets, her arms at her sides, and steeled herself for the discomfort of entry. He slid inside, filling her completely. Painlessly. Her eyes flew open.

His eyes were squeezed shut, his face contorted, his mouth moving but she couldn't make out the words.

Had she done something wrong?

He bent his elbows, resting more of his weight on her, his mouth close to her ear. "So good, Sylvia," he murmured, "feels so good."

Apparently, he was not in pain. She relaxed, and waited for it all to be over soon.

He nuzzled her neck. "You all right?"

She nodded.

"Good, because I think I'm going to die if I can't—" He moved, barely, in and out, and groaned.

Her husband used to make similar sounds, just before he finished. But this time she didn't feel as though she were being pounded through the mattress.

Tony's movements increased in range, and so did the pleasant sensations rippling through Sylvia. She fought to keep from crying out.

With his weight on his elbows, he continued to caress her with his hands, his mouth. "You can touch me, if you want," he whispered.

Tentatively, Sylvia stroked his muscular shoulders, feeling the slightly raised marking of his tattoo. She let her hands roam lower, down the curve of his spine, now slick with sweat, to the hollow of his back, and lower still, feeling his muscles clench and relax with each movement.

Now she realized the inarticulate sounds Tony was making were definitely from pleasure. Emboldened, she stretched her arms their full length and cupped him with her hands, just as he had done to her. Oh, very nice, indeed. Why would anyone want to pinch when a handful was ever so much better?

She had never lifted her heels from the bed before. She bent one knee and caressed his lower leg with her foot. The feel of his muscles, the dusting of hair along his legs, was so different from her own. She lifted her other leg, slid them both along the backs of Tony's legs, trying to discover how high she could go. Ooh, that far.

The pleasurable sensations at her core changed, increased, intensified, and she felt him plunge even deeper inside her. She moaned and tightened her legs around him, needing him still deeper. She was beneath him, writhing in pleasure, just as Tony had promised that night in the kitchen, when he had been naked in the tub.

Suddenly he pulled back and rolled them both over, putting her on top.

She cast her eyes down, waiting for his rebuke, restraining a growl of frustration. It had all been going so well, the most fun she'd had in her life, and she'd ruined it.

"Oh, yes, even better," he murmured.

Startled, she looked up, saw his head on the pillow below her, brown eyes smoldering. With his hands on her hips, he adjusted her position and slid inside again, groaning his pleasure. He helped her rise up, resting her weight on her hands, freeing his to caress her. He lifted his head for a kiss.

From this position, she could pull back, out of his reach. If she wanted.

He had given her that choice.

No one had ever done that for her, either. She bent to give him a quick kiss, but then sat up, drawing her knees close, tight against his side.

Instead of voicing a protest, he cupped her breasts, massaging the sensitive flesh, murmuring his appreciation, sending tingles down her spine. She curled her toes. She became aware of cool air against her bare skin in this new position, but the heat from his hands banished the cold, made her warm all over.

The urge to move became irresistible. Tony slid his hands down her sides, to her hips, and helped guide her movements. He exerted only a slight pressure—a suggestion, not an order. She could resist, change, if she wanted. She rocked from side to side just because she could. Freedom was exhilarating, almost as much as sliding up and down.

"Yes, sweetheart, that's it. Don't fight it." He slid his feet up the sheets, raising his knees.

"This is almost like . . . sitting on your lap."

He rocked his hips in rhythm with her movement. He grinned, his white teeth flashing in the candlelight. "You can sit on my . . . lap . . . anytime, sweetheart."

She almost laughed, but he thrust deeper on the next stroke, and she thought she would scream from the overwhelming pleasure of it all.

Something built within her, growing, expanding, invading every muscle, every fiber of her being, until she squeezed her eyes shut against the intensity, until she felt like . . . like she was going to explode.

"That's it, sweetheart, let it happen. Give in to it. I'll catch you when you fall."

She sped up her movements, intensifying the pleasure, increasing the buildup, until she . . . exploded.

It tore moans from her throat, reverberated off every cell within her, made every muscle convulse. Her fingers clenched his upper arms, digging into his flesh.

At last she collapsed on Tony's chest, gasping for breath.

Gradually she became aware of him stroking her hair, murmuring soothing nonsense in her ear. She lifted up, barely able to look him in the eye after such a wanton display.

He shifted his hips, reminding her that he was still fully aroused. "Want to do that again?" His tone was playful.

Explode again, so soon? It would probably kill her. "Perhaps later."

"Fair enough." He grinned and rolled them over

while they were still joined. "My turn now, sweetheart." He adjusted everything to his satisfaction, and continued touching her, stroking, kissing, his tongue mimicking his other actions.

She was floating on clouds, held in place by his comforting weight, solid but not oppressive. She lightly raked her nails down his back, thrilled with his moan in response. She became more active, exploring, touching, tasting, participating as his excitement built, his movements increasing in speed and intensity.

Suddenly he pulled out and lay on top of her. Heat spread between their bellies as he groaned, his panting stirring the hair beside her ear.

As their passion cooled, she was quite content to lie there, her arms around him, his heart beating next to hers.

Eventually Tony rolled to the side, still leaving one of his legs draped over hers, and nuzzled her neck. "At the risk of shattering your illusions, my dear, I'm afraid I am a typical man, in that I'm about to fall asleep."

Was that what Hubert had done as soon as he'd left her each time?

Should she leave now?

Tony reached over the side of the bed, and came up with the kerchief they'd used earlier for her tears. He wiped her clean, dropping several kisses on her chest in the process, then cleaned himself. He tossed the kerchief back to the floor, blew out the candle, and tugged the blankets up over them both. He sighed as he pulled her close. "You don't have to go," he whispered against her neck.

Go back to her cold, lonely bed? Or snuggle up with Tony, who was busy nuzzling and stroking her bare skin?

"No, I don't have to." She had never before slept naked. Had never before spent the entire night in a man's arms.

Two more new experiences, in a night full of them.

Sylvia awoke just before dawn. She was not alone in bed, which was fairly common. She was used to Macbeth crowding her on the pillow, and having to push his fluffy tail away from her face. He finally settled with his tail draped over her ear, purring softly.

But this was not her bed. She lifted her head to have a look around, only to bump it against something hard.

Tony's chin.

Memories of last night came rushing back, and her cheeks flooded with warmth. Almost as warm as the solid, masculine, utterly male body spooned up behind her.

Tony's arm tightened around her middle for a moment, before his hand wandered up and cupped her breast. "Oh good, you're awake," he whispered, his beard stubble grazing her nape. "Didn't know how much longer I could restrain myself."

"You want to . . . again? Already?"

He wiggled his hips, and she felt proof of his arousal. "It's been at least five hours, sweetheart." He pounced on her, growling, making her laugh.

Macbeth leaped to the floor and stalked away in a

cloud of offended dignity, which only made Sylvia laugh even more.

Soon Tony had her gasping for breath, sizzling with pleasure, her laughter forgotten, totally unashamed in the pale dawn light, and holding him close as he found his own release.

The cat jumped up again when they stopped making the bed shake.

Sylvia felt like purring, too. "I could wake up like this every morning for the rest of my life," she said with a sigh, threading her fingers through Tony's hair, his face nuzzled against her neck.

Tony went still.

She closed her eyes. How could she have been so foolish as to say that out loud?

He moved.

When she opened her eyes, he was staring down at her, his intense expression unreadable. She swallowed, and decided to make light of it. "You already have Macbeth's approval."

She felt the pillow dip as Tony stroked the cat, making Macbeth purr even louder.

"Yes, I have that." Tony dropped a kiss on her mouth, and sat up. "You should probably get back to your room before Galen comes upstairs."

Sylvia sighed. "Galen knew what I was going to do even before I did."

He winced. "If I were Scottish, I'd think she had the sight."

"No, just several decades' more experience than us."

Tony's turn to sigh. "Well, we have a lot of work to

do, things to figure out." He swung his legs over the edge, and Sylvia got a good look at the bruises on his back.

"Stay right where you are." She patted a spot that wasn't bruised, and dashed to her room for a bottle of liniment.

He gave a soft whistle as she came back. She looked down, and realized she hadn't even bothered to grab her wrapper. His look was openly admiring, though, so she lifted her chin and stepped forward with confidence.

"Lie down, please."

He did.

"On your *stomach*."

He grumbled a bit, but rolled over. She knelt on the bed, straddling his legs, and massaged the liniment into his back. With such uninhibited access, she massaged the oil into his shoulders, down his back, even carefully, thoroughly, tracing the bruise that dipped low on his hip. Massaged it into both hips, for good measure. He lay still with the pillow tucked under his head, Macbeth off to one side, both of them looking content, their eyes closed. She really could get used to this every morning.

She capped the bottle. "Does that feel better?"

Tony moved swiftly, and Sylvia suddenly found herself on her back beneath him. "Let me show you how much better," he growled in her ear.

He couldn't possibly, again, so soon after . . . Oh.

He could.

Chapter 17

When they both finally sat up, Tony saw the red marks around Sylvia's mouth, on her neck and chest—whisker burn—and grinned. It quickly turned to a grimace, though. Galen would have no doubt whatsoever what they'd been doing.

Perhaps if he shaved before the housekeeper saw him, she wouldn't make the connection. Farfetched, perhaps, but an ideal excuse to keep touching Sylvia a while longer, and her touching him. "Ever shaved a man before?"

Sylvia paused on the edge of the bed, beside him. "No." She raised her eyebrows.

He rested his whiskered chin on her lovely bare shoulder. "Want to?"

Good thing neither of them were wearing any

clothes, because they managed to get shaving soap all over each other. But they had oh so much fun wiping it off, and even managed to remove his whiskers in the process, without drawing blood.

He sat still while she removed the bandage wrapped around his head, brushed his hair, and applied a fresh bandage. Well, almost sat still. His hands, which seemed to have a mind of their own, kept exploring whatever part of Sylvia they could reach, as if trying to find all the places and ways to make her blush and giggle and sigh.

Finally he could think of no other good excuses to keep her naked in his room, and they began to get dressed. Sylvia searched for her wrapper, which Tony had kicked far under the bed. He watched her while he tried to find clothes that fit him. His own were gone, except for his spare linens. Galen must have collected them last night during dinner, and tried to save them from the seawater.

He resigned himself to again borrowing Hubert's ill-fitting breeches and coat, and shrugged into the garments. It wasn't that he minded wearing someone else's clothes—as the youngest, he'd often worn his big brother's hand-me-downs. He just didn't want Sylvia to see the clothes and be reminded of Hubert. He wanted her to see him, Tony.

She was on her knees now, peering under the bed. If he whistled now, she'd kill him for sure. But my, what a beautiful sight.

He, too, could get used to this every morning for the rest of his life.

He'd been shocked when she'd let that slip out earlier. It was only yesterday afternoon that he'd made his decision to stay. He hadn't even had a chance to mention it to Sylvia yet, explore its repercussions. Figure out how he fit into her life, her small community, what his permanent role would be.

Prior to coming to Lulworth Cove, his place in life had always been temporary and uncertain. After Papa died, Ben inherited the title, but almost immediately ran off to fight Napoleon. Tony had—temporarily—taken Ben's place. Tony had been the one to make sure that the crops were planted, the servants paid, and he had tried to help Mama adjust to being a widow and the uncertainty of not knowing if Ben would survive.

After five years, Ben had come home, slightly worse for wear. As soon as he'd proven the doctors wrong by not dying, he'd sent Tony back to finish his interrupted schooling. Now Ben was happily married, undoubtedly had an heir already on the way, and Tony had struggled to discover his direction in life.

He wasn't the only one in that position. Because of Teague and Ruford, the direction of the whole village was uncertain.

Whatever his future held, Tony was certain it was here, with Sylvia.

"Strange. I wonder how that got way over . . ." She retrieved her wrapper from beneath the bed and stood up so quickly she caught him staring. "You're incorrigible."

He gave her his most innocent expression.

They heard the door to her room open.

Sylvia's eyes widened in panic.

Footsteps in the dressing room.

Sylvia darted behind the chair by the fireplace, pulling on her wrapper and tying the belt. Tony sat down before the mirror, one boot in his hands.

The door opened after the briefest of knocks, and Galen poked her head in, seeming unsurprised to see him up at such an early hour. There were still streaks of red in the sky. "Beg pardon, sir, but have you seen my lady? She's not in her room, and her bed's not been slept in."

He paused, pretending to give the matter some thought. "Perhaps she's already gone down to her stillroom."

Galen nodded, glanced at his mussed bed, then closed the door.

Tony dropped his boot. Where was Sylvia? In his stocking feet, he padded over to the chair and peered behind. Not hiding there. Nor was she under the bed.

Macbeth was gone, too.

Hmm.

Tony examined the adjoining wall more thoroughly, thumping it here and there. A hollow spot, down low, beside the fireplace bricks. He pushed, and a panel swung open. Inside the small space was an opening in the floor and ceiling off to one side, and a crude ladder attached to the wall.

He got up, dusted off his knees and palms, and strode through the dressing room to Sylvia's chamber.

She had just pulled a day gown over her head, gray of course, and was struggling to pull it down into place. Her room was a mirror image of his own, but done in faded rose and washed-out blue, where his had once been rich browns and earthy greens.

While she fought her voluminous gown, Tony checked the wall beside the fireplace, and found the panel that swung open. Satisfied, he tugged on Sylvia's gown.

She gave a startled yelp.

He put a finger to her lips. "Just me. She's gone."

Sylvia nodded, and reached to fasten the buttons up the back. Tony spun her around and did them for her, dropping kisses on her flesh before it disappeared from view.

Once done, he wrapped his arms around her waist from behind, one last chance to hold her close for who knew how long. "Soon, sweetheart, you must allow me to demonstrate my skill at *removing* your garments," he whispered in her ear, making her blush. He nuzzled a kiss just below her ear, in the spot that made her shiver with arousal, an excuse to lean in and inhale her sweet scent one more time.

Sylvia patted his hands, and he let go. "I'll go down the back stairs," she said, sitting at her dressing table, "and you go down the main stairs, several minutes later."

"Not a problem. It will take a while to get my boots on, if I *can* get them on again after their soaking yesterday."

She began rolling a stocking onto her foot. "Oh, your lovely boots. I'd forgotten about them."

He barely heard her words, focused as he was on the stocking she was pulling over her shapely ankle, up the strong calf he'd caressed just minutes ago, to her knee. The backs of her knees were ticklish. How many of her body's secrets had he discovered? Not nearly enough.

"Stop that." She slid her second stocking on.

"Stop what?" He missed her bare toes dreadfully. So pink, so delicate, so ticklish . . .

"Looking at me like a wolf eyeing his prey." She stuffed one foot into her sturdy half-boot.

He swooped down to steal a kiss. "But you are good enough to eat."

She batted him away, laughing.

With a martyred sigh, he returned to his room, to the disaster that was his boots.

Fortunately, Baxter or Gerald had thought to stuff them with newspaper before turning them over the boot form to dry yesterday. Tony pulled the wads of damp newsprint out and tossed them into the fireplace.

At home in London, he had a champagne-based boot polish that might save the stained leather. And footmen who would gladly spend the entire day polishing to restore the luster and sheen.

Here, however, he had none of that. He did the best he could with the supplies on hand, and forced his feet into the boots. Ouch. They'd probably stretch back to their original shape and soften up again after he wore them a while.

He'd heard Sylvia's footsteps on the stairs several minutes ago. His stomach grumbled, reminding him of the need for nourishment after so much exertion.

He headed down to breakfast, whistling despite the fact his boots were pinching his feet.

Galen set a plate in front of him with such force that half the eggs slid off the far edge. "You was right. My lady was in the stillroom, with a silly grin on her face."

He glanced up, trying to reconcile the pleasant words that had been spoken in the tone of a challenge.

She sat down, the better to wag her finger at him. "She didn't look that happy even when she first got here and still had all her hopes and illusions."

"I'm thinking 'you're welcome' is not the response you're looking for." He ate a forkful of scrambled eggs.

"She was content. Not happy, maybe, but she weren't unhappy, neither."

Tony opened his mouth, intending to swear he would never make Sylvia unhappy, but realized he couldn't make that promise. He stuffed another forkful of egg in.

He was uncertain what he intended to do this afternoon, never mind the rest of his life. He wanted to stay here in Lulworth Cove, but wasn't sure how he'd fit into the tiny, close-knit community.

He had given Sylvia pleasure last night, and twice this morning. He may not have been her first lover, but he was obviously the first to help her reach the height of ecstasy.

Before he came along, she'd had to fight off the advances of a smelly, lecherous sea captain, after being widowed by a cold, unfeeling sea captain. The villagers had welcomed him, or at least they'd welcomed his strong back and willingness to indulge in manual labor as they rebuilt from the storm. Without him, many of them would still have no home to call their own.

Pounding on the front door interrupted his thoughts, and he followed Galen out into the hall. Gerald was still inching down the stairs when the visitor swung the door open himself, shouting for Lady Montgomery. It was one of the boys Tony had seen in the taproom his first night.

"Teague's gang was on our beach. Some of our men are hurt bad. She has to come quick!"

"Who's hurt?" Gerald finally reached the bottom step.

"Baxter, and some of the other tub men. They're on the beach. There's blood everywhere."

Tony turned to go get Sylvia, but she was already running toward them, wiping her hands on her work apron. Jimmy appeared up on the landing, barefoot, tucking his shirt into his breeches, his red hair sticking up.

"I'll go have Farleigh hitch up the cart, my lady," Gerald said.

"No, the tunnel is faster." She spun on her heel, running back toward the stillroom.

"My lady, you sure you want to go that way?" Galen touched Sylvia's elbow as she passed.

"Quite sure. I'm just going to fetch my bag."

"Wait for me," Jimmy called. "I'm coming, too!"

In the stillroom, Sylvia threw tins and jars of preparations into her bag, snapped it shut, shoved it into Tony's arms, and grabbed another portmanteau from a low cupboard. "I worried the day would come that I'd need this one."

He ran out the door after her. "What's in it?"

"Bandages. Nothing but bandages and splints."

Galen swung open the cellar door as they skidded into the kitchen. "Godspeed, my lady."

Sylvia clattered down the stairs, with the lad who'd brought the message at her heels, and Tony close behind. They'd just reached the bottom when Jimmy thundered down the steps, shielding a lit candle.

Sylvia picked her way past empty shelves and crates. She pushed on one of the rough stones in the far wall, and a section swung inward. Unlike the secret passage upstairs, the tunnel opening was four feet wide, and at least six feet high. No one would have to crawl.

From his candle, Jimmy lit the wall sconces, and removed one that turned out to be a torch. "Want me to go first?"

She grabbed another torch, lit it from Jimmy's, and stepped into the passageway. "I'll be fine."

Her smile had seemed shaky to Tony, but he chalked it up to worry about her injured men on the beach.

"She's terrified of the bats," Jimmy confided as he lit another torch. "Has been since the time I tricked her into going in there without a light, and shut the door on her."

Tony snatched the torch out of Jimmy's hand and ran after Sylvia.

With both of them carrying a portmanteau in one hand and a torch in the other, he couldn't take her hand as he wanted. "Right behind you, sweetheart."

"I knew you would be." Her back was straight, her voice strained from the effort of running.

The tunnel was even colder than Spencer's cellar, with an irregular, uneven ceiling. Tony ran slightly bent over, not wanting to discover exactly what was overhead.

Behind them, Jimmy was questioning the lad about what to expect when they reached the beach. He answered in gory detail, describing some of the injuries.

He didn't prepare them for the state of the boats.

Sylvia gasped as she left the tunnel and stepped around the boulders that camouflaged its entrance at the base of the cliffs. "Oh, dear heaven."

The cove's beach was awash with people, most of whom were up and moving about, hovering around the half-dozen men who were sitting or lying in varying stages of consciousness.

But the boats had been dragged together into bonfires, roaring columns of flames edged by heaps of charred timbers. The fishing boats, the luggers, even the little skiffs—no vessel had been spared.

Sylvia was the first to rouse herself from the shock. She jammed her torch into the sand and ran to check the wounded. Hayden was sitting up, being tended by his wife, as Mrs. Doyle tended her husband. Monroe had his wife tucked under his arm for support, and was making his unsteady way toward the path that led to the inn.

Corwin stood off by himself, bruised, bloody, and a little wobbly, staring up at the east side of the cove. Tony followed his gaze. The path on that side led to Tyneham.

Teague's territory.

The path was empty.

Tony ran across the beach, skidding around the fires, searching.

Baxter was sitting propped against the cliff face, one leg at an unnatural angle in front of him. His left eye was swelling shut, barely noticeable amidst all the blood dripping from a cut above his eye, and from his broken nose.

Tony knelt beside him. "What the hell happened here?"

Baxter shook his head. "One minute we was working, same as always, next minute there must have been at least two dozen of 'em. I know why they stole all our tubs, even ransacked Spencer's cellar to get 'em, but why'd they burn the boats? My fishing boat. My wife helped me build it, God rest her soul." He pointed at the largest of the bonfires.

Sylvia had worked her way over to them, handing out bandages and splints, and now knelt on the other side of Baxter.

He lifted his hands, rubbing at his bloody knuckles. Proof they hadn't given up the tubs easily. "Big fellow said to give a message to my lady."

"What message is that?"

Baxter coughed, and spat blood. "He said to tell you not to interfere no more, or next time a lot more people than just your husband will die."

By noon, they had the wounded men cleaned and bandaged, their broken bones set, and carted them home. Rain began to fall just as they loaded the last injured man onto a door and hauled him up the path. A few would be weeks or months in recovering, and might never be the same, but no one had died. Those with no one else to care for them were taken upstairs at the inn, watched over by Mrs. Spencer and her daughter.

Tony sat in the taproom apart from Sylvia, trying to clean the blood off his hands. He'd washed at the pump, but it was still there, under his nails. The blood of Sylvia's gang, spilled because of him.

"We're going to starve," Mrs. Hayden wailed, and buried her face against her husband's uninjured shoulder. He patted her knee.

With Hayden's arm broken, he wouldn't be doing any fishing anytime soon, even if his boat hadn't been reduced to a pile of ashes.

"They didn't kill the dairy cattle, so we still have the cheese," Sawyer said. "Don't we?"

Jimmy quietly groaned. Sylvia buried her face in her hands.

"I s'pose I'll be heading to Swanage, then," Corwin said. "Bound to be work at the docks somewhere. Maybe I'll sign up as crew again, see some of the world."

"Well, I guess I'm off to my nevvy's." Mrs. Pitsnoggle drained her tankard of ale and set it down with a thump. Monroe beside her didn't even jump, so engrossed was he in watching rain slide down the windowpane. She filched his tankard and drained it, too.

"We ain't got the brandy," Trent said. "We ain't got the coin to buy another load. Which really don't matter none, since we don't got a captain to sell us a load, or a ship to go get it our ownselves." He signaled Mrs. Spencer to refill his tankard. "We might can catch a few fish off the beach, and until the next batch is ready, if we get really hungry, there's the briny cheese these lackwits ruined."

Sylvia raised her head from her hands. She had hoped they would only have to do smuggling runs this summer, and then be able to quit. That would have enabled them to make enough money to rebuild their homes, stock their pantries and cellars, and have enough in reserve to comfortably get everyone through the winter. She'd hoped to come up with a viable alternative to smuggling by spring, a legal source of income.

Well, that plan was out the window.

The night Tony had arrived, she'd been thinking she needed to act more like a smuggler. Now she had no other option. "There isn't enough time to find another captain, or another ship. We'll have to make do with the one we've got."

"My lady?" Several men spoke at once.

"Syl, what do you mean, the one we've got?"

Jimmy ran his fingers through his hair. "We don't have so much as a skiff anymore."

"Ruford does." The more Sylvia thought about it, the more outrageous, the more desperate it seemed. But didn't desperate times call for desperate measures?

Murmurs rippled through the room.

"Are you suggesting what I think you are?" Tony stared at her in shock. "You want to steal Ruford's ship?"

"Of course!" Corwin jumped up. "We have pistols and swords. We'll just take what we need. He'd do the same, in our position."

"I don't *want* to steal his ship," Sylvia said. "But he's left us no choice."

More murmurs went up through the crowd. Sawyer rapped his tankard on the table, and they quieted down again. "It's Ruford's fault we're in this predicament. Least he can do is help us out of it."

"You can't just steal his ship." Tony leaned toward Sylvia. "There must be some other way, some other solution."

"Why?" Jimmy demanded. "You said it yourself. The local authorities are as crooked as corkscrews, paid off by Teague. Why should they all profit, while we starve?"

"We won't let Ruford starve," Sylvia said. "We'll keep him and any of his crew who are willing to sail with us, pay them fair wages for their work. He simply won't be making the decisions about who he sells his cargo to anymore." She turned back to Tony. "Don't you think I've been searching for some other way, some other solution? There is nothing else that will feed the people of this village, no other source of income. We have to have a ship."

"You're calmly discussing something that is much more dangerous than moving a few casks in the dark of night past underpaid Revenue agents. Ruford's men are not going to give up without a struggle. Some of you may be hurt, or even killed."

"We can take 'em," Sawyer said, puffing out his chest.

Tony looked at everyone in disbelief. "Doesn't anyone else think this is madness?"

Trent broke the silence. "My lady's right. It's what needs to be done."

Tony rubbed his temples. "I'm not going to let you get hurt. Smuggling is one thing, but I won't help you get yourself killed. I can't let you do this."

Sylvia's heart squeezed in anguish. This was it. She'd known this day was coming—she just didn't expect it to hurt this much. Tony was abandoning her, even though he still sat on the bench beside her. Just when she needed him most, needed his strength, his intelligence, he was deserting them all. Good thing she had not come to rely on him.

"When shall we do it?" Doyle said. "When shall we take the ship?"

"Next time he delivers a load to Worbarrow Bay," Jimmy said. "While his men are busy unloading the longboats on the beach, we can row out, and take over the ship before he gets back."

"Row out in what, laddie?" Trent said. "Teague's men burned every last one of our boats."

"We'll swim, then."

"We should have at least a week before he's due back with another load for Teague," Sylvia said. "Perhaps we can borrow, buy, or build something by then. Not all of us can swim."

Mrs. Spencer made another round with her pitcher, refilling tankards. "My sister works near the docks in Swanage," she said. "I can send word, if you like, have her let us know when Ruford comes and goes."

"Please do." Sylvia took a deep breath, steeling her nerves. "Before we work out more details, I need to know that everyone present is committed to the success of this undertaking. Tony's right—this is much more dangerous than what we've been doing. We likely will suffer casualties. Anyone who does not want to take part should leave now."

All eyes in the taproom swiveled to Tony.

Corwin pointed at Tony. "That means you, chum."

"But—"

Sylvia clenched her fists until her nails bit into her palm. "We appreciate the help you've given while you've been here. But it's time for you to go back to your own world, where you belong."

Tony's jaw worked, but no sound came out.

"Good-bye." Sylvia's eyes and throat burned with unshed tears.

Doyle and Sawyer stood up, as did several others, ready to help Tony depart.

Without another word, Tony spun on his heel, and slammed the door behind him.

Jimmy took the paper and pencil Spencer offered. "Now, where were we?"

Tony stormed across the inn's yard, his blood boiling. Go back to where he belonged, she'd said. He had begun to think he could belong here, in Lulworth Cove. With Sylvia.

Obviously that bullet to the temple yesterday had rattled his brains more than he'd thought.

He marched up the High Street toward the manor house, passing the neat little cottages he'd helped repair after the storm. At Doyle's cottage, sunlight glinted off the new windows that Tony had set in place and glazed with care so that no rain could sneak inside. The roof was snug, the stairs did not creak, the doors closed tight to keep out the chill winter winds.

Just before the road curved and the rhododendrons blocked the village from sight, Tony turned for one last look at Lulworth Cove. The stiff breeze blowing in off the Channel whipped his hair, tugged at his clothes. Even the wind was pushing him away.

Once again, he'd stepped in during a difficult time, willing to help, only to discover his help was wanted on just a temporary basis. Once again, he was extraneous. Not needed.

The sole sign of his having passed through this place would apparently be his workmanship on Doyle's cottage, and the roof of Sylvia's house. He'd made no impression on the villagers themselves, heading off as they were on an insane course, intent on their plan to steal Ruford's ship. He thought he'd made a connection, personal ties with the people—Jimmy, Baxter, Marge—but those ties were apparently as ephemeral as footprints on the cove's beach.

And he'd obviously made no impression on Sylvia, the way she had on him. His plans to stay here with her, plans he had for their future, meant nothing to her.

Well, fine.

He clenched his fists. If she wanted to get herself killed, he was washing his hands of her.

An hour later, Sylvia left the chattering crowd in the inn and stepped outside. The more they'd talked about the plans for stealing the ship, the more excited they became, and the more wretched she felt.

She walked to the edge of the cliff and stared down at the ruins on the beach. Wind blew the cold rain against her cheeks. Seagulls soared overhead and dipped down over the piles of ash on the pebbles—dirty heaps sullying the clean beach, embodiment of all their losses.

She'd known all along that Tony would leave someday, and someday had come. It shouldn't hurt. But misery weighed her down, crushing, nearly suffocating her. The fact she'd been the one to point out it was time for him to go just twisted the knife in her gut.

She walked back to the manor house on leaden feet. Galen and Gerald sat at the kitchen table, staring silently, morosely, into the bottom of their teacups.

Sylvia couldn't bear their company. Where was

Macbeth? Stroking his warm fluffy body would calm her. She needed his unconditional affection, his soothing purr. Her cat would never question her actions, never abandon her.

She searched the ground floor, then climbed the stairs. Holding her hand against her chest to calm her pounding heart, she opened the door to Tony's bedchamber and stepped inside.

Assailed by memories of last night and this morning, she gazed around the room. The bed where they'd made love together with such abandon just hours ago was now neatly made. The dressing table where she had shaved him was bare of his brushes and razor. His haversack, which had been slung over the chair back, was also gone.

She slumped against the doorframe and covered her eyes with her hands. She would *not* cry. Since he would not help them anymore, he had to leave. He'd done as she asked, had only done what she'd expected him to do since the day he'd arrived.

Sylvia shut the door and sat on the edge of the bed, where she imagined she could still smell a hint of his sandalwood soap. Through the sparkle of her tears, something bright and shiny on the pillow caught her eye.

A gold ring.

The ring Tony had worn, symbolizing their temporary, make-believe marriage.

It was not his fault she had started to imagine what it would be like to be married to him for real. Wondered what it would be like to wake up in his arms every morning, and go to sleep tucked in his embrace every night. Make love with him—loud, vocal, lively lovemaking that sent her senses soaring—whenever they wanted.

Not his fault that she had grown accustomed to having him at her side, facing problems together, making the insurmountable seem surmountable, the impossible merely difficult, the difficult easy.

She clutched the ring in her fist and held it to her chest.

Not his fault she couldn't stop crying.

That evening, a cart loaded with hay rumbled to a halt just outside Weymouth. Tony jumped down from the back, wincing in pain as soon as he put weight on his feet, and called his thanks to the driver.

The farmer waved, then slapped the reins on the cart and moved on, leaving Tony beside the muddy road. He hefted his haversack on his shoulder and started trudging toward the docks. He was two days past the date they'd agreed to meet. If Alistair or Nick were still in town, they'd be staying at the Duck and Drake Inn.

Tony limped through the front door of the inn. Smoke and noise assailed him, along with the scents of unwashed bodies and the evening meal. His stomach grumbled, reminding him he hadn't eaten since early that morning, and it was now past sunset. Hoping to spot Alistair, he wandered through the large crowded taproom, wincing with every step.

"Well, look what the cat dragged in," called a familiar voice.

Tony squinted through the smoke, peering at every face until he recognized one. "Didn't really expect you to still be in town, Nick." Tony pulled out a chair and sat at the table across from his friend. His feet still throbbed, but not as fiercely as before.

"Obviously."

Remembering how short of funds he was at the moment, Tony helped himself to his friend's tankard and drank the contents down in one gulp.

"Had a rough day, did you?"

"That's not the half of it." His stomach rumbled again. Would it be beyond crass to ask if his friend planned to finish his meal?

Nick waved at the serving wench, and ordered a meal for Tony and drinks for them both. "My treat. All you have to do is regale me with the details of your conquest." Nick leaned forward, his elbows on the table, a leering grin on his face. "I want to hear all about your pretty young widow."

Tony leaned back. "What did Alistair tell you?"

"Only that you abandoned his company in favor of a pretty blonde who appeared in need of a dashing hero and a male body to warm her bed."

Tony snorted. Hero, indeed.

Alistair joined them at the table and patted Tony on the shoulder. "You give up on her so soon?"

Tony shrugged.

Nick laughed. "The widow kicked you out of her bed!"

Alistair shook his head. "No, no, no, that can't be it.

That widow wasn't going to let him into her bed in the first place."

"Thank you both very much for your vote of confidence." Tony was spared any further ribald comments by the appearance of the serving wench with their food and drink. He dug into the roast mutton, though he had no taste for it. He just wanted to eat enough to settle his stomach.

Alistair ordered a tankard of ale for himself. "So, does this mean you're going to continue on around the coast with me on my journey, or head back to London?"

Tony chewed and swallowed. "Haven't decided yet."

Nick gave a sad, slow shake of his head. "Looks like our boy here still doesn't have a direction for his life, despite our best efforts."

Tony tried to dredge up the energy to be angry or upset with his friend. But Nick was right. He thought he'd discovered his direction, but Sylvia had corrected his mistake.

"I thought you said he wanted to be a rake? Here he is, ignoring a perfectly willing, not to mention buxom, maiden." Nick pointed at the departing serving wench.

Alistair shrugged. Tony realized he had no interest in the serving wench beyond the meal she'd brought. He hadn't even noticed if she was blonde or brunette, young or old.

"What did the pretty widow think of your seduction technique?"

Tony considered giving Nick an anatomically challenging suggestion. Instead he finished his mutton.

"He's not going to tell us." Alistair slapped his palms on the table and leaned forward. "This must be serious."

"You're right, he won't even look up to stare daggers at me. Serious talk calls for serious drink." Nick waved down the serving wench and ordered a bottle.

"No brandy." Tony never wanted to see or smell brandy again.

"Whiskey it is. And since I'm guessing there's to be no talk of brandy, either, we better take this conversation up to Alistair's room or down to my ship. Too many ears in here."

"We're not going to take him down to your ship. Poor lad's barely had time to recover from the last time he was on board." Alistair gave Tony a reassuring thump on the shoulder.

They didn't know the half of it.

"Upstairs, then." Nick pushed his chair back and stood. "Shall we?"

Alistair led the way up to his room, Nick pushing Tony from behind. Every step felt like walking on broken glass. At last they reached Alistair's room at the end of a hall that seemed to go on for miles.

Tony ignored the two large chairs in front of the fireplace in favor of sprawling on the big bed. He tossed his haversack aside and lifted one booted foot up. "Somebody mind giving me a hand with these? I seem to have left my valet behind in London."

Nick stared at Tony's water-stained, ruined boots. "What did you do to Hobson's lovely boots?"

Tony almost laughed at the look of abject horror on Nick's face. "Would you believe I went for a swim in the cove?"

Nick's jaw dropped. He closed it with a snap. "In June? Don't you know you're supposed to wait until August? It's much too cold this early in the year to swim in the ocean."

"Ignore the dandy." Alistair bent to the task of assisting Tony out of his boots. "By the way, you look like hell. And you smell like . . ." He took another sniff. "Is that lavender?"

Tony untied his cravat. Even his linen smelled like Sylvia. A sense of loss washed over him, unexpectedly strong. "Liniment."

Alistair folded his arms over his chest. "Liniment smells harsh and nasty. This smells like m'lady's eau de toilette."

"M'lady made the liniment, and she's partial to lavender."

Nick and Alistair exchanged glances.

Tony shrugged. "Said it has medicinal properties."

Alistair tugged on the boot again. "Right. If you say so."

"*I* don't say so, she—"

"Enough with the damn lavender liniment." Nick ran his fingers through his hair. "Did you forget that you're supposed to strip down before you go swimming so you don't get waterlogged and drown?"

Tony grabbed on to the bedpost to keep from being dragged off the edge of the mattress by Alistair's enthusiastic tugging. "I was a bit tied up at the time, and didn't have much say in the matter."

Alistair finally managed to get the left boot off. "Tied up, as in, with rope?"

Tony nodded. He pulled his knife from his right boot before raising it for Alistair to remove.

"Oh, this is going to be good. Tell all, and I do mean all." Nick poured three glasses of whiskey.

"Why didn't you give me the knife before? Should have just cut them off in the first place, because I'm telling you now, you're never going to get these boots back on your feet." Alistair pointed to the bloodstains on Tony's white stocking.

Ah. That explained the broken-glass sensation.

"Don't let him distract you. You were tied up, and went for a swim in the cove. Go on."

"What am I supposed to wear if you cut off my boot?"

"Never mind that!" Nick practically shouted. "There is a cobbler down the street, and I have a pair you can wear in the morning when we go see if he has something to fit you."

Alistair tugged on the boot with such force that when it suddenly came free he staggered back two steps and sat down hard with a grunt.

Nick heaved a sigh of impatience as Alistair and Tony settled themselves, each with a glass of whiskey in their hand, Alistair in the other chair by the fireplace, Tony on the bed with his aching feet propped up on pillows.

"All right," Alistair said. "How did you end up in the cove if you were tied up?"

Tony shrugged. "Apparently the impact from the pistol shot pushed me over the railing."

"Railing?" Nick sat forward. "You were on a ship out in the middle of the cove?"

"Forget the ship." Alistair set his glass down with a *thunk*. "You were shot at?" He pointed at the bandage wrapped around Tony's head. "I thought the widow just hit you over the skull with a skillet."

Tony narrowed his eyes. "Your confidence in my address with the fairer sex underwhelms me."

"Gentlemen, gentlemen." Nick refilled their glasses. "I want all the particulars, if you please, from the beginning." He rubbed his hands together. "Leave nothing out."

Chapter 18

⁓⟡⁓

It required several hours, and the better part of the bottle, for Tony to relate his adventures of the last week and a half. His audience sat enthralled as he told them about the motley band of smugglers led by a plucky widow and her bantling brother-in-law.

"Bullets, blisters, bruises, and a make-believe bride." Nick finished off his drink. "Tell me, was your wedding night make-believe, too?"

Tony threw a pillow at Nick's head. He batted it aside, laughing.

"What do you think they're all going to do now?" Alistair threw more coal on the fire.

"Sylvia's plotting for them to steal Ruford's ship."

Nick stopped laughing. "Really?"

"What else can she do? Even the cheese is ruined." And she wanted nothing more to do with Tony.

"Ooh, she has bottom," Nick said. "I want to meet her."

Alistair tilted his head to one side. "I've never tasted low tide before."

Tony reached for his knife and his haversack. "I can fix that." Before he'd left the manor house, Galen had given him a round of cheese. As the number of miles he'd walked increased, several times he'd almost tossed it into a ditch to lighten the pressure on his feet. But he couldn't bring himself to part with any reminder of Sylvia, no matter how painful the memories. Or briny. Now he cut into the round and handed a piece to Alistair. He sat back and waited for the expression of disgust.

Alistair chewed, slowly and thoughtfully. He shook his head. "What do you mean, ruined? This is delicious."

Nick reached for the cheese. "Give me a hunk of that."

Tony obliged.

"Oh, my." Nick's expression could only be described as euphoric.

"It has a certain piquancy," Alistair said.

Nick nodded. "Get a nice bottle of wine to go with it."

"Perhaps some walnuts."

"Pears. Pears would go well with this."

Tony watched them, his brow furrowed.

Alistair took the knife from Tony's lax hands and cut off more cheese for himself and Nick. "I don't know what you're talking about, old chum," Alistair said around a mouthful of cheese. "This is the best I've ever had."

Nick mumbled his agreement, as well.

Tony took a cautious sniff of the cheese. No hint of the harbor. He broke off a tiny piece and tasted it on the the tip of his tongue.

Pure ambrosia, even better than anything he had tasted while in Lulworth Cove. This must have come from the batch that was ripening in Sylvia's stillroom. As he took a bigger bite, he had to swallow past the lump that formed in his throat.

"Since you don't want it," Nick said, "I'll be happy to take it off your hands."

"Not a chance," Alistair said. "I want it."

Tony looked back and forth between the two in amazement. He sat back on his heels. "I'll sell it to you," he said to Alistair, "in exchange for my half of the lodging expense for tonight."

Nick chuckled. "A little light in the purse, are we?"

"If she was feeding and housing you and tending to your various injuries, what did you possibly spend your coins on?"

Tony answered while he was digging through his haversack.

"Didn't quite hear that." Alistair cupped his hand to his ear.

"Roof tiles!"

Nick almost doubled over in laughter.

There was something heavy in the bottom of his

haversack. Tony pushed aside his linen to get at it, with the idea of throwing whatever it was at Nick's head.

"Other men buy flowers and fans and gewgaws for their ladies. Our friend here buys . . . building supplies." Nick broke out in another burst of laughter.

Tony finally got his hands on the unfamiliar object at the bottom of his haversack and pulled it out. He turned it over in his hands, examining it from every side.

Nick finally stopped laughing. "I say, what are you doing with a mariner's compass?"

Alistair sat on the edge of the bed beside Tony, and took the compass in its ivory case from his hands. He turned it over a few times. "She saw your tattoo, didn't she?" he said quietly.

Tony didn't answer.

Nick came over to take a closer look, as well. "Was this her husband's?"

"I don't know." When had she placed this in his haversack? Must have been after he'd given her the spool of ribbon. He took the compass back from Alistair, feeling an unexplained need to hold it.

Nick placed his large hand at the back of Tony's neck and gave him a gentle shake. "Someone else trying to give you a direction for your life, too?"

Tony thought he'd found his direction, but Sylvia had disagreed.

Fortunately Alistair broke the serious mood by grabbing for more of the cheese. He yawned before he could stuff it in his mouth.

"I best be getting back to the *Wind Dancer* before it

gets too late." Nick got up, shrugged into his coat, and gave them both a mock salute before he let himself out the door, with the promise to return in the morning.

"Don't forget to bring the spare shoes!" Tony yelled after him.

Within minutes, Alistair had slid under the sheets on his side of the bed, and began snoring soon after that.

Tony lay staring up at the ceiling, hands behind his head, for what felt like hours. After trudging along the road from Lulworth for so long before getting a ride on a passing farmer's cart this afternoon, not to mention the exertions of last night and this morning, he was beyond exhausted and should have fallen asleep immediately.

In the soft light cast by the fire, he glanced over at Alistair, whose expression was peaceful in repose.

This was not the bed companion Tony wanted. He'd hoped to spend every night for the rest of his life holding Sylvia. He'd had no idea she had other plans until she'd dismissed him this afternoon at the inn.

In time he would get over her, and look at other women with renewed interest.

That's what a true rake would do.

He got up, retrieved the compass from his haversack, and limped over to one of the chairs before the fire. In the glowing light from the coals, he watched the needle spin and finally settle. Now he knew in which direction north lay.

What kind of compass could help him figure out the direction for his life?

* * *

Alistair sat up, stretched and yawned, and stared at Tony, who was sitting in the armchair by the fire. "Couldn't sleep?"

Tony had the compass in one hand, a chunk of cheese in the other. "You know, land-based smugglers are really in a transportation and retail business." He held up the cheese. "This is what they should be selling instead of brandy. No ships or lecherous captains required."

Alistair cocked his head to one side. "And it's legal."

Tony stared at the cheese. "Yes, there's that."

They began to get ready for their day. Tony was just pulling on his only pair of clean stockings when Nick arrived and dropped a pair of dancing slippers in Tony's lap.

"I had no idea we were to attend a ball." Tony should have known the shoes would be much too large for him, since Nick towered over him by at least six inches. "Anyone ever tell you your feet are enormous?"

Nick gave a comical leer. "You know what they say about men with big hands and big feet." He pointed at Tony's dirty stockings. "Wad those up and stick 'em in the toes. You're only going to wear them long enough to get to the shoemaker's."

Tony finished getting dressed, and stopped in front of the mirror, hairbrush in his hand. His hair was mussed, but Sylvia's bandage was still neatly in place. He should remove it. It was just a piece of cloth, after all. But Sylvia had put it there.

He sighed.

"Boy's got it bad," Nick muttered from his chair by the fire.

"Beg pardon?" Tony looked at him in the mirror's reflection.

"Take it off. Let's see the bullet wound."

Alistair paused in the act of pulling on his boots. "Yes, let's see it."

"You're balmy, both of you." But Tony unwound the bandage. He started to toss the cloth onto the coals, but wadded it up and shoved it into his haversack instead. He pushed the hair back from his forehead, revealing the jagged, torn flesh on his right temple. It was the dark pink of a healing wound, not the angry red of an infection. Sylvia's herbs had done their work.

Alistair gave a long, low whistle. "A hair's breadth to the other side, and they'd have put you to bed with a shovel."

"You're one lucky bugger," Nick said.

Baxter had said the same thing, just two days ago. With Sylvia at his side, Tony had heartily agreed. Now, however . . . He quickly swiped the brush through his hair and shoved it into his haversack, eager to get going, to get away from memories that were still too fresh.

They went downstairs for breakfast, then headed out to the cobbler's shop, with a detour to the bank. Tony had his packed haversack over his shoulder, to carry the spare shoes later.

Just as he'd asked, Ben had arranged for a draft to be waiting for him at the bank, the amount of his next quarter's allowance.

His good luck continued—the cobbler had a pair of

boots that fit as if they had been made expressly for Tony, and were nearly identical to his ruined pair.

The transaction concluded, Nick hauled them outside into the sunshine. "I need to check on my carpenter's progress," he said. "We lost one of our masts in that storm last week." He began walking toward the docks, knowing the other two would be right beside him.

"You were out on the ocean in that mess? Several of our villagers lost their homes in that. I can't believe you survived it."

Both men stopped and gaped at Tony.

"What?"

"You said 'our,'" they said in unison. "'Our villagers,'" Alistair added.

"No I didn't."

"Yes you did." Nick threw his arm around Tony's neck in an affectionate gesture that threatened to suffocate him, and towed him toward the docks.

They were still several streets away from the waterfront, but Tony could see the tall masts of the ships above the roofline in the distance.

At last they turned a corner, and the harbor was laid out before them. Nick quickened his pace, practically dragging the other two along with him.

"You'd think we were going downstairs on Christmas morning," Tony said to Alistair.

"It's always gratifying to see a grown man so eager to see his toy."

"Knock it off, you landlubbers." Nick grinned from ear to ear as they drew abreast of his ship.

"Ahoy, Captain!" Jonesy, the first mate, let down

the plank. "Carpenter's mate says we'll be ready to sail by the next tide."

Nick rubbed his hands together. "Excellent, excellent." He stepped onto the plank.

"You're not expecting us to follow you up there, are you?" Tony eyed the ship with antipathy. Tied up at the dock, the ship's movement was rather limited, but Tony had no wish to experience again the joys of being on board. The memories of Ruford's ship, not to mention his method of departure, were still too fresh.

Nick just laughed and went aboard.

Tony looked away from the bobbing ship, at the people swarming around the docks. There was so much more activity and people here than in the cozy, calm village of Lulworth Cove. There was no Betsy making cow eyes at him, no Mrs. Miggins trying to pinch him, no Baxter trying to get him to taste the overproofed brandy.

No Sylvia.

He gazed at the other ships tied up at the docks— brigs like Nick's, galliots, fishing smacks, barques, and more. Each was an anthill of activity as their crews and dockworkers scurried here and there, loading and unloading cargoes, restocking the ship's stores.

Ships.

Sylvia needed a ship, and here was a banquet of them.

"I wonder how much it would cost to buy one," he said, almost to himself.

Alistair followed Tony's gaze to the rows of ships. "You can't be serious. You hate ships."

"It would have to be a fast one, to outrun the Revenue cutters." He turned in a half circle, looking over each of the possibilities.

Alistair frowned. "Fast, like Nick's brig?"

Tony stared at his friend. "Perfect! Alistair, you're a genius." Tony yelled for Nick.

He had to keep Sylvia from committing a foolhardy act, doing something that might get her or her men seriously hurt. Or worse. There was no way her motley crew could succeed in taking over Ruford's ship.

But if Tony *gave* her a ship, there would be no need for her to steal one. She could still be a smuggler, a rogue, without having to turn pirate.

"You want to *what*?" Nick gaped a few moments later.

"Buy your ship. Name your price, and please hurry. We have to get it to Lulworth before they go after Ruford's cutter."

Nick folded his arms over his chest. "You want to buy my ship, but you want me to sail it to Lulworth?"

Tony nodded. "To deliver it to its new master."

"And who would that be?"

"Sylvia, of course."

Nick tugged on his earring. "Suppose I don't want to sell. Maybe I want to transport brandy, and sell the cargo to your fair Sylvia."

"You, become a smuggler?" Tony shook his head. "Your sisters would never forgive you for besmirching the family name."

Nick briefly bowed his head. "There is that consideration, though it would be awfully fun. All right, I suppose I can find Lulworth Cove."

Tony nodded. "Good. I'll hire a horse and meet you there."

"I haven't agreed to sell, yet." Nick glanced over at Alistair, and back to Tony, a calculating gleam in his eye. Tony braced himself. "Tell you what. I will consider selling you the *Wind Dancer* if you sail with us to Lulworth instead of riding there."

Tony clutched his churning stomach. Nick stood with his feet apart, fists on his hips. "All right." Tony nodded. "Deal."

"I'll be damned," Nick said softly. "He's really serious."

Alistair stepped closer. "Let me make sure I understand. You, a man who heaves his guts out every time he steps on board any waterborne vessel, not only wants to own a vessel, but is willingly going to get on board it and sail for several hours? Out on the open ocean?"

Tony grimaced. This trip couldn't possibly be any worse than the last time he'd been on board a ship. "What else can I do?"

Alistair rested his hand on Tony's shoulder. "Does she know you love her?"

Tony blinked at him.

"Oh, dear Lord, even you didn't know you're in love with her. You poor sod." Alistair shook his head. "That poor girl." He turned back to Nick, and they discussed Tony's apparent mental deficiencies.

Tony sat down with a thump on the nearest bollard, untangled his feet from the mooring rope, and tried to sort things out.

Love?

Must be. Why else would he want to spend the rest of his life with her? Why else had it felt like a knife had been plunged between his ribs when she told him good-bye?

He thought back on the tempestuous ten days he had spent in Sylvia's company. Thought of all the bruises and blisters he'd developed, the blood he'd shed. The hard manual labor he'd performed, the adventures he'd had, the risks he'd taken.

The most wonderful night and morning of his life he'd spent, with Sylvia in his arms. The hours and minutes spent in her company.

He'd do it all over again, in a heartbeat, for the chance to spend more time with her.

He didn't want to be a rake. He wanted to be a husband. A *real* husband, this time.

Sylvia's husband.

Tony jumped to his feet. "How soon can we cast off?"

Chapter 19

❦

Sylvia paced on the tiny beach of Arish Mel in the center of Worbarrow Bay, and peered through her spyglass. Still no sign of Ruford.

Mrs. Spencer's sister, a serving maid at Ruford's favorite inn in Swanage, had sent word that he planned to meet with Teague today. Based on the tide tables and wind, he should arrive any time now.

They would have to execute their plan perfectly. Subdue Ruford's men, take over the ship, and sail out of the bay before Teague arrived for their meeting. Every second would count.

This idea had a much better chance of succeeding than taking over while Ruford delivered a load to Teague. Had they overlooked any detail? For the hundredth time, she wondered if their preparations were adequate. This had come together much too fast. They should have taken days, perhaps even weeks, to plan such an attack.

But if they had more time to contemplate their actions, they would never go through with it.

She glanced at the rocks on the beach and cliffs that lined the bay. Even knowing where they had concealed themselves, she could barely make out her men, all barefoot and ready to swim out to the *Polly Anne*. Jimmy wore a scarf to hide his shock of red hair. He crouched beside Trent, who was practically chortling with glee at the prospect of boarding Ruford's ship.

Since they were the youngest and the oldest in the gang, respectively, she had tried to discourage them both from participating. But Jimmy would not be denied, and Trent reminded her that he swam the width of Lulworth Cove every morning before breakfast, and had done so for the past sixty years. It was Trent who taught Jimmy how to swim like a seal beneath the water's surface.

They saw her staring, and each flashed a reassuring grin. In return she lifted the corners of her mouth and bared her teeth, the closest she could come to a smile.

Doyle and Sawyer stood nearby, their bulk and coiled strength offering some comfort and hope for success. As soon as the *Polly Anne* was sighted, they'd row Sylvia out in the skiff. It was the only seaworthy vessel left in Lulworth Cove, saved from the bonfires because it had been in the inn's workshed to be re-caulked. Spencer had assured her it was now seaworthy.

With what they had planned for today, a leaky row-boat was the least of their concerns.

How she wished Tony were here. He would have a quip at the ready for the men, would whisper something outrageous in her ear guaranteed to make her blush. His strength and leadership would assure their success.

But Tony was gone.

She'd sent him away before he had the chance to leave her.

She lifted her chin and swallowed down the lump in her throat. She would not cry over him anymore.

She'd wanted to think beyond the boundaries of her upbringing, act more like a smuggler in order to solve her own problems. Stealing a smuggler's ship certainly fit the bill. She could do this without Tony's help.

"There she is, my lady." Sawyer pointed at the cutter trimming sail and making for the bay.

Sylvia took a deep breath. This plan was insane, and surely she belonged in Bedlam for having suggested it. But she had been tossed about by the whims of men and fate all her life, and given little or no say in the events that shaped her future. Until now she'd been resigned, if not actually content, to make the best of whatever situation befell her.

Now it was time she took the helm. With their own ship, they would not be at the mercy of a spineless sea captain or a cutthroat smuggler.

Sawyer and Doyle checked their weapons—knives tucked into their boots, pistols and a cutlass tucked in the sashes at their waist, hidden under their coats.

Time for her to do the same. She checked the dagger in her half-boot, and hoped the folds of her cloak would conceal Montgomery's ancient dueling pistol tucked into her own sash. Its twin was nestled beneath the folds of cloth in her basket.

Reluctantly, she removed her fichu and dropped it into the basket. Her gown's neckline was everything that was proper, yet still exposed more décolletage than she was comfortable with for a meeting with Ruford. With any luck, the flesh on display would distract him from her true purpose until it was too late.

The *Polly Anne* grew close enough to see the men on deck without the aid of her spyglass. Both of her men were working near the railing on the main deck, as planned, within reach of the rope ladders. They had hired on while the ship was docked in Swanage yesterday.

"All right, gentlemen. Let's go." Waiting any longer would only make her more jittery, and she didn't want to lose her nerve in front of her men.

Doyle assisted her into the skiff, and Sawyer pushed off. They quickly settled into the smooth swing-and-pull motion, rowing with powerful strokes.

She set her basket at her feet. Staring down at the planks, she couldn't help thinking of the last time she'd been out on the water. Was that only two days ago? It seemed a lifetime.

She could still see Tipton's lifeless body, his sightless eyes staring up at the sky. Remembered her overwhelming sense of relief when she saw Tony pop up in the water, alive and vibrant, how she had wept tears of joy. How she had curled up against his side on the sofa, in full view of the villagers congregated in the salon, her need to hold him and feel his heartbeat overriding all else.

Tony had made her feel like the most beautiful, most cherished woman in the world. Had helped her reach heights of pleasure she'd never before attained, had never even known were possible. Made her feel powerful and skilled as a lover, as though she gave him as much pleasure and joy as he gave her.

But that was all part and parcel of being a rake, wasn't it? Part of what made a man a rake was his ability to make each woman feel like she was the most important woman in the world to him. Until he moved on to the next woman, his next conquest.

She was sure he'd moved on to his next conquest by now.

They pulled close enough to the port side to hear the men on deck. Ruford gave the order to heave to, and Crowther and McCutcheon passed along more commands.

Sylvia took a deep breath to steel her nerves. "Ahoy, Captain!"

Several men leaned over the bulwarks. A moment later Ruford joined them, his familiar lecherous leer in place. "My, my, my, what a welcome surprise."

"The ladies from the village have sent a gift of smoked mackerel. May I come aboard?" Sylvia held her basket aloft.

Ruford gestured for his men to let down the rope Yes, of course, my dear." His expression of delight clouded briefly when Doyle climbed the ladder first, but returned when Sylvia slung the basket handle over her arm and headed up. Sawyer secured the skiff and hurried after her before the ladder could be retracted.

Sylvia took a moment to get her bearings. It had been a long time since she'd been aboard this large a ship. There was half a forest of wood making up the decking and railings and masts, and a mile of ropes in the rigging and neatly coiled on the deck. Several men were balanced on the ratlines high above, furling the sails, while others tended to chores on the deck.

The ship was big, clean, had lots of cargo space below, and was very fast, according to Ruford's claims. Perfect for their needs.

Corwin and Monroe were among those hurrying to and fro on the deck. She hoped they had already dropped another rope ladder over the starboard side.

Knowing Ruford would follow, Sylvia casually strolled toward the stern of the ship. Doyle followed close behind, though Sawyer stayed near Crowther. The first mate hardly spared him a glance, so busy was he reprimanding two mates who had not belayed ropes properly.

Doyle had his hand on the butt of his pistol. Sylvia gave a slight shake of her head. She wanted to give Ruford one more chance. She held out a package of mackerel to the captain. "The ladies of the village feel that we can offer you an arrangement that would be much more beneficial to you than that offered by Mr. Teague."

Ruford paused in unwrapping the fish. "The ladies?"

"Because of the shipwreck that claimed Montgomery and so many other men last year, there are several widows in the village. Lonely women." She allowed Ruford a moment to ponder the implications. "If you were to reprovision your ship's stores in Lulworth Cove, Spencer can provide you goods at a cost comparable to what you pay in Swanage. And while you are at anchor, your men could have the advantage of home-cooked meals."

Ruford rubbed his chin. "Home-cooked meals, eh?" He caressed her shoulder. "And would there be . . . other advantages . . . of being in the home?" He sidled a little closer to her.

Sylvia swallowed down the bile that rose in her throat. "That would be open for negotiation on an individual basis." She took a few steps back, until her backside pressed up against the stern railing. "In exchange, we would expect, of course, to be the recipients of all of your cargo loads each month."

Ruford's hand dropped to his side. He darted his gaze to the cliffs that rimmed the bay, as though he expected to see someone. Sylvia half expected to see Teague there, too. She could almost hear Ruford weighing the consequences of his decision, his lust for her and fear of Teague fighting for dominance. At length he shook his head. "I'm very sorry, my dear. T_____ pting as your offer is, I must decline."

_____ia hadn't really expected him to give in, but it

still twisted something inside her to have to actually go through with their plan. She was crossing a line, one that she'd never thought she'd get anywhere near. There would be no going back after this.

She took a last glance around the ship, hoping everyone was ready and in place. She reached under her cloak. "Then I'm very sorry, too." She pulled out her pistol and pointed it at Ruford's heart. "You've left us no choice. Please ask your men to stand aside, Captain. We're taking over the ship."

Ruford laughed. "Very amusing, my sweet little vixen." He reached for the pistol. "Give me the gun."

Sylvia cocked the pistol.

Ruford lunged for the weapon. Doyle wrapped his arm around Ruford's neck. At the same time, Sawyer hit the first mate on the back of the head with the butt of his pistol. As Crowther crumpled to the deck, Corwin and Monroe each pushed two crew members over the side. Jimmy and Trent scrambled aboard, sopping wet, and shoved a few more sailors over the side. As the rest of her men climbed up, more of Ruford's men were shoved over the railing or pushed down below the hatches.

Doyle wrestled Ruford down to the deck. Sylvia pointed her pistol at the men up in the rigging who had started to climb down. "Stay right where you are!" she shouted. She brought her other hand up to help steady the weapon.

They looked uncertain, but to her great relief stayed where they were, at least for now. Sawyer and the others had their hands full with the remaining sailors on deck.

Jimmy took a blow to the belly and doubled over, but then rammed his shoulder into his opponent's stomach and shoved the much larger man backward over the railing. Trent grabbed one man by the arm and swung him around until he knocked heads with his crewmate. Both sailors fell to the deck, unconscious. So far, everyone had used only their fists. There were a lot of bloody noses, but no one had been stabbed or shot. Yet.

She spared a glance for the beach and the paths down to it. Oh, blast. At least a dozen men were filing into boats and heading toward the *Polly Anne*. Sylvia pulled out her spyglass.

Teague was in the lead boat with four other men.

Doyle had pinned Ruford to the deck, arms behind his back. Sylvia plucked Ruford's tricorne from the deck, straightened the feather, and put the hat on her head, symbolizing the change in authority.

The brawling continued on the deck, though the number of men still conscious had dwindled.

Teague drew closer.

Sylvia tried to make a two-fingered whistle, but got nothing but a huff of air for her efforts. "Listen to me!" The fighting continued unabated.

She rang the ship's bell, clanging it until her ears rang with the echoes. The men gradually stopped fighting and stared at her. "Listen to me!" Satisfied she had everyone's attention, Sylvia held her pistol shoulder-high, the other hand resting possessively on the ship's wheel. "We're taking over the *Polly Anne*. You can either sail with us willingly, or go overboard now."

"But I can't swim," whined one of Ruford's men.

"There is a skiff tied to the port side. Help yourself." Sylvia waved the pistol in the general direction of the port bow. "The rest of us are going to head for Cherbourg."

"You've gone daft in the head," Crowther said, sitting up and rubbing the back of his skull.

Sylvia shook her head. "Toss him over."

Sawyer and Monroe helped Crowther to his feet. When he realized they were serious, he shook them off and climbed down the rope ladder to the skiff, muttering curses as he went.

"Anyone else?" Sylvia scanned the faces of the men turned toward her. Everyone stayed where they were, including McCutcheon, the second mate.

Ruford sputtered. "You're actually stealing my ship?"

"Borrowing. Just for the season." She adjusted her hat. "Now give the commands that will get us moving out into the Channel, please."

Doyle allowed Ruford to sit up. "You can't be serious." Ruford glared at Sylvia, or rather at his hat on her head.

"You can either be my first mate, or fish bait. I leave the choice entirely up to you."

Ruford folded his arms across his chest. "You don't have a chance without me. You'll run aground before you can even get out of the bay. If by some miracle you do make it out to the Channel, you'll be dismasted the first time the wind changes direction."

She shook her head. "Trent knows these shores even better than you do. He is happy to come out of retirement to pilot us across the Channel and back. And between the two of them, Trent and Doyle have forgotten more than you've ever learned about sailing a ship." She leaned a little closer, making sure to still stay upwind of him. "So again, I offer you the choice, *Mister* Ruford. Give the commands to get us moving, or go for a swim."

She held her breath, waiting to see if Ruford called her bluff. Trent had never been aboard anything bigger than a fishing smack, and neither Corwin nor Monroe knew how to navigate.

His eyes widened. "You've gone mad from grief." He slowly shook his head. "I am so sorry, my dear. I tried to prevent them from shooting your husband, really I tried." He started to reach for Sylvia, but heard Doyle's warning growl. He dropped his hand and continued in a tone so sincere, Sylvia almost believed he meant it. "He died bravely, with dignity, and I am persuaded he did not suffer, but was dead before he hit the water. Scant consolation, I know, but—" He stopped babbling at Sylvia's growl.

"Toss him over," she said to Doyle. She briefly shut her eyes against a fresh wave of grief. Tony was as gone as if he really had died.

"Wait, wait!" Ruford muttered some words that she was probably better off not understanding, then got to his feet and dusted off his hands. "I capitulate." He cocked his head to one side. "I've never taken orders from a woman before. It could be quite interesting."

He lowered his voice. "Tell me, my dear, do you enjoy ordering men about? Does it give you a sense of power to make men submissive? I've heard of such appetites, but never before met a practitioner."

Sylvia retrieved her dagger. "Give the commands *now,* or I'll gut you stem to stern."

With his index finger, Ruford pushed the tip of the blade to the side. "No need to get hostile, my dear." He cupped his hands to his mouth and began shouting orders. His remaining crew sprang into action, and soon the ship began to move again.

Monroe ran to Sylvia's side. "Beg pardon, my lady, but Teague is about to board us." He pointed at the port side.

She dashed to the railing, where she was afforded some protection by the mass of rigging, and leaned over the side. "Your agreement with Captain Ruford has been canceled, Mr. Teague. I am now in command of this vessel." She put away her dagger, to use both hands to steady the pistol as she pointed it at Teague. "Kindly move away."

"I don't bloody think so," Teague growled. "Get up there!" he shouted. Two of his men leaped to the *Polly Anne* and began climbing up the side.

"They're coming up the starboard side, too, my lady," Sawyer reported.

"Call them off, Teague, or I'll put a ball between your eyes."

Despite the rocking of the skiff, Teague stood up and held his fists to his hips, barrel chest thrust out, shoulders back.

Bugger. Even if she aimed for his shoulder, she might accidentally shoot him between the eyes after all.

She gritted her teeth. She was a smuggler and now a thief, but she refused to cross the line to murderer. She would *not* be like Teague.

She aimed the pistol a little lower, squeezed her eyes shut, and pulled the trigger. Wood fragments flew up, and the skiff bobbed from her shot and Teague's flinch. He lost his balance and fell overboard. Water bubbled up through the hole in the bottom of the skiff.

Teague's men swarmed over the sides of the *Polly Anne*. Corwin, Monroe, and Sawyer engaged them, along with her other men. Even Jimmy and Trent still held their own. Ruford's men climbed higher into the rigging, out of the way. They weren't helping her men, but at least they weren't helping Teague, either. A few of them called out, urging on the combatants. Coins changed hands.

"We are impartial observers," Ruford called to his men, and gave an apologetic shrug to Sylvia. "I find myself conflicted, my dear. I'm not sure who I want to win. Teague only wants my cargo, not my entire ship." He shouted more commands, which his crew carried out, and the ship began to head out to the Channel.

Sylvia saw another of Teague's men swing his leg up over the starboard railing. Everyone else was already engaged. She darted across the deck and hit his fingers with the butt of her pistol, then smacked him on the forehead and sent him splashing back into the bay.

Before she could congratulate herself, she was accosted from behind, hauled up against the brick wall of a man's chest, his meaty arm around her neck, the steel blade of his dagger just under her chin. Her hat fell to the deck. Breath froze in her lungs.

"I've had enough of your interference," Teague growled in her ear. The cold from his wet clothes soaked into her back, chilling her to the bone. "Stealing your brandy, burning the boats, even shooting your husband wasn't enough of a warning. Never thought I'd have to kill a woman, but you leave me no choice. Why couldn't you stay at home, cooking and mending, like a proper female?"

"My cooking skills are abysmal, I'm afraid." She had to raise her voice to be heard above the fight. Ruford's men had been content to use their fists, but Teague's gang were fighting with cutlass and dagger, forcing her men to do the same. She heard the clang and hiss of metal against metal, the occasional grunt and cry of pain as a blade found its target. Corwin, Jimmy, and the others were still valiantly holding their own.

Was this the end? She couldn't even pretend to faint in order to slip out of his grasp, because Teague's blade would slit her throat.

How ironic that she, the one who had warned the villagers what a dangerous path they'd chosen when they decided to return to smuggling, should be the first to fall.

Could she somehow get to her own dagger? And then what? She had never tried to harm anyone on purpose before. She had always tried to heal, to end the suffering of others, not to inflict it. Besides, Teague was twice her size, with hands like hams and arms like tree trunks.

Then again, this was the man who had shot Tony, the only man she had ever truly loved.

She would cut off Teague's ballocks and slit his throat.

"Let her go." Doyle aimed his pistol at Teague.

Sylvia's heart beat even faster. Doyle was a genius when it came to fixing carts and wagons, but everyone knew he couldn't hit the broad side of a barn. Well, perhaps not everyone. With any luck, Teague didn't know.

"Sails ho, astern!" someone shouted from the topsail yardarm.

Teague turned his head to investigate, and loosened his hold on her. Sylvia stomped on his instep and kicked the side of his knee. He grunted in pain and swore. His grip shifted, allowing Sylvia to reach the dagger in her boot. She slammed the blade into Teague's thigh.

He howled in pain and let go of her to clutch at his bleeding leg, and fell to the deck, swearing.

She jumped back, well out of his reach, her breath coming in harsh pants.

"Sylvia!"

She looked up, startled to see another ship had pulled alongside the cutter. Its crew had tossed grappling hooks into the *Polly Anne*'s rigging and heaved on the ropes, pulling the two ships together.

"Oh, not again," Ruford groaned. "We've already been boarded twice today," he shouted. "Come back some other time, won't you?"

Chapter 20

The fight going on around Sylvia was still fairly evenly pitched, no one was down, and the deck was not yet covered in blood, as Ruford had predicted with a moan. She looked back at the new ship.

It had pulled closer and furled her sails. Individuals on board were now discernible, including . . . No, it must be her imagination. Could it be?

"Sylvia!"

"Tony!" Laughter and joy bubbled up within her.

He stood high in the ship's rigging, wind tousling his hair, holding on to a rope with one hand, a cutlass in the other. He pointed beside her. "Look out!"

Teague had regained his feet. He roared and lunged at her with his dagger.

She parried the blade aside, but lost her balance and

her dagger. She sprawled on the deck. Her knife skidded away, through the scuppers and over the side.

Teague staggered but stayed upright. She rolled onto her back and fumbled for the pistol in her sash. He stared at her, pure hatred in his eyes. "Now I'm going to finish you, you damn bit—"

With a cutlass clenched between his teeth, Tony swung aboard, feet first, and slammed into Teague.

Teague crashed to the deck, face-first, and was still.

Tony let go the rope and dropped lightly to the deck beside her, and reached a hand to pull her to her feet. With the cutlass in his right hand, he pushed her behind him with his other, shielding her with his body.

He nudged Teague with the toe of his boot, and rolled him over.

Teague's shirt and right leg were covered with blood. His own dagger handle stuck out of his chest, right over his heart, if he'd had one. Even in death, his face was frozen in an angry snarl.

Sylvia tried to dredge up some sense of loss for a human life, but couldn't find it. Not for this life.

Tony reached back for her hand and laced his fingers with hers, and gave her a squeeze. Looking into his warm brown eyes, very much alive and real and *here,* she managed a shaky smile. He raised their joined hands and dropped a kiss on her knuckles.

Shouts and thumps on the deck nearby yanked them back to the ongoing conflict.

"Cease and desist!" Tony shouted. Only a few men paid him any attention. Tony waved his cutlass in a signal to the brig, and seconds later its starboard bow cannon fired. At such close range, the explosion of powder was nearly deafening, but harmless since there was no cannonball.

The fight stopped immediately. As though frozen by the dissipating smoke, men were still holding each other by the lapels, fists drawn back to strike, or cutlass held high, ready to swing downward. They all looked at Tony and Sylvia astern.

"Cor blimey!" one of Teague's men shouted, and quickly made the sign of the cross.

Ruford sputtered. "But—but I saw you get shot! You're dead!"

Tony shifted his stance, and Sylvia heard the smile in his voice. "I'm feeling much better now, thank you."

Still holding his hand, she darted out and picked up the captain's hat, put it back on, and stepped forward. "This ship is under my command." She glanced over at the captain of the brig, then gave a nod to Tony. "Thank you for your assistance, kind sirs." Raising her voice, she continued. "Those of you who worked for Teague, kindly absent yourselves." She gestured at her men. "Please assist any of those who are in need of help in disembarking from my ship."

With a little encouragement from Sylvia's gang, there was a brief flurry of activity as men jumped over the sides or climbed down the rope ladders, and joined the others already swimming or rowing for the shore. Ruford sputtered a protest at the term "my ship," but soon quieted after a threatening rumble from Doyle.

With Teague's men routed, the enormity of what they had just done began to sink in. The back of her dress was still cold and wet where Teague had pressed up against her. Sylvia started to shiver, and struggled to take in enough air.

She was suddenly enveloped in a warm embrace. Tony had taken off his coat and wrapped it around her. She hugged herself, drawing in his strength, inhaling his scent.

"Once again, your timing is impeccable," she said through her chattering teeth. Tony had his arm around her shoulders, standing there in his waistcoat and shirtsleeves, the cutlass in his free hand. "By what miracle did you arrive in the nick of time?"

Tony was suddenly yanked away, pulled backward.

"Did someone say Nick?" The brig's captain was pulling on a rope tied around Tony's waist, tugging him closer to the railing, taking him away from Sylvia.

Tony slashed the rope with one strong swipe of his cutlass and pointed the tip of the blade at the other gentleman. "I'm warning you, Nick . . ."

Nick laughed and thumped his companion on the shoulder. Sylvia was startled to recognize the other man, Alistair.

Seconds later both of them had swung aboard the *Polly Anne* and stood on the deck. "I've never met a female pirate captain before," Nick said. "Won't you introduce me to your lady love, Tony?" He straightened the knot in his cravat. The gold ring in his left ear glinted in the sunlight.

Lady love?

"No." Tony wrapped his arm around Sylvia's waist and pulled her back a step. "You stay away from her."

Nick was jesting, teasing his friend in the way that boys do. His words had no deeper meaning. But Tony was standing with his arm possessively around her waist, in full view of the world. She glanced up at his face. His jaw was set, his expression that of grim determination. If he had tender feelings for her, he was hiding them well at the moment.

"I have the honor of already being acquainted with the lady." Alistair gave an elegant bow. His blue eyes were sparkling with humor when he straightened.

"I must confess I never expected to see you again. But I'm very glad of the fortuitous timing in your return."

Nick pointedly cleared his throat.

"You wouldn't have gotten here in time without his help," Alistair said softly to Tony.

Tony gave an inarticulate growl. "Fine. Lady Sylvia Montgomery, may I present Nicholas, Viscount Sheffield."

"Enchanté." Nick gave an elegant bow. "I have heard the most marvelous and fantastic things about you, my lady."

From the corner of her eye, Sylvia could have sworn Tony was blushing. "You're the one responsible for getting Tony drunk and tattooed."

"Just so." Nick's blue eyes sparkled with mischief. "After all, what are friends for?"

"Will you stop?" Tony placed the tip of his cutlass against one of Nick's waistcoat buttons.

While they had been talking, Nick's crew had been removing the grappling hooks from the *Polly Anne*'s rigging. Nick shouted for his men to tidy things up, then turned back to Sylvia. "May I inquire where we are sailing?"

"Beg pardon, my lady." Doyle stood a few feet away. "Are we actually sailing for Cherbourg?"

"No, not yet. We're headed back to Lulworth Cove. Please pass that along to Ruford."

"Did y'hear that, Jonesy?" Nick shouted to his brig. "Meet us in Lulworth Cove."

"Aye, Captain."

"Sail all the way back to the cove?" Tony gestured at the receding beach with his chin. "We could just row ashore right here, and walk to Lulworth."

"You've made it this far, chum," Nick said, as serious as she'd heard him so far. "Less than an hour now, we'll have you on dry land again." Alistair murmured similar reassurances.

Of course. It couldn't be pleasant for Tony, being on the ship where he'd almost died just two days ago. She shuddered. When the breeze was just right, it lifted the hair at his temple, revealing his wound. He should still have a bandage on it.

"Beg pardon, my lady." Doyle had returned. "Capt—er, Mister Ruford says his limit is three boardings per day, and he's not going to pilot us anywhere."

She glanced over at Ruford, who was sitting on a locker, arms folded, roman nose stuck high in the air. Now what? She couldn't pilot so much as a skiff. Per-

haps Trent or one of her other men really did know
how to operate a large ship with so many sails.

Then again, the brig alongside them had just as
many sails as the cutter, and its captain was standing
on the deck beside her. "Sheffield, could I impose
upon you?" She gestured at the wheel.

"Me, take the helm?" Nick preened. "I'd be hon-
ored, my lady." He slapped Tony on the shoulder. "I'll
have you on solid land in no time at all." After only a
slight hesitation, Ruford's men responded to Nick's
commands and they got under way.

Tony grabbed Sylvia's hand and led her toward the
bow, away from Teague's corpse. "Doyle, would you
be so kind as to wrap up the rubbish?" Tony said.

"Aye, sir." Doyle dislodged Ruford from his perch
in order to retrieve a spare sail from the locker. Corwin and Sawyer helped him roll Teague's body up in
the canvas.

Holding Sylvia's hand, Tony ducked under the un-
furled foresail and pulled her after him, giving them
some measure of privacy as they stood in the bow of
the ship. Once he'd secured his cutlass in the belt at
his waist, he patted her shoulders and down her arms,
and lifted her chin, inspecting both sides of her neck.
"Are you all right? Unharmed? Uninjured?"

"I'm fine," she said. "The only thing injured when I
fell was my dignity."

Tony had taken a step back, and was examining her
gown. "But there's blood." He pointed at the large
stain on her gown, at the side of her leg.

Her heart skipped a beat. One couldn't draw another's blood without expecting to get covered with
it, as well. Tony started to lift her skirt. "It's not
mine." She pushed his hand away. "I stabbed Teague
in the leg."

"Oh, sweetheart," he groaned. He pulled her into
his arms, wrapping her securely in his embrace.

Her hat slipped off backwards and fell to the deck,
unheeded. She buried her face against his chest, knowing instinctively that his anguish was remorse for what
she'd gone through, not recrimination for her actions.

The cool linen of his cravat quickly warmed to her
touch, and she felt the reassuring beat of his heart beneath her cheek. She thought she'd never experience
this again.

She sniffed, and blinked back a tear. "Not that I'm
not overjoyed to see you, but why are you here? I sent
you away."

"You can't get rid of me that easily. I had an idea,
and came back to share it with you."

That was it? "You came all this way on Nick's ship
to share an idea with me?"

"Well, there was this, too." He cupped her cheeks
and claimed her lips in a long, deep, mind-dissolving
kiss that left her gasping for breath, her heart pounding. He kissed his way along her jaw toward her ear
and nuzzled a kiss under her earlobe. "Oh, how I
missed you, sweetheart," he whispered.

Sylvia tilted her head back, allowing him better access. "I missed you, too," she whispered. She closed

her eyes and wrapped her arms around his back, not too tightly, mindful of his myriad bruises.

The ship started to come about, heading into the cove. As Nick ordered the crew to adjust the sails and strike the foresail, some of their privacy went away. Sylvia reluctantly took a step back from Tony. "Well, what is it?"

"What is what?" His eyes were still glazed from passion, and he looked more than a little perplexed.

Sylvia took some pride in having put that dazed expression on his face. "You said you had an idea to share with me."

He nodded. "Right. It's about the—" The ship rolled slightly, and Tony clutched the railing with one hand.

"Are you all right? You look a little unwell."

The ship righted itself, and Tony groaned. "I'll be fine as soon as we get ashore." The ship broached the breakwaters just outside the cove. As the bow lifted, Tony groaned again. He grabbed her hand and led her back to amidships, keeping his free hand on the ship's railing. When they were at the midpoint, he leaned against the railing and pulled her in close. He held on to her tightly, as if someone were trying to take her away from him.

She hugged him back, not caring who saw.

"Well, I've never seen *that* used as a cure for mal de mer before," Nick said from his stance at the wheel.

"Shut up," Tony said.

Sylvia leaned back in his embrace. "You're seasick?"

"Can't even set foot in a rowboat without getting violently ill," Alistair offered.

"Shut up," Tony repeated.

"But you came in the *Wind Dancer*—"

"Do you like it?"

Sylvia glanced over Tony's shoulder, at the ship following just off their stern. "I'm sure it's a very nice boat."

"It's yours."

"Excuse me?"

"I didn't want you to steal a ship. Still don't. But you needed one to continue your smuggling operation. So I bought the *Wind Dancer* from Nick. She's a brig—very fast, Nick claims—and now she's yours."

She put her hand over her pounding heart. "I—I don't know what to say. No one has ever given me something so valuable. I'm not sure I can accept it." She stared at the brig. "It must have cost a fortune."

Tony shrugged. "Nick and I were still discussing terms when we spotted Ruford's sails, and thought we might be needed to help in the fight. You and your men acquitted yourselves quite admirably, by the way."

Sylvia grinned. "They did well, didn't they?" She grew more serious. "And the only casualty was Teague."

Nick gave the orders to heave to, and the anchor splashed into the water. Crewmen began lowering the longboats so they could row ashore—the Lulworth Cove beach was now just a hundred or so yards away. The *Wind Dancer* hove to nearby.

Tony moved out of the crew's way, pulling Sylvia with him. "With Teague no longer a threat, everything's changed."

She looked up in surprise. She'd been so busy, so focused on the fight and then Tony's return, she hadn't even thought of the implications of Teague's death. There was a chance things could return to the way they were.

But did she want that? Give Ruford back his ship, and buy their brandy from him just as before. Would a smuggler such as he forgive the affront of taking over his ship, however briefly?

Tony stroked his thumb over the back of her neck. "We could change things again, though."

"How?"

"The idea I mentioned. Though I'm not sure how well everyone is going to take to it. It will be quite a change from what they're used to. Hold off on telling them about the ship, until after we see what they think."

Sylvia was pretty sure she knew what had brought Tony to her side. "I think I like your idea," she said. Her heart swelled.

"I haven't even told you yet."

"That's all right. I'm sure the answer is going to be yes."

Trent came up to the railing and peered over the side, at the longboats ready to go. "Meet you at the Happy Jack for a mug of ale?" he said to Tony.

"Looking forward to it."

Everyone began climbing down into the longboats, though Corwin, Monroe and a few others stayed behind to make certain the *Polly Anne* didn't go anywhere. Doyle ordered Ruford to precede him down the ladder, and Tony helped Sylvia down.

"Where do you think you're going?" Tony said when he saw Nick descending the ladder.

"I'm dying to meet your Mrs. Miggins."

Alistair came down next. "As am I."

Doyle and Sawyer pushed away from the cutter and began rowing. Soon the boat skidded up onto the beach.

Nick was the first one out, and offered his hand as Sylvia stood. But instead of just helping her keep her balance, he grasped her under the arms and swung her high into the air before setting her gently down on the beach. She couldn't help laughing at the sensation.

Tony stood up, hands on his hips as he glared at Nick. He cleared his throat. Loudly.

"Oh, sorry, didn't mean to keep you waiting." Nick hoisted Tony up and out of the boat, though he didn't swing him quite as high.

"That's not what I meant and you know it, you blockhead." Tony smacked Nick on the back of his head. "Keep your hands off her."

Sylvia felt a tiny thrill at his display of jealousy.

"You're lucky he didn't puke on you for that," Alistair said, stepping onto the beach without any assistance. The others spilled out of the boat, as well.

"There's nothing left," Nick said. "Couldn't possibly be."

Tony clapped his hand to his forehead, closed his eyes, and took deep breaths. His lips moved as though he were silently counting to ten.

Sylvia stood on tiptoe and gave Nick a kiss on the cheek. "Thank you for bringing him to me so quickly."

"Happy to be of service, my lady." He winked.

Jimmy, Trent, and the others pulled ashore in their boat, and started up the cliff path.

Tony held his arm out for Sylvia, his warm brown eyes full of promise. As soon as she tucked her hand in his arm, he started up the path to the inn, too.

"What about us?" Nick called.

Tony waved for them to follow. "Ale's this way."

"Right-o."

Sawyer met them in the yard of the Happy Jack. "We've put Teague down in the cellar next to Tipton, my lady."

For a moment, her blood ran cold. Two bodies to dispose of now.

Tony patted her hand. "If you haven't already made plans for them, may I make a suggestion?"

Sylvia made an encouraging gesture.

"Take both bodies to Danielson, Tipton's supervisor in Weymouth. Remind him that Teague shot Tipton. He'll see to it there's no trouble with an inquiry."

Sawyer nodded. "We'll take them at first light."

Sylvia heaved a sigh of relief.

Soon after, they stepped into the inn's taproom. The loud buzz of conversation turned to cheers and applause when those gathered realized who had entered. Tony took a step to the side, joining in the applause. Jimmy's cheeks flushed a bright red, but he made an elegant bow. Sylvia curtsied, her cheeks heating at the unexpected praise.

People started to quiet down and take their seats again. In the corner, Doyle guarded Ruford, who was sulking. "Damn pirates," he muttered. Baxter leaned on his crutches, near Hayden with his arm in a sling.

"How soon are we going to sail for Cherbourg, my lady?"

"Do we know who we're going to get the brandy from?"

"I want to be part of the crew."

"Me, too."

The questions and comments flew faster than Sylvia could answer them, or even identify the speaker. The noise started to get out of hand.

Tony pierced through the hubbub with a two-fingered whistle. She'd have to get him to teach her how to do that. "Let the lady at least take a seat before you bombard her with questions." Tony ushered her toward a spot that suddenly became vacant.

Spencer hustled over with three full tankards and set them down on the table. "Something to wet your whistle, my lady, my lord. Sir."

Sylvia gratefully took a sip, as did Jimmy and Tony. It seemed that at least half the village was gathered in the taproom, in addition to Ruford and Tony's two friends. Mrs. Miggins was seated between Alistair and Nick, a broad grin on her face.

Tony leaned close. "Mind if I tell them about my idea now?"

Here? Now? In front of everyone? She took another sip. "Go ahead."

Chapter 21

Tony cleared his throat and stood up. After a moment, everyone looked at him expectantly. He had done so much and earned their trust and friendship in such a short period of time. Sylvia's heart swelled with pride. Everyone had all but forgotten the disagreement over stealing Ruford's ship.

"I realize I am a newcomer to your way of doing things," he began. "But perhaps that gives me the ability to see things from a different perspective. I know smuggling is a time-honored tradition around these parts, and offers the potential for great profits. I've also seen how dangerous it can be. I want to propose an alternative."

This was his idea? Sylvia had expected an entirely

different kind of proposal. She tried to not let her disappointment show.

"In selling the brandy to your inland customers, you essentially have a transportation and distribution business. I propose that you simply transport and distribute a different product. Cheese."

She had been trying for months to convince the villagers to try alternatives. But her recipe experiment had gone horribly, horribly wrong. Cheese could not be the answer.

There were whispers and mutterings, and a few outright laughs.

"Your double Dorset blue vinny has a wide and growing reputation for excellence." He ignored the snort from Ruford in the corner. "Even the folks up in Shaftesbury have heard of it. With a small investment, you could expand your facilities and herds, and increase production. You can sell to a much wider market than you have been with the brandy. And it's legal."

Mrs. Pitsnoggle stood up. "That's a fine idea, laddie, but we can't even replace all the roofs we lost in the last storm yet. Where are we going to get the coin to make improvements?"

"Me."

There was a moment of shocked silence.

"I have the coin. Just, ah, not with me at the moment. I've been looking for a new investment opportunity. I'd much rather invest it in expanding a dairy than buying a ship."

There was renewed whisperings and mutterings. Several people shook their heads.

Nick stood up. "Our boy here has been hiding his light under a bushel. I can attest that not only does Tony have the coin to invest, but so does his brother, the Earl of Sinclair."

There was an awed hush, followed by more whisperings, as people looked at Tony in a new light.

His brother was an *earl*? Sylvia slid down in her seat. She'd known from his clothes that there was money in his family, but never suspected they ranked so high. How foolish, thinking he was planning to marry her, the widow of an insignificant country baron. Since she had succumbed to his charms, he was probably planning to make her his mistress. Sylvia buried her face in her hands.

"And I'd like to be your first customer," Nick continued. "I'll take fifty pounds of cheese for my ship. Today. I might even share it with my crew."

There were a few laughs.

Ruford stood up, hands on his hips. "Have you even tasted the vile concoction they call 'cheese' around here?"

"Excellent point." Tony gestured for Alistair, who retrieved the round of cheese from his haversack. Tony withdrew the knife from his boot and sliced into the cheese, and passed a chunk to Ruford. "The piece you were offered the other morning was an aberration. There was a slight error with that batch that has since been corrected." He glanced at Sylvia for confirmation. She nodded. "Try a taste from this batch."

Tony kept cutting until everyone had a piece. The noise level dropped while everyone tasted.

"Damn, that's good."

"There's something else in it."

"Herbs?"

"Best I've ever had."

Sylvia finally took a bite of it herself. She looked at Tony in surprise.

He looked exceedingly pleased with himself as he smiled back at her. "This is from the batch that's aging in Lady Montgomery's stillroom. I believe it's her own variation of the local recipe."

Sylvia reluctantly nodded.

Tony pulled a slip of paper from his pocket. "I've done some initial calculations, and figured that you could be running Lavender Hill Farms as a profitable venture within a year."

"Lavender Hill Farms?"

Tony glanced at her. "Just a suggestion." He looked back at the crowd. "By fall, there should be enough to go around for everyone's cottage to have been repaired before the winter storms set in, see to it that your cellars are well stocked, and perhaps even replace the lost fishing boats. There should also be enough for Lord Montgomery to return to school and finish his education."

Jimmy looked up. "Me, go back to school?" He beamed.

Tony flipped the paper over. "I've done some sketches of changes to make to the barns and production rooms, some things that should improve efficiency. The operation will still require pretty much everyone in the village to be involved, to make it successful."

"Everyone will have work?" Hayden said.

"If they want it, yes."

There was an excited buzz of conversation. Trent snagged the paper from Tony, and held it out so he and Baxter could study it by the fire. Several other men crowded around, studying the drawings, discussing the document.

Tony sat beside Sylvia. "Well, what do you think?"

"You've just suggested a viable alternative to smuggling, something I've struggled to come up with, in vain, for months. And you've only been pondering the problem for a day or two—"

"Week and a half. I started thinking about it the night you introduced me to Ruford."

"I'm not sure if I want to hit you or kiss you."

He grinned. "I know which of those two choices *I* favor."

His expression was eager yet worried, as though his entire happiness depended on her approval. "I was right. I like your idea," she said at last. It wasn't the idea she'd hoped for, but this idea would benefit many more people. She would just have to swallow her disappointment.

With the majority of men in the room still chattering over Tony's notes, Nick and Alistair moved to the table and helped themselves to more cheese. "You were right about Mrs. Miggins," Nick said around a mouthful.

Tony grinned. "Get you, did she?"

"Got us both." Alistair popped another piece in his mouth.

"Can't say I didn't warn you." Tony turned in his seat to face Sylvia and took her hands in his, some of his eagerness fading. "I thought you would be more excited."

"I am excited. This is an excellent idea." She tried to force more enthusiasm into her voice.

Tony still looked troubled but plunged ahead. "We could spend the winters at my estate in Berkshire. It's not that large, but it produces enough to keep me, and the tenants, comfortable. Or we could live here in Lulworth year round and just make periodic visits to my steward there. Whichever you prefer—just so long as we keep an eye on both the estate and the cheese production."

"We?"

Nick leaned over Tony's left shoulder. "I think you may have left out one facet of your brilliant plan, Sir Genius."

Tony's brow furrowed. "I don't think so."

Alistair leaned over the other shoulder. "Why would Lady Montgomery go with you to your estate in Berkshire?"

"Because she—" Tony's eyes widened. "Oh."

"Precisely." Alistair grabbed Nick by the elbow, and dragged him, protesting, across the room.

Sylvia and Tony were left in a quiet bubble, separate from everyone else's excited chatter. Her heart began to beat faster again.

Tony tightened his grip on her fingers. His smile was tinged with apprehension. "I've made a muddle of this, haven't I?"

"Muddle of what?"

"I never thought I'd be doing this so soon, so early in my life." He took a deep breath. "But I don't want to wait a moment longer." He slid out of his seat and down on one knee, and pulled a small jeweler's box from his waistcoat pocket.

Sylvia couldn't help but gasp at the sight of the ring—an emerald, surrounded by small diamonds—and more importantly, what the ring represented.

The noise level in the taproom suddenly dropped, but Sylvia had eyes only for Tony. Her heart was pounding so hard, surely everyone could hear it.

"I love you, Sylvia. Would you do me the great honor of becoming my wife?"

Now *this* was an idea to get excited about. With tears of joy blurring her vision, she wrapped her arms around his neck.

"I think that generally means yes," Nick announced.

Sylvia nodded. "Yes," she whispered against Tony's neck. "I love you, too."

He stood and carried her up with him, until her feet left the floor and he spun in a circle. Her skirts flared out, but she didn't care. She was in Tony's arms. He loved her. He set her down and cradled her cheeks in his hands, and claimed her lips in a tender kiss.

Gradually she became aware that the roaring in her ears was the cheering villagers.

"This is all well and good," Ruford shouted. The crowd quieted and moved closer to him, the men reaching for their weapons. "I'm happy for you both, really I am. Very touching. But what about my ship?"

Sylvia considered. "It would seem I have no need for it after all."

"You're just going to give it back?" Doyle asked in shock.

Sylvia tilted her head to one side. "I don't know how to sail it. Do you?"

"Well, no, but . . ."

"After all the effort you went through to take it, that's it?" Baxter said.

"After all the effort *we* went through, you mean," Jimmy groused. His left eye was swelling, and the bruises were starting to show up on his jaw. The other men were also beginning to show signs of the fight they'd been in.

"It was an act of desperation." Sylvia smiled at Tony. "We are no longer desperate." He pulled her close for a quick kiss. Sylvia turned to Sawyer. "Please let Corwin and Monroe know that the *Polly Anne* is free to sail at her captain's convenience." Sylvia held out her hand to Ruford. "No hard feelings?"

Ruford stood with his arms folded across his chest. "I lost my first mate and several crew members when you told them to jump overboard. Who knows where they've got to by now."

"Crowther was an unpleasant fellow, and the others were cowards," Tony said.

After a thoughtful pause, Ruford inclined his head in acknowledgment.

"McCutcheon is due for a promotion, don't you think?" Sylvia said.

"Well, he has been with me almost as long as Crowther." Ruford rested his hands on his hips.

Sylvia held her hand out again.

Ruford wagged a finger at her. "It was an act of piracy, and you don't even have a letter of marque from King George. There is only one thing that can atone for such an act." He had his nose high in the air again.

The men who had been eavesdropping gathered in a circle around Ruford and Sylvia. Tony straightened to his full height at her side, his hand a reassuring presence at the small of her back.

"Fifty pounds of cheese and ten pounds of smoked mackerel should cover it."

They shook hands and the buzz of conversation resumed.

With everything else that had gone on, Sylvia hadn't noticed until now that Jimmy was by himself in a corner, staring into his tankard.

"Jimmy? Something wrong?" She sat down next to him.

"I'm happy that you're happy, and I like Tony—he's great guns—but . . ."

"But what?"

She barely heard his whisper. "If you marry him, that means you won't be my sister anymore."

"Oh, Jimmy." She pulled him into a hug. "You'll always be the brother of my heart."

"I'll try to remember that when your Uncle Walcott makes me move in with his houseful of brats. He only let me stay here because *you* were here."

Jimmy was right. Once she married, Jimmy would be alone, except for servants. Uncle Walcott took his court-appointed role of guardian quite seriously. He would undoubtedly insist Jimmy live under his roof until Jimmy reached majority status, three years away.

She shuddered.

Tony joined them. "This looks serious."

" 'Tis nothing." Jimmy pasted a bright smile on his face.

Sylvia explained the situation.

"A fate worse than being keelhauled, to be sure." Tony scratched his jaw. A moment later he snapped his fingers. "All you need do is petition the courts for a change of guardian. Offer up some sobersides married chap, a stuffy fellow with good breeding and old money. A title in the family tree wouldn't hurt."

"Stuffy?" Jimmy wrinkled his nose.

Sylvia bit back a grin. She squeezed Tony's hand, barely able to contain her gratitude.

Tony nodded, his expression grave. "Think we could fool them into thinking I fit that description?"

Jimmy's jaw dropped. "You'd do that for me?"

"Seems only fair, since you've been taking care of Sylvia."

"What's this?" Nick had wandered over. "Trouble in paradise already?"

"Seems I'm about to acquire a ward as well as a wife." He ruffled Jimmy's hair.

Nick's brows rose in surprise. "A wife and a cub in one day. You don't mess about, do you?"

"Once you know what you want, there's no point in

dawdling." He kissed Sylvia's hand. "Do you want to wait three weeks for the banns to be read, or shall we get a special license?"

"Or you could elope to Scotland. I can have you there in just a couple days on the *Wind Dancer*. I'll even let you have use of the captain's cabin." Nick grinned. "Though I suppose it wouldn't be very romantic if the bridegroom were perpetually sick, would it?"

Tony stood, pulling Sylvia with him. "Come, sweetheart, we'll leave the court jester to amuse himself."

Unfazed, Nick slung an arm over Tony's shoulder. "May I kiss the bride? I've never kissed a lady pirate before."

"No. And she's not a pirate anymore."

"Oh, come on, give. You kissed your sister-in-law at her wedding breakfast."

"No."

"But—"

While Nick and Tony argued, Alistair tapped Sylvia on the shoulder. When she glanced up at him, his normally serious expression was full of mischief, his brows raised in query. Before she knew what he was about, Alistair tipped her head up with one finger under her chin, and gave her a light, quick kiss on the lips. He winked as he pulled away.

"You are not going to kiss my wife. Make peace with that, and move on."

Nick's sudden gasp proved Alistair's action had not gone unnoticed. "Oh, that's just bloody unfair," he complained. "Alistair gets to kiss her but I don't?"

Alistair grinned.

Sylvia didn't want to be the source of discord. "But I kissed you, on the beach, remember?"

Tony whipped his head around to face her. "You what?"

"On the cheek. To thank him for bringing you to me so quickly."

"Oh."

Nick grinned.

Tony wrapped his arm around her, drawing her close. "If either of you come anywhere near her, I'll cut your tongues out. No one else is ever going to kiss her again. Except me."

As Tony gave her another long, deep kiss, Sylvia decided that was just fine with her.

Coming in March 2006 from Avon Books...
Four amazing love stories, by four
outstanding authors!

Portrait of a Lover by Julianne MacLean
An Avon Romantic Treasure

She met a stranger on a train . . . and suddenly Annabelle
Lawson was swept away by a passion she could not control.
But Magnus Wallis is a scoundrel—a man who would seduce
a young lady and then leave her to face the consequences.
And when the two meet again, Annabelle is the lady scorned,
while Magnus is determined to show her that he has
reformed. And everyone knows there is no better lover than
a reformed rake.

Running for Cover by Lynn Montana
An Avon Contemporary Romance

Cole Bannon is handsome, rugged—and perhaps unscrupu-
lous . . . but Lexie Chandler needs this dangerous man. She's
on a mission that threatens her life…and she's not about to let
anything go wrong. Cole is her best bet when it comes to facing a small army and a tiger or two—but even if she makes it
out alive, she faces a greater danger than mere gunfire:
seduction by Cole himself!

A Study in Scandal by Robyn DeHart
An Avon Romance

Lady Amelia Watersfield is over twenty, very unwed…and
longing for adventure. So when a priceless family heirloom is
stolen, she is determined to retrieve it. And the help of the
breathtakingly handsome inspector, Colin Brindley, is most certainly welcome! Not only is he sharp-witted and brave, but he's
unleashed a wild desire in Amelia . . . a desire she has no intention of taming!

The Bewitching Twin by Donna Fletcher
An Avon Romance

Aliss is being held against her will—by Rogan, a strong, sexy
Scotsman who insists she use her bewitching healing powers to
save his people. He swears to return her home once her task is
complete, but he doesn't want to let her go. And when it comes
to being captured in a game of seduction, Aliss begins to wonder
just *who* has captured *whom*!

Avon Romantic Treasures

Unforgettable, enthralling love stories, sparkling with passion and adventure from Romance's bestselling authors

Avon Romances
the best in
exceptional authors and unforgettable novels!

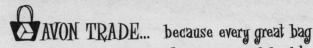

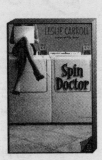